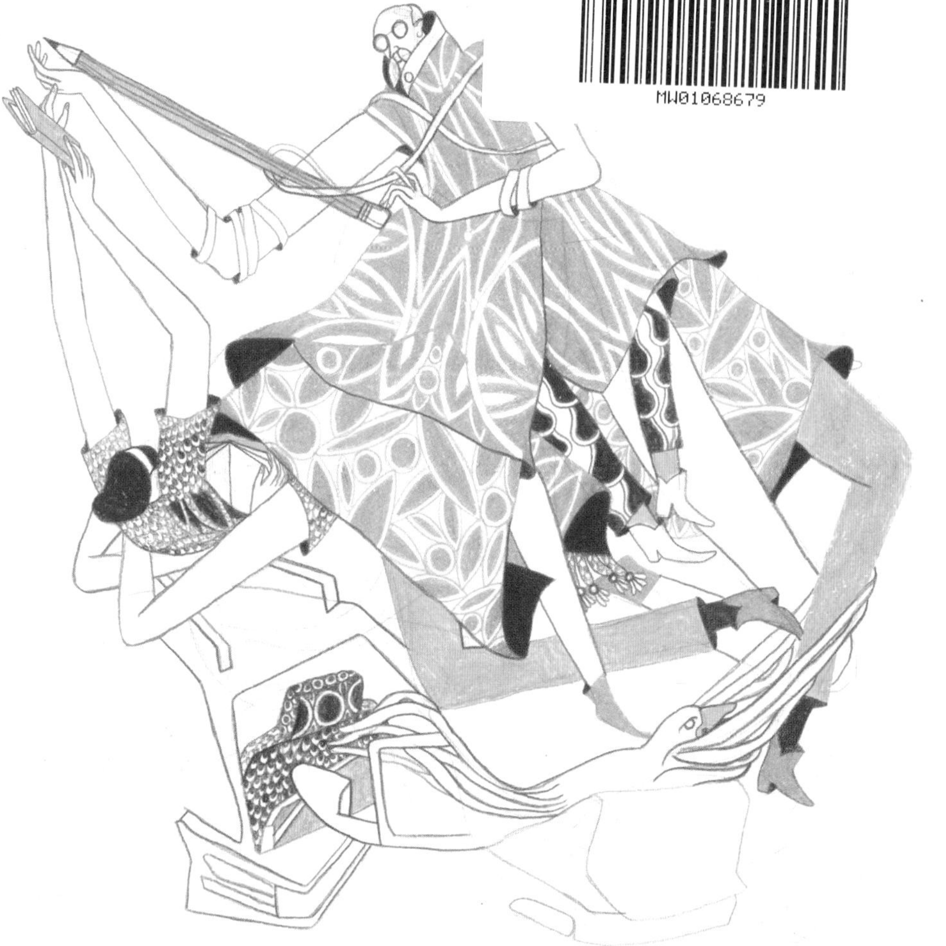

The Academic Hour

Keren Katz

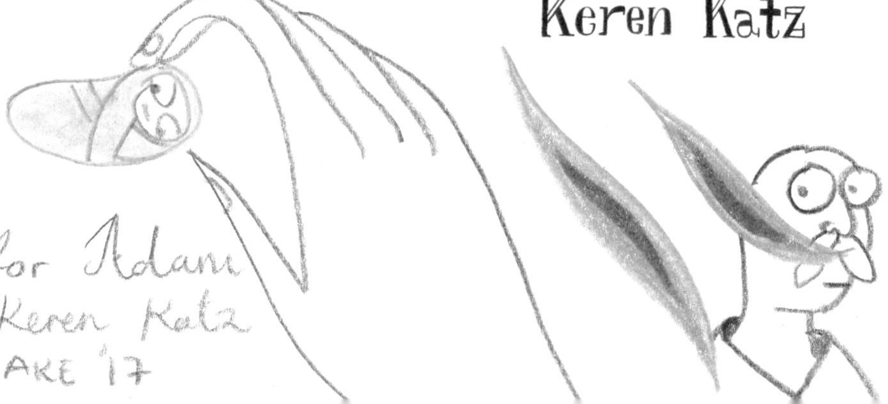

for Adam
Keren Katz
CAKE '17

THE ACADEMIC HOUR

FIRST EDITION. April 2017.

Printed in China.

SOME WORK IN THIS BOOK HAS
BEEN PREVIOUSLY PUBLISHED
(WITH VARIATION) BY:
SMOKE SIGNAL
PATHOS MATHOS COMPANY
LOCUST MOON COMICS
RETROFIT COMICS/BIG PLANET COMICS
THE BROOKLYN RAIL
INK BRICK
ROUGH HOUSE COMIX
THE SUNDAY COMICS
HA-PINKAS, HOTEM
ASUFA HAGGADAH
YOU ARE HERE
REGA ECHAD, TLV MUNICIPALITY
DOCTORS FOR HUMAN RIGHTS
PARDES PUBLISHING
THE JEWISH QUARTERLY

THANK YOU TO: GABE FOWLER, BOX BROWN, BOB SIKORYAK,
JOSH BURGGRAF, JOSH O'NEILL, ANDREW CARL, RUSS KICK
CHRIS STEVENS, MONTE BEAUCHAMP, MOLLY BROOKS
ALEXANDER ROTHMAN, PAUL TUNIS, BIANCA
STONE, MARC GOLDNER, LILACH DEKEL-AVNERI, KEITH KAHN HARRIS
TAMAR HOCHSTADTER, LIOR YAMIN, AUSTIN ENGLISH,
BILL KARTALOPOULOS, CHRIS COUCH, TOM MOTELY, SETH KUSHNER,
BEN KATCHOR, TOM HART, LEELA CORMAN,
NAAMAN HIRSCHFELD, BRENDAN KIEFER, JOSH BAYER, GREGORY BENTON,
JOHN MALTA, THE SOCIETY OF ILLUSTRATORS,
PAT DORIAN, JESS WORBY, STEVEN GUARNACCIA, LI-OR ZALTSMAN,
ANELE MILLER, KURT HOSS, JAMES ROMBERGER, JESS RULIFFSON
THE NYC COMICS SYMPOSIUM, ROBYN CHAPMAN, ELI VALLEY
WHO HAVE SUPPORTED, ENCOURAGED AND
WELCOMED ME INTO COMICS.
     MY DESSERT ISLAND FRIENDS:
KAREN, KRIOTA, CONNIE AND ANDREA

ISBN-13: 978-0-9962739-5-4
ISBN-10: 0-9962739-5-6

SAB-034

LIBRARY OF CONGRESS PCN: 2016960532

PUBLISHED BY SECRET ACRES
237 FLATBUSH AVENUE, #331
BROOKLYN, NY 11217

THANK YOU BARRY AND LEON FOR
MAKING A DREAM COME TRUE
THANK YOU TO ALL MY TEACHERS
AT BEZALEL AND S.V.A, AND
MY MFAII3 FAMILY.
THANK YOU DAVID SANDLIN AND MAIRA KALMAN
FOR HELPING ME TELL THE STORY OF
ROOM 1001.
THANK YOU RICHARD MCGUIRE FOR
TAKING ME (AND MAELLE DOLIVEUX)
ON THE GREATEST COMICS ADVENTURE.
TO MY FRIEND SHAHAR SARIG WHO
KNOWS POTHEL AND KNOWS HOW TO
MAP THIS SCHOOL. I COULDNT
HAVE MADE THIS BOOK WITHOUT YOU.
THANK YOU FOR HUNTING LEOPARDS,
HIDING MUSEUMS, DESIGNING
BUTTON FACTORIES, DISAPPEARING
UNDER HORSES AND FLYING FROM BIKES.
AND FOR THE BIRD SUITCASE OF BOOKS
FOR LYLE, THE CATALOG OF EVERYTHING
AND YOUR DRAWING AND YOUR WRITING THAT INSPIRES ME.
FOR
LIANA FINCK (NO RELATION TO OTHER LIANA), THANK YOU
I AM THANKFUL FOR OUR GRAPE DIARIES.
TO MY FRIENDS WHO "ALSO TRADE
IN STOCKS" "AND ARE TIGERS": ALON GOLDSTEIN
AND MY STUDIO MATE/SINGING TEACHER
HADAR REUVEN, AND THEIR CAT Patton SAMANDRIEL
WHO SITS ON MY DRAWINGS AND GIVES ADVICE W TAIL.
THANK YOU AVIA NORMA FOR GIVING
ME THE KEYS TO AN ALTERNATE UNIVERSE,
GIVING ME THE MAGICAL ARTIFACTS I
REQUIRE TO TRAVEL SAFELY THROUGH IT,
AND KEEPING MY HANDS FROM CRACKING.
THANK YOU TO THE SEQUENTIAL ARTISTS WORKSHOP
(SAW) WHO AWARDED ME THE GRANT THAT I USED
TO PUBLISH THE FIRST BOOK IN THIS SERIES:
PLANS TO TAKE UP ASTRONOMY"
THANK YOU TO MY SPIRIT SOCK GUARDIANS
ANDREA AND ALEXANDER.
THANK YOU LIRON COHEN, "M₂ Ping."
THANK YOU TO MY LOVING GRANDPARENTS:
JACOB AND BRURIA, WHO ARE ALSO MY
MODELS AND PROP SUPPLIERS.
TO MY WONDERFUL FAMILY, AND MY BROTHERS.
THANK YOU MOM AND DAD FOR ALWAYS
BEING THERE FOR ME NO MATTER WHAT.
THANK YOU RAFAEL AND DANIEL KATZ.
PETER J. COHEN FOR YOUR INSPIRATION
AND GENEROSITY OF SHARING YOUR COLLECTION.
THANK YOU TO MY "HUMDRUM" FAMILY:
HILA, OMER, DAN, HADAR AND ALSO OVADIA.
THANK YOU TO MY DANCE TEACHERS.
THANK YOU TAMMUZ FOR REVERSE URBAN
EXPLORATION AND ASTRONOMY REPORTS.
THANK YOU YANAI PERRY FOR THE COLOR PENCILS.
I'D LIKE TO ALSO THANK: MY BEZALEL FAMILY AND
MY FIRST COMICS TEACHERS, ASAF HANUKA
MICHEL KICHKA, MERAV SALOMON
ZEV ENGELMAYER, RUTU MODAN
MARSHAL, CHRIS, VIKTOR, MIRKO,
CARL, CAROL, GREG, MICHELE AND KIM.
THANK YOU ILAN MANOUACH FOR
TEACHING ME SO MUCH AND
INSPIRING ME,
I LIKE TELLING YOU STORIES.

TO THE PEOPLE AND PLACES IN
MY LIFE WHO MAKE MY WORLD
MAGICAL, THANK YOU.

THANK YOU LOKCHOT LA-REOT
ITAI RON GILBOA, MEIRA MOOSE,
ODED MENDA LEVY,
OREN FISCHER,
LIOR ZALMANSON
NETALLY SCHLOSSER
YUVAL SAAR
ROY CHICKY ARAD
KENNETH GOLDSMITH
DEREK BEAULIEU,
ERAN GLOBUS
SIVAN SHIKNAGY
LIHI CHEN
HILA LAHAV
MICHAL WEINBERG
RUSS SPITKOVSKY
NADAN BIN-NUN
TAHNEER OKSMAN
HAGILLER
ORIT GIDALI
KARMIT GALILI
BRAW WILER
AVRAHAM BERKOWITZ
MEGHAN TURBITT
SVA ALUMNI SOCIETY
THEATRE 80 BONNIE SLOTNICK AND
LEBOWSKY 'STORE.
CHEN HERMAN
CHANA KUBAN
NOMA LEVINSON
ELI SHAMIR

FOR ERAN HADAS, AHUVI SHE-YICHYEH
AL HA-KOL, HA KOL.

THIS IS THE STORY OF PROF. POTHEL AND LIANA SET IN A SCHOOL FOUNDED AND DESIGNED BY A TEAM OF RENOWNED ARCHITECTURE PROFESSORS ACCEPTING ONLY STUDENTS WHO HAVE BEEN INVOLVED IN TRAFFIC ACCIDENTS BUT WHO HAVE NEVER BROKEN ANY BONES. THE SCHOOL WAS DESIGNED SO THAT DURING THE COURSE OF THEIR STUDIES, AND BY WAY OF THEIR CONDUCT WITHIN CAMPUS, THEY WOULD BREAK EVERYTHING THEY WERE SUPPOSED TO BREAK BEFORE.

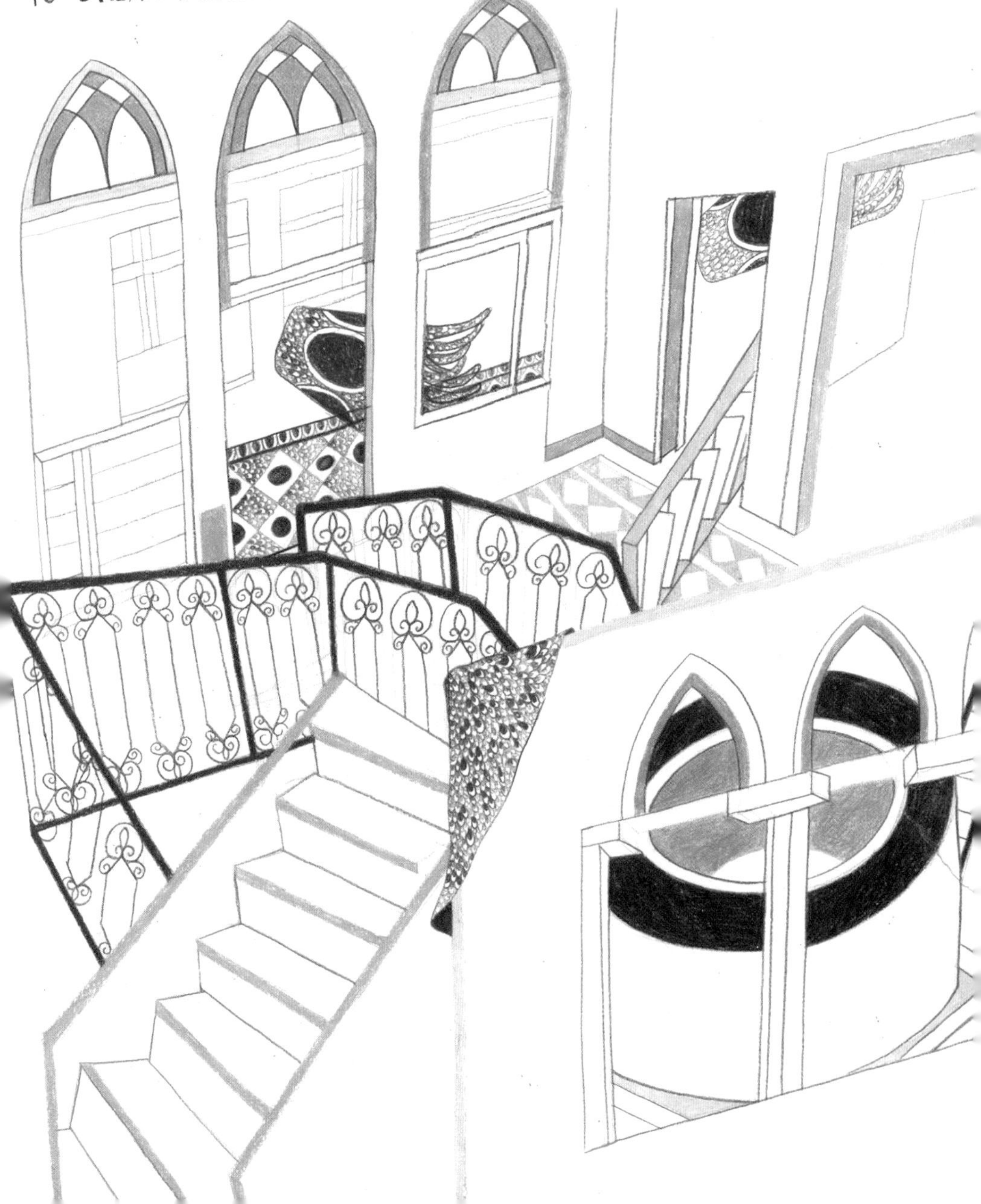

SCULPTURES OF WAITING
PROLOGUE

THE LESSON WILL BEGIN IN FIVE MINUTES.
WE MUST ALL GET RID OF A HORSE.

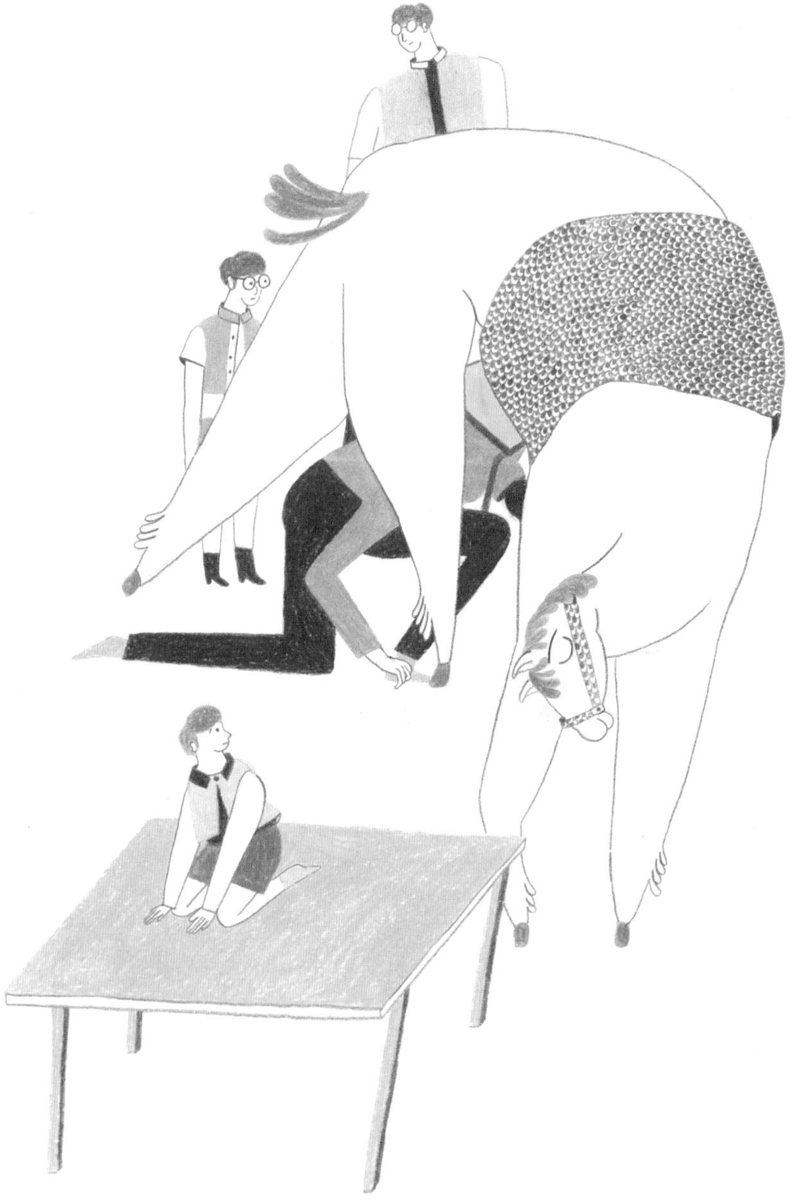

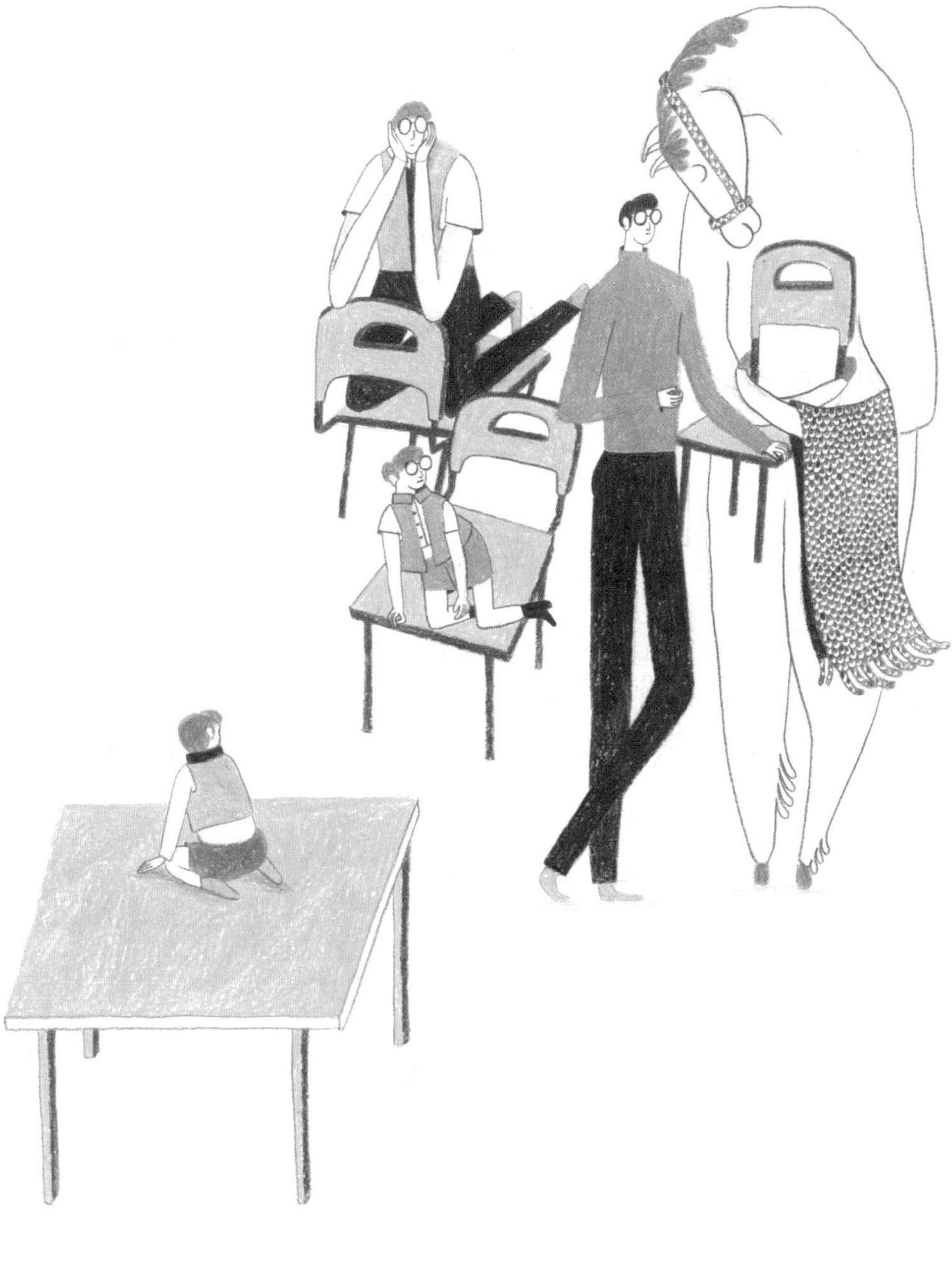

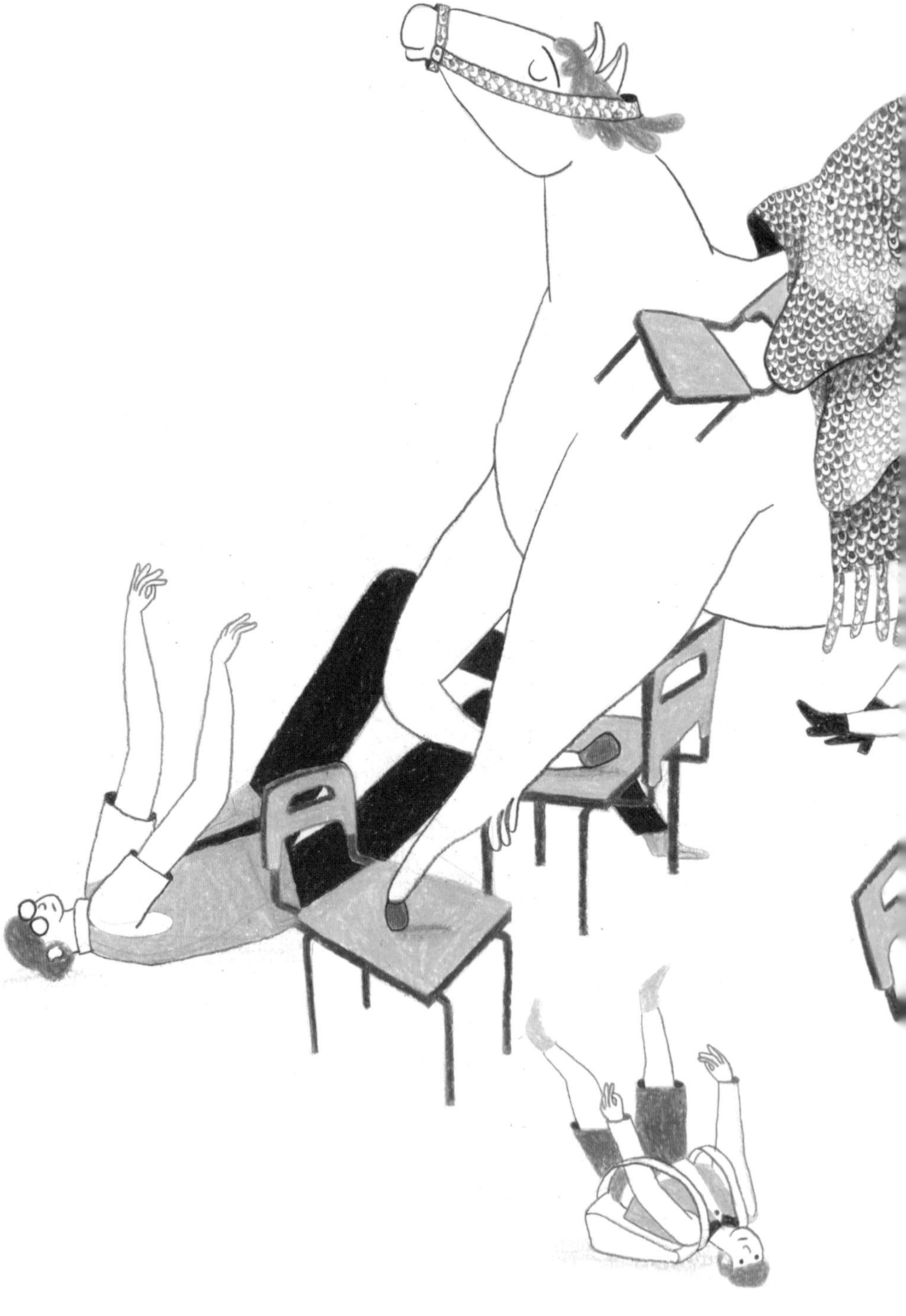

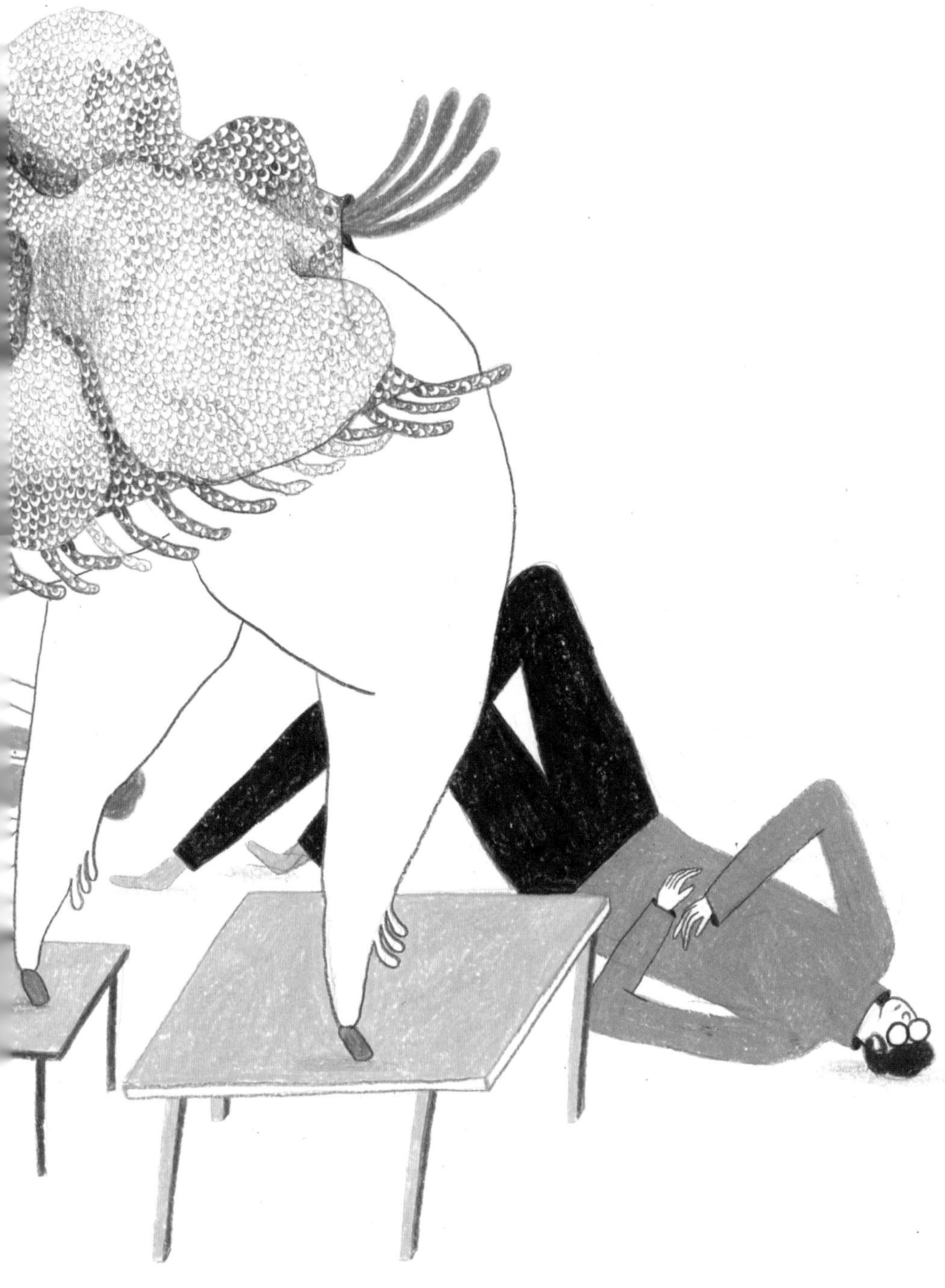

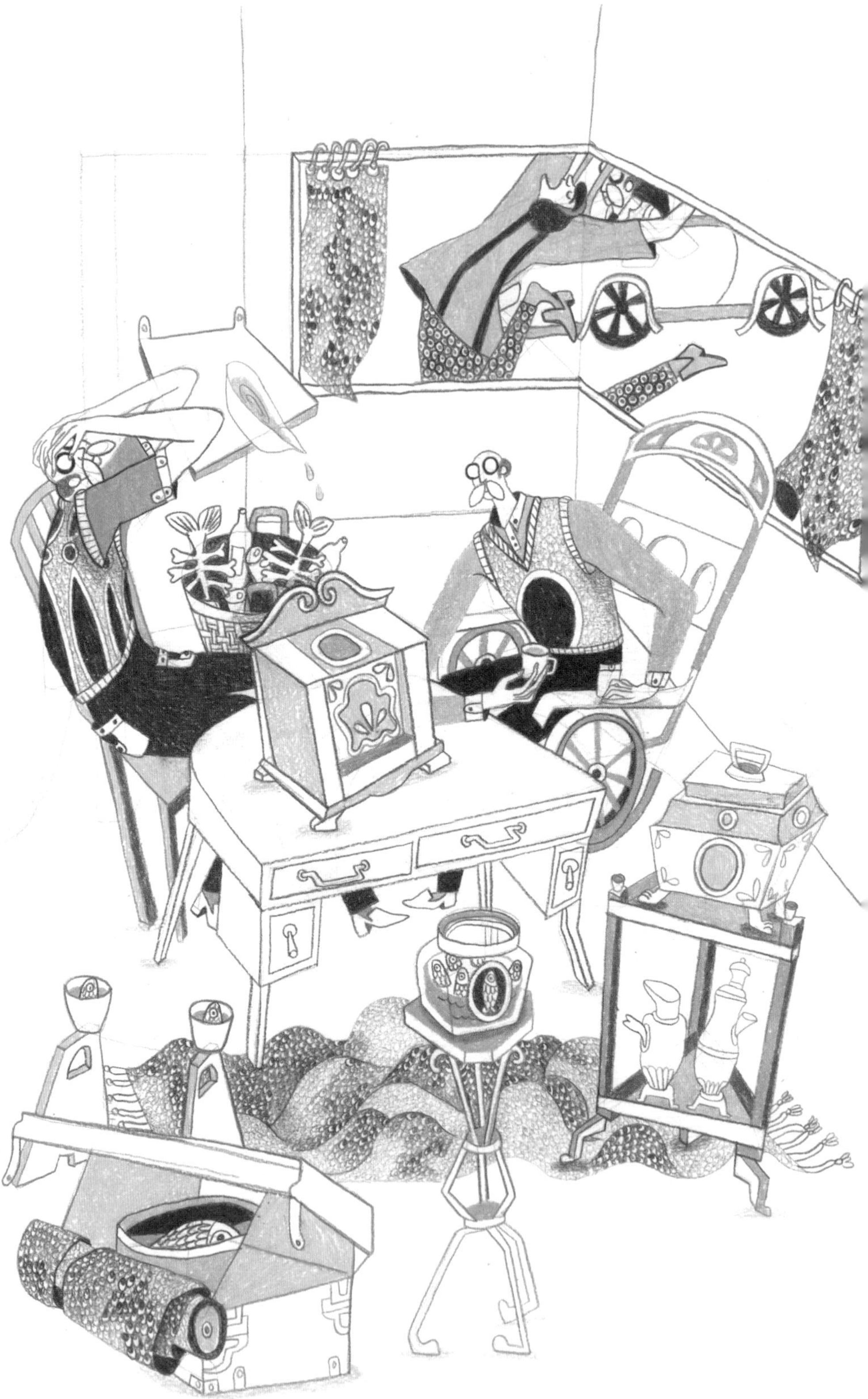

AN ANATOMY LESSON

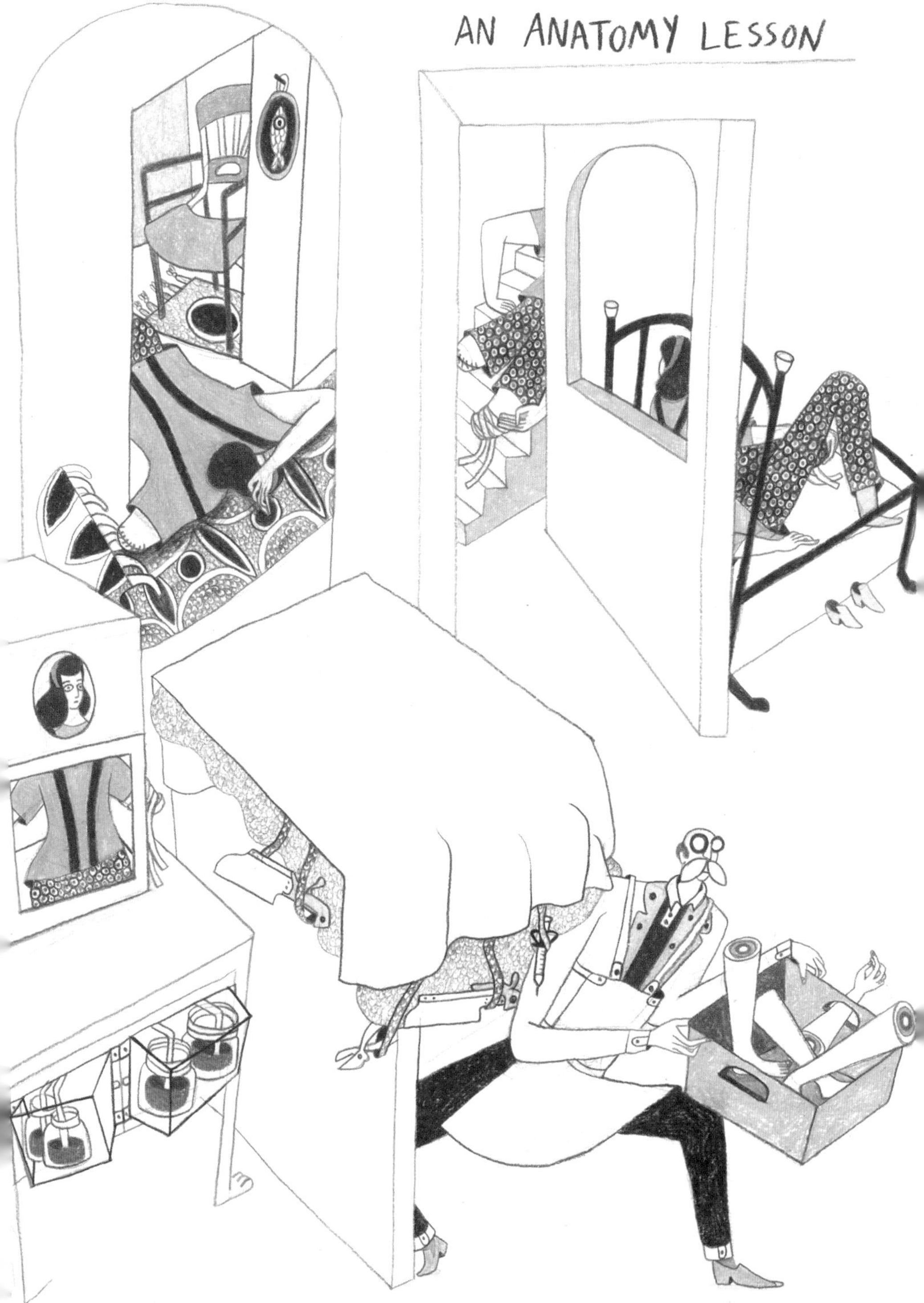

PATELLA WAS IN
THE PROCESS OF
CURLING HER SPINE
BACKWARDS TO GET
TO HER ANATOMY CLASS—

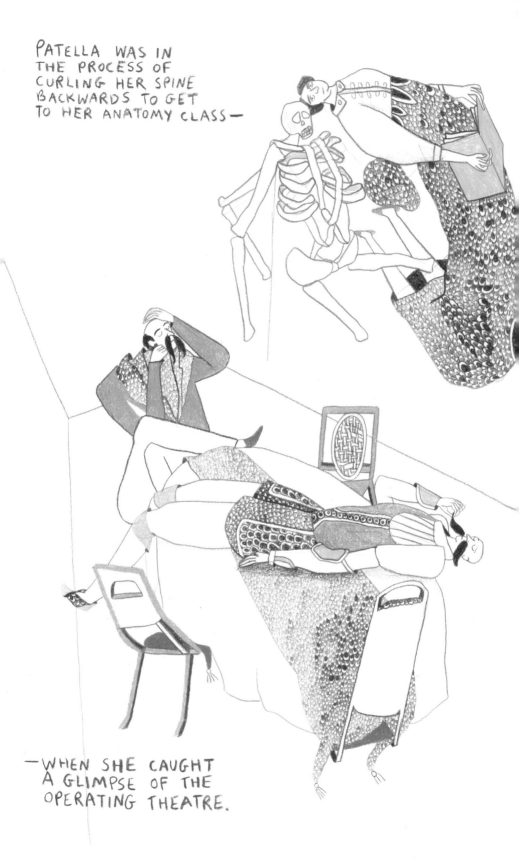

—WHEN SHE CAUGHT
A GLIMPSE OF THE
OPERATING THEATRE.

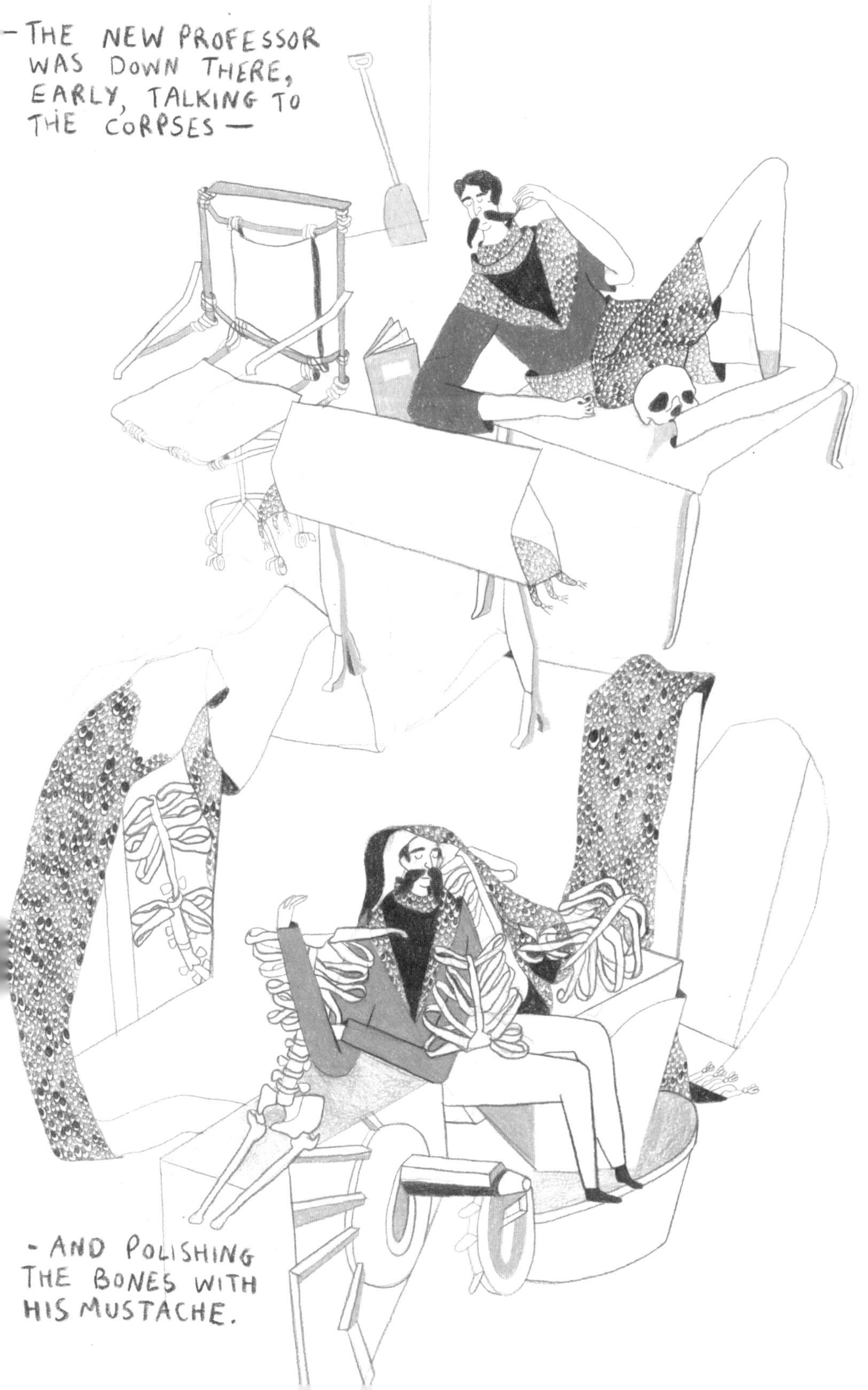
-THE NEW PROFESSOR WAS DOWN THERE, EARLY, TALKING TO THE CORPSES—
-AND POLISHING THE BONES WITH HIS MUSTACHE.

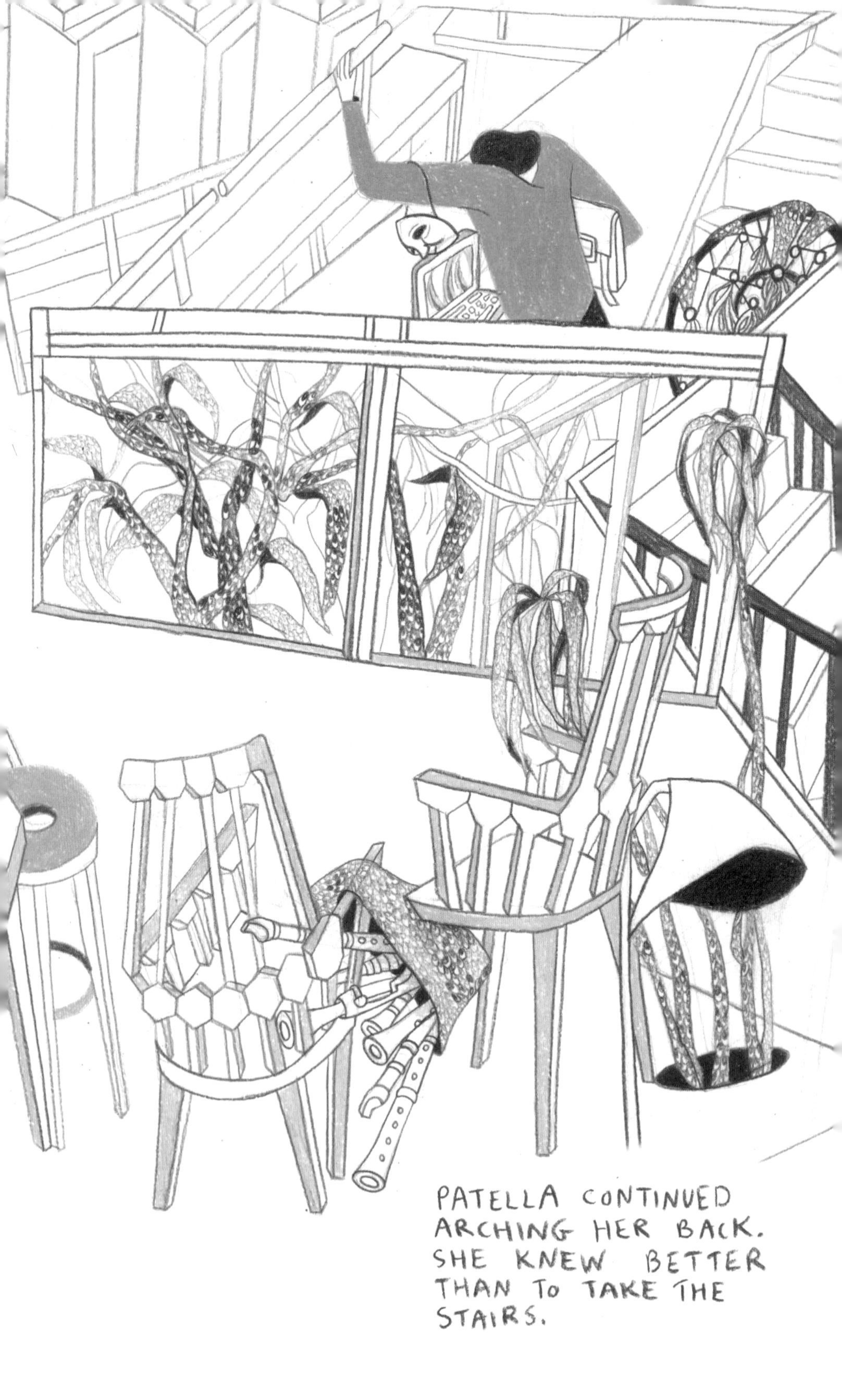
PATELLA CONTINUED ARCHING HER BACK. SHE KNEW BETTER THAN TO TAKE THE STAIRS.

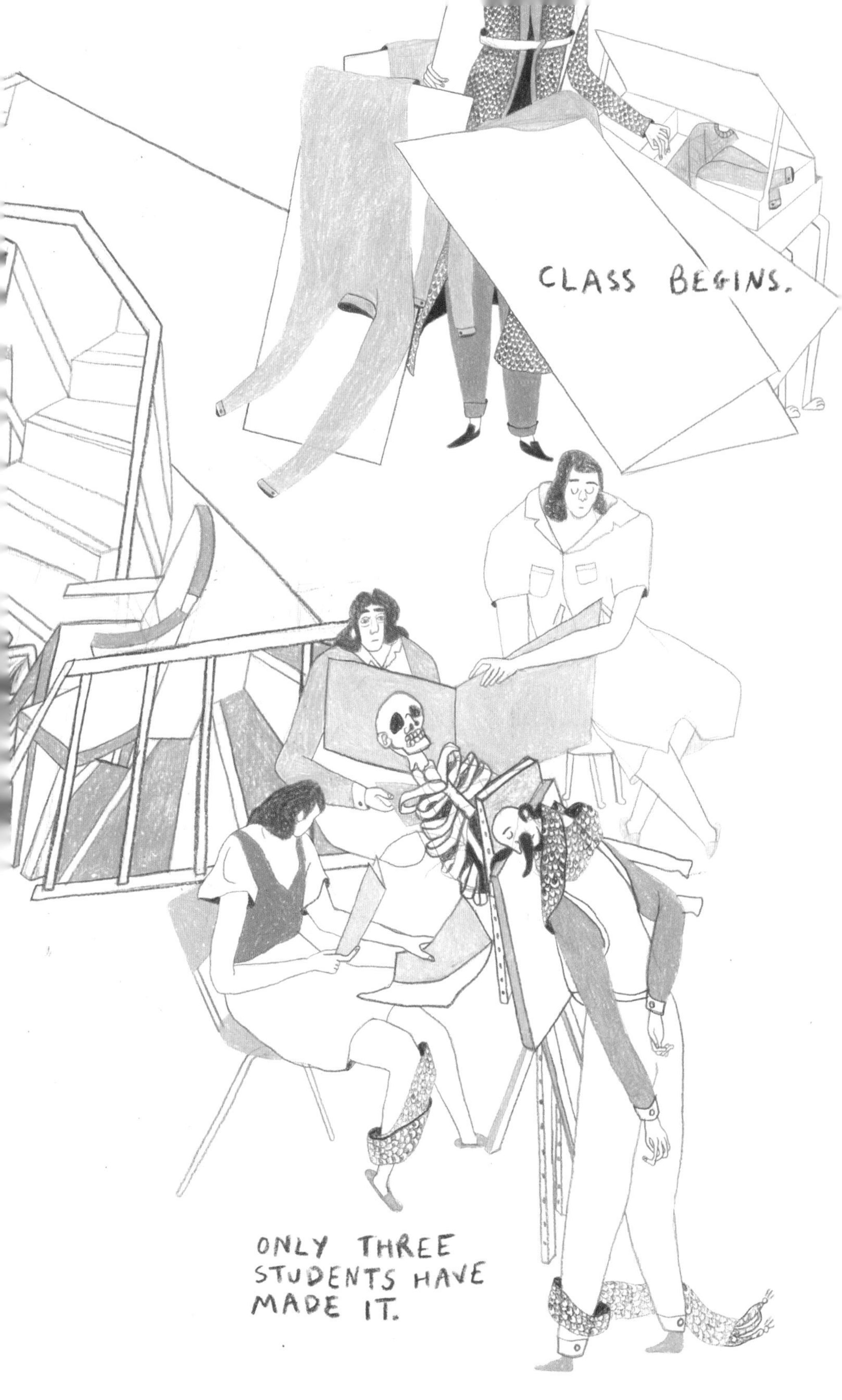
CLASS BEGINS.
ONLY THREE STUDENTS HAVE MADE IT.

Dear Pothel,

I imagine a time in a paper city. There are balconies with tiny awnings, windows, dogs, guards, angles and citizens. The most lovely figure is a woman whose dress weighs her down. Her dress spills through a window all the way down to the street. I can tell she wants to remain inside, and the long dress seeping out is only there to lead me away from her. She is also the most lonely.

I open the door to her room; a tiny pigeon feather hangs from an exposed piece of tape. In other cities I've been to, these feathers are the only things that move. Here, it's the buildings. Every morning they need to be pressed back against the tape. The dogs here are larger than the buildings, but they don't bow over as much, probably because of their sturdier silhouettes, narrower at their tops.

The windows are not cut open where the citizens are standing in their rooms looking out. There is an overlapping. I conclude the windows serve as a ruler of sorts, to bring everything else to scale. When I lean forward, they make the buildings seem closer together, like they've gathered for cover in stormy weather.

A woman named Renata walks in to my room and tells me there was once a man where there is now a piece of exposed tape. She points at the paper city and says she used to sneak out past her curfew and run across the rooftops to meet him. I ~~recog~~ recognize this place now.

Didn't you enter on the back of a horse?

If I hear music and I'm standing in a place where I can't move my arms, I usually begin to cry. I usually decide to move without knowing. Dancing to music does not necessarily mean avoiding a straight line. I remember you getting off your horse and walking in a straight line towards a sleeping lion. You were making sure to dance every movement larger than the lion. The proportions of the paper city are all wrong, but the lion is miraculously measurable simply by moving toward it. When your letters stop coming, I imagine you got swallowed by the lion.

Liana.

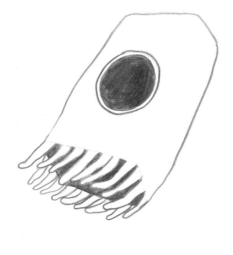

THE FIRE THEATRE

THE STUDENT:

SHE WRITES A MYSTERY ABOUT A PROFESSOR DISAPPEARING. TWELVE CHAPTERS. THE PLOT MOVES THROUGH THE LIBRARIES, CLASSROOMS, STAIRWAYS, CAFETERIAS, OFFICES AND CORRIDORS. AS MANY PLACES AS THE STORY NEEDS FOR IT TO HAPPEN OR UNFOLD.

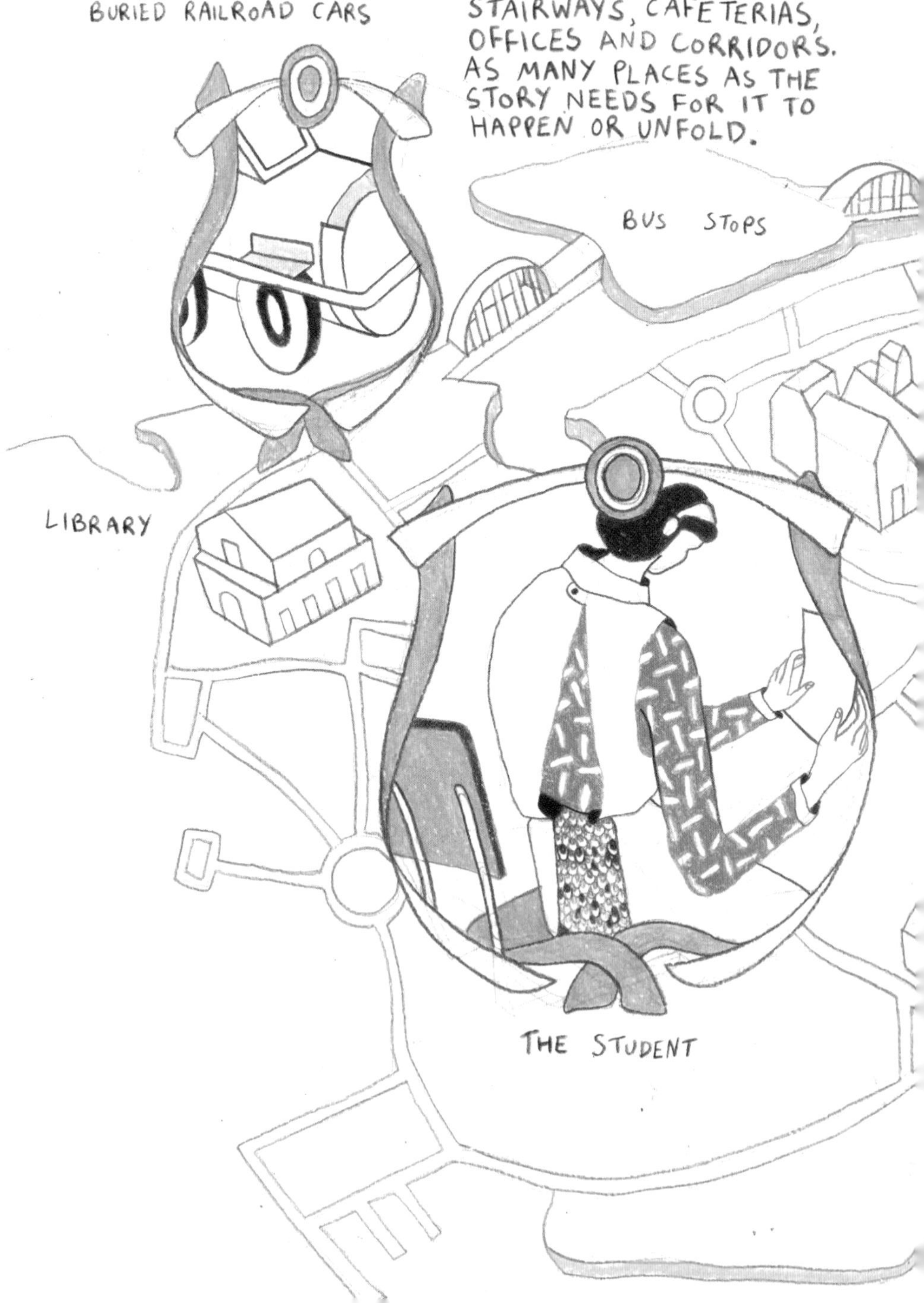
BURIED RAILROAD CARS
BUS STOPS
LIBRARY
THE STUDENT

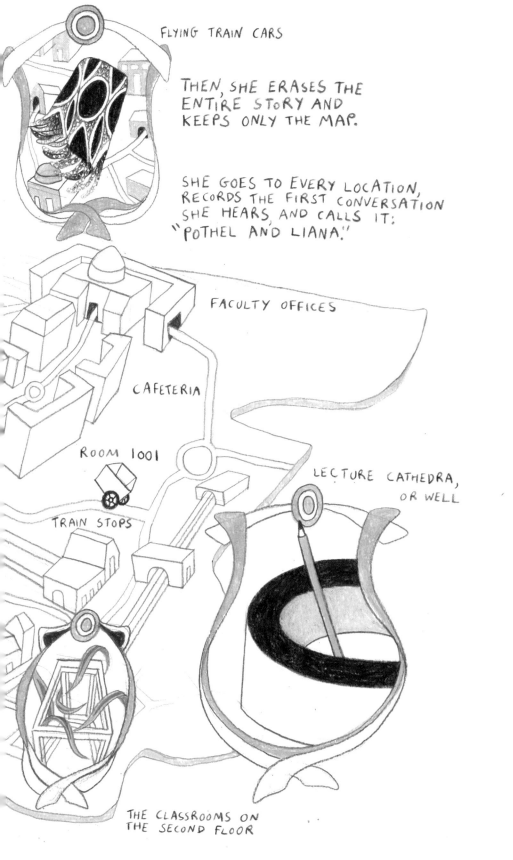

FLYING TRAIN CARS

THEN, SHE ERASES THE
ENTIRE STORY AND
KEEPS ONLY THE MAP.

SHE GOES TO EVERY LOCATION,
RECORDS THE FIRST CONVERSATION
SHE HEARS, AND CALLS IT:
"POTHEL AND LIANA."

FACULTY OFFICES

CAFETERIA

ROOM 1001

LECTURE CATHEDRA,
OR WELL

TRAIN STOPS

THE CLASSROOMS ON
THE SECOND FLOOR

THE CAMPUS:

A BURIED UNDERGROUND RAILROAD WAS PROPOSED BY AN ARCHITECT BY THE NAME OF POTHEL.

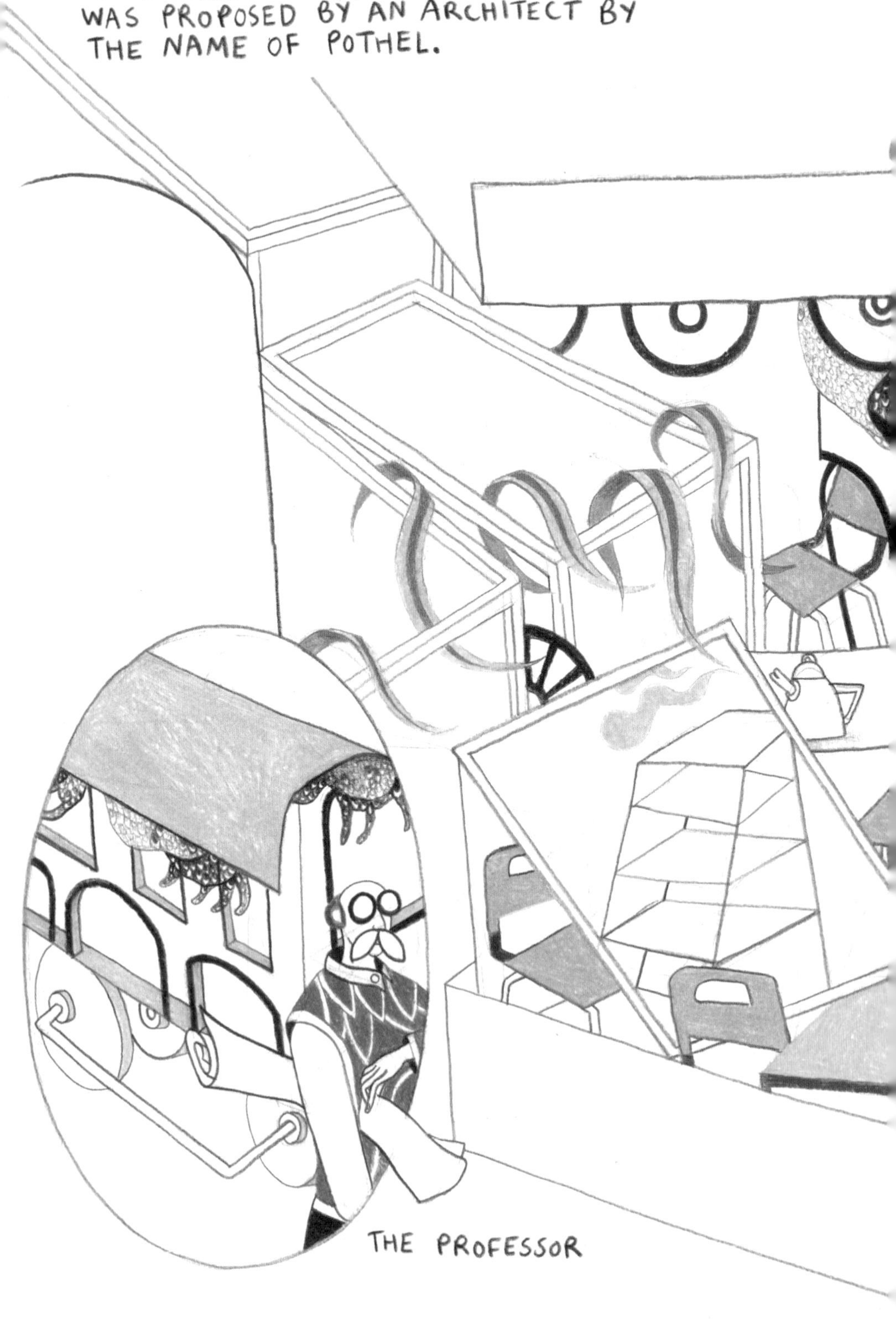
THE PROFESSOR

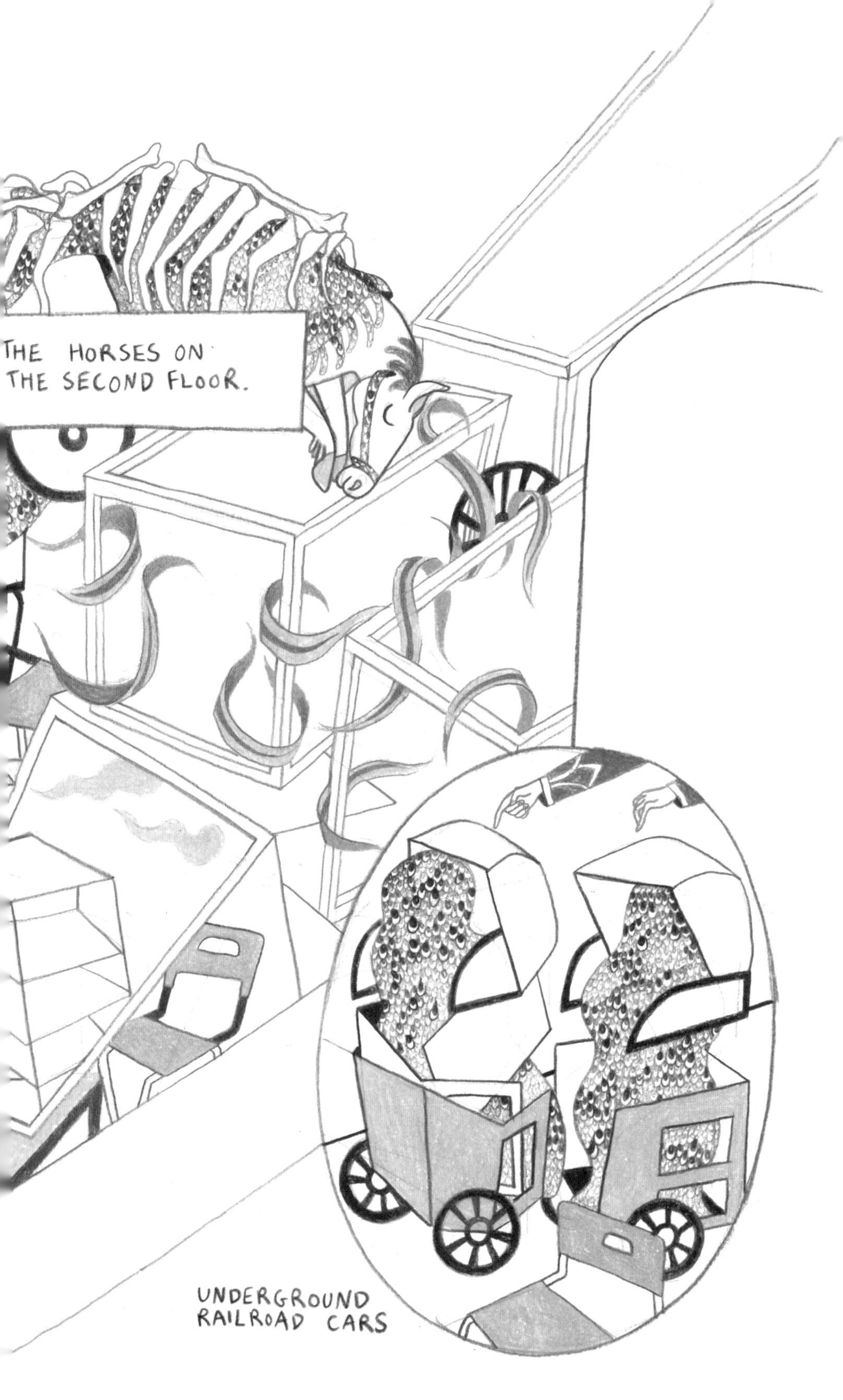
THE HORSES ON
THE SECOND FLOOR.
UNDERGROUND
RAILROAD CARS

HIS PLAN WAS TO BURY DOZENS
OF UPRIGHT, IMMOBILE RAILROAD
CARS DEEP BELOW THE FOUNDATIONS
OF THE UNIVERSITY—

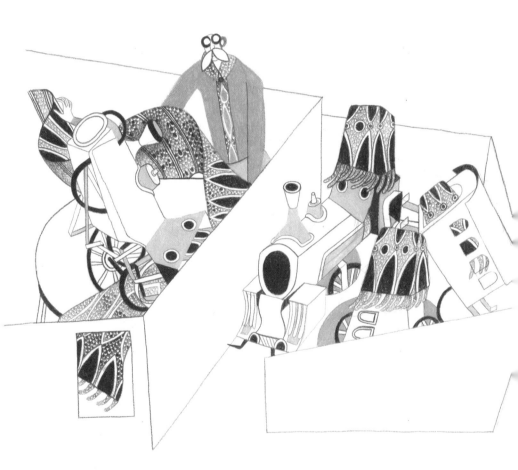

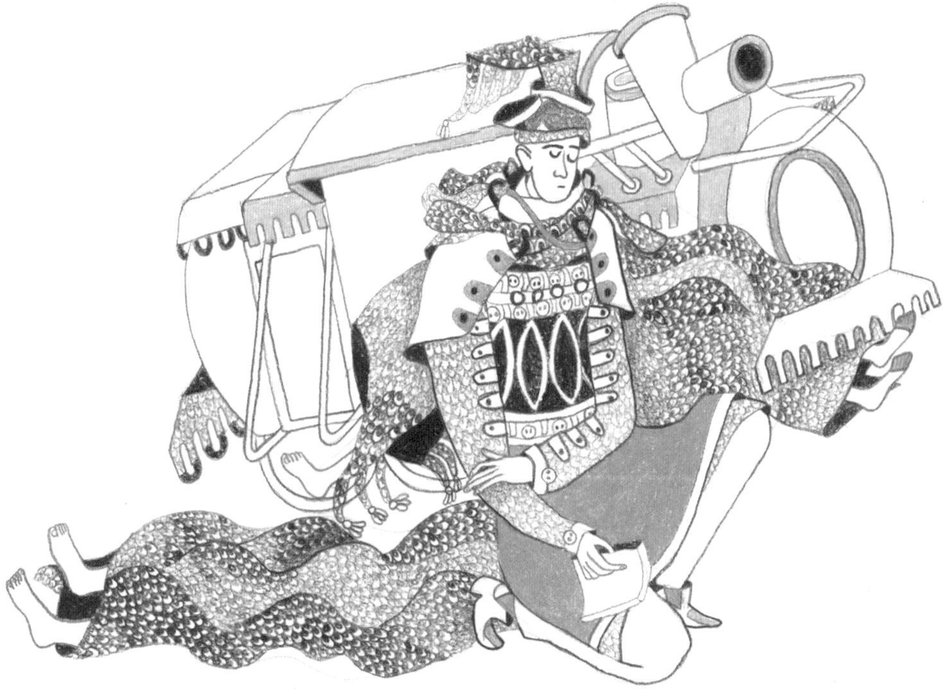

- AND HAVE THE STUDENTS LEARN OF THEIR EXISTENCE -

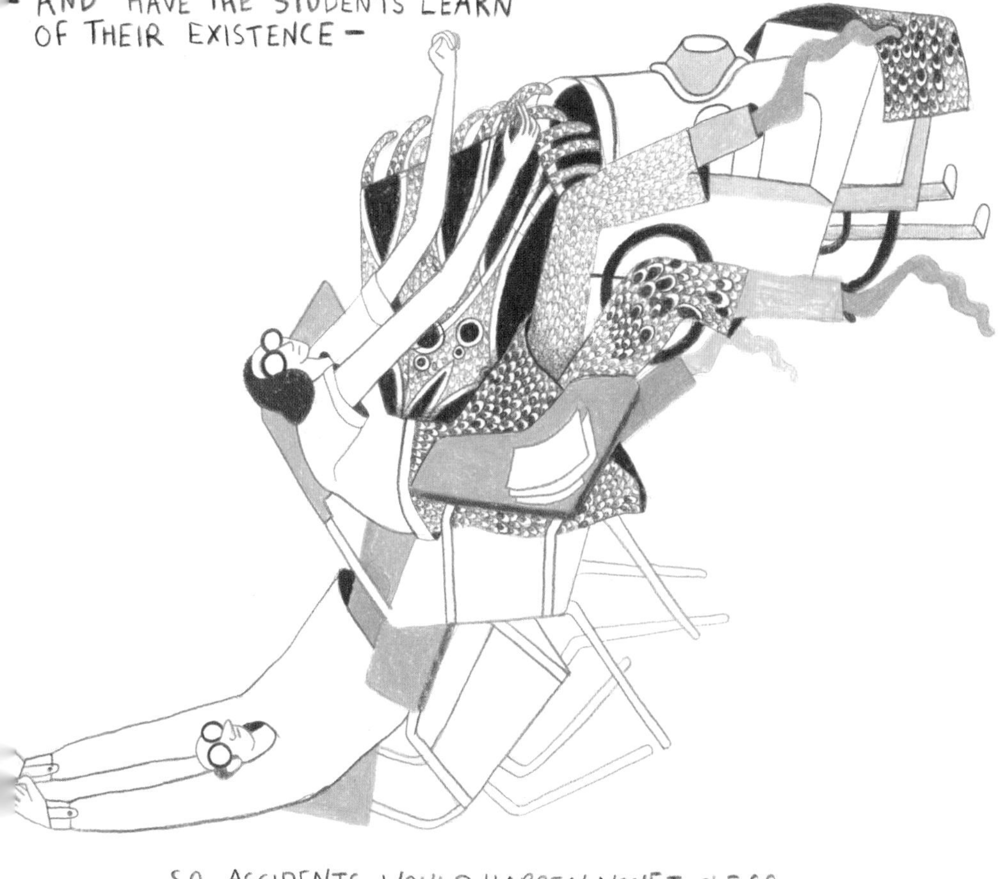

— SO ACCIDENTS WOULD HAPPEN NONETHELESS.

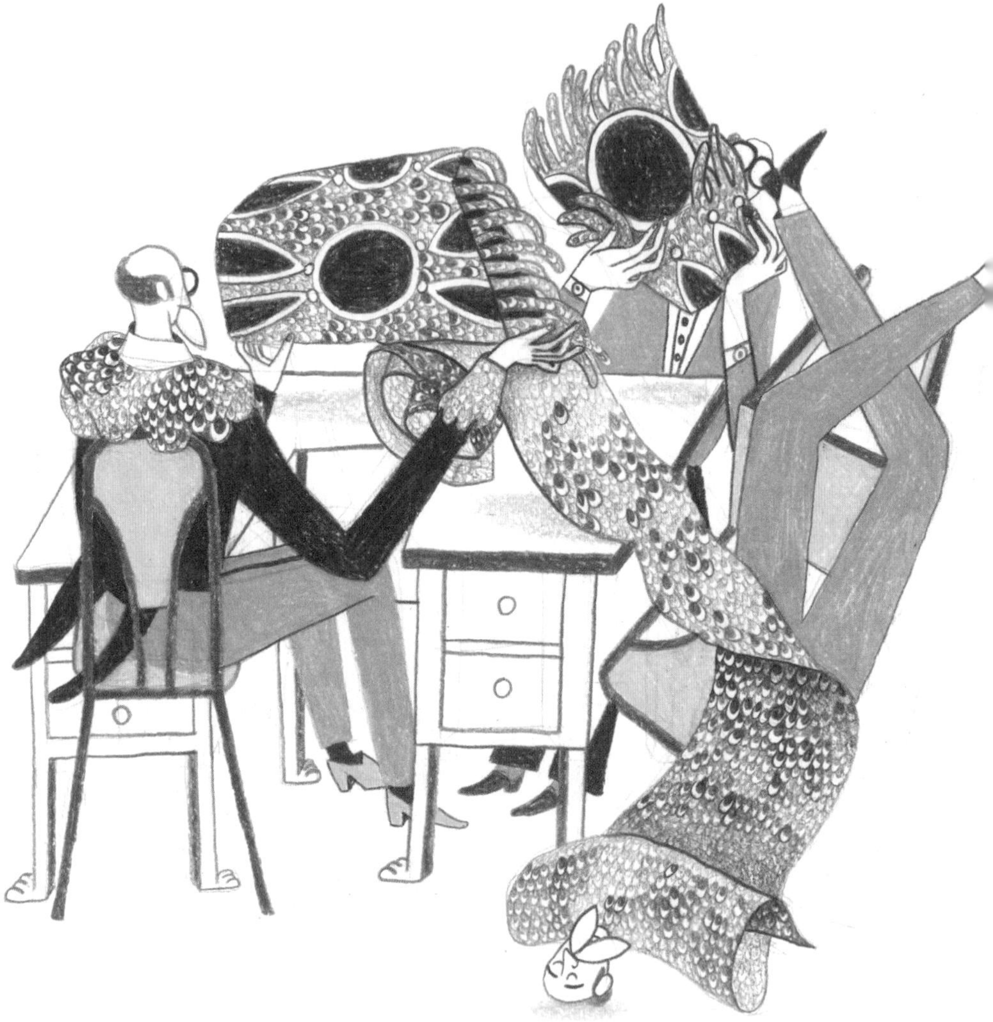

HE WAS IMMEDIATELY FIRED
FROM THE DESIGN TEAM.

THEY KEPT HIM ON AS FACULTY,
BUT BANNED HIM FROM TEACHING
IN THE ARCHITECTURE DEPARTMENT.

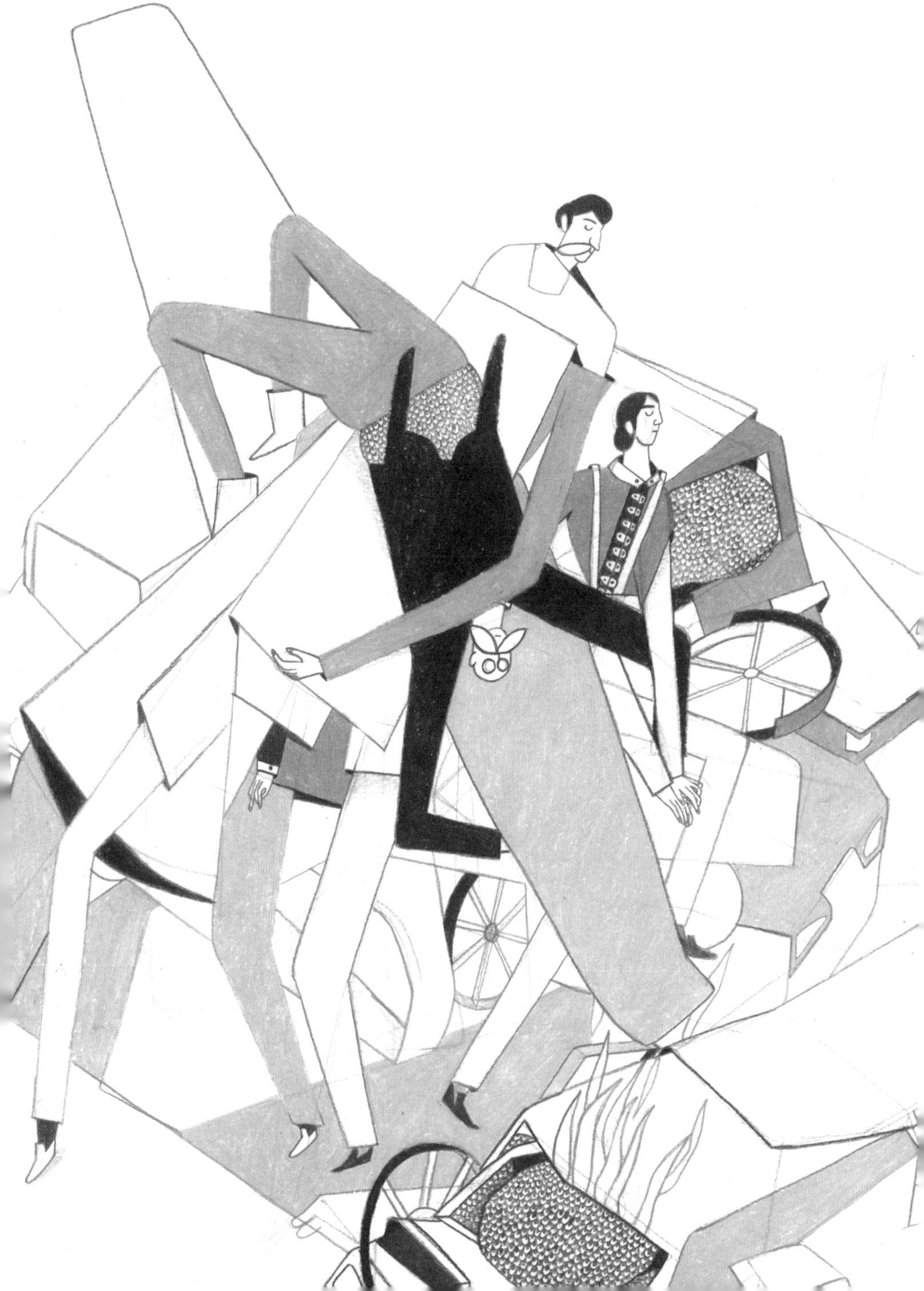

HOWEVER, POTHEL'S PLANS SOMEHOW RESURFACED AS PART OF THE OFFICIAL DESIGN PROTOCOLS OF THE CAMPUS.

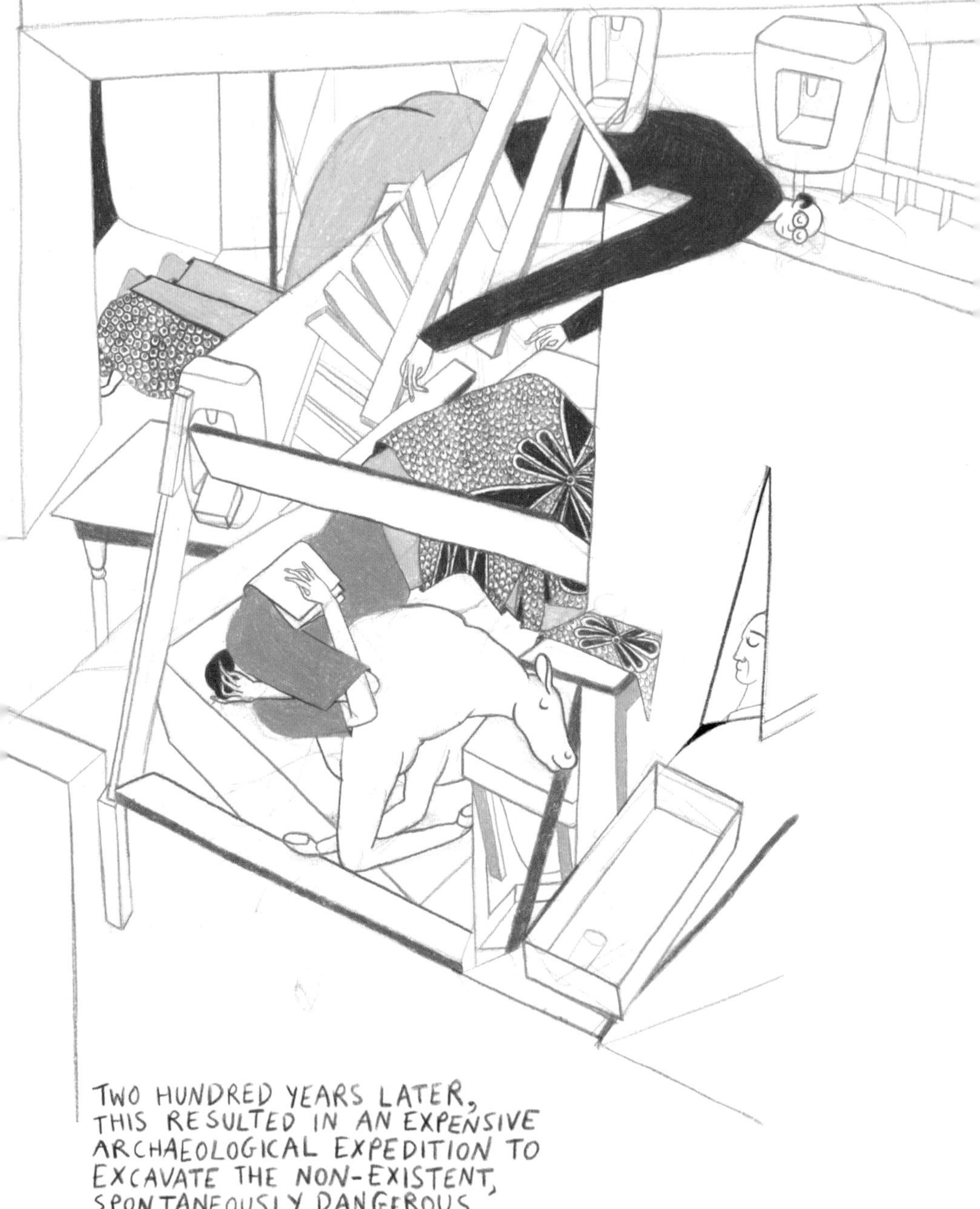

TWO HUNDRED YEARS LATER, THIS RESULTED IN AN EXPENSIVE ARCHAEOLOGICAL EXPEDITION TO EXCAVATE THE NON-EXISTENT, SPONTANEOUSLY DANGEROUS RAILROAD CARS. THEY FOLLOWED POTHEL'S BLUEPRINTS, WHICH THEY CONSIDERED THE MOST CURIOUS AND WORTHY FEATURE OF THE LEGENDARY SCHOOL.

THEY FOUND LIANA,
TRAPPED IN THE RUINS OF A CLASSROOM
WITH A GIANT PENCIL GROWING
BEHIND HER EAR.

THE PROFESSOR:

AFTER HIS FIRST CLASS TEACHING
OUTSIDE HIS DEPARTMENT, PROF. POTHEL
DISAPPEARS FROM CAMPUS WITHOUT
A TRACE.

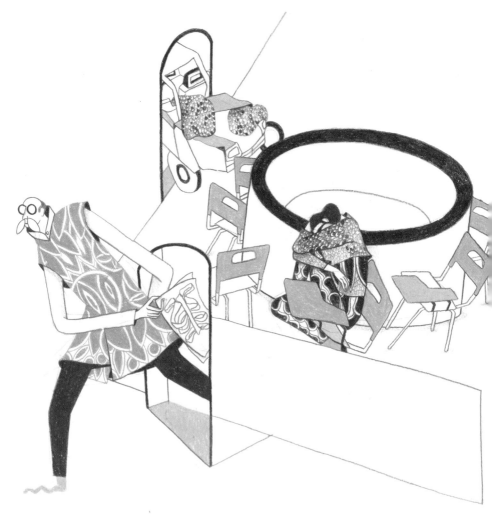

A MONTH LATER, HE RETURNS TO CAMPUS
AS A CRASHED CAR AND RESUMES TEACHING
HIS ANATOMY COURSE EXACTLY WHERE
HE LEFT OFF.

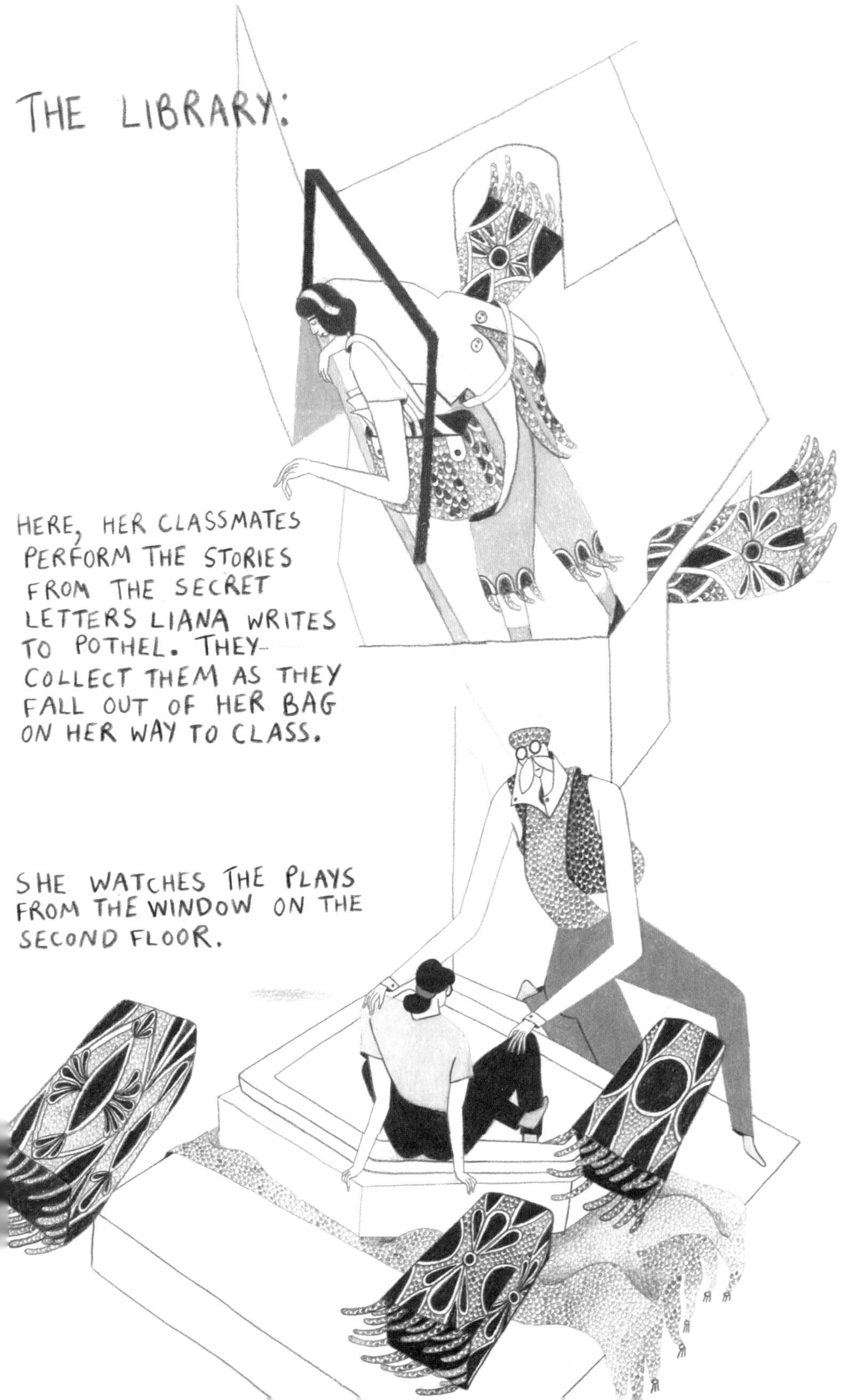
THE LIBRARY:
HERE, HER CLASSMATES PERFORM THE STORIES FROM THE SECRET LETTERS LIANA WRITES TO POTHEL. THEY COLLECT THEM AS THEY FALL OUT OF HER BAG ON HER WAY TO CLASS.
SHE WATCHES THE PLAYS FROM THE WINDOW ON THE SECOND FLOOR.

THE EFFECT OF THE ANATOMY PROFESSORS ON THE ARCHITECTURE DEPARTMENT:

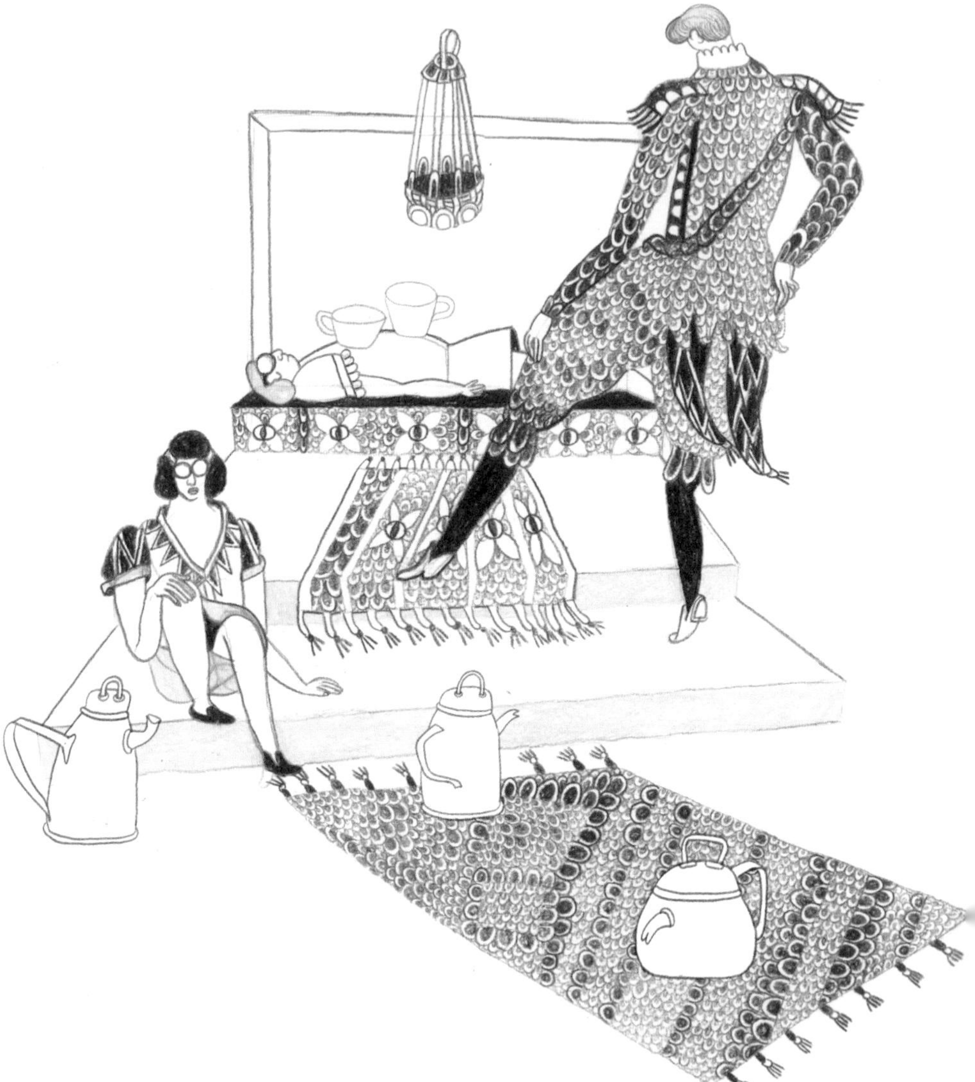

THEY HAVE NO OFFICE OF THEIR OWN, SO THEY BOIL WATER FOR THEIR TEA IN THE CORRIDORS.

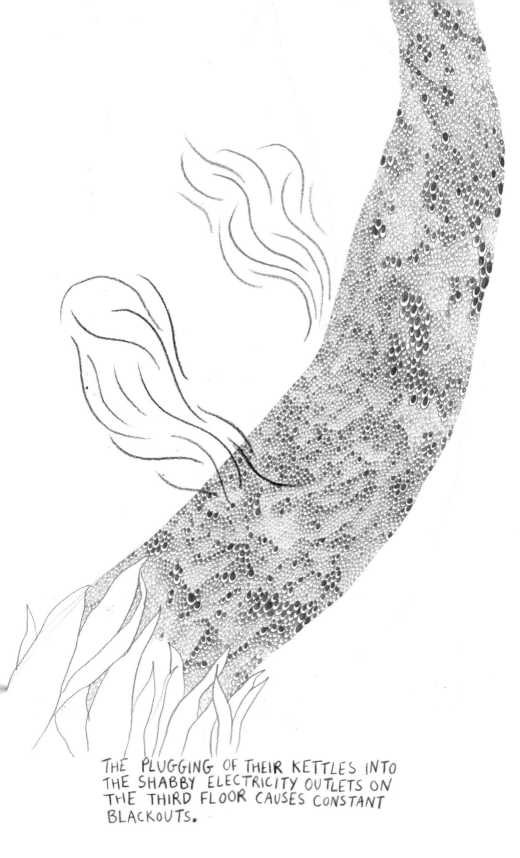

THE PLUGGING OF THEIR KETTLES INTO
THE SHABBY ELECTRICITY OUTLETS ON
THE THIRD FLOOR CAUSES CONSTANT
BLACKOUTS.

THE CLASSROOMS ON THE SECOND FLOOR:

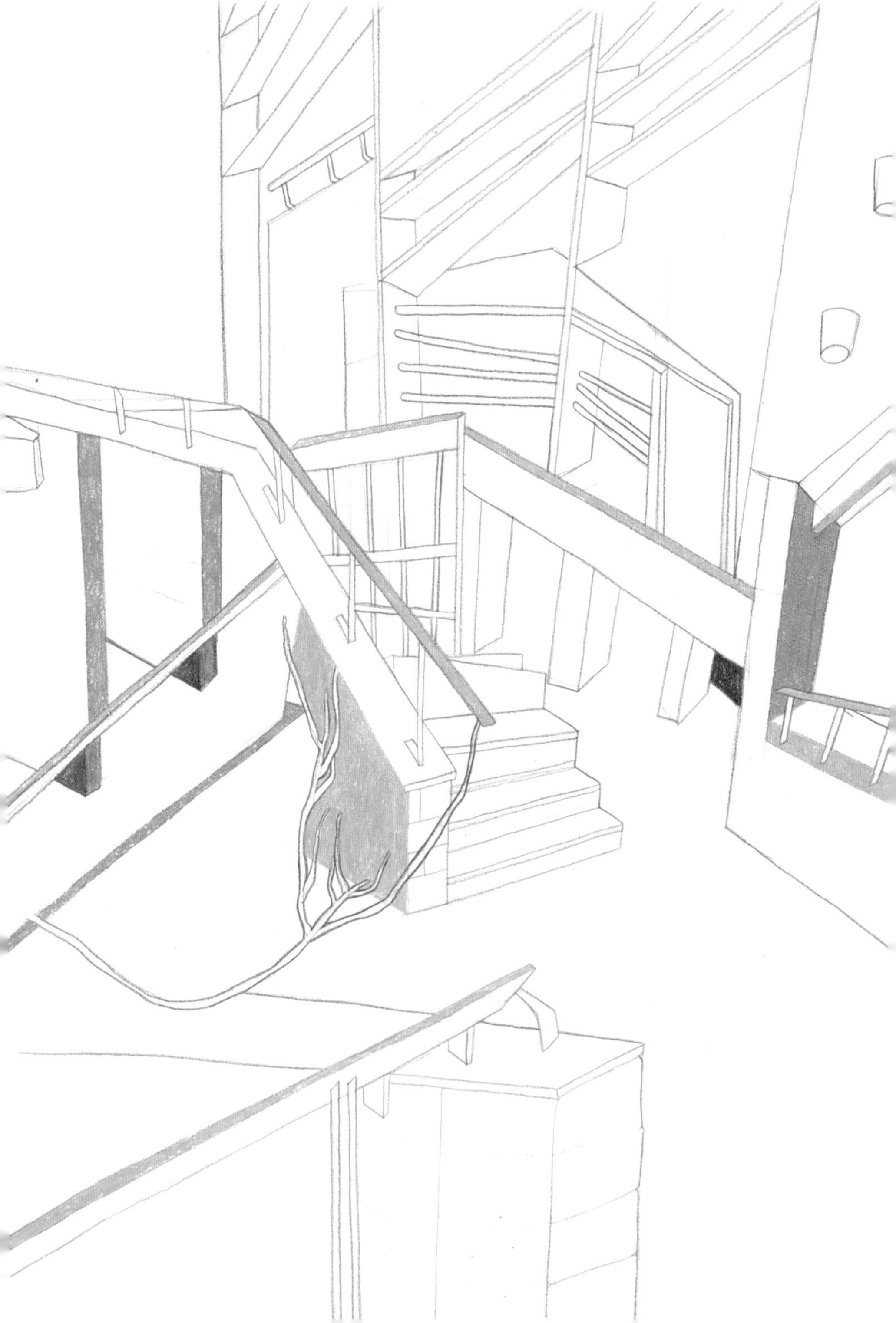

IF TWO OR MORE PEOPLE ARE ABLE TO FIND THEIR WAY UP THERE WITHOUT USING THE STAIRS, THEN THAT MEANS THEY ARE THE SAME PERSON. THERE ARE NO STAIRS LEADING UP THERE.

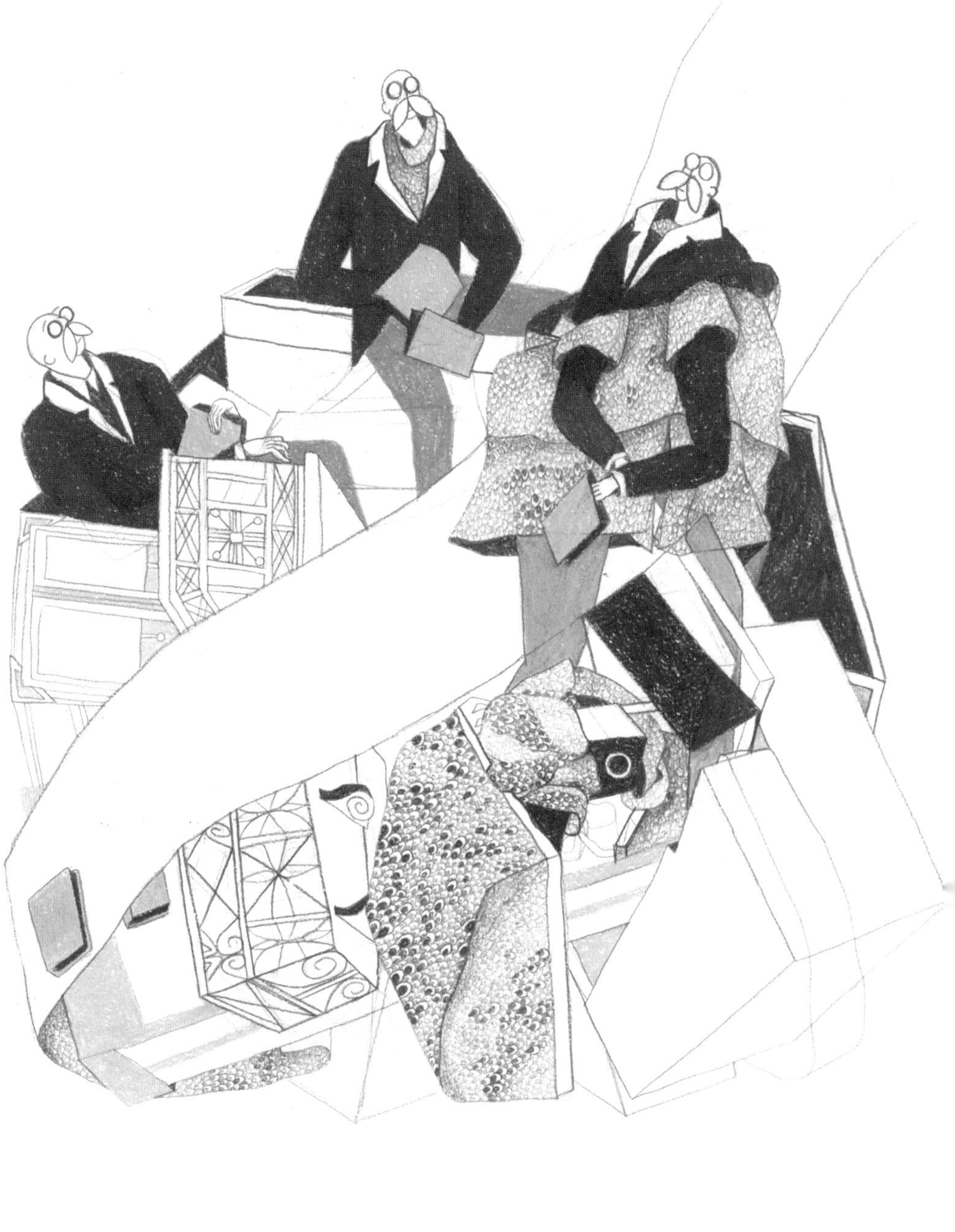

THE LECTURE CATHEDRA:

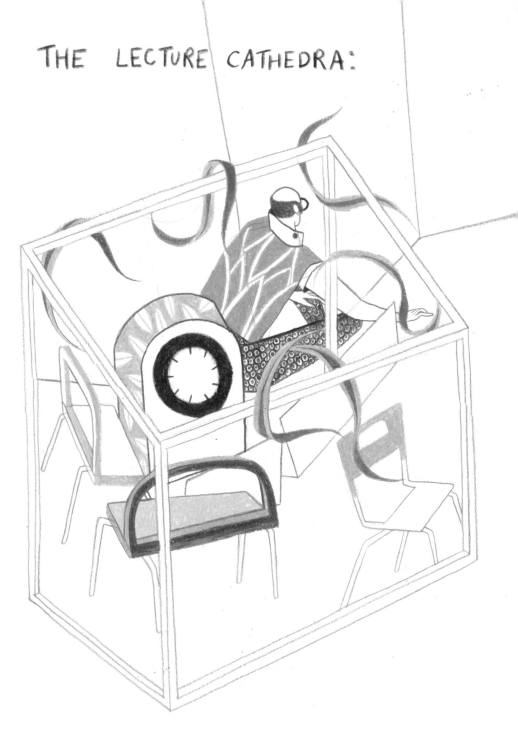

HE WAKES UP ON THE HOUR.

AFTER A MINUTE PASSES, HE REALIZES;
I AM ON STAGE.

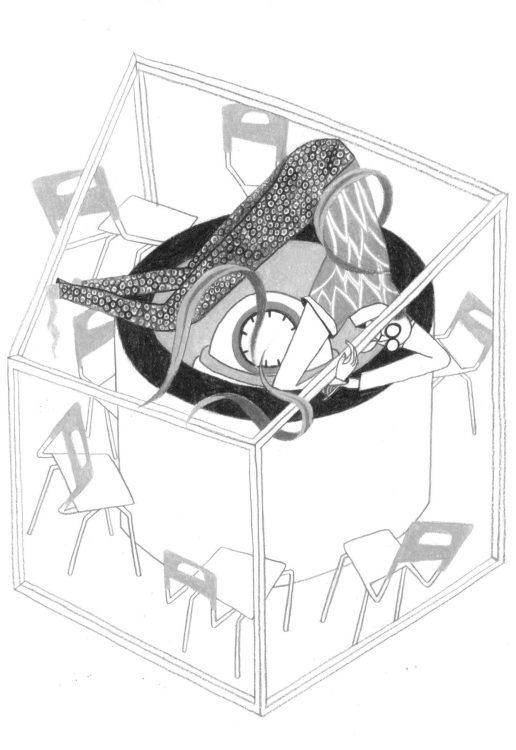

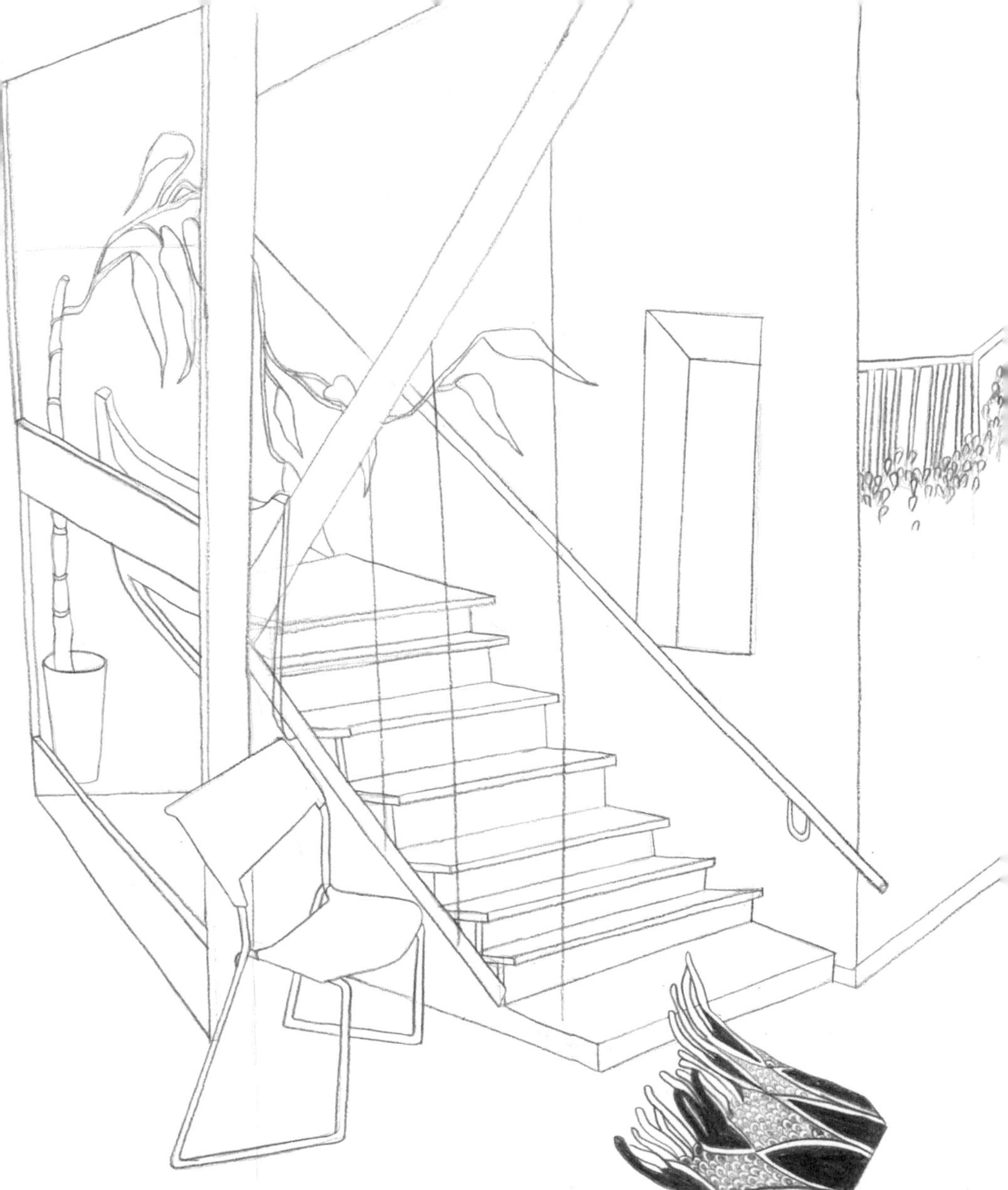

THE STAIRWAYS:

STAIRS, EVEN MORE SO THAN SLEEP, ARE THE MOST SIGNIFICANT SWITCH FOR LIANA'S IMAGINATION, LEADING HER TO HER THEATRE OF SEARCHING. EVERY CLASSROOM WHICH HAS EVEN A COUPLE OF STEPS LEADING INTO IT, WOULD TRANSFORM, IN HER MIND, INTO POTHEL'S OFFICE —

—EVEN WHEN POTHEL HAD LONG RETURNED, AND THERE WAS NO ONE LEFT TO SEARCH FOR.

ROOM 1001:

LIANA TELLS POTHEL STORIES ON THEIR WAY TO HIS ANATOMY COURSE IN ROOM 1001 IN THE HOPES THAT HE WILL FALL IN LOVE WITH HER BEFORE THEIR ARRIVAL.

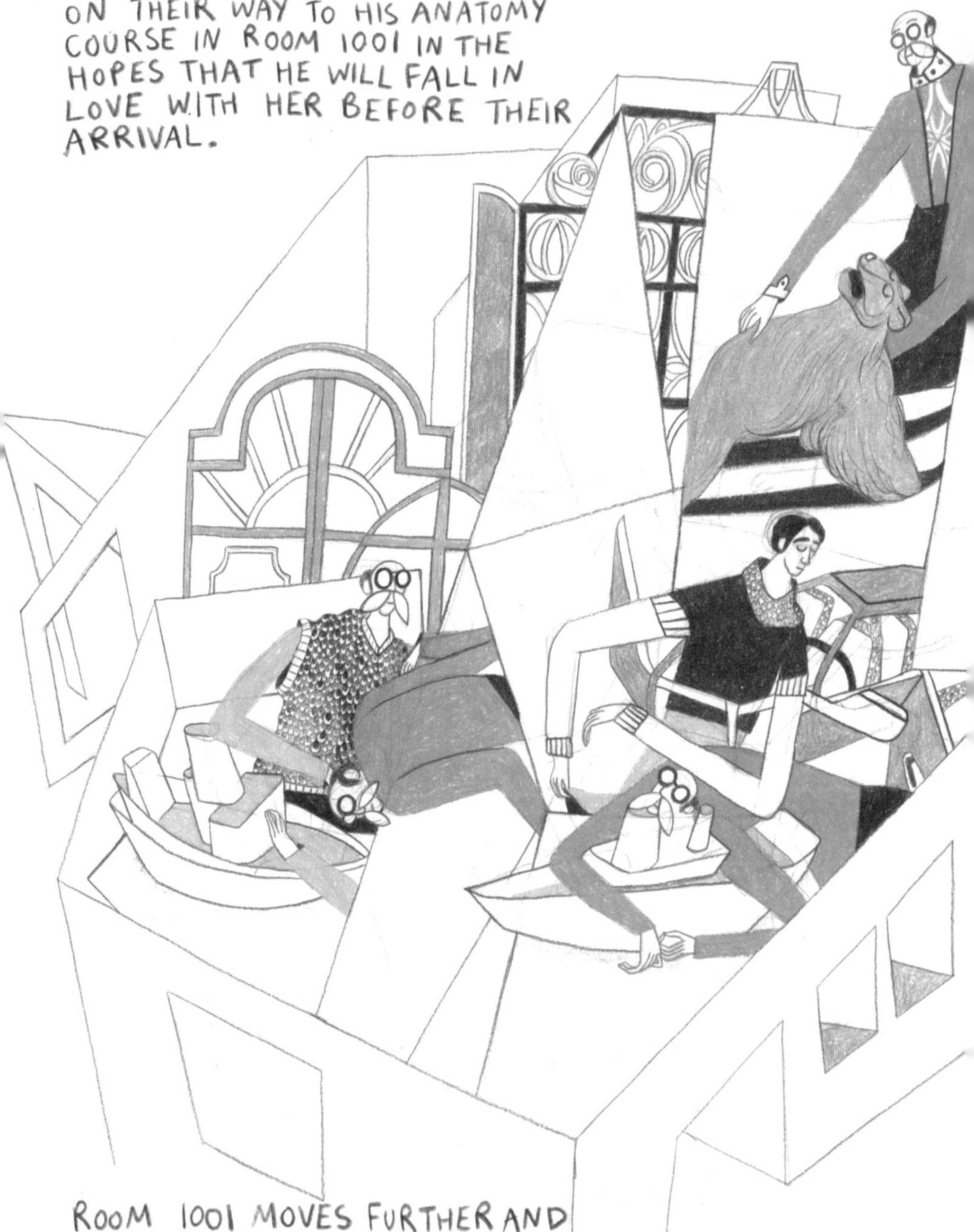

ROOM 1001 MOVES FURTHER AND FURTHER AWAY FROM THEM AT THE END OF EACH STORY.

(THIS IS THE HARM A ROOM CAUSES WHEN IT MOVES.).

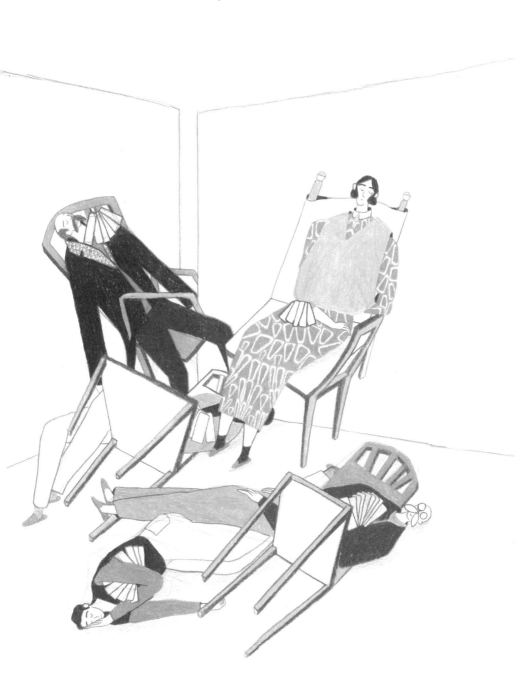

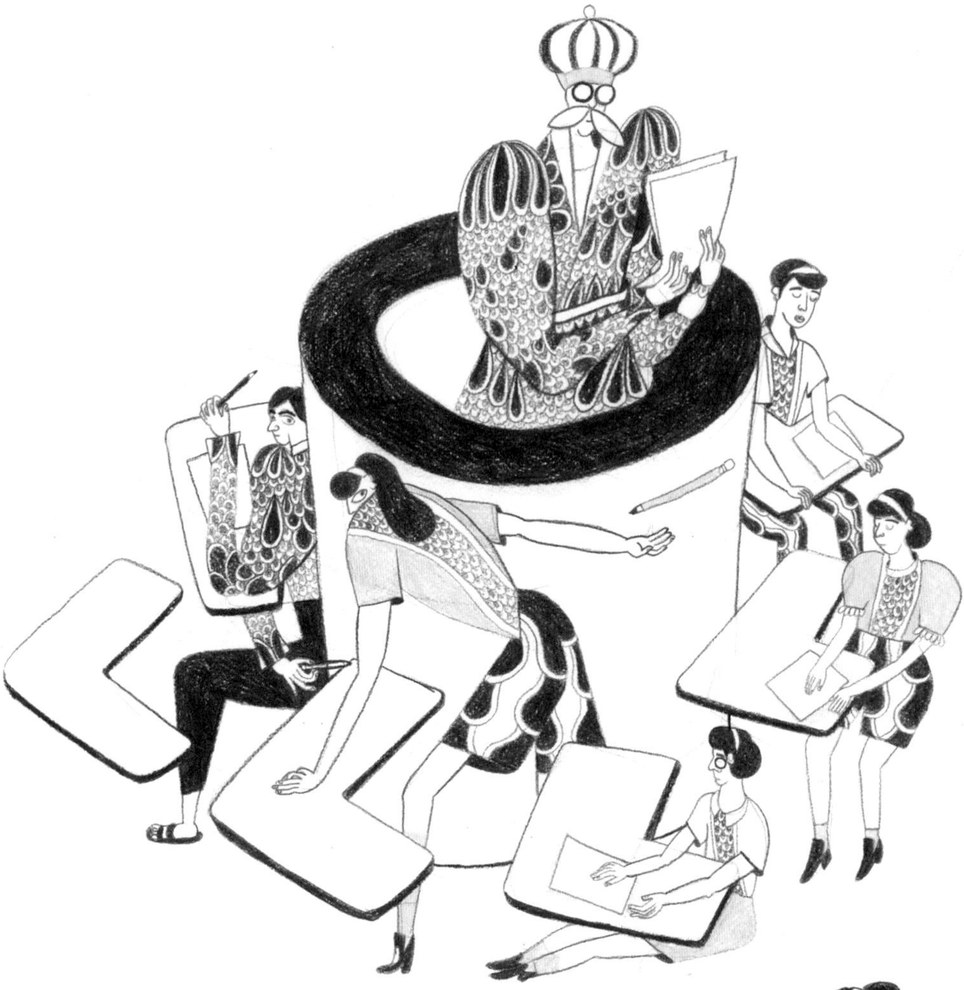

SHE TELLS HIM ABOUT THE GIRLS WHO LEAVE PENCILS TO GROW BEHIND THEIR EARS.

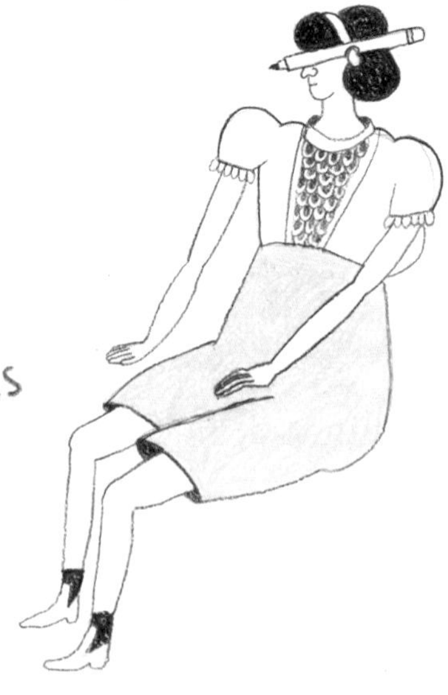

SHE TELLS HIM HOW THEY ALL WAIT AROUND DURING THE BLACKOUTS TO SEE HIM JUMP IN THE AIR FOR EIGHT SECONDS AT A TIME TO CHANGE THE LIGHT BULBS. NO LADDER REQUIRED.

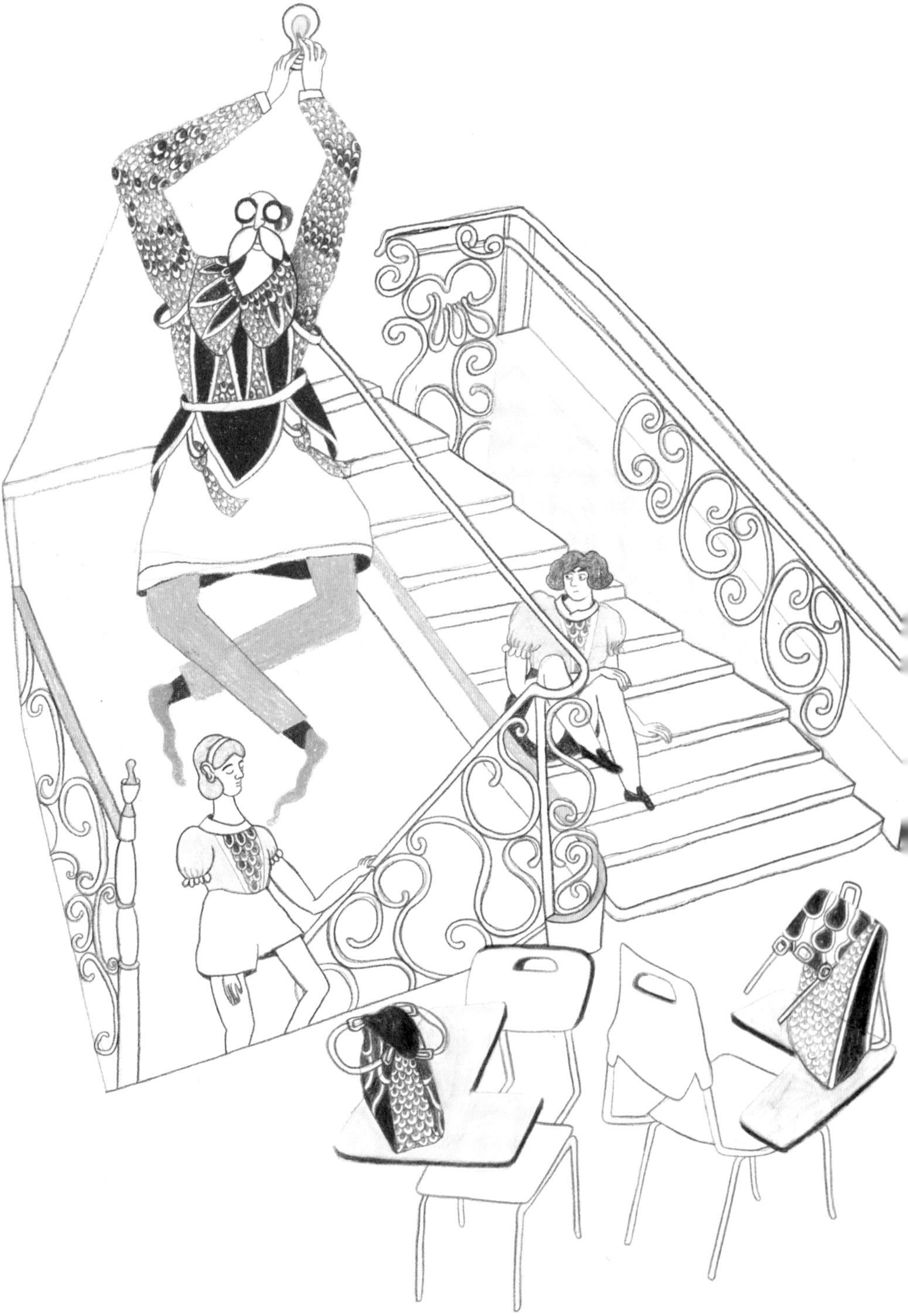

SHE TELLS HIM ABOUT THE GIRL WHO
HAS PERFECTLY GOOD EYESIGHT
BUT CANNOT SEE CHAIRS.

UNLESS THEY ARE BEING USED IN A PLAY.

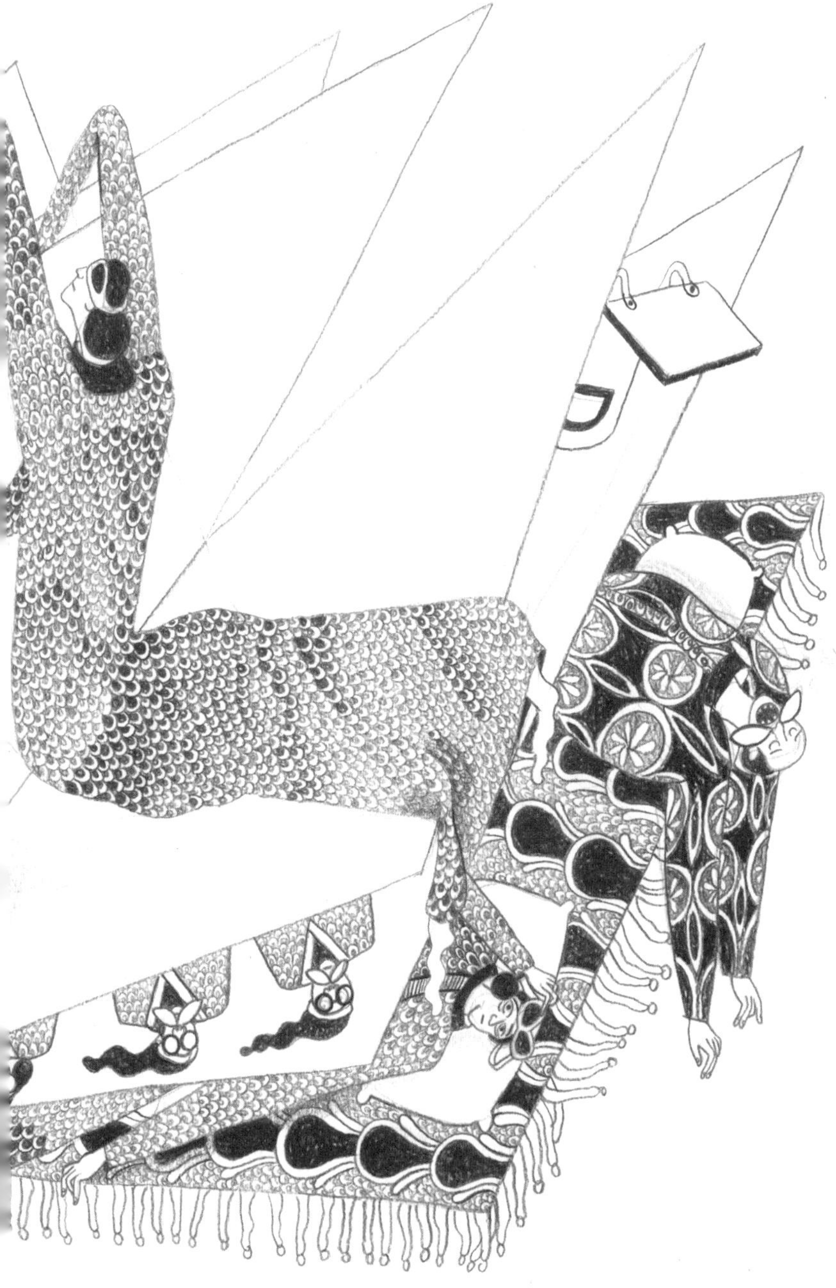

SHE TELLS HIM ABOUT THE ROOM CURSED WITH SHADOWS OF FALLING WOMEN.

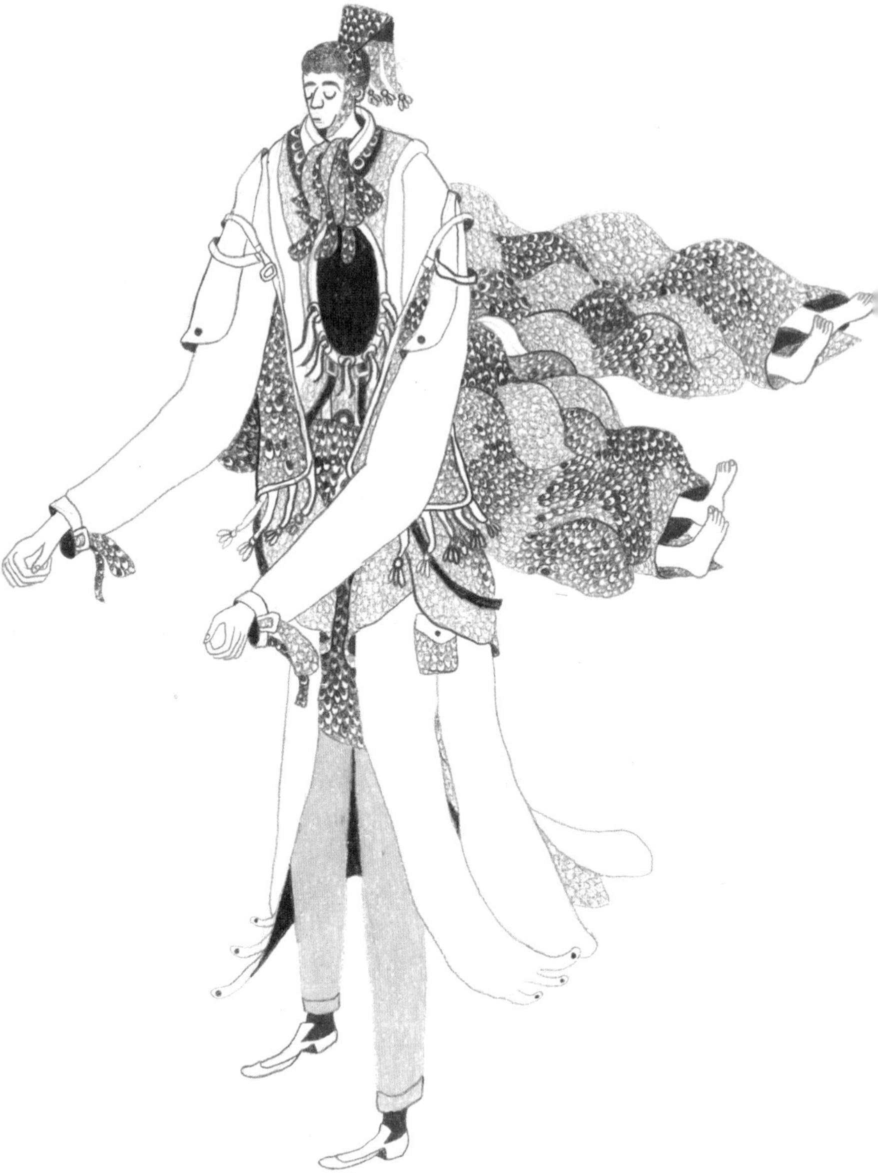

SHE TELLS HIM ABOUT THE RAVEN MASTERS WHO KEEP COUNT OF ALL THE RAVENS IN THE SCHOOL, LEST IT SHOULD FALL APART—

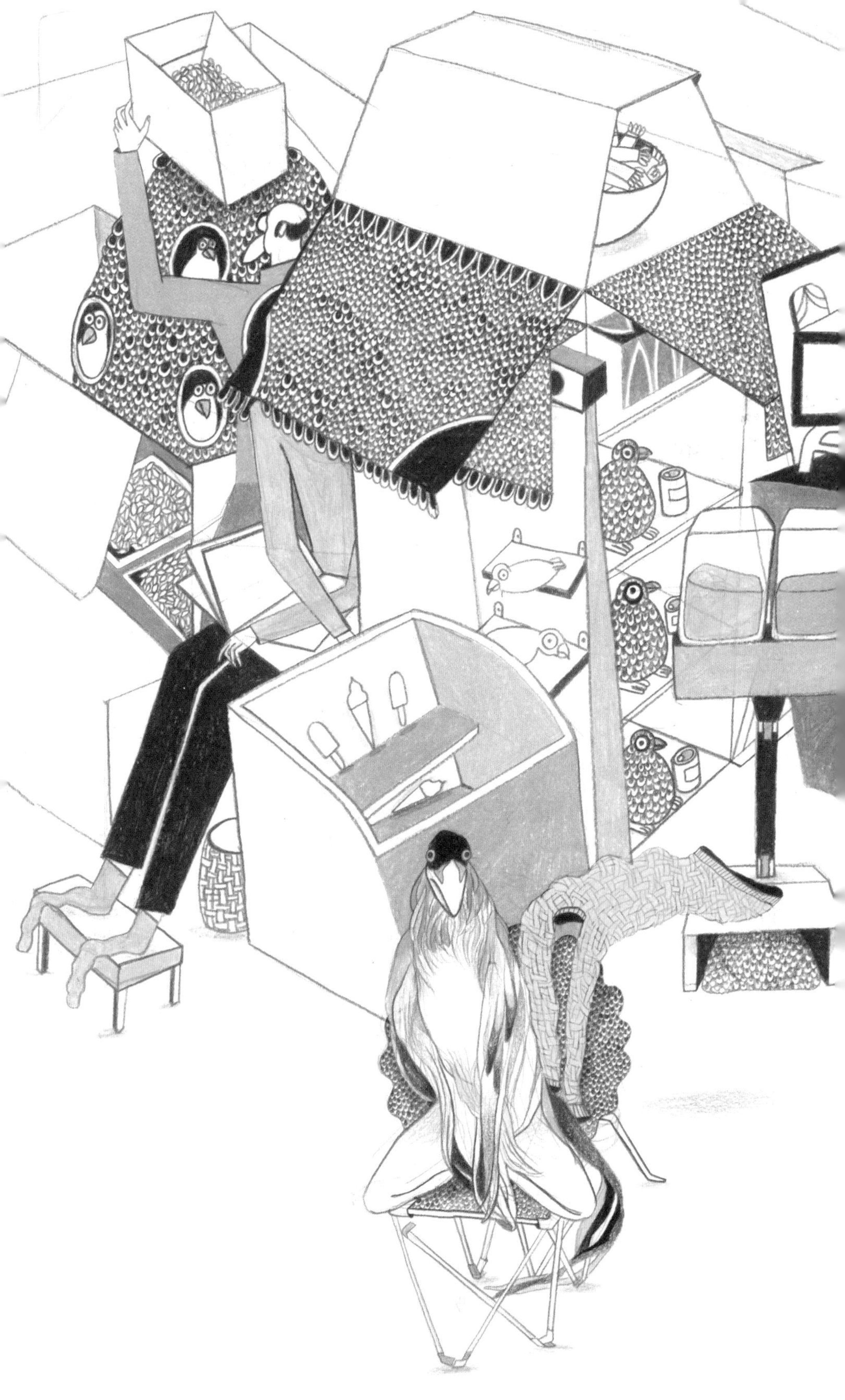

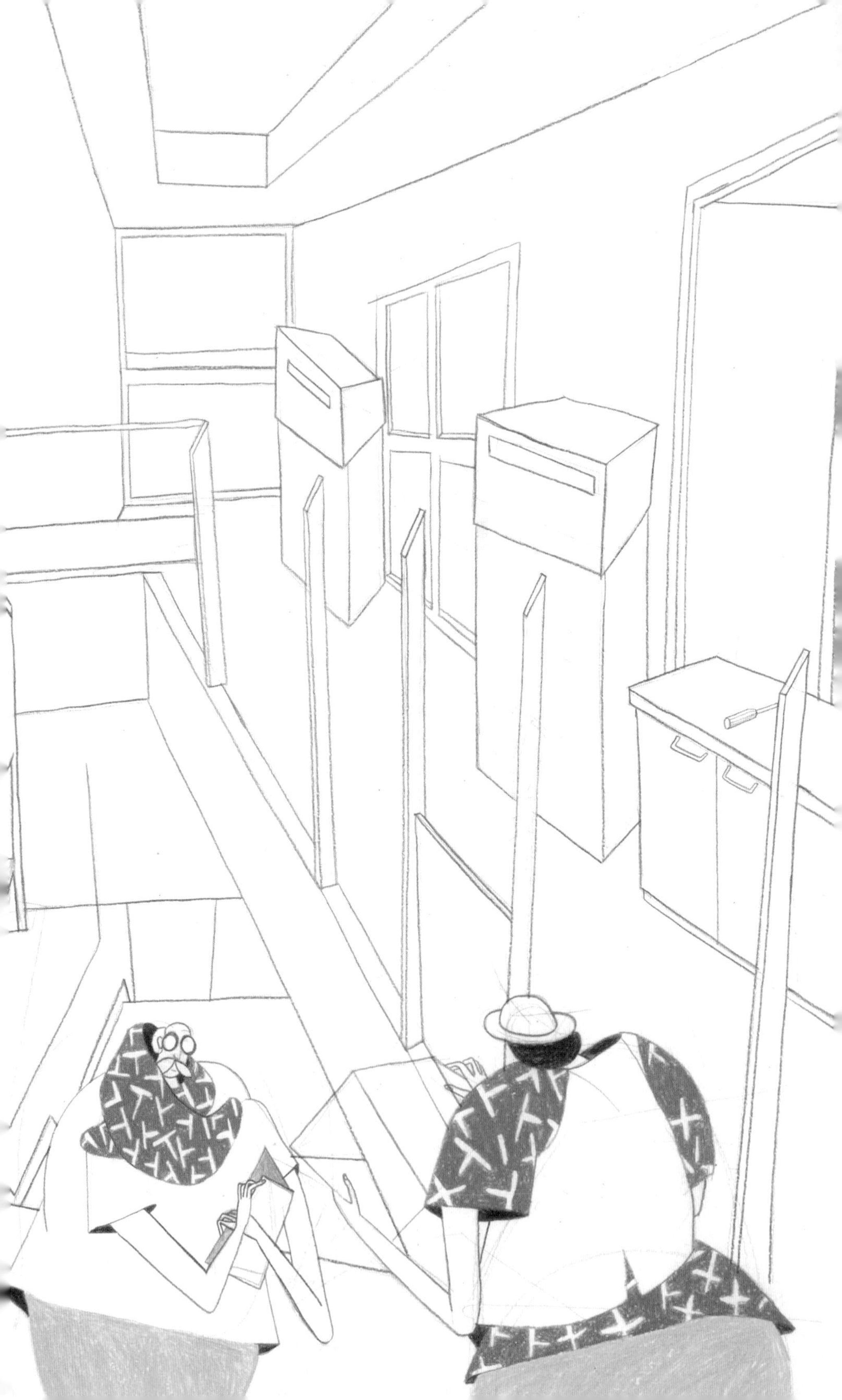

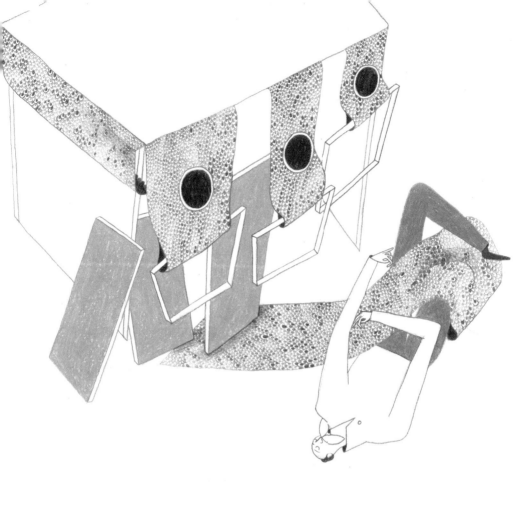

—AND ROOM 1001 SHOULD DISAPPEAR
INTO THE HORIZON.

THE ACADEMIC HOUR:

IT IS LIANA'S FAVORITE BOOK, THOUGH SHE HAS NEVER READ BEYOND THE FIRST CHAPTER AND SHE CONSTANTLY FORGETS IT ON THE BUS ON HER WAY TO SCHOOL.

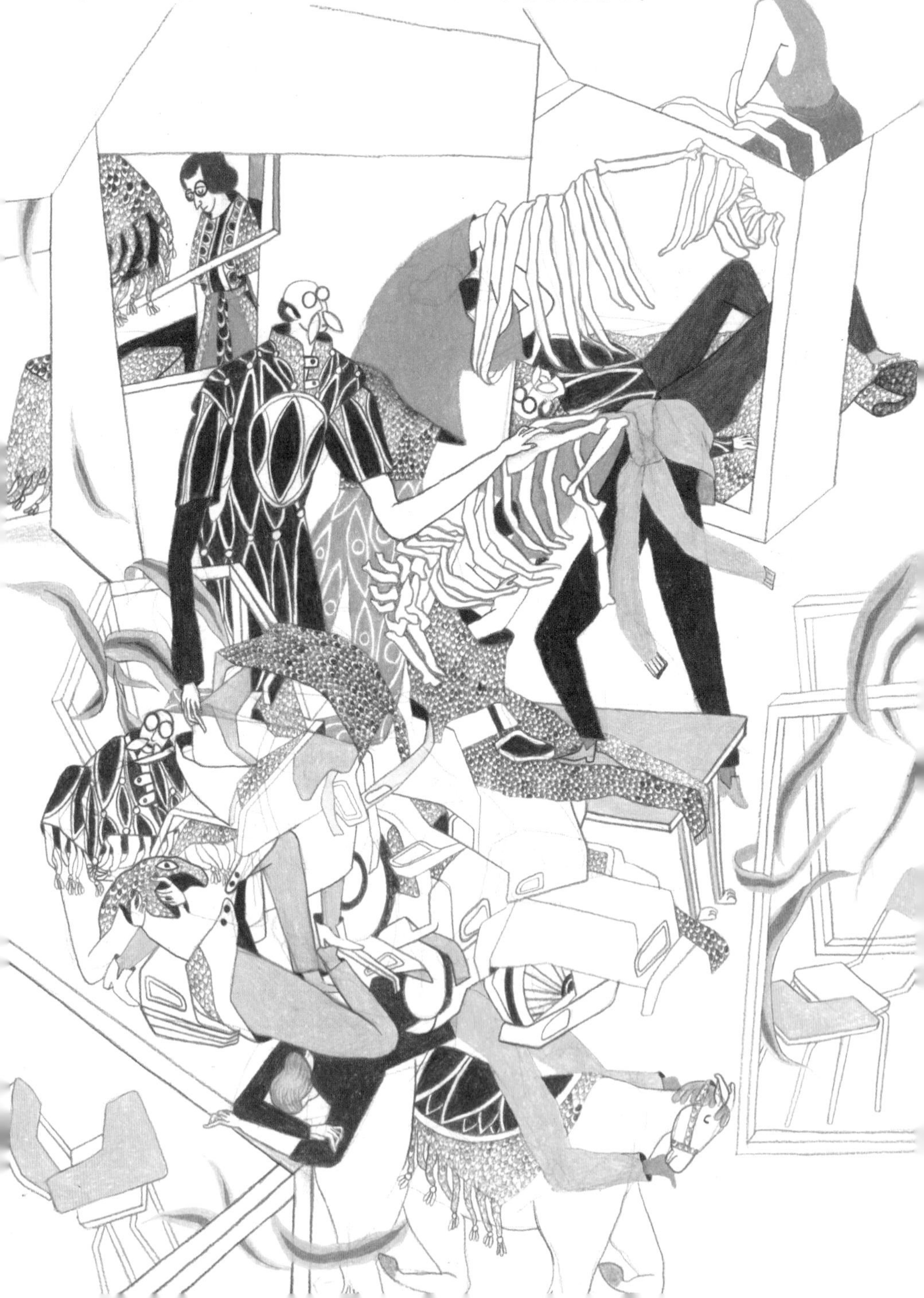

BUT EVERY SCENE SHE ENCOUNTERS ON CAMPUS, SHE LATER DESCRIBES TO POTHEL IN HER LETTERS AS IF THEY WERE CHAPTERS FROM THE BOOK.

SHE IS SAVING THE ACTUAL READING FOR WHEN SHE FINDS HERSELF SOMEDAY WITH TIME TO KILL, ALONE, BEFORE CLASS BEGINS.

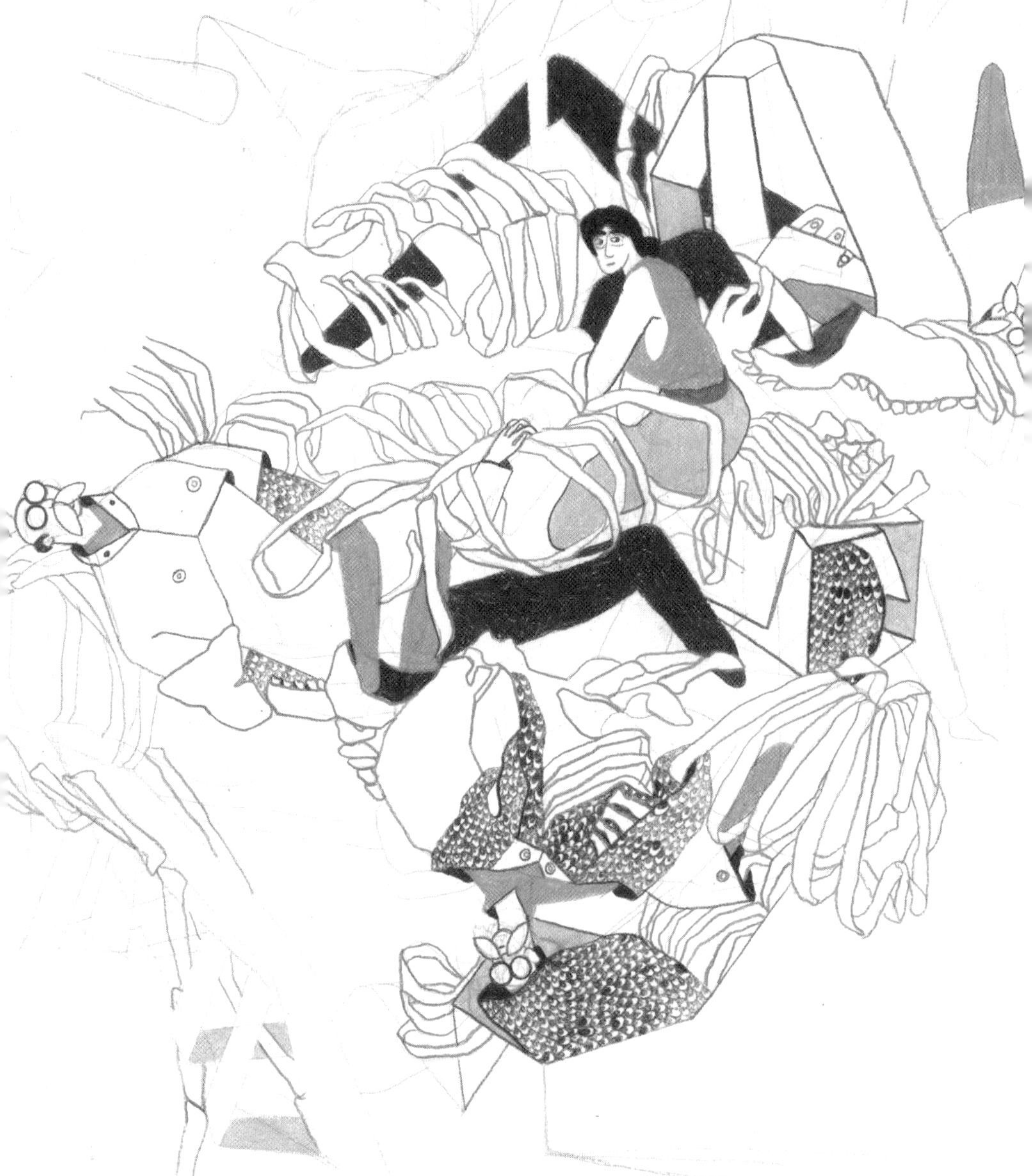

ONE DAY SHE WILL FIND OUT THE BOOK ENDS IN A GRAVEYARD FULL OF LION BONES.

Pothel,

This is a list of the things I did with my teachers in the Fire Theatre—

- We laughed at the feet.
- We talked about men and proceeded to follow them as we left the museum; they were, somehow, conjured by our conversation.
- My mom served them biscuits in the living room (but I was not allowed.)
- They took me to a dinosaur museum.
- They set a room for me.
- I picked out shirts for them.
- I crawled on the floor to lock the door at midnight, so they wouldn't hear that I was home.
- I cried.
- I danced in Margaret's dorm with the windows open.
- We drove around in circles.
- I smoked in my grandmother's living room while she was away and I let them smoke and I gave them an ashtray.
- We hitchhiked.
- I picked them up at the airport instead of the people I was supposed to pick up.
- I saw them hit and run some cars.
- Gave dumplings to.
- Got set up.
- Met after a break.
- The button they press to the top floor. The light humming in the ceiling. The light that goes out in their eyes. The glare of the computer screen. The fake bulbs in the chandelier.
- Babysat their rabbits.
- Extinguished a fire.
- Visited.
- Asked a question.
- Shot a firework gun.
- Gave them my firework gun license.
- Spoke on the phone. I said "Hello, Tower!"
- Got tricked.
- Reenacted their classes at night.

Liana.

POTHEL, WERE YOU WATCHING?

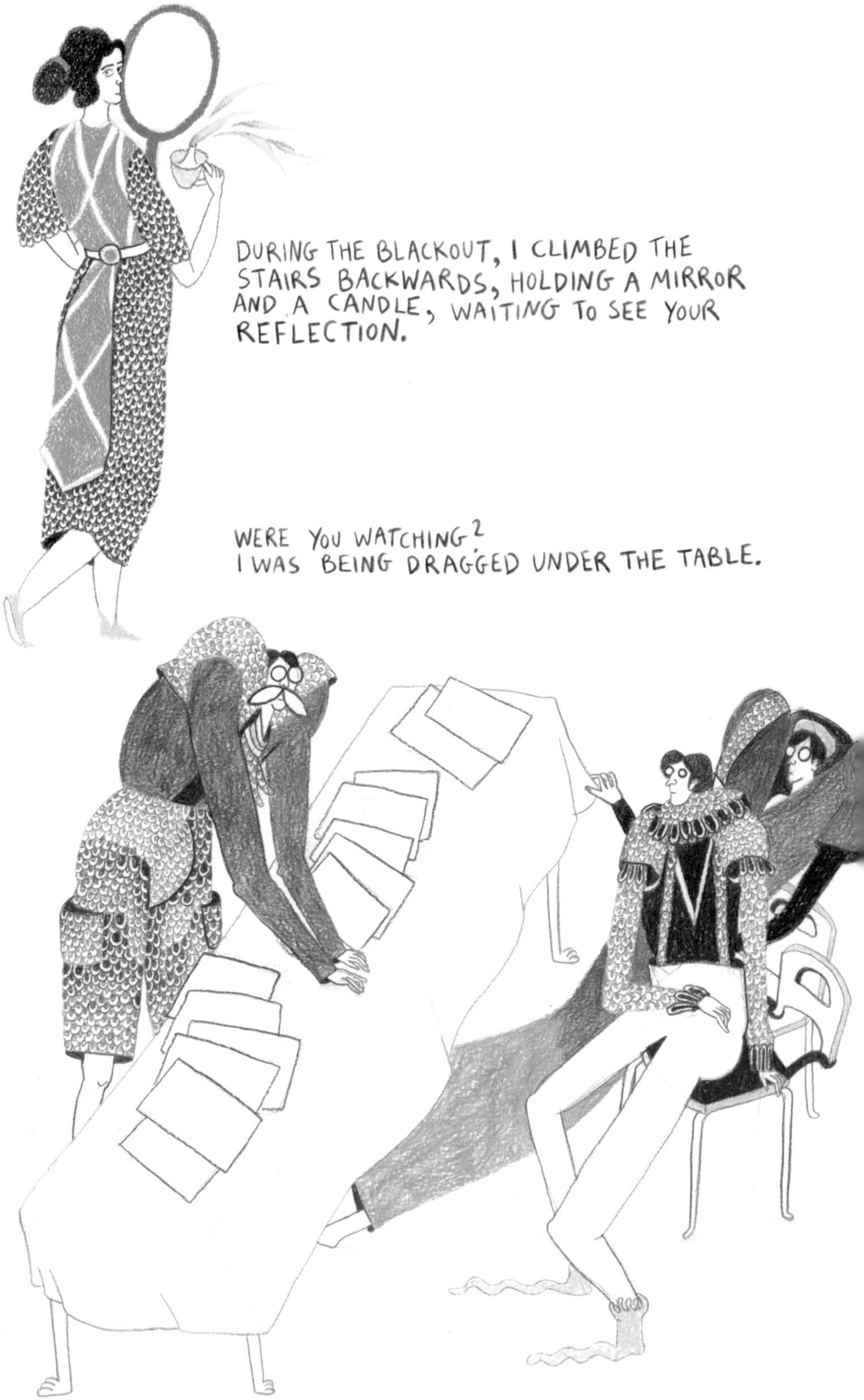
DURING THE BLACKOUT, I CLIMBED THE STAIRS BACKWARDS, HOLDING A MIRROR AND A CANDLE, WAITING TO SEE YOUR REFLECTION.
WERE YOU WATCHING?
I WAS BEING DRAGGED UNDER THE TABLE.

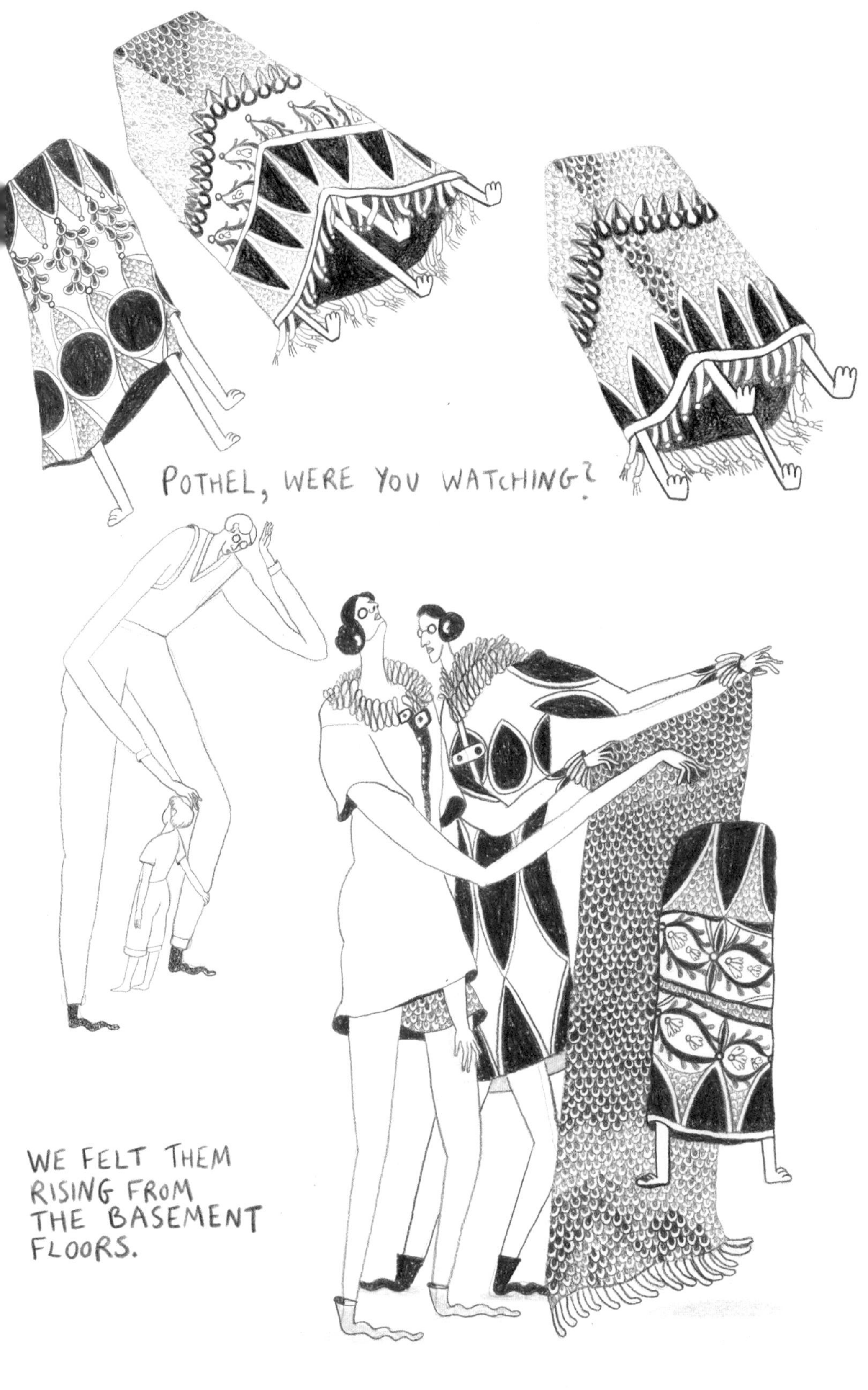
POTHEL, WERE YOU WATCHING?
WE FELT THEM RISING FROM THE BASEMENT FLOORS.

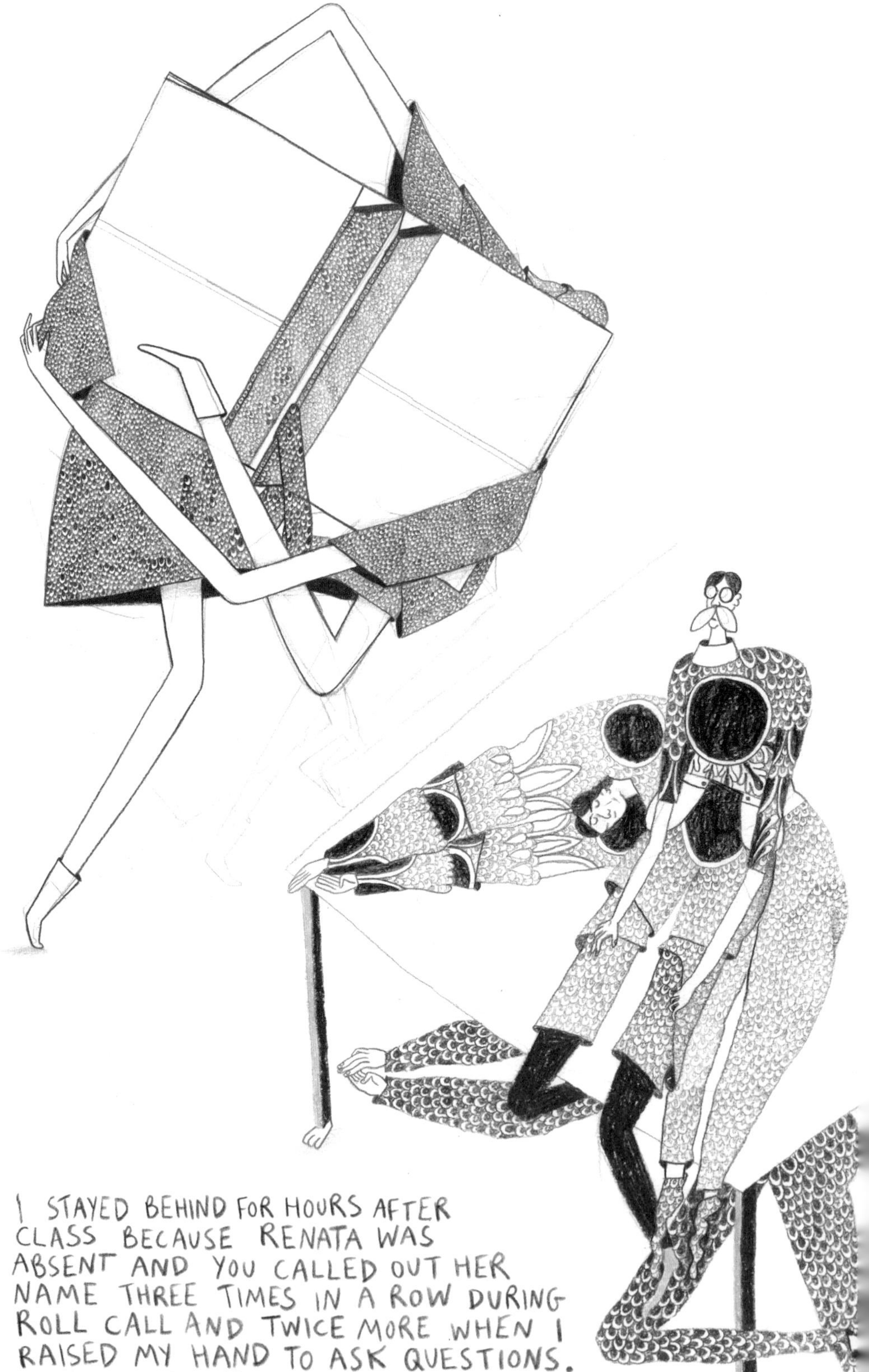
I STAYED BEHIND FOR HOURS AFTER CLASS BECAUSE RENATA WAS ABSENT AND YOU CALLED OUT HER NAME THREE TIMES IN A ROW DURING ROLL CALL AND TWICE MORE WHEN I RAISED MY HAND TO ASK QUESTIONS. WHAT WERE YOU THINKING ABOUT?

WERE YOU WATCHING?

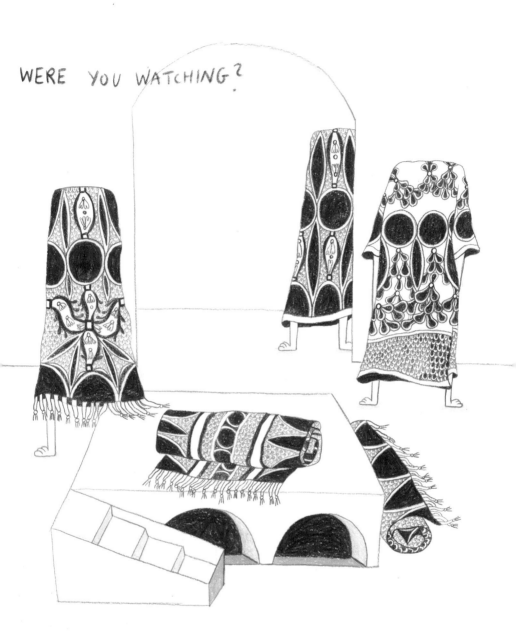

I WAS THE ONLY ONE WHOSE CHIN
CHANGED YELLOW, AND THEY ROLLED
ME UP IN A CARPET AND
BURIED ME.

WERE YOU WATCHING?

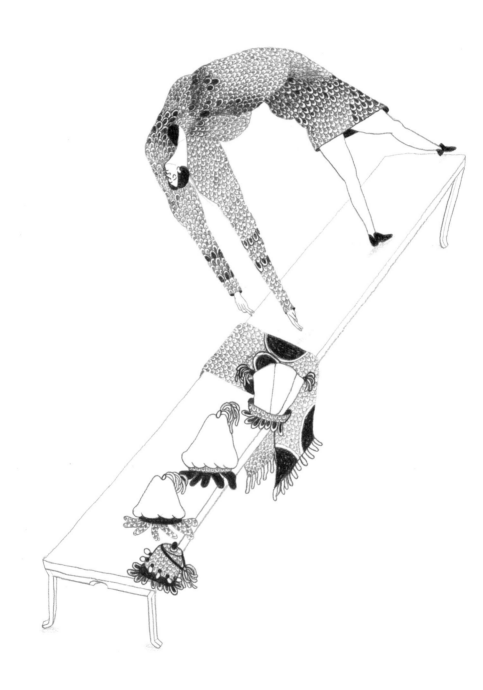

I WENT LOOKING FOR YOU IN THE
CEDAR FOREST.

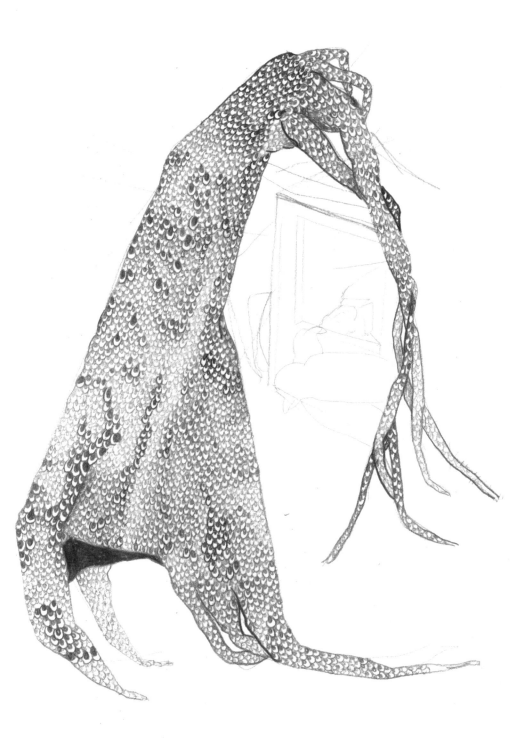

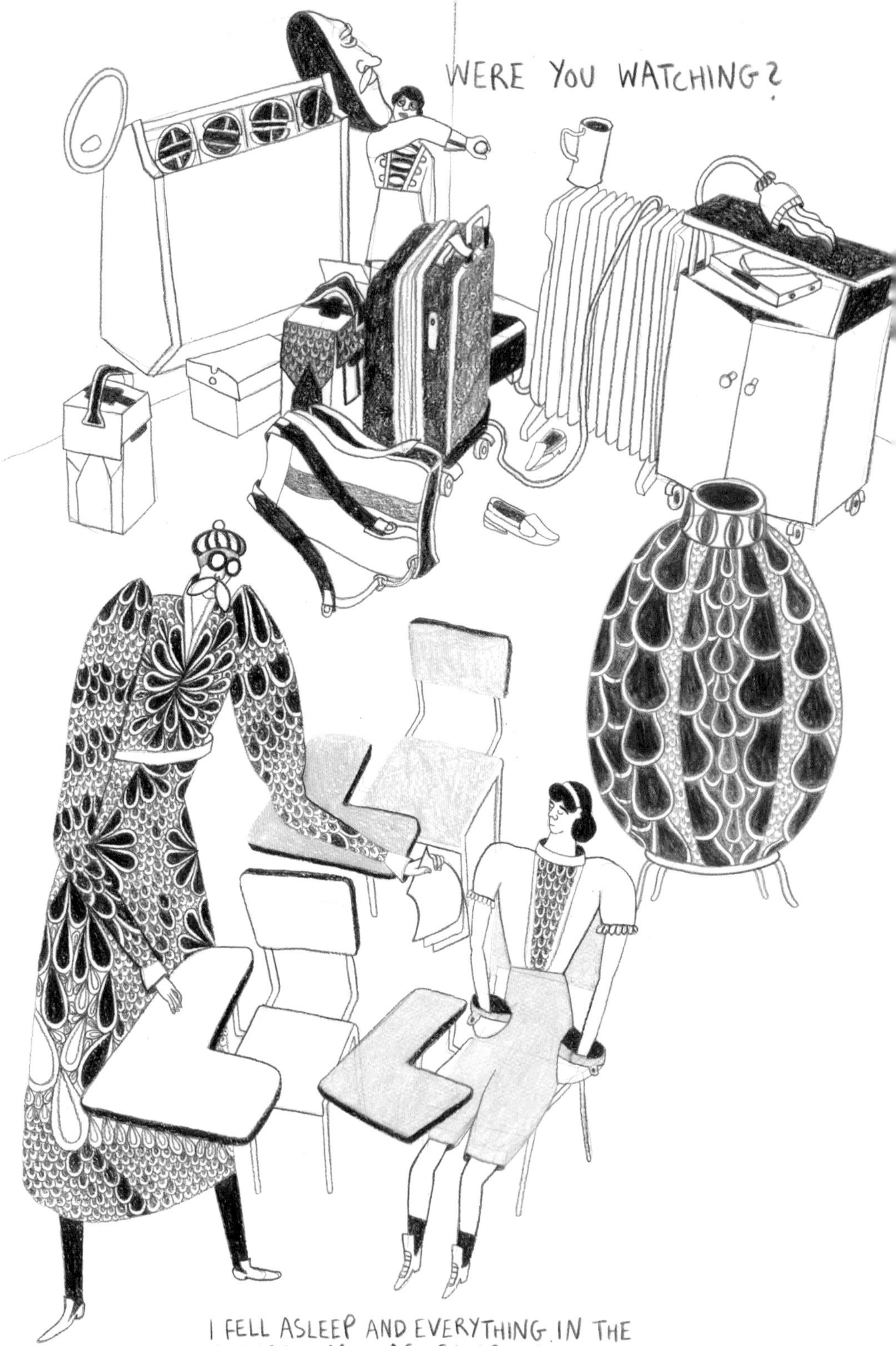
WERE YOU WATCHING?

I FELL ASLEEP AND EVERYTHING IN THE CLASSROOM WAS SLIPPING TOWARDS ME.

DURING THE TIME YOU WERE GONE, WE WERE AFRAID TO MOVE. OUR ARMS BEGAN TO GROW AGAINST OUR WISHES. WE FOUGHT THE MOVEMENT BY COVERING OURSELVES WITH CARPETS AND DRAPES WHICH WE TOOK FROM THE STUDY HALL.

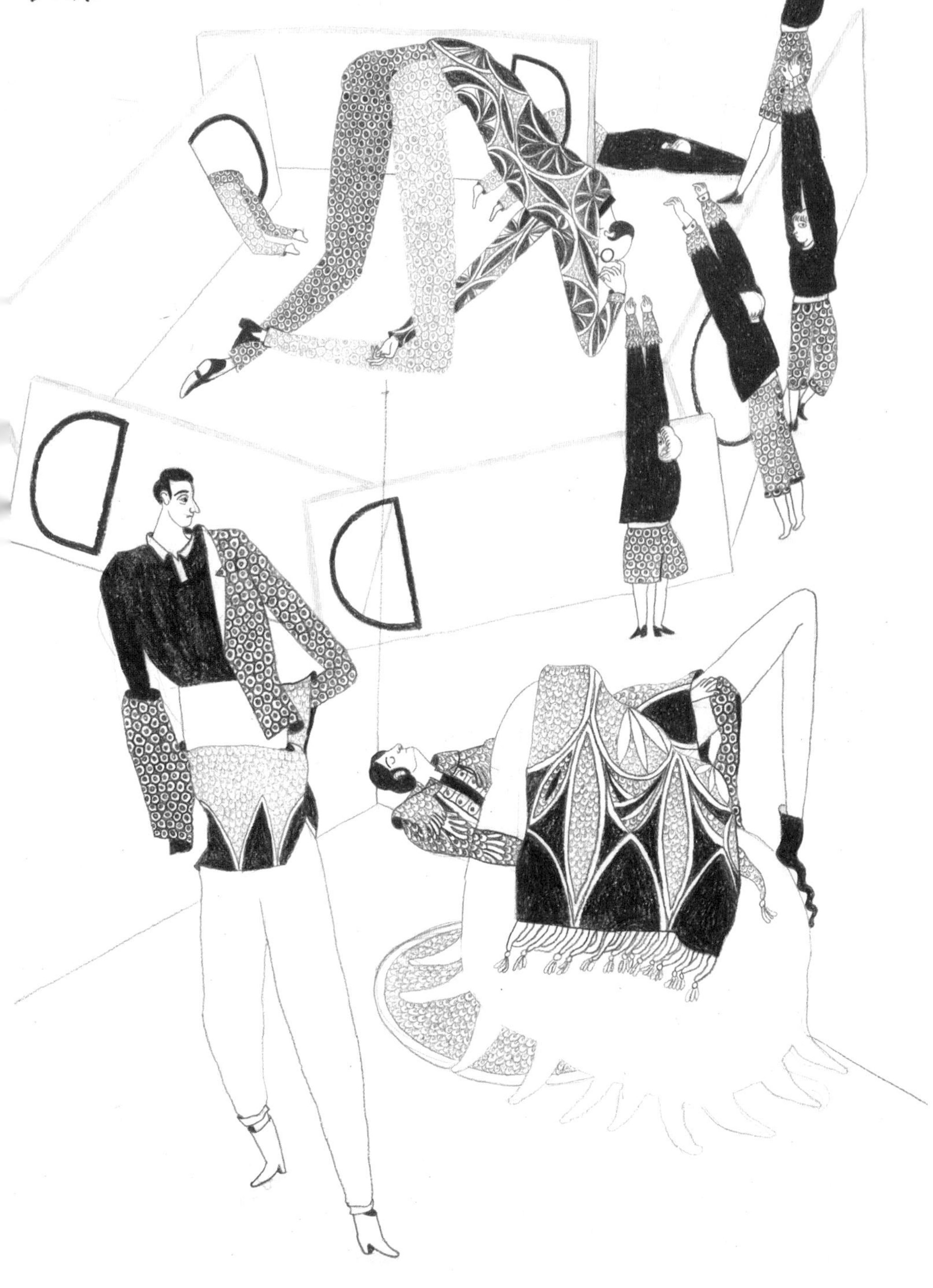

WERE YOU WATCHING?

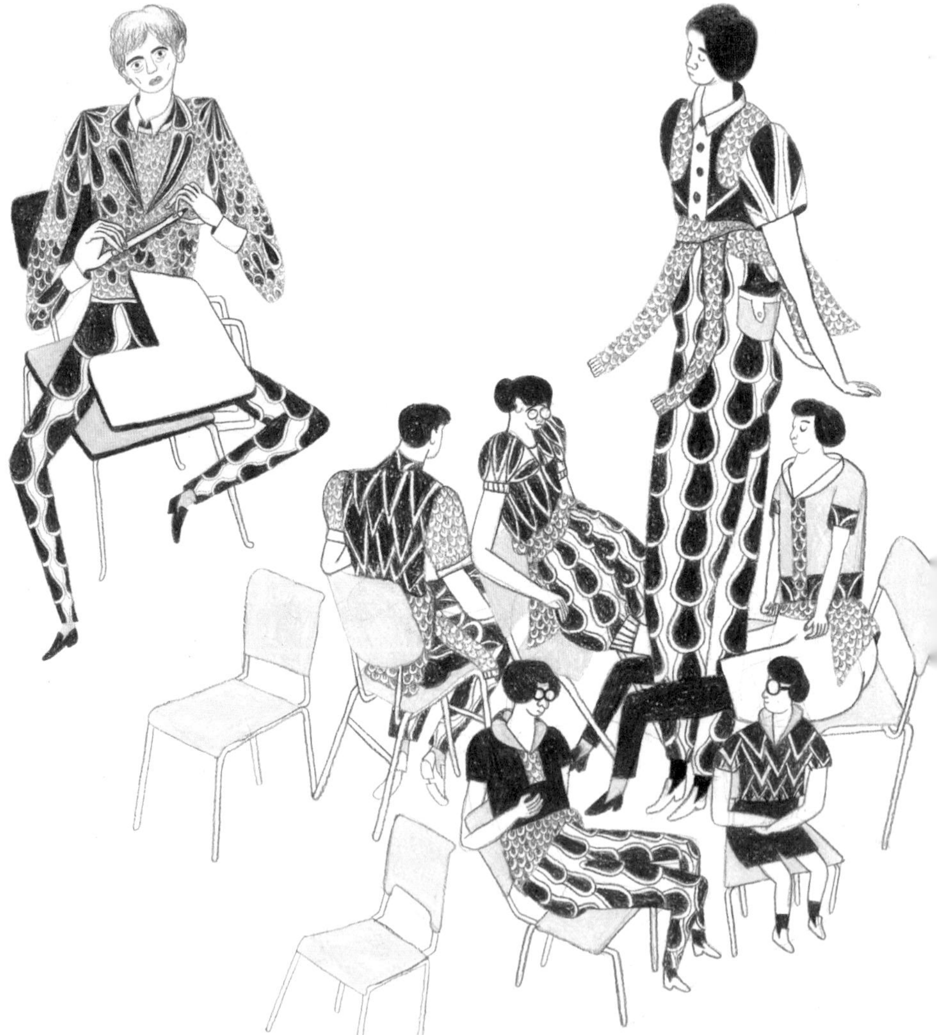

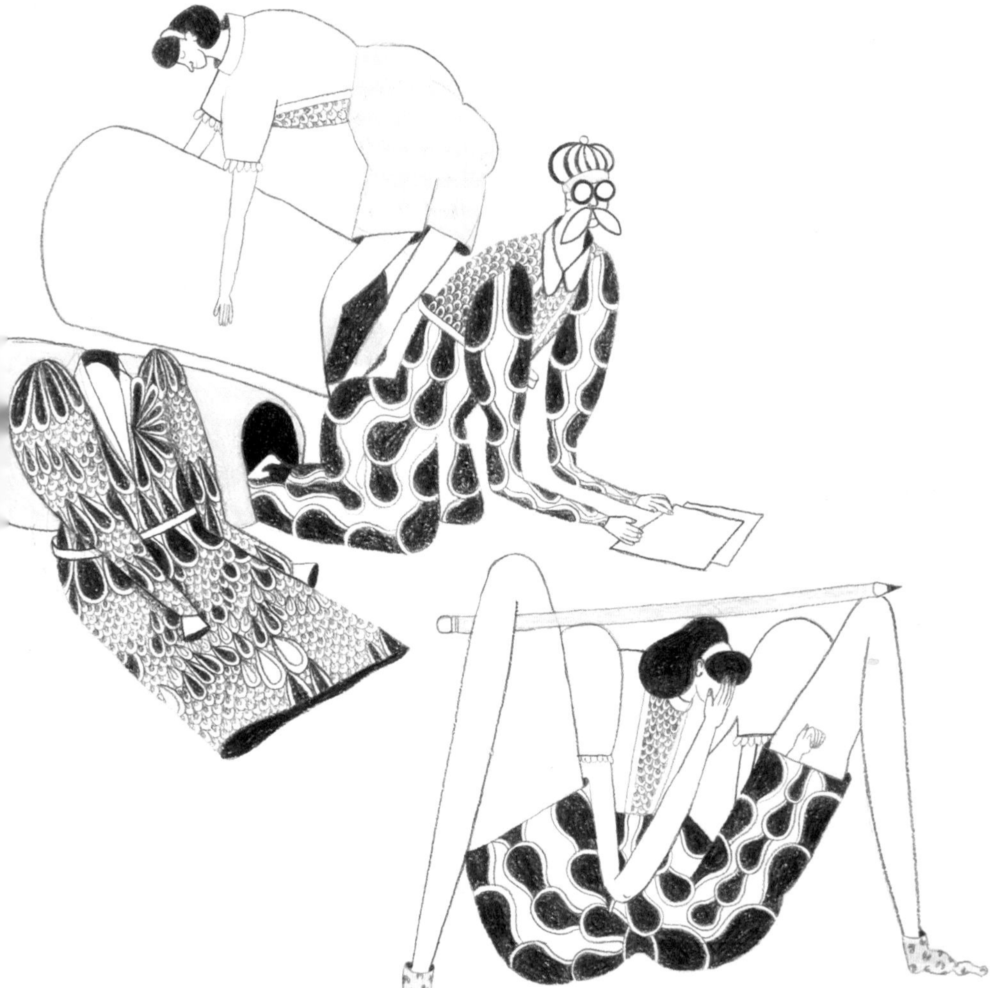

WERE YOU WATCHING WHEN I STRUGGLED TO
LEAVE THE CLASSROOM BECAUSE THE PENCIL
YOU LOANED ME FOR THE TEST GREW SO LONG,
IT WOULDN'T FIT THROUGH THE DOORWAY?

WERE YOU WATCHING?

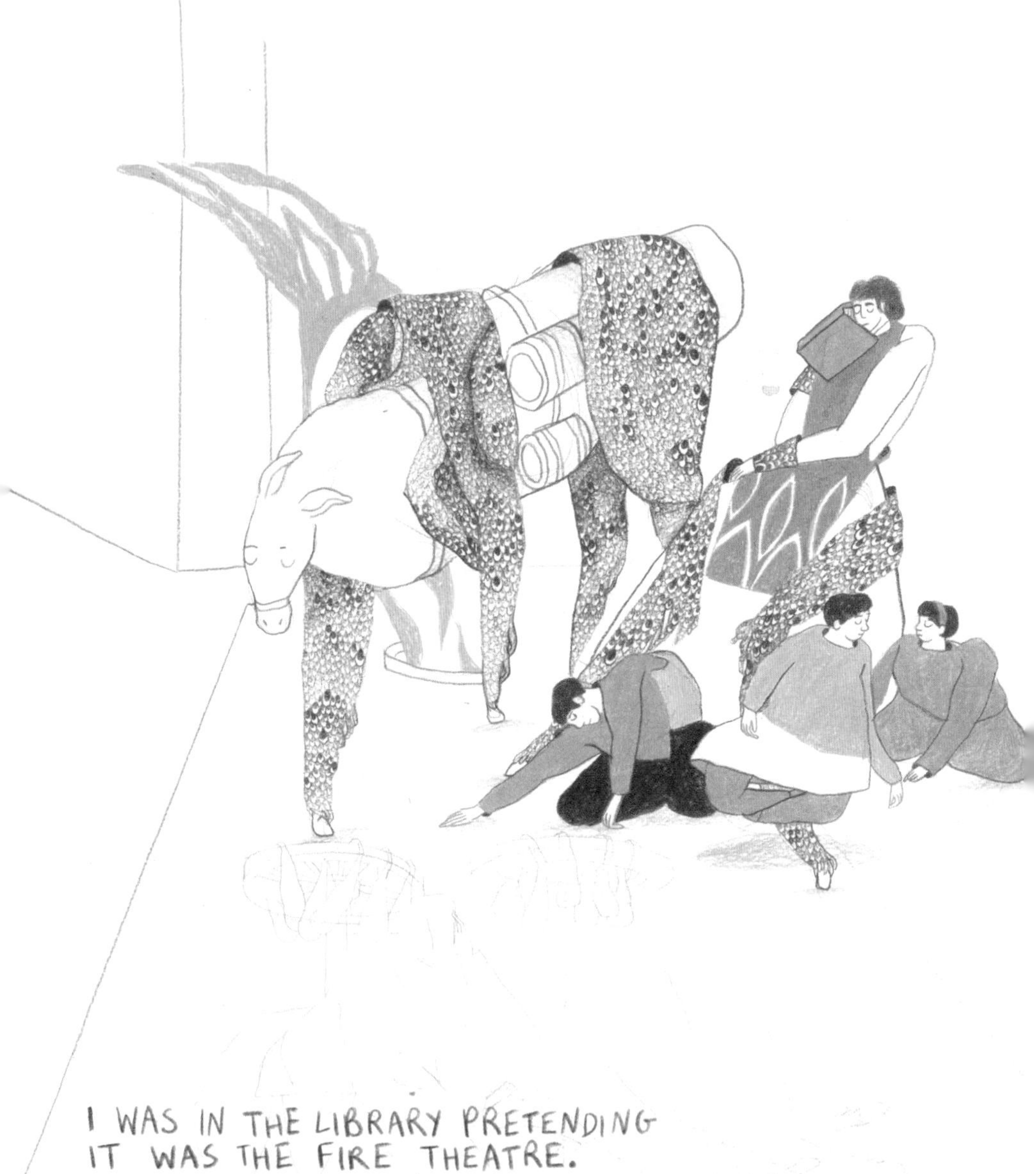

I WAS IN THE LIBRARY PRETENDING
IT WAS THE FIRE THEATRE.

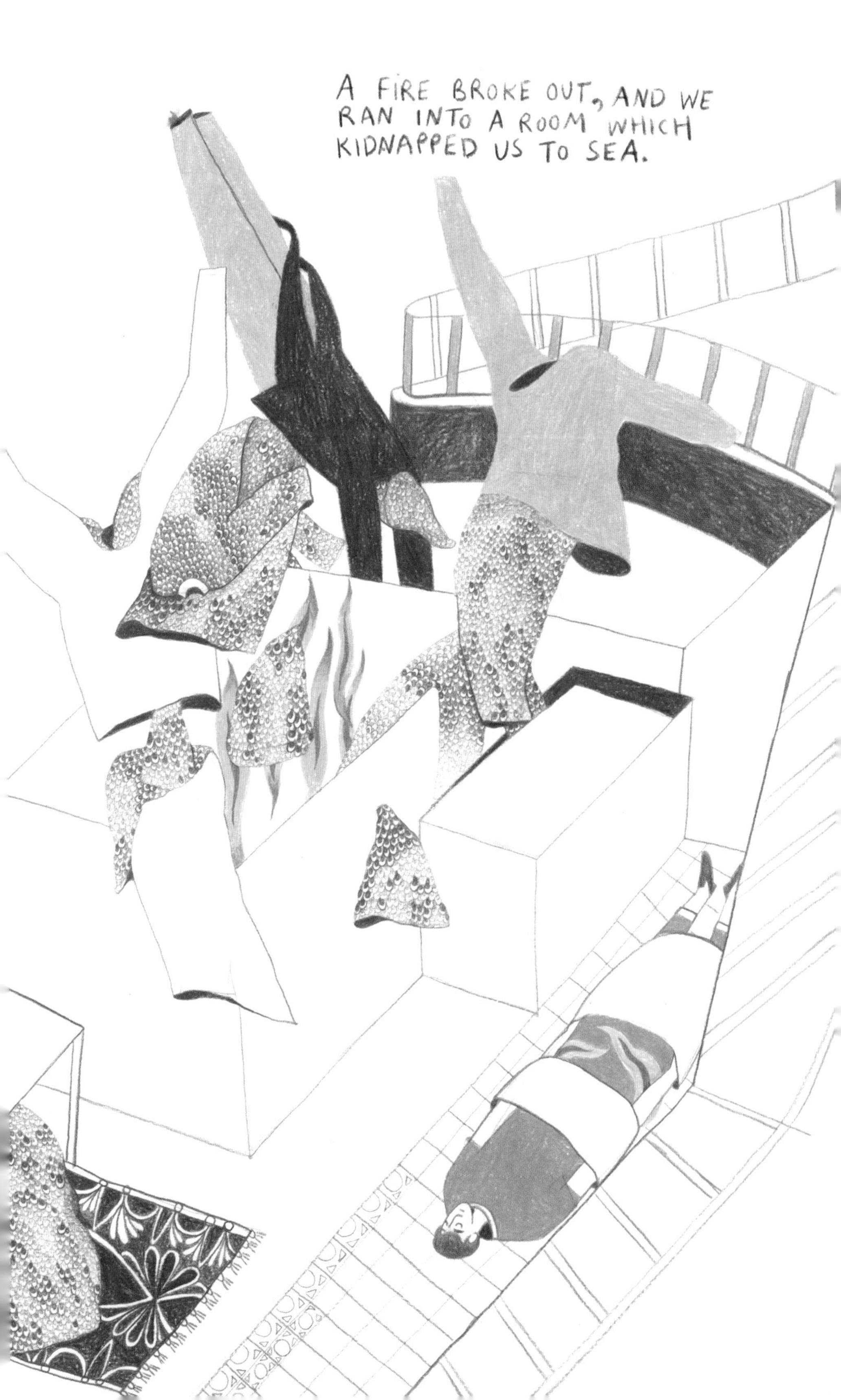
A FIRE BROKE OUT, AND WE RAN INTO A ROOM WHICH KIDNAPPED US TO SEA.

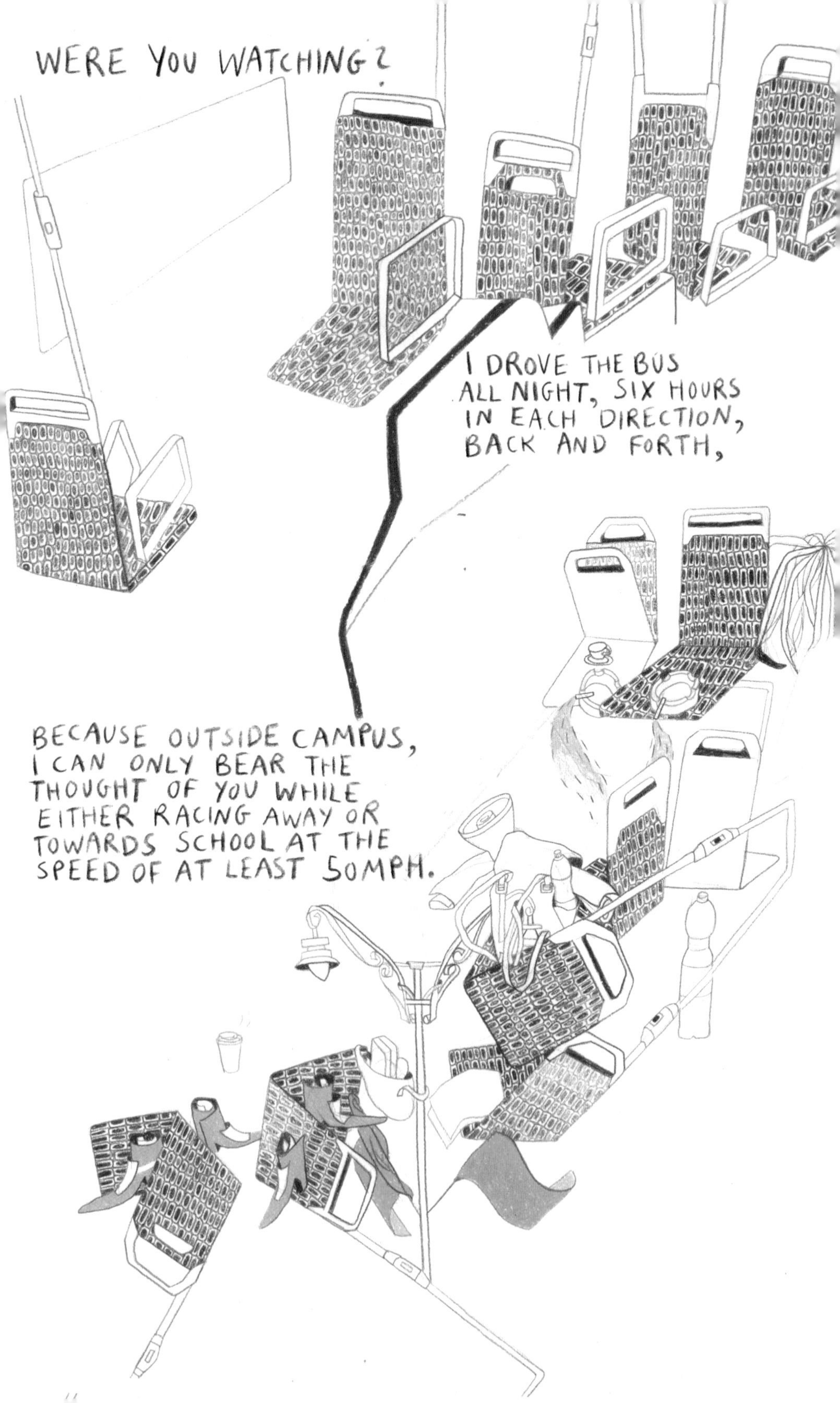
WERE YOU WATCHING?
I DROVE THE BUS ALL NIGHT, SIX HOURS IN EACH DIRECTION, BACK AND FORTH,
BECAUSE OUTSIDE CAMPUS, I CAN ONLY BEAR THE THOUGHT OF YOU WHILE EITHER RACING AWAY OR TOWARDS SCHOOL AT THE SPEED OF AT LEAST 50MPH.

I SNUCK INTO THE RAVEN MASTERS' OFFICES AND TOOK THE BREAD LEFT THERE TO BRIBE THE BIRDS FROM LEAVING THE SCHOOL GROUNDS.

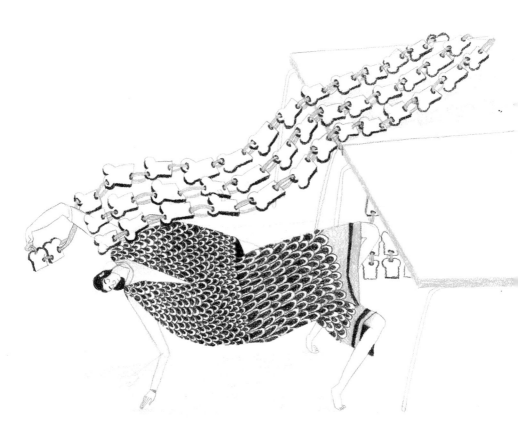

I COVERED MYSELF WITH IT AND WALKED OUT.

WERE YOU WATCHING?

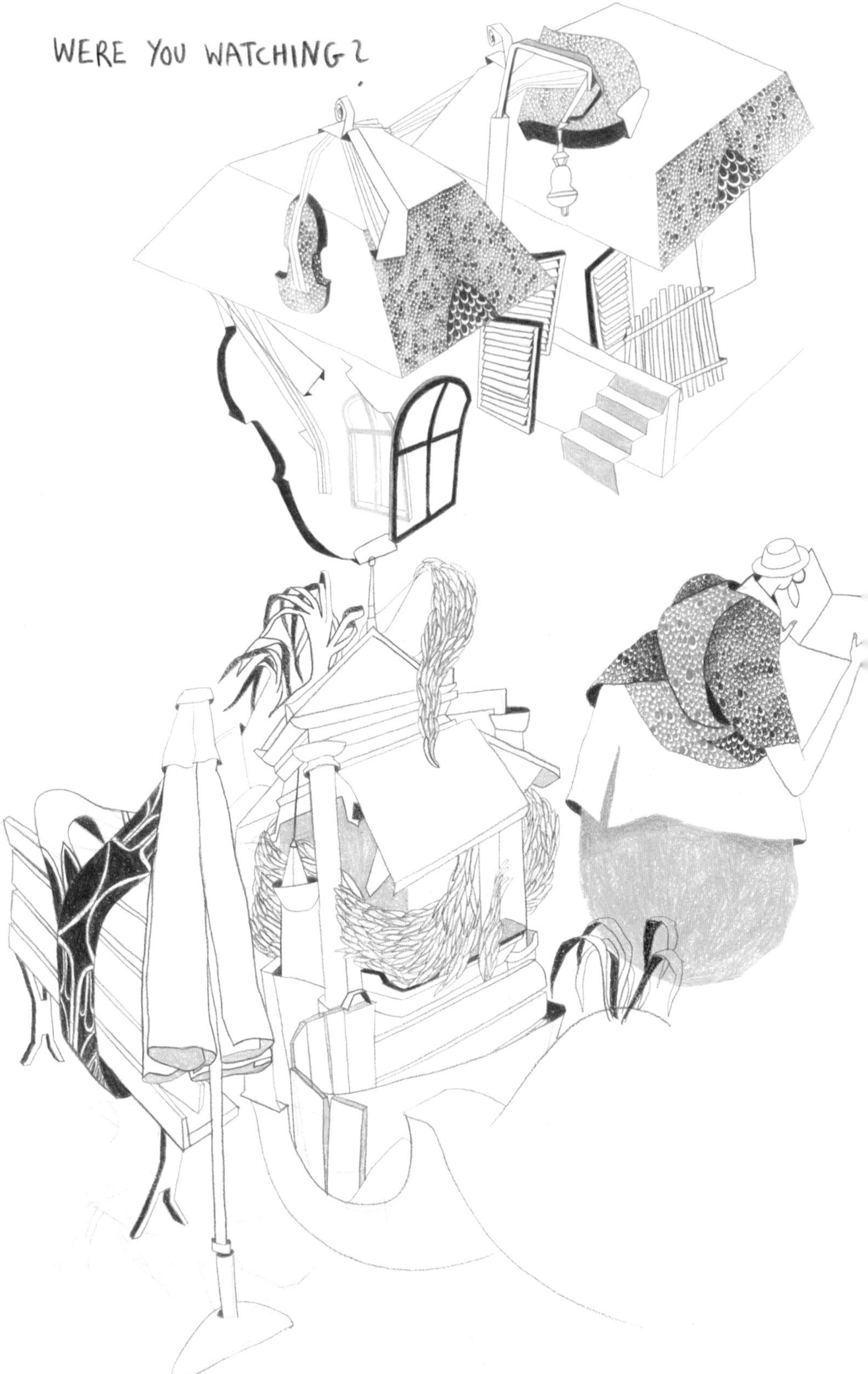

I WAS ABLE TO MOVE ROOM 1001 JUST BY TELLING STORIES.

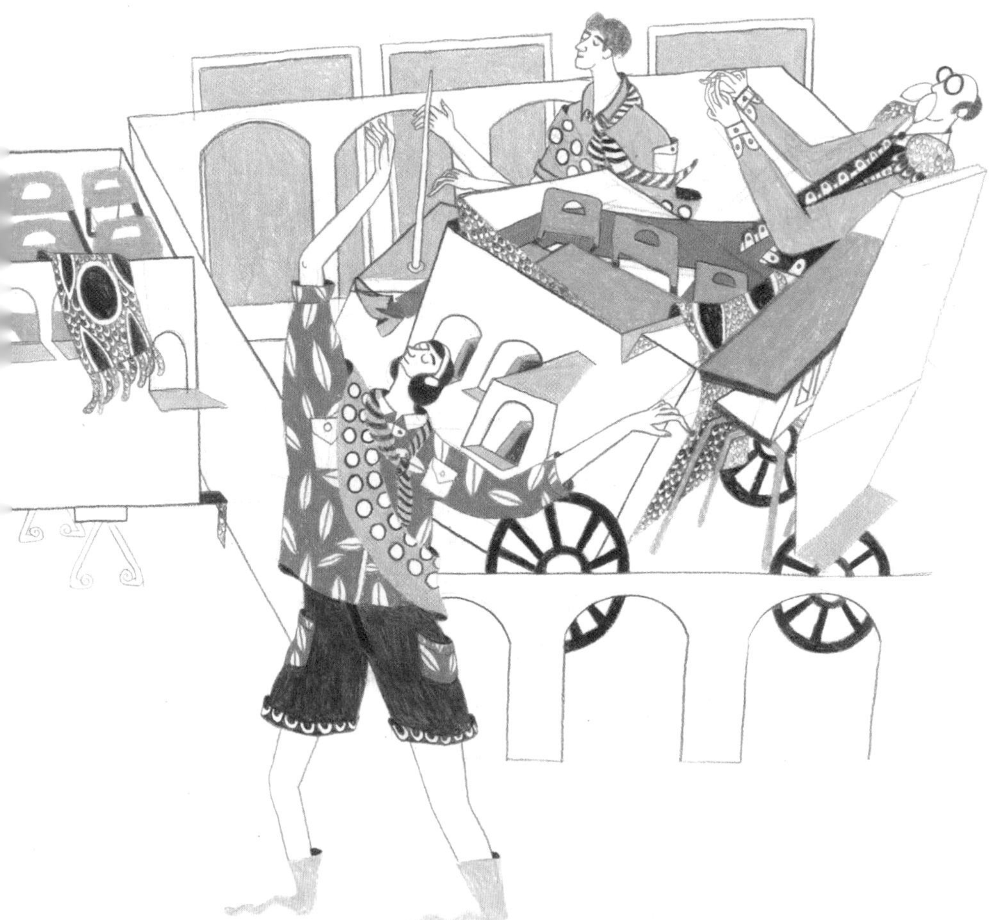

WERE YOU WATCHING?

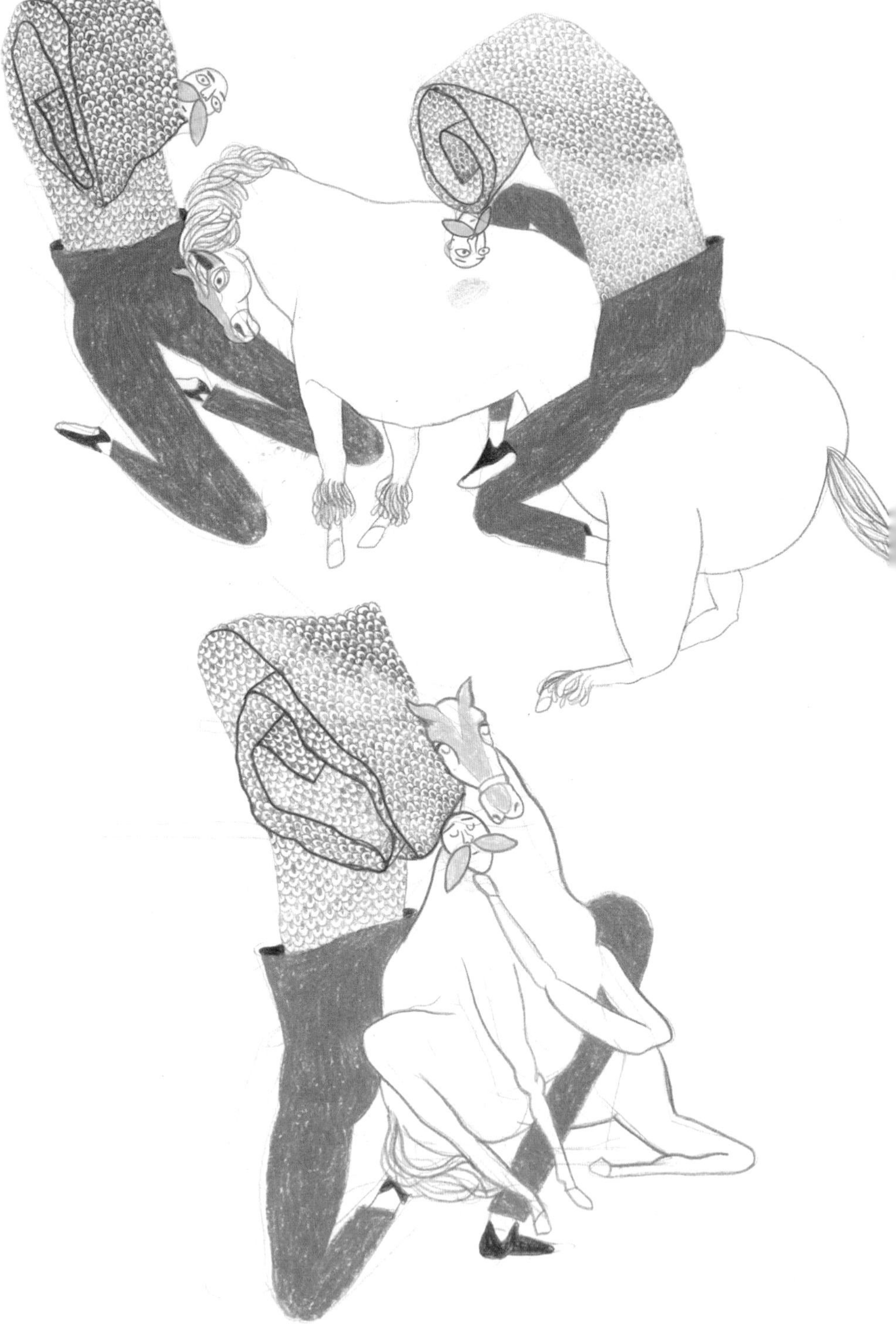

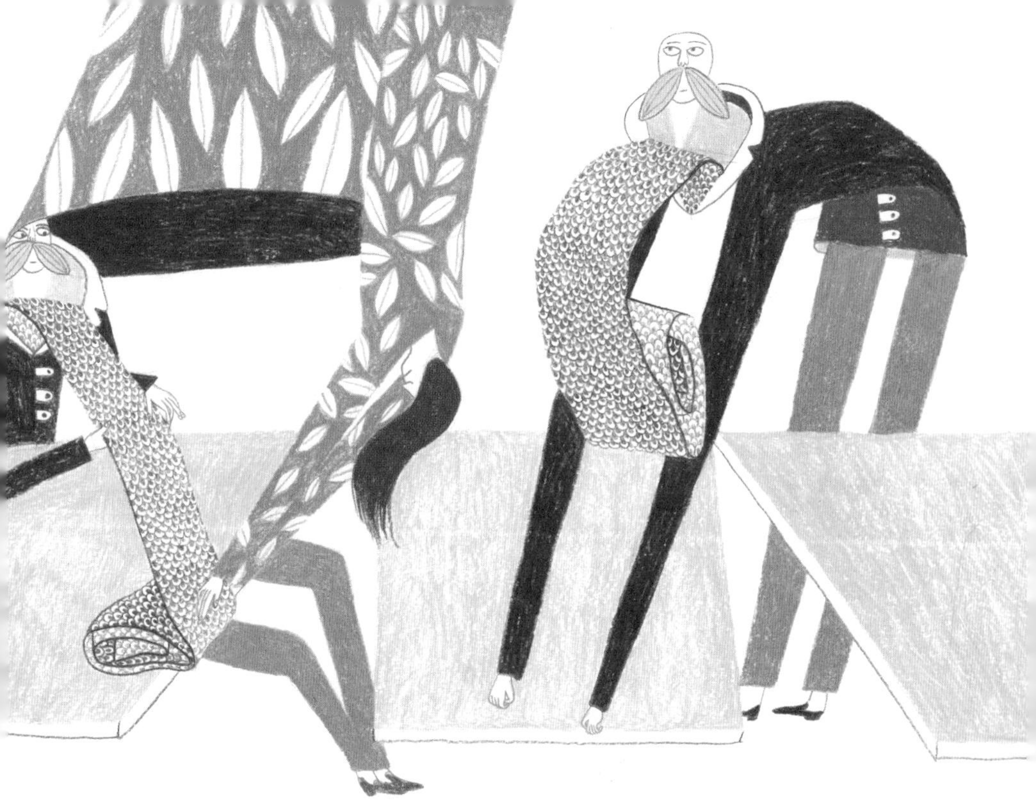

I CUT MY HAIR DURING CLASS.

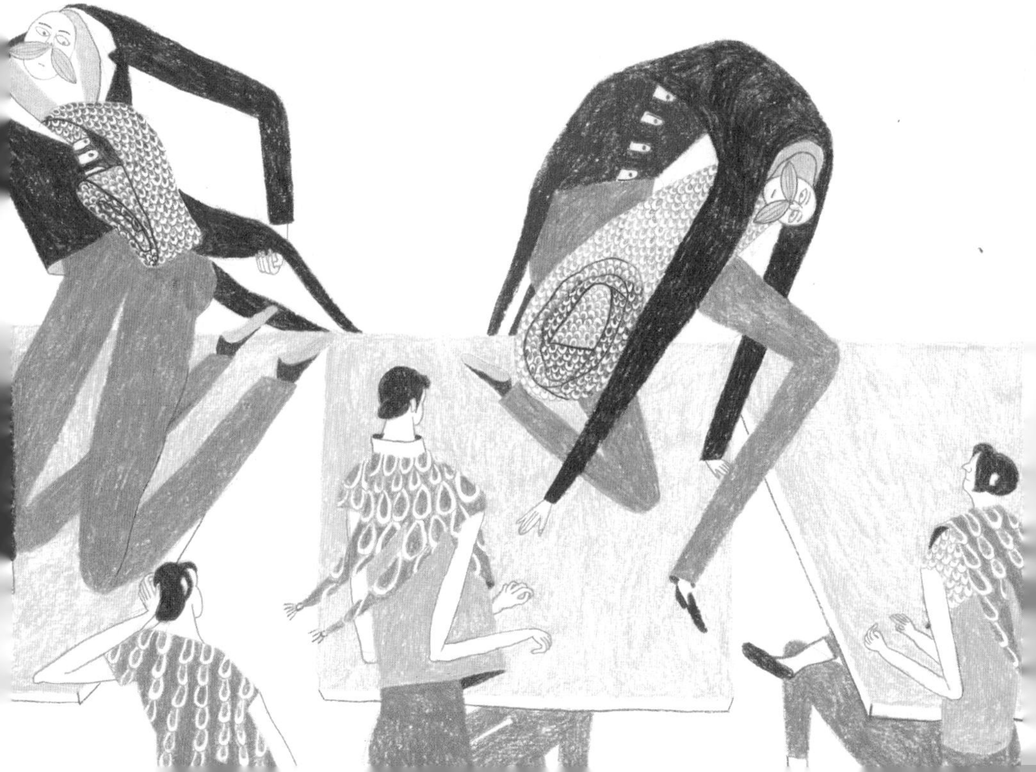

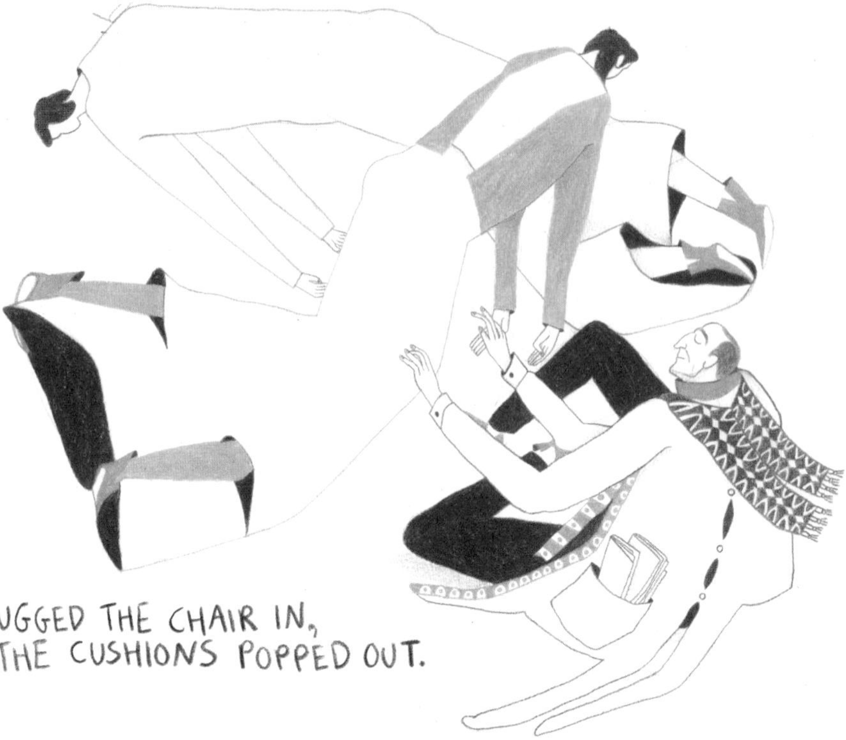

I PLUGGED THE CHAIR IN, AND THE CUSHIONS POPPED OUT.

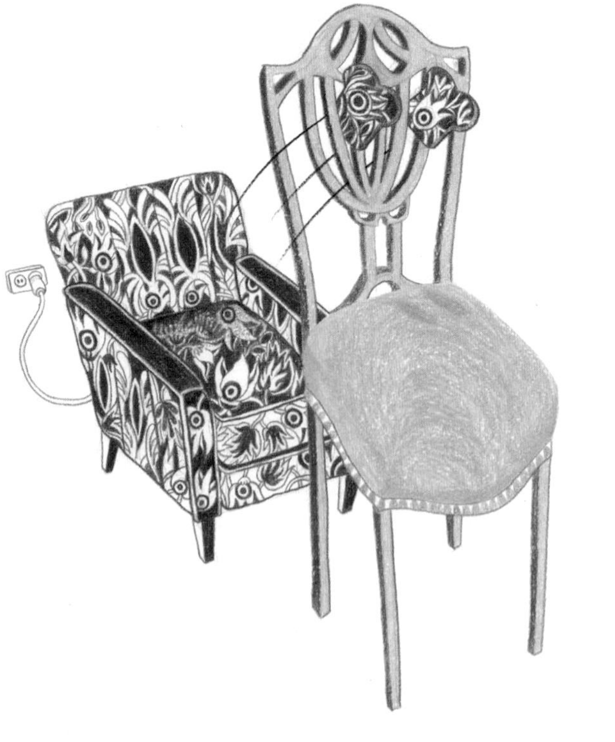

THE HEAT CAUSED A FUSE TO EXPLODE
AND CAUSED A FIRE IN THE LIBRARY.
I WAS THE LAST ONE TO BE SAVED.

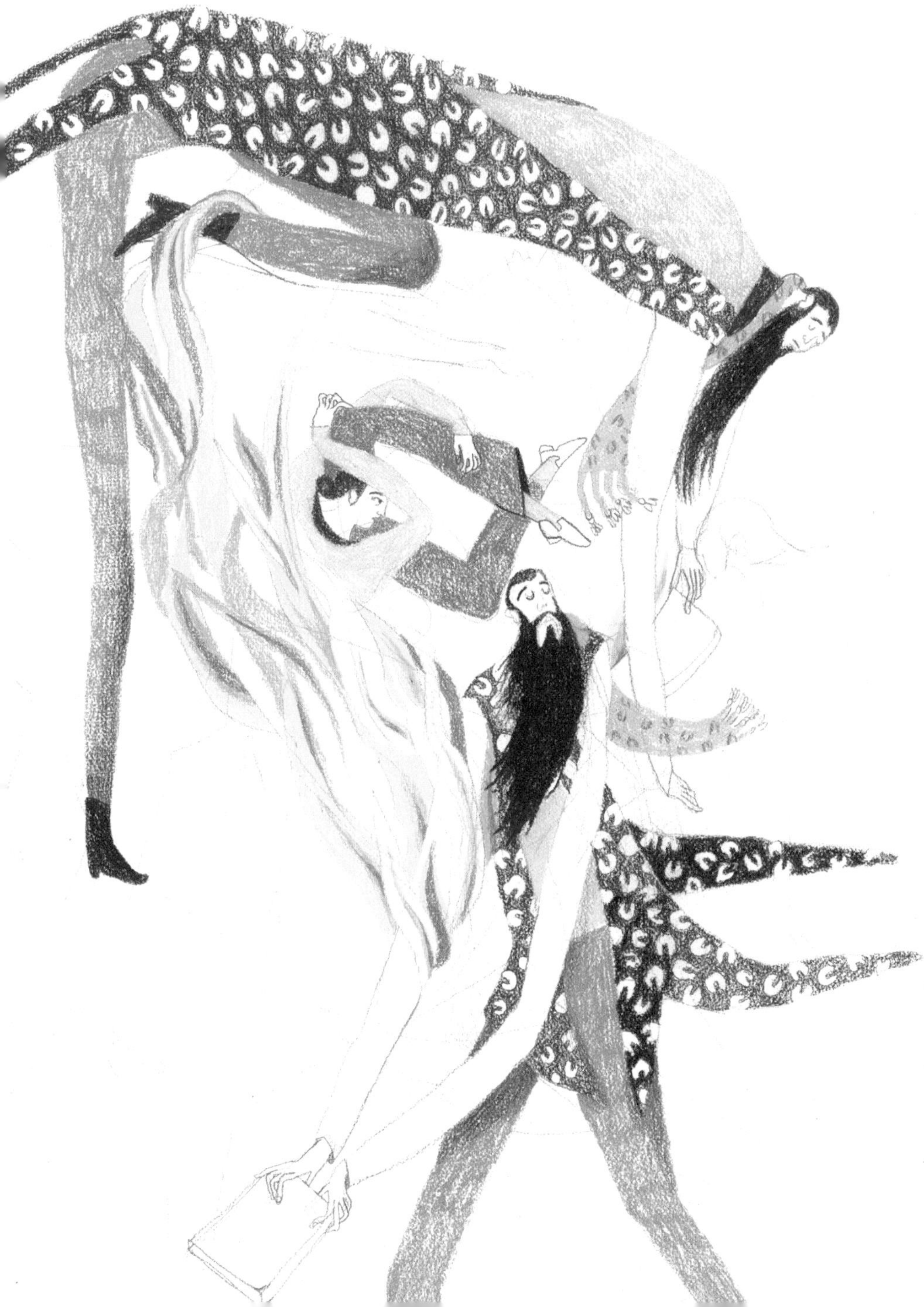

WERE YOU WATCHING US IN FRONT OF THE
WINDOW OF THE EMPTY CLASSROOM?

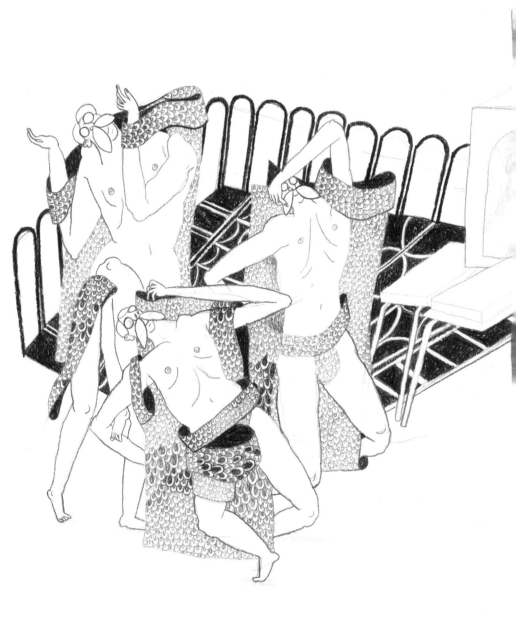

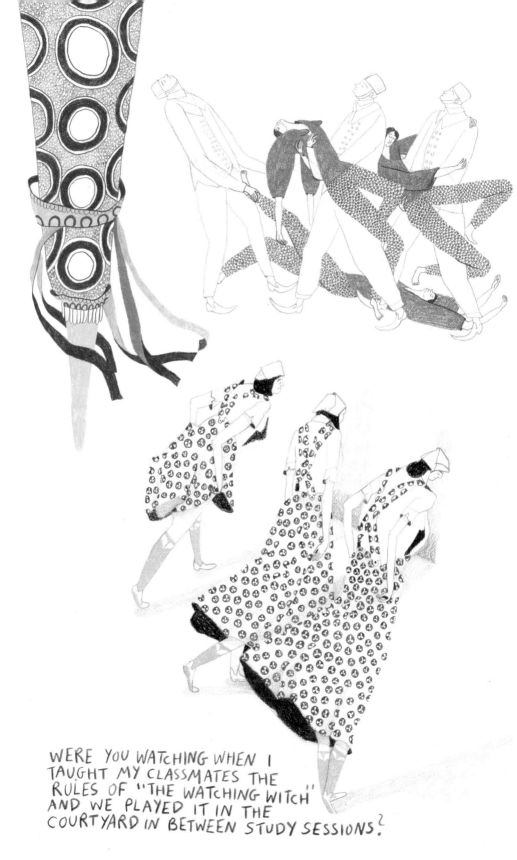

WERE YOU WATCHING WHEN I
TAUGHT MY CLASSMATES THE
RULES OF "THE WATCHING WITCH"
AND WE PLAYED IT IN THE
COURTYARD IN BETWEEN STUDY SESSIONS?

Dear Pothel,

   Before, I looked up from my desk, because someone opened the door and stuck their head in. Then, two trains... they crashed a few miles from here, and I was distracted again. Then two airplanes, moving rapidly through the sky, not even close to crashing one into the other, but even so, I had to stop what I was doing.

   I've flipped through the entire book, back to front! There are drawings of parked cars in the margins, and a few birds, a rib cage. What you see most is that it's the descriptions of the wounded parts (of everything, and not just birds) which tell you most about how a certain bird moves. Wings aside.

   I havent decided on a color for the walls yet. I fell asleep imagining colors. The weight of the color catalog on my chest kept me down.

   In the notebook, in the margins, there are several cars. Might be moving or might not. It's hard to tell from your drawings. It's hard to tell how long you were there, especially since I know that you are someone who was hit by a car, so there might be truth involved in at least one. And I will only know when you've finally broken that arm which you should have broken back then.

   I turn the pages quickly after the notations of cars, assuming you stay longer with buildings and horses. You stay longer in the room, the room where she falls asleep more often than you do. She wakes up in it more often than you do, as well. So you will draw a feathered crown on her head when you draw her in that room, where, if you fall asleep at all, you do so just to catch up with her Theatre of Sleep.

                                    Liana.

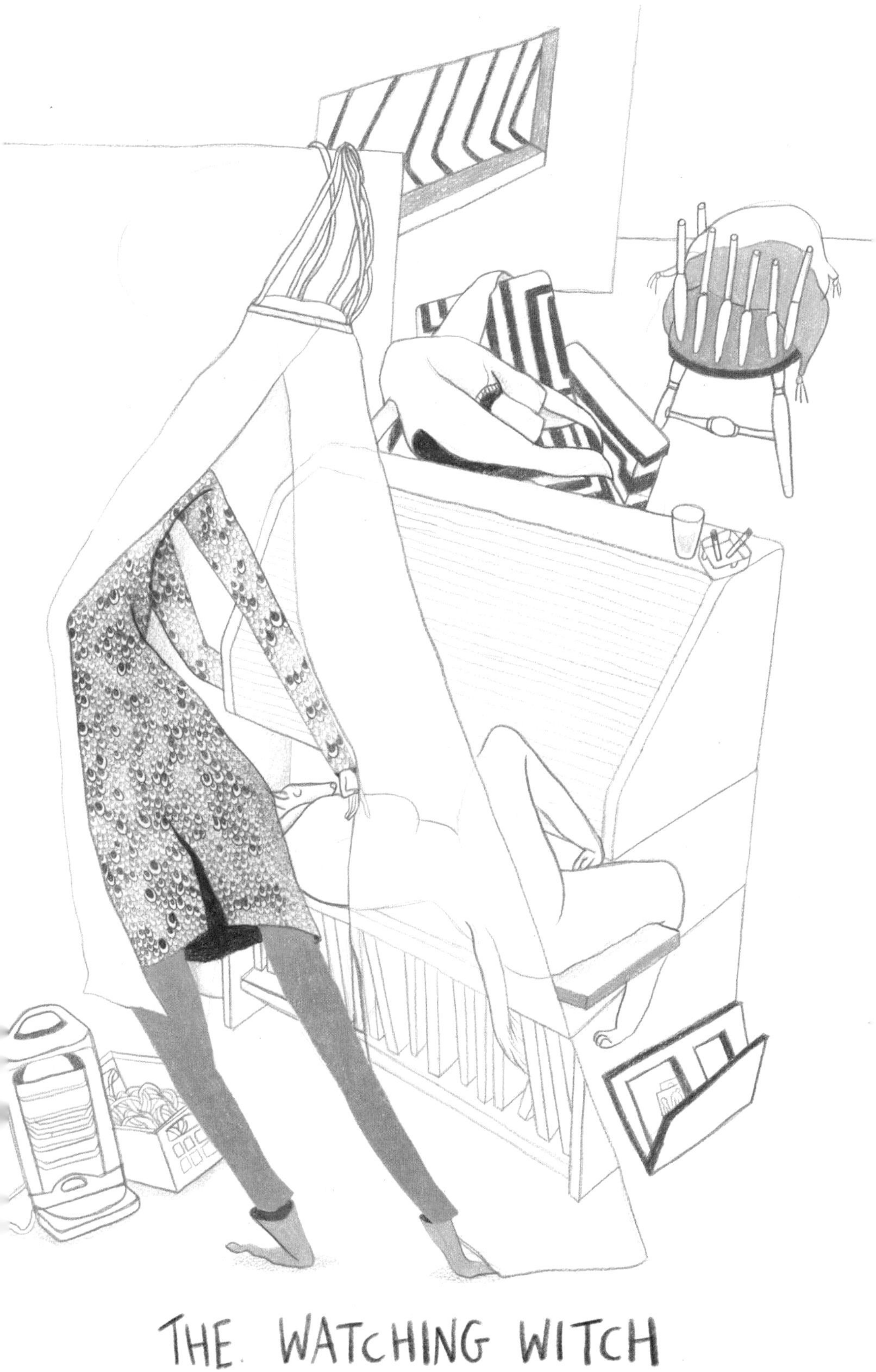

THE WATCHING WITCH

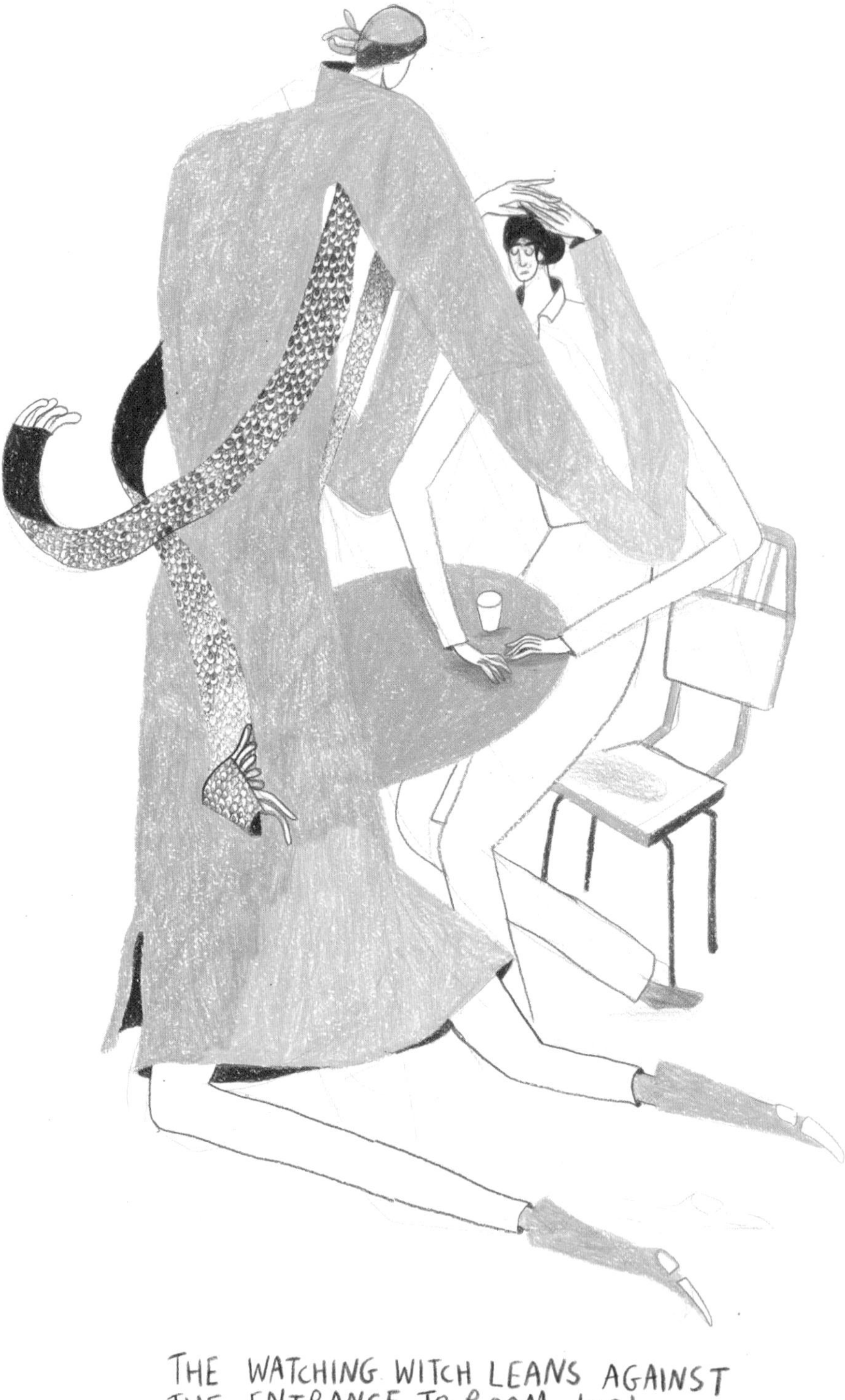

THE WATCHING WITCH LEANS AGAINST
THE ENTRANCE TO ROOM 1001 –

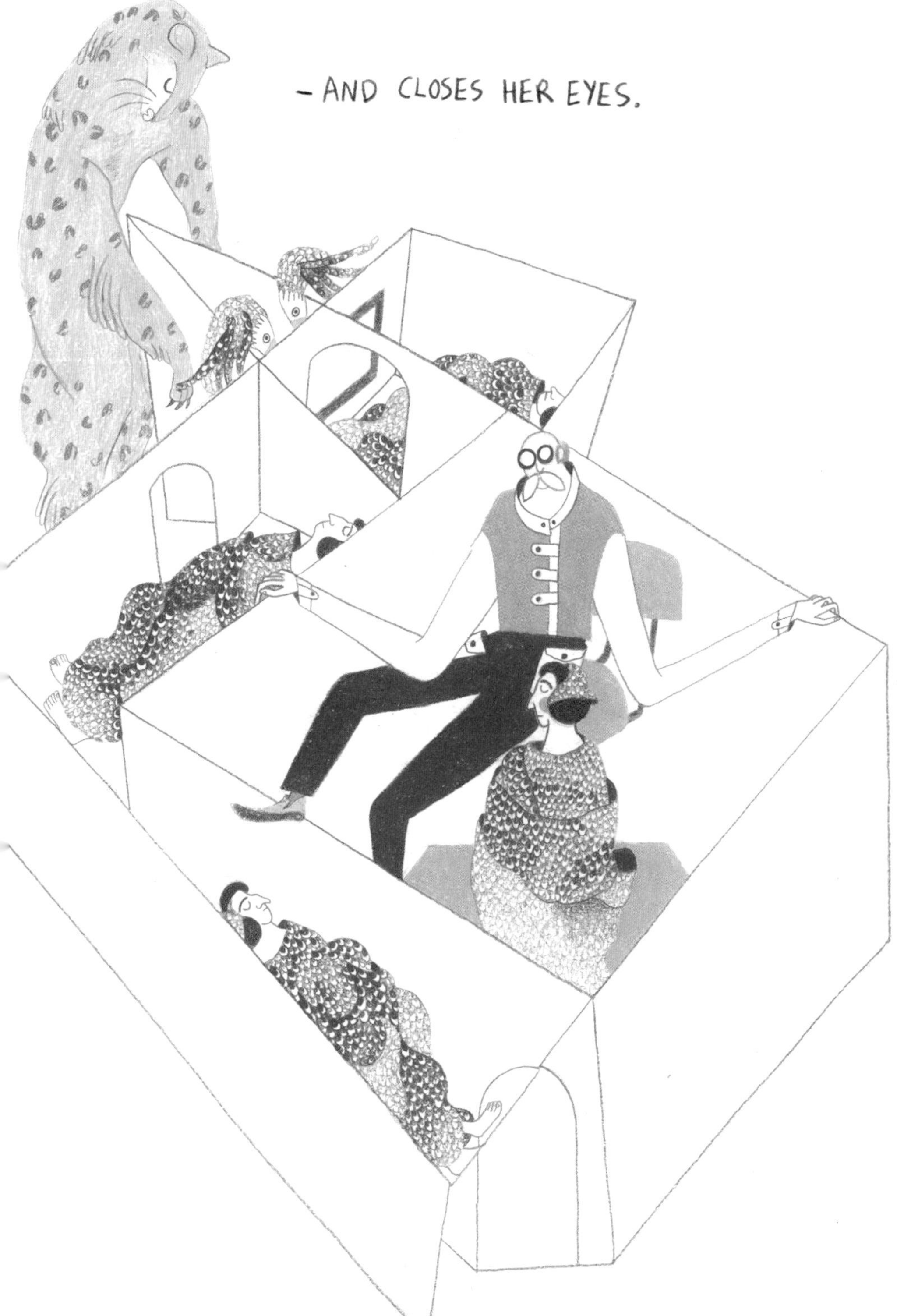
–AND CLOSES HER EYES.

WHEN SHE TURNS TO LOOK AT US, WE HAVE TO FREEZE IN PLACE.

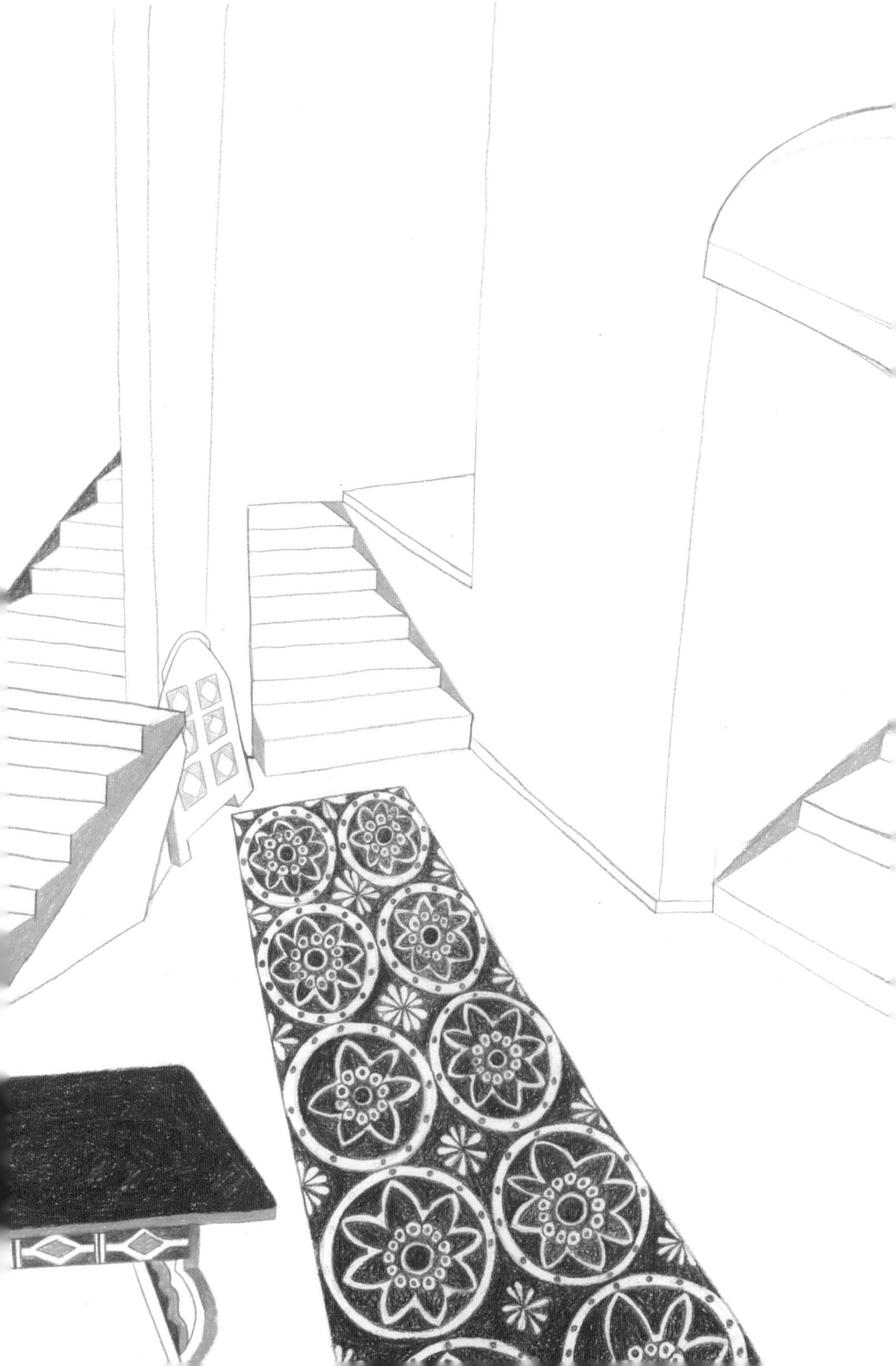

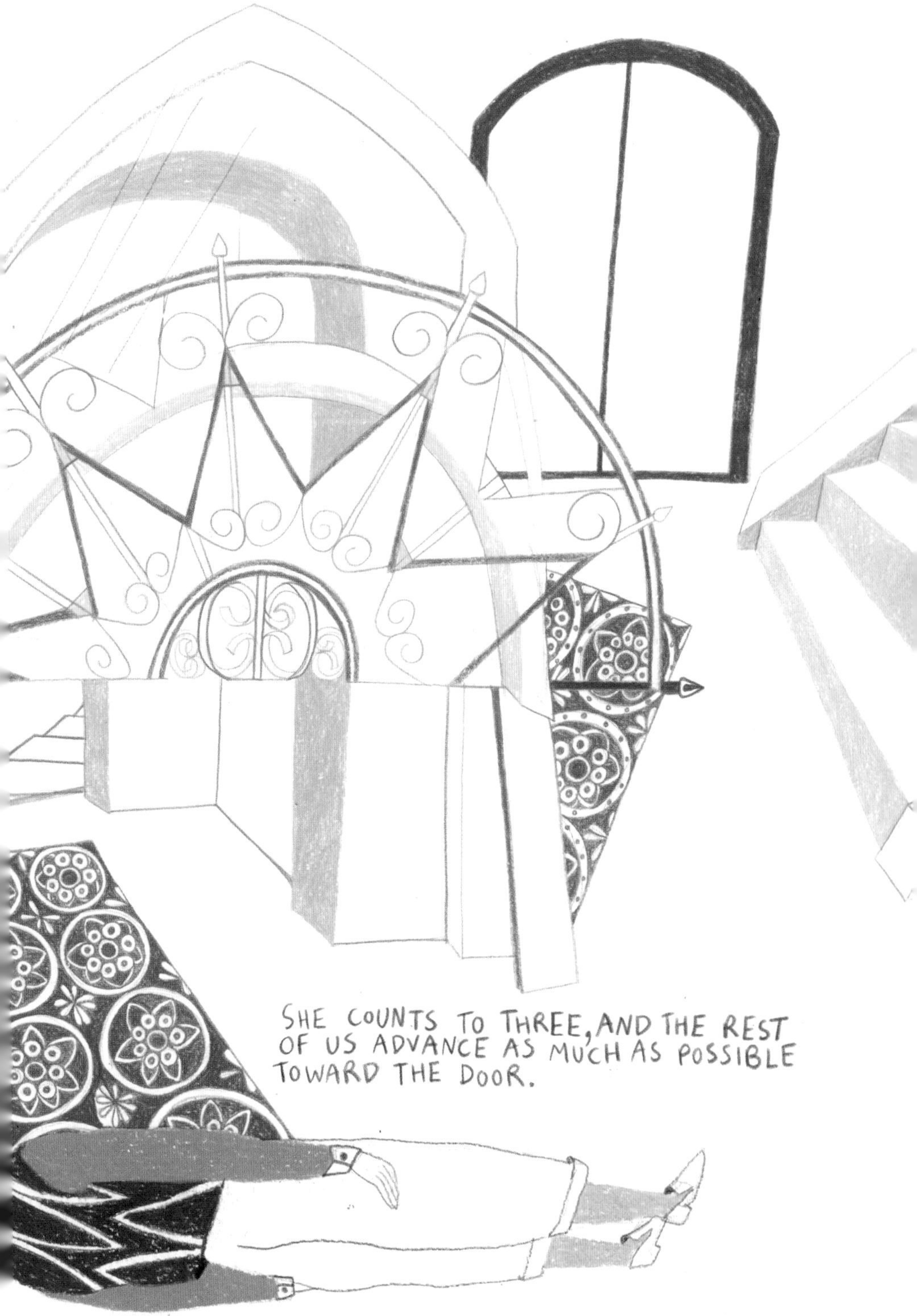
SHE COUNTS TO THREE, AND THE REST OF US ADVANCE AS MUCH AS POSSIBLE TOWARD THE DOOR.

THE WITCH IS FREE TO MOVE AROUND US
AND RESCULPT US AS SHE PLEASES.

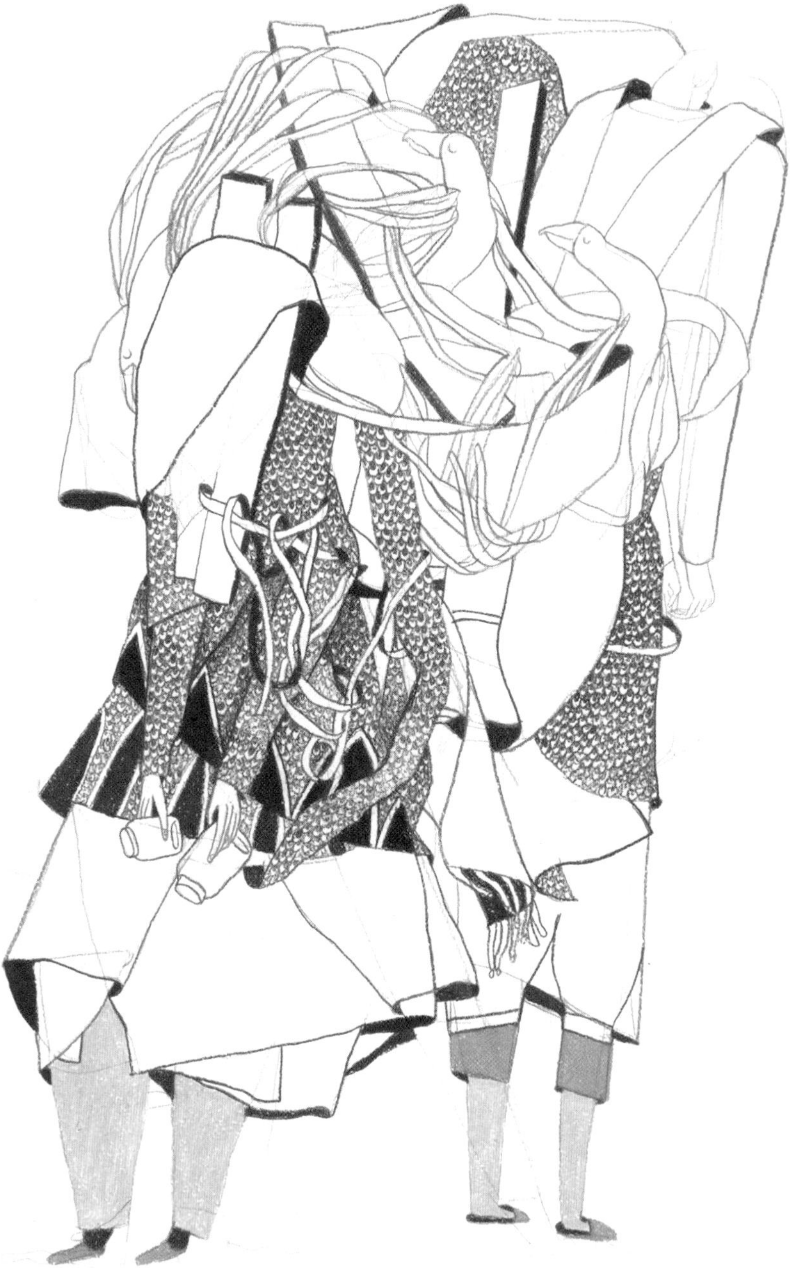

SHE MAY MAKE US STAND ON ONE LEG.
OR PLACE US BACK TO BACK.

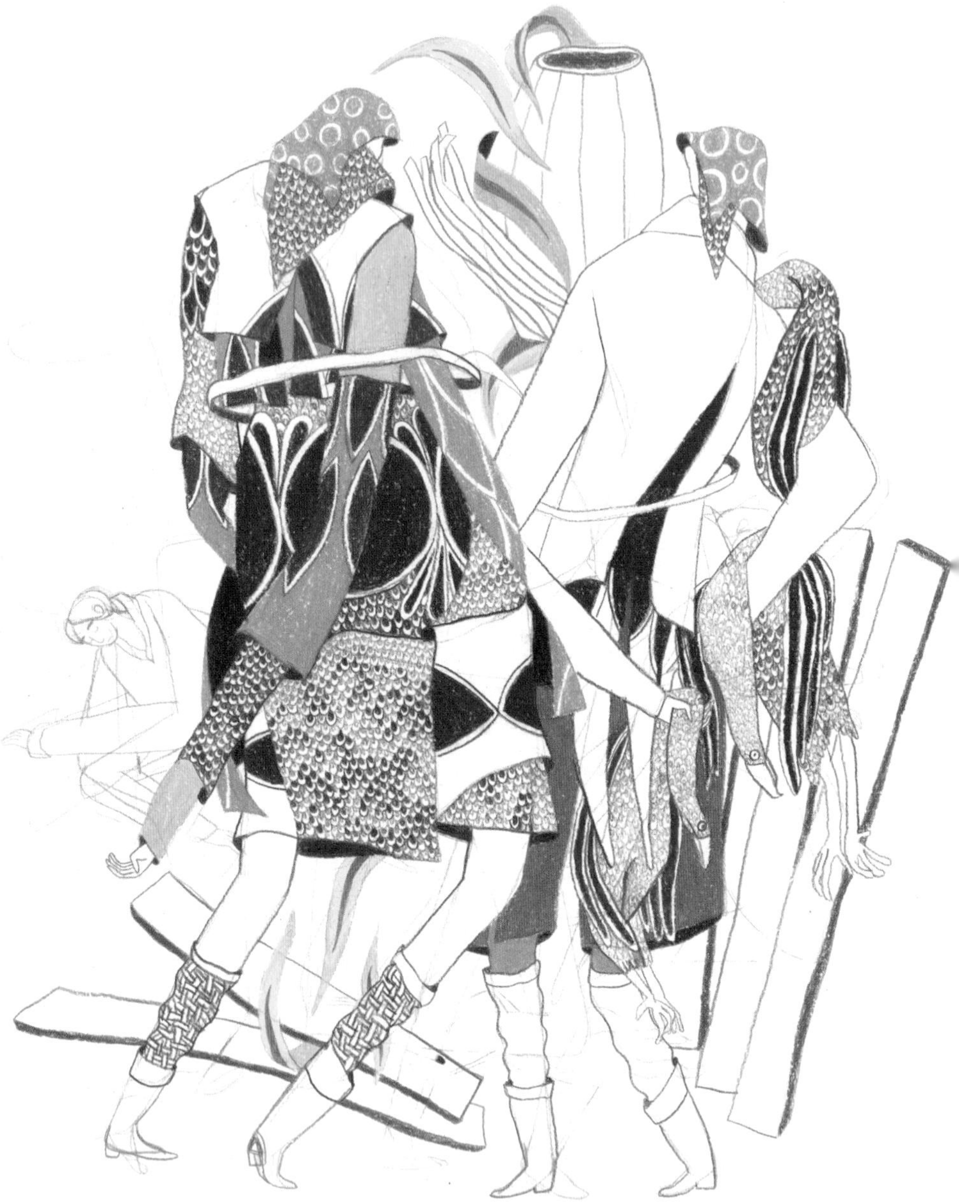

OR STARE INTO OUR EYES UNTIL WE BURST INTO FLAMES.

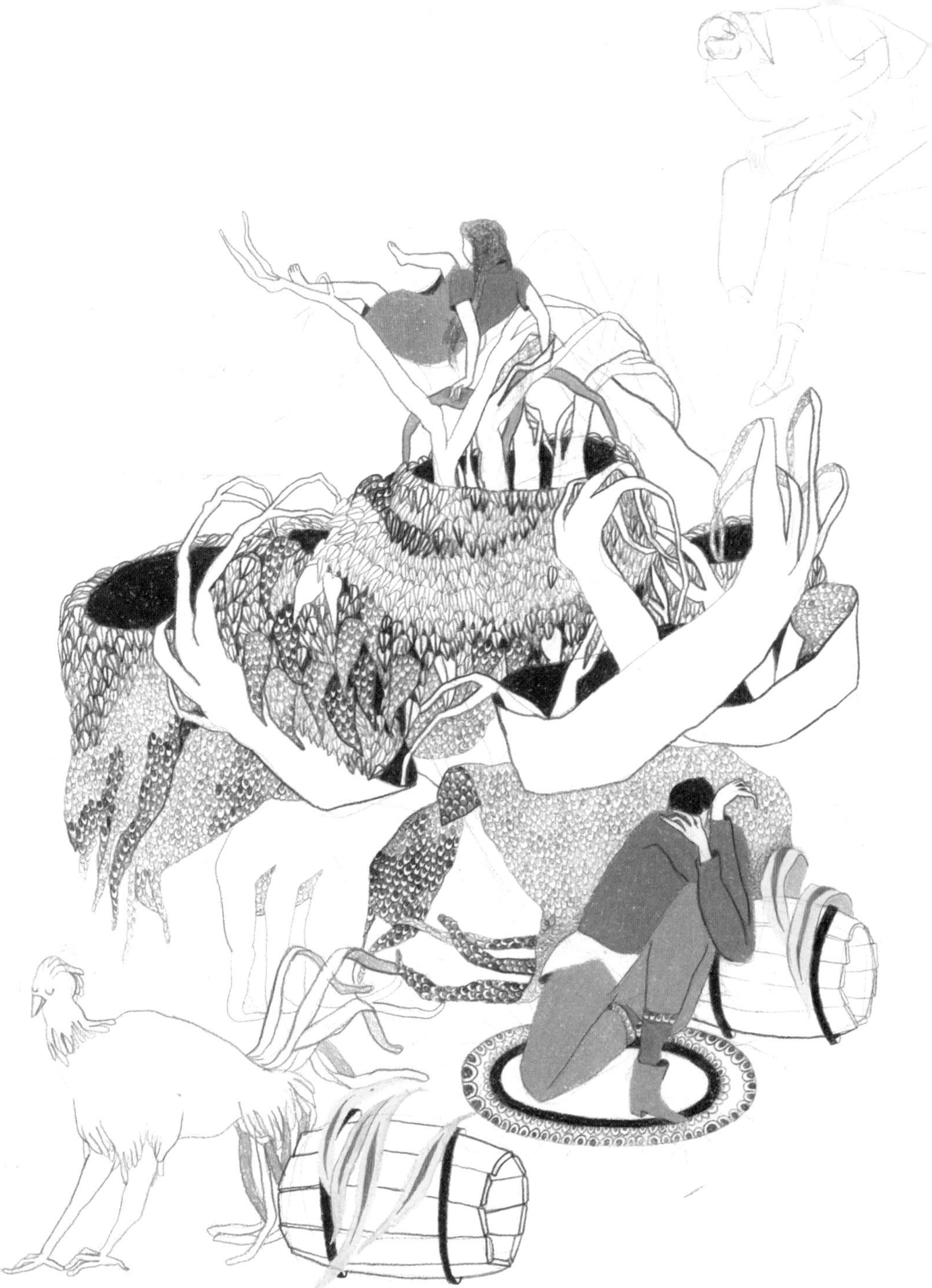

IF WE ARE SPOTTED FLINCHING —

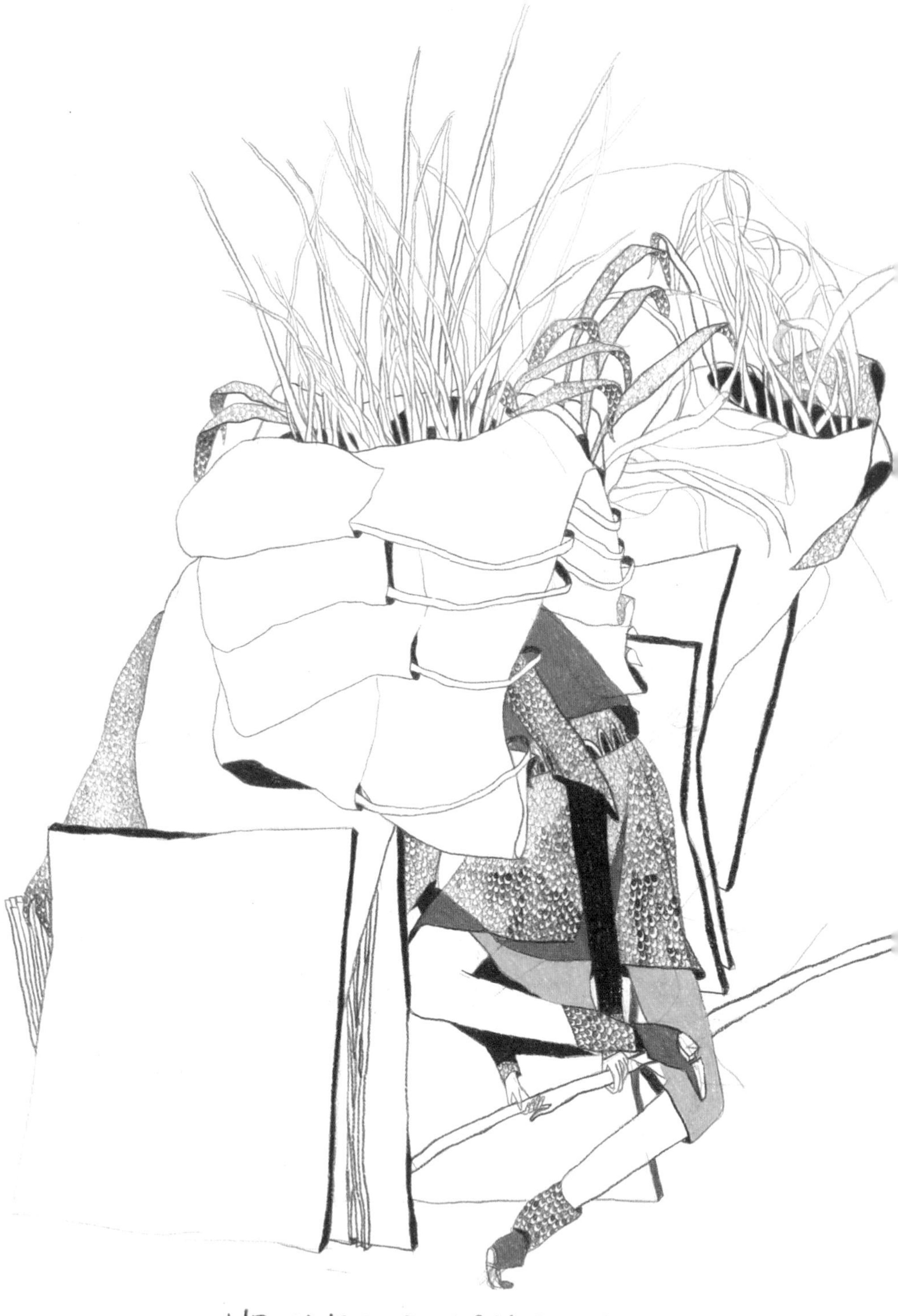

—WE MUST RETURN ALL THE WAY
BACK TO THE STARTING POINT.

IF ONE OF US SUCCEEDS TO SNEAK OUT FROM UNDER HER GAZE AND REACH ROOM 1001 THEN THE WITCH IS OBLIGED TO TELL US A STORY.

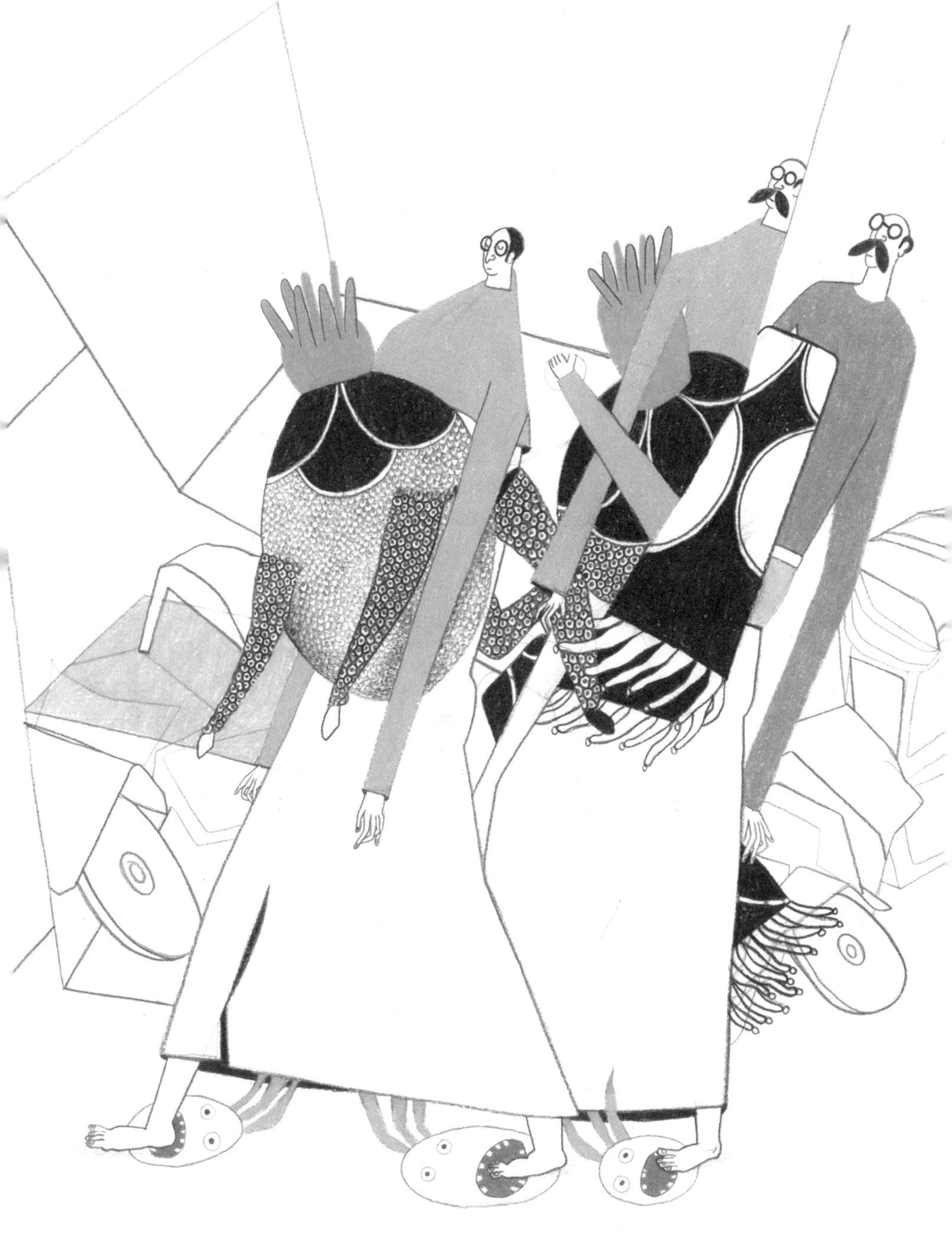

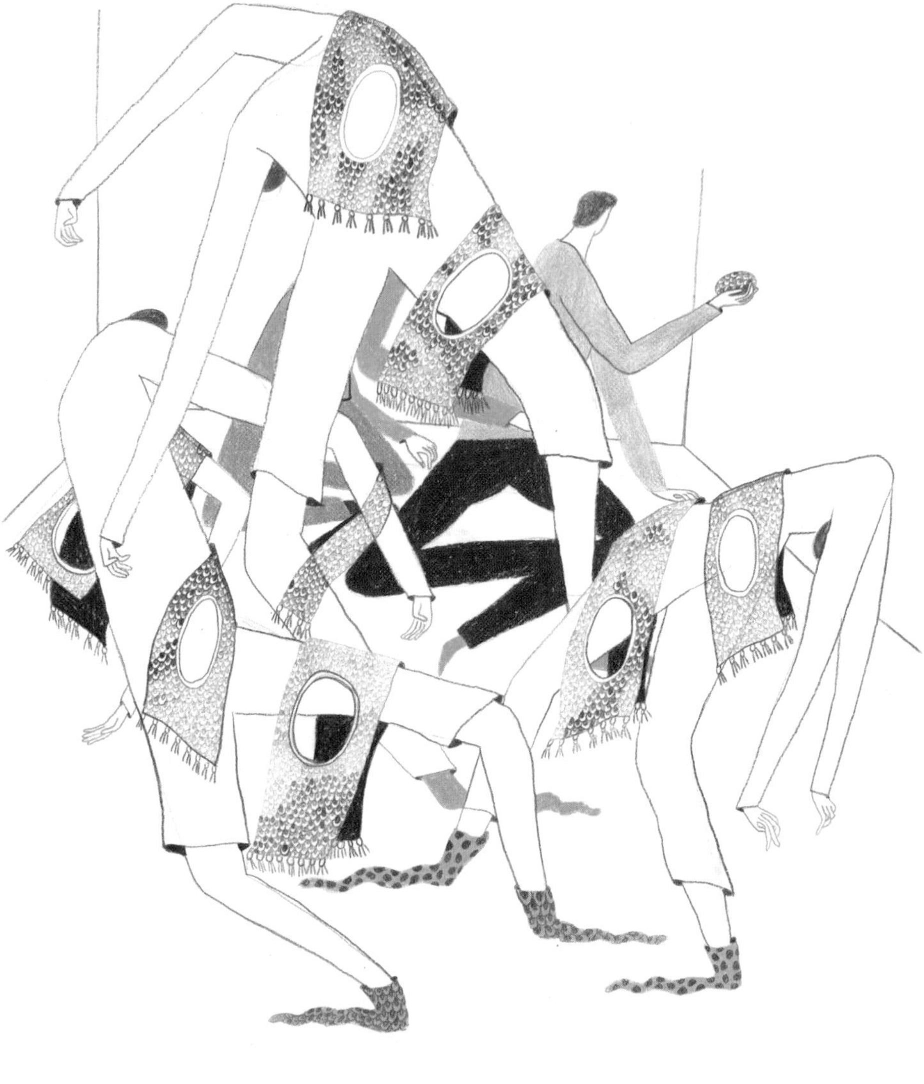

WE MUST LISTEN CAREFULLY BECAUSE THE LAST WORD IN HER STORY SETS US ALL FREE TO RUN INTO THE ROOM. BUT WHOMEVER SHE CATCHES UP WITH AND TAGS—

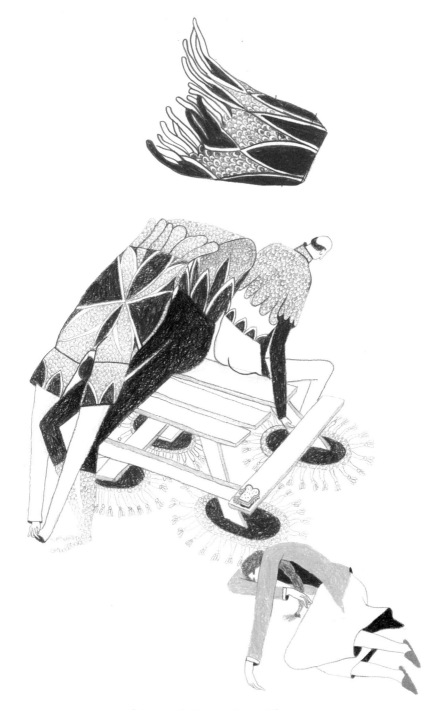

—WILL BECOME THE NEXT
WATCHING WITCH.

Dear Pothel,

On our way to school, we practice a ritual of shutting our eyes and closing our mouths and pinching our nostrils together when the bus rides past the cemetery.
A tradition to ward off accidents.
It's quite a large stretch of cemetery sprawling uphill.
If anyone is asleep at this point, we yell, "STOP BREATHING! STOP BREATHING!" to make sure no one is jinxing the ritual.

Today, approaching the cemetery, it's cold. It's still pitch dark outside and the air looks dense, foggy. We all squeeze into the left side of the bus to get a good view of the "starting line". At the sight of the first white cross protruding over the fence, the tallest boy on the bus cries "NOW!" and we shut our eyes. He volunteers to keep his eyes open under penalty of holding his breath for an extra 30 seconds after the cemetery is well out of sight so that he can inform us when it's okay to resume breathing and seeing. A time passes which seems too long in which he does not speak again. The bus is still traveling forward at the same speed, so this makes no sense.

I finally open my eyes and shriek. The rest follow. The cemetery is still right there, in full view in the window, in front of us. The bus is still moving fast and the cemetery is moving with it, as if it were dragged along by a magnetic field, uprooted and ripped from the earth. I scream "STOP!" but the driver ignores me. The rest of us remain silent. We notice each other's breathing slowing down. The sun is in full rise, and now we can read all the names on the gravestones. The inscriptions are as close and as steady as if the bus is not moving at all. The road is smooth.
I am reading your name.

Liana.

P.S Thank you for the book.

GETTING TO SCHOOL

OUR ANATOMY PROFESSOR
VANISHED ONE DAY AND
RETURNED TO CAMPUS
AS A CAR.

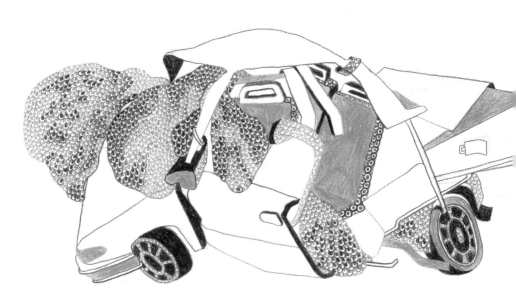

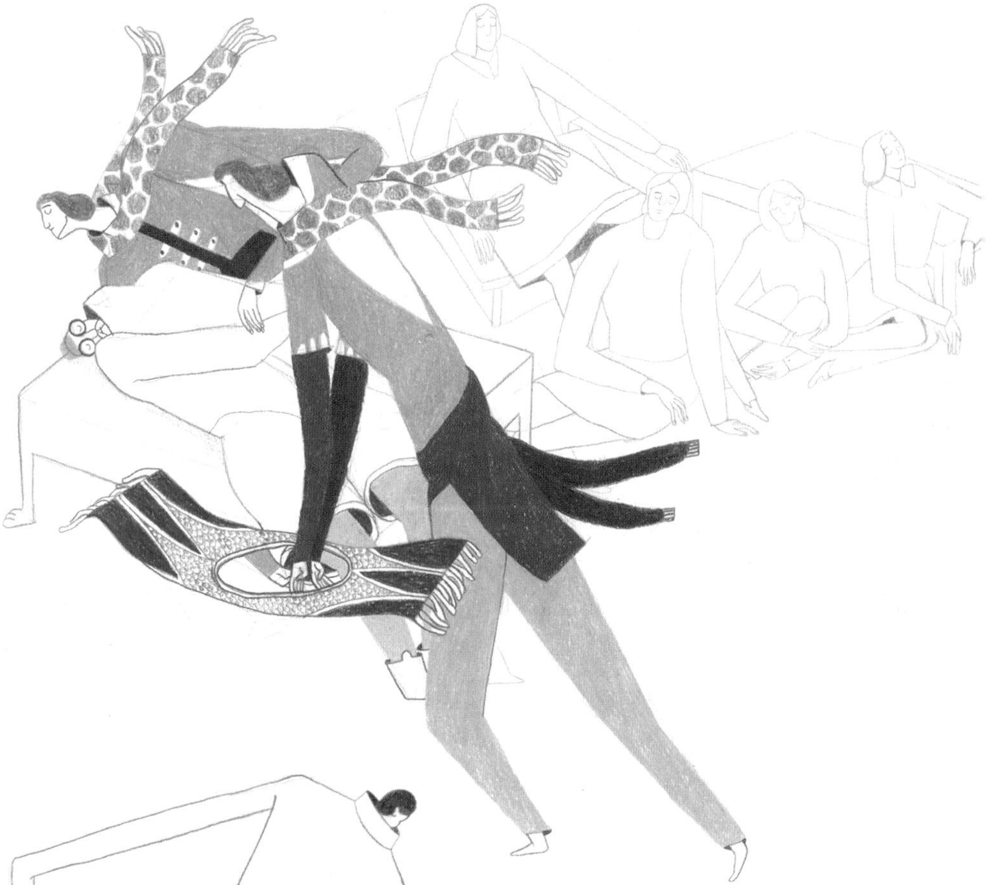

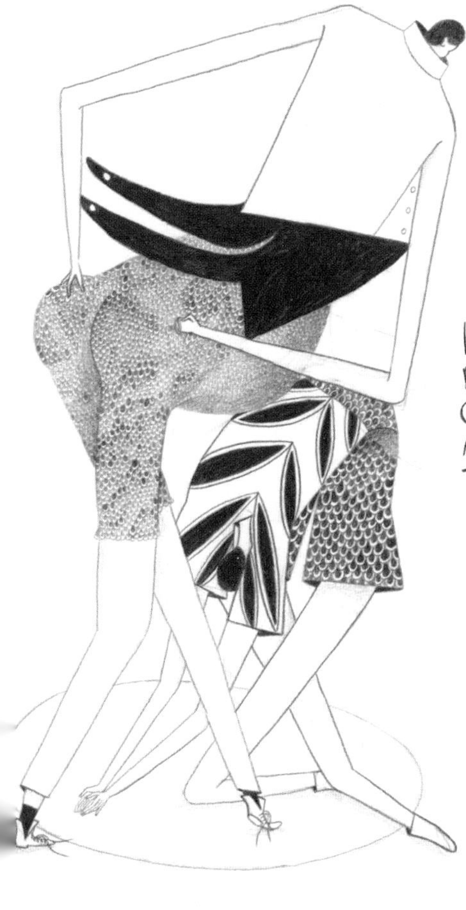

IT WAS QUITE SHOCKING
BUT EVERYONE WAS TOO
CAUGHT UP IN THEIR OWN
AFFAIRS. SO THINGS RETURNED
TO NORMAL PRETTY QUICKLY.

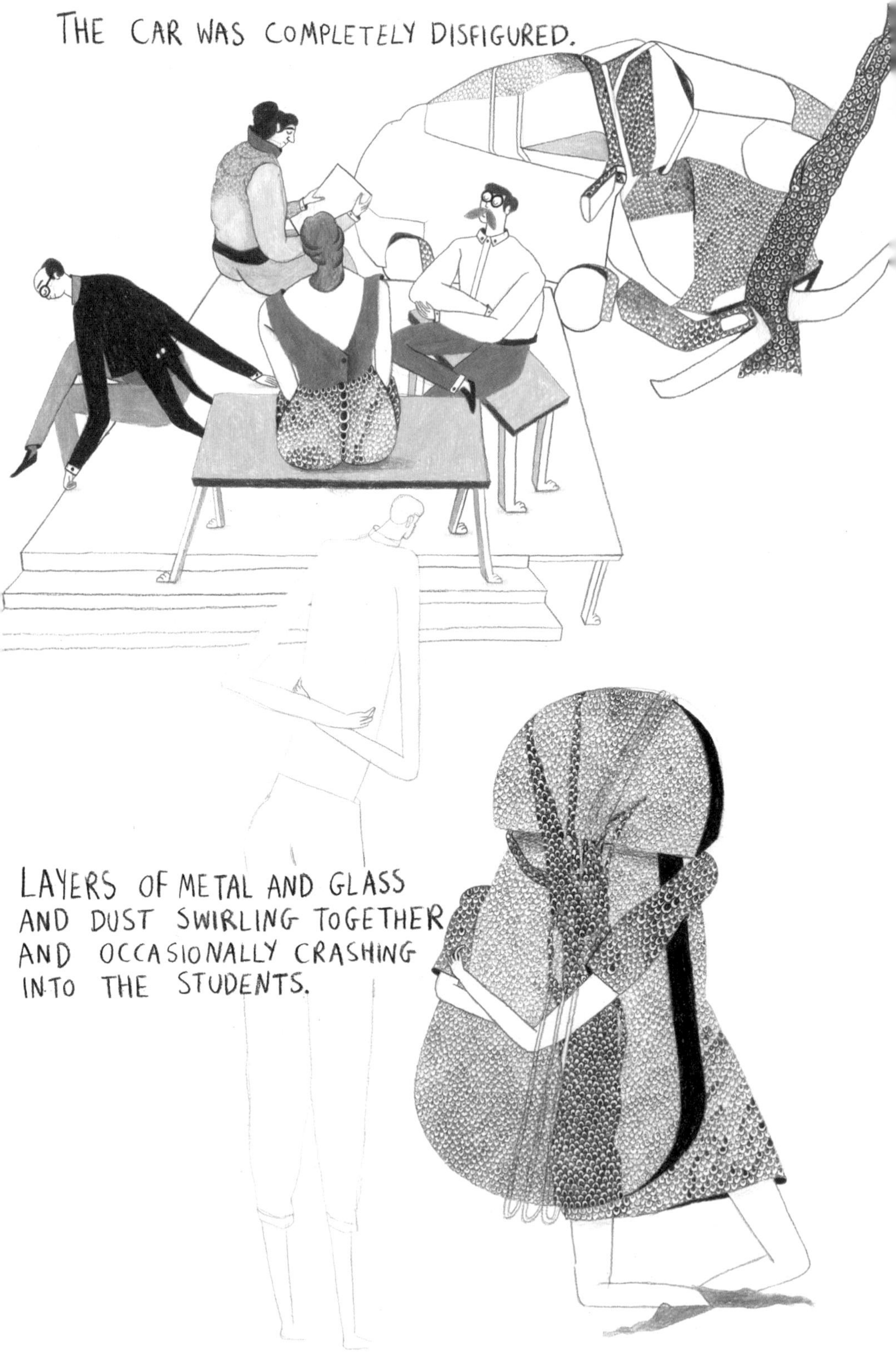
THE CAR WAS COMPLETELY DISFIGURED.
LAYERS OF METAL AND GLASS AND DUST SWIRLING TOGETHER AND OCCASIONALLY CRASHING INTO THE STUDENTS.

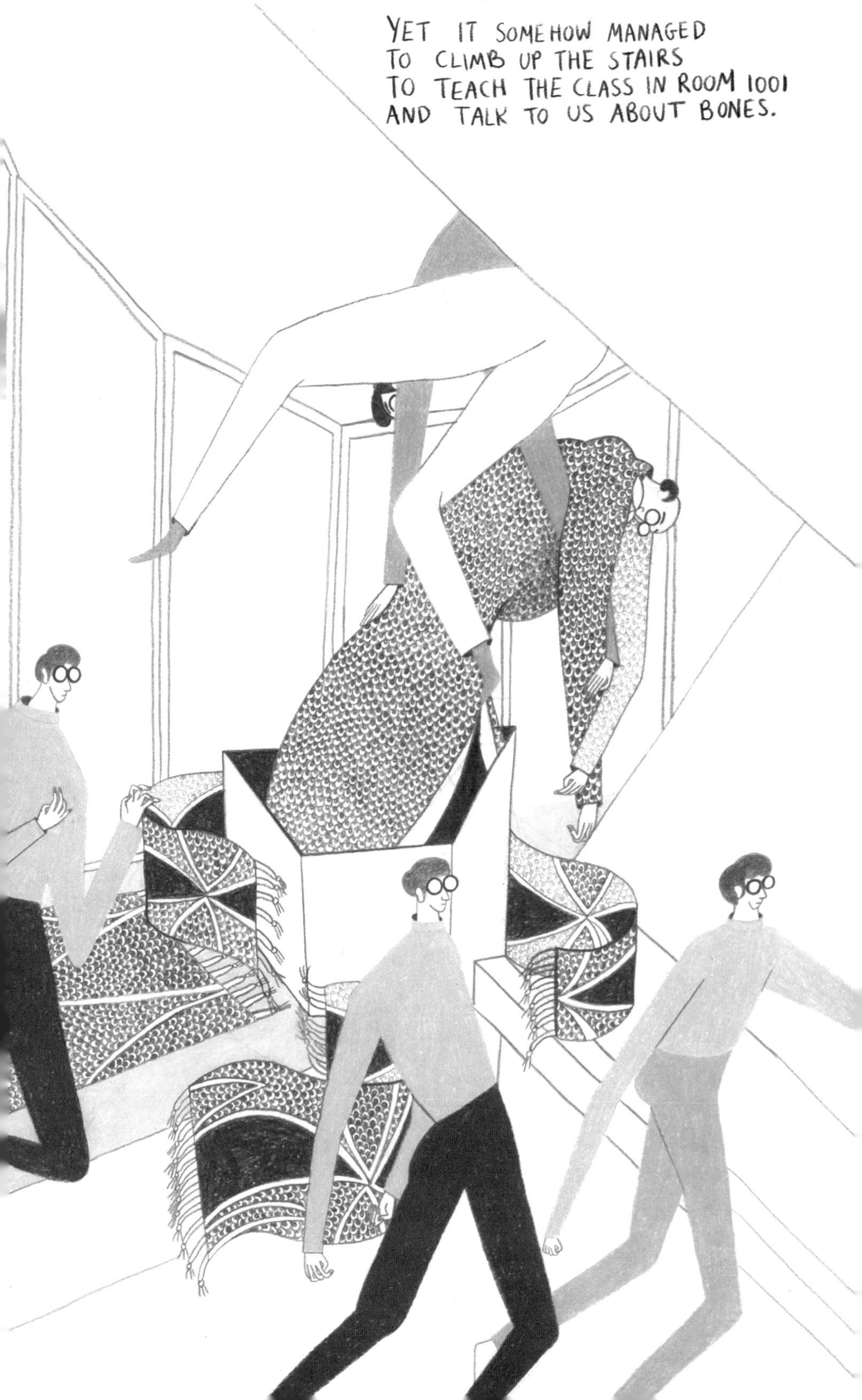
YET IT SOMEHOW MANAGED
TO CLIMB UP THE STAIRS
TO TEACH THE CLASS IN ROOM 1001
AND TALK TO US ABOUT BONES.

WE WERE ALL ALWAYS BREAKING
THEM SO THIS WAS A CLASS
NO ONE COULD AFFORD TO MISS.

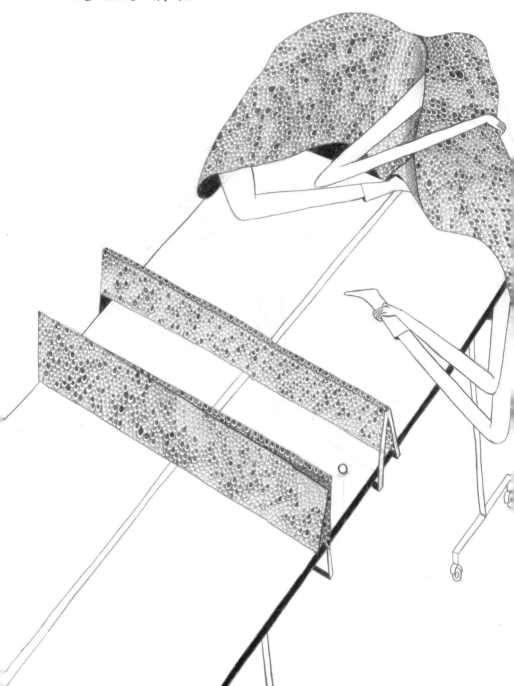

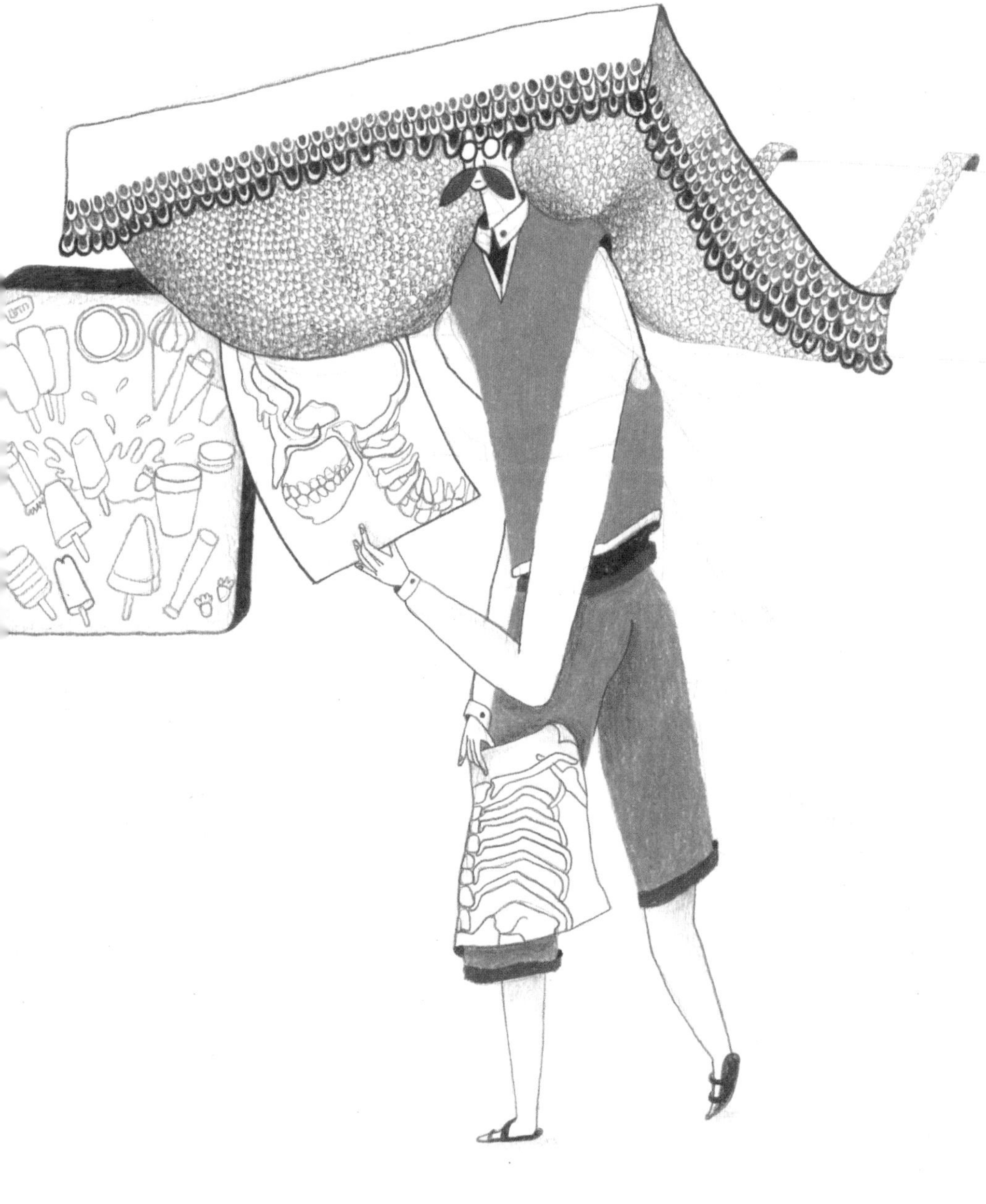

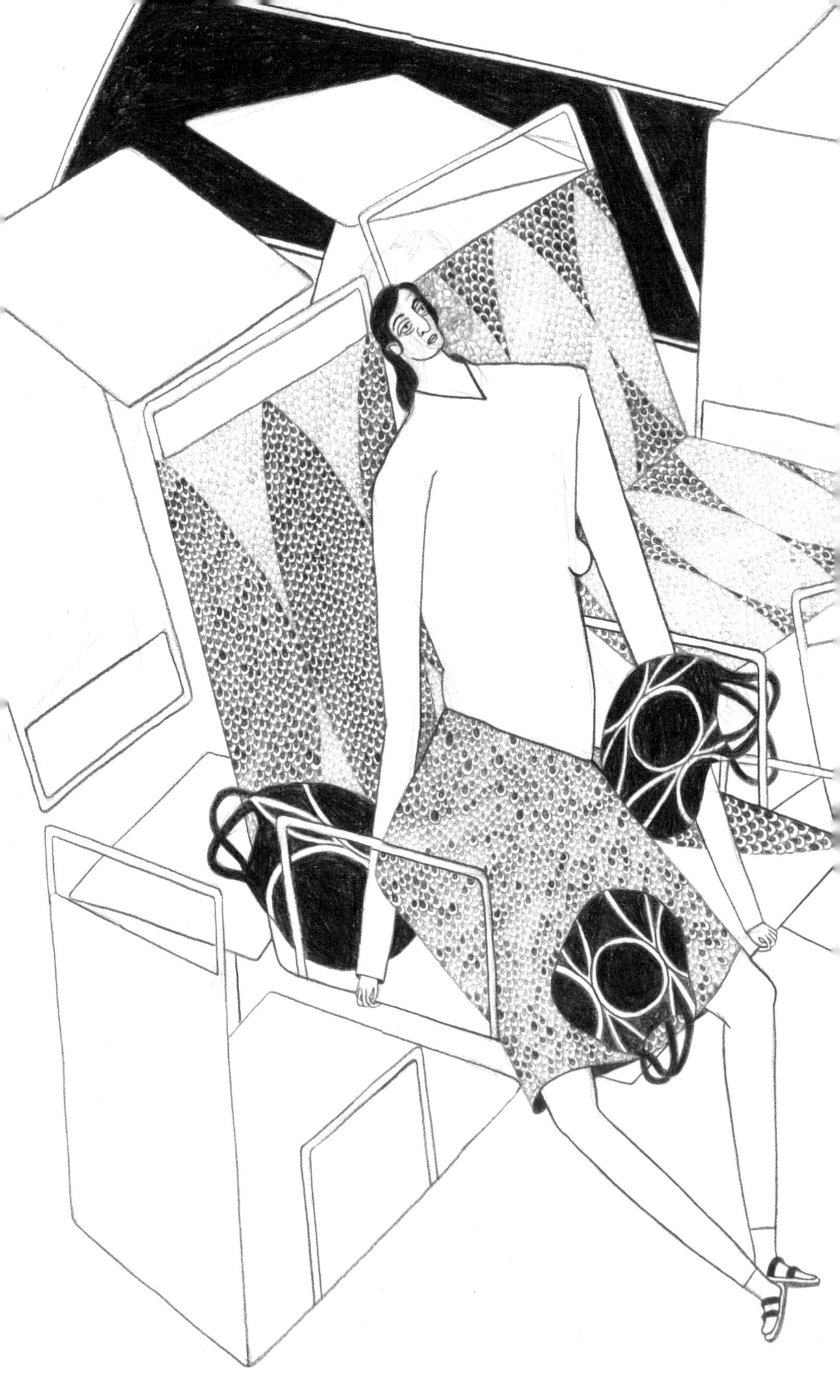

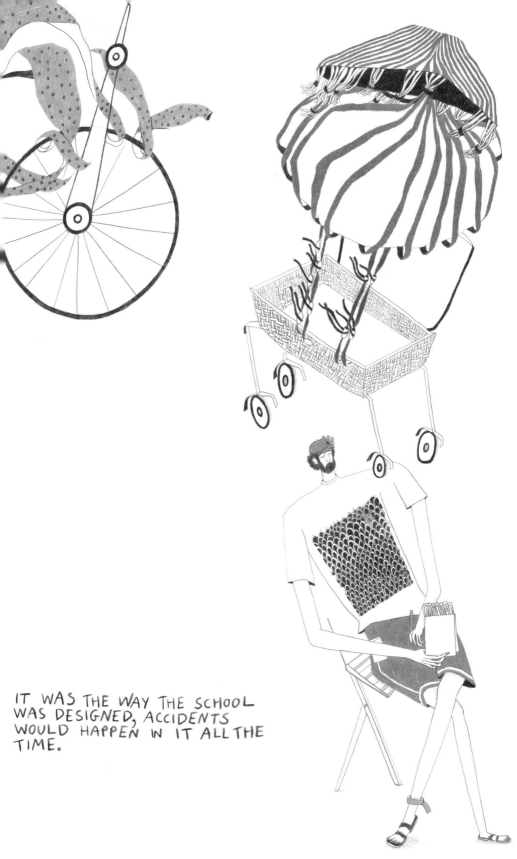

IT WAS THE WAY THE SCHOOL
WAS DESIGNED, ACCIDENTS
WOULD HAPPEN IN IT ALL THE
TIME.

MOST DAYS I WOULD TAKE THE
5AM BUS TO SCHOOL.

I LIKE TO AVOID THE
COMMOTION OF THE CHILDREN
AND THE SWINGING DOORS.

STILL, EVERY NOW AND THEN, A MAN BOARDS AND BREAKS HIS COLLARBONE.

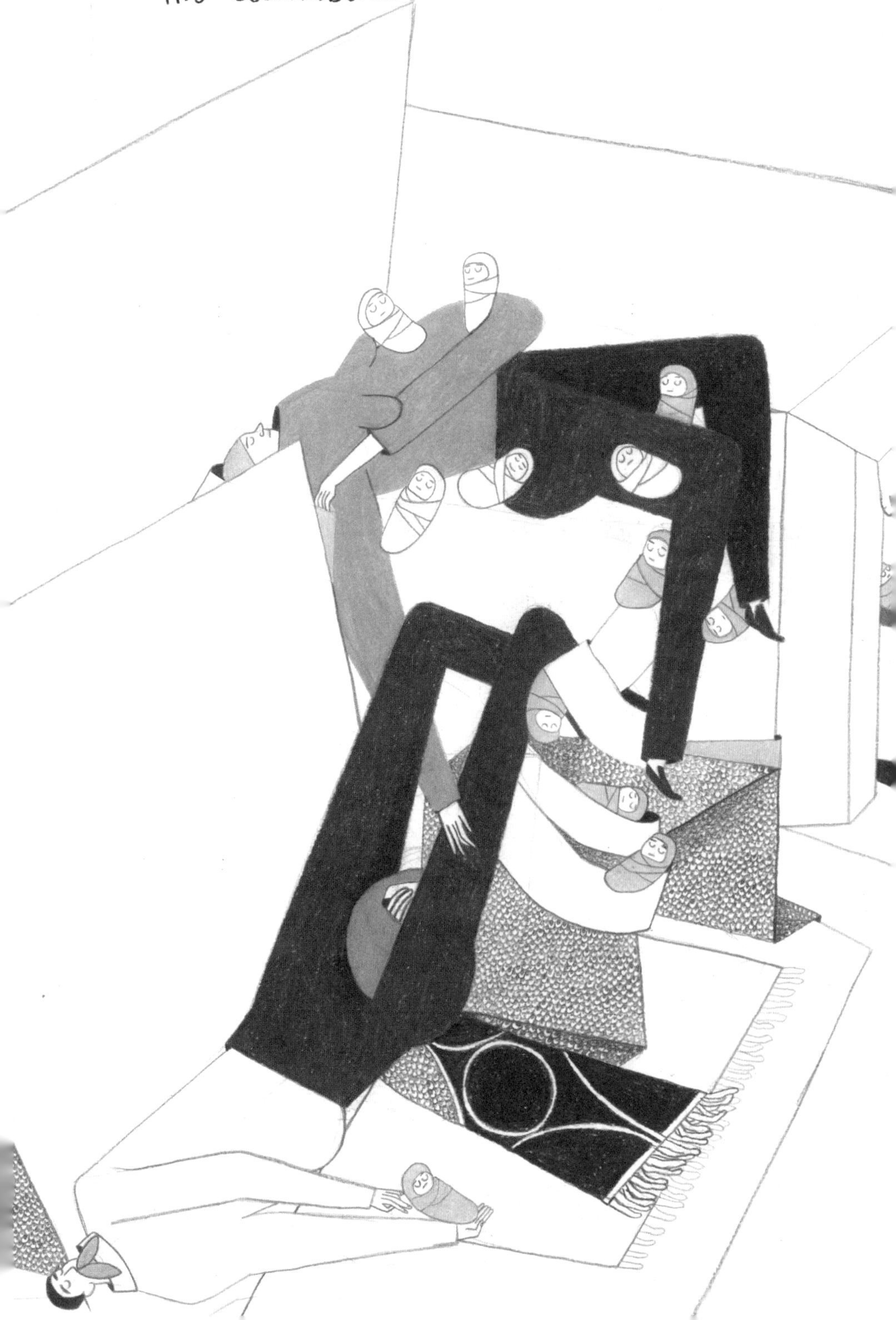

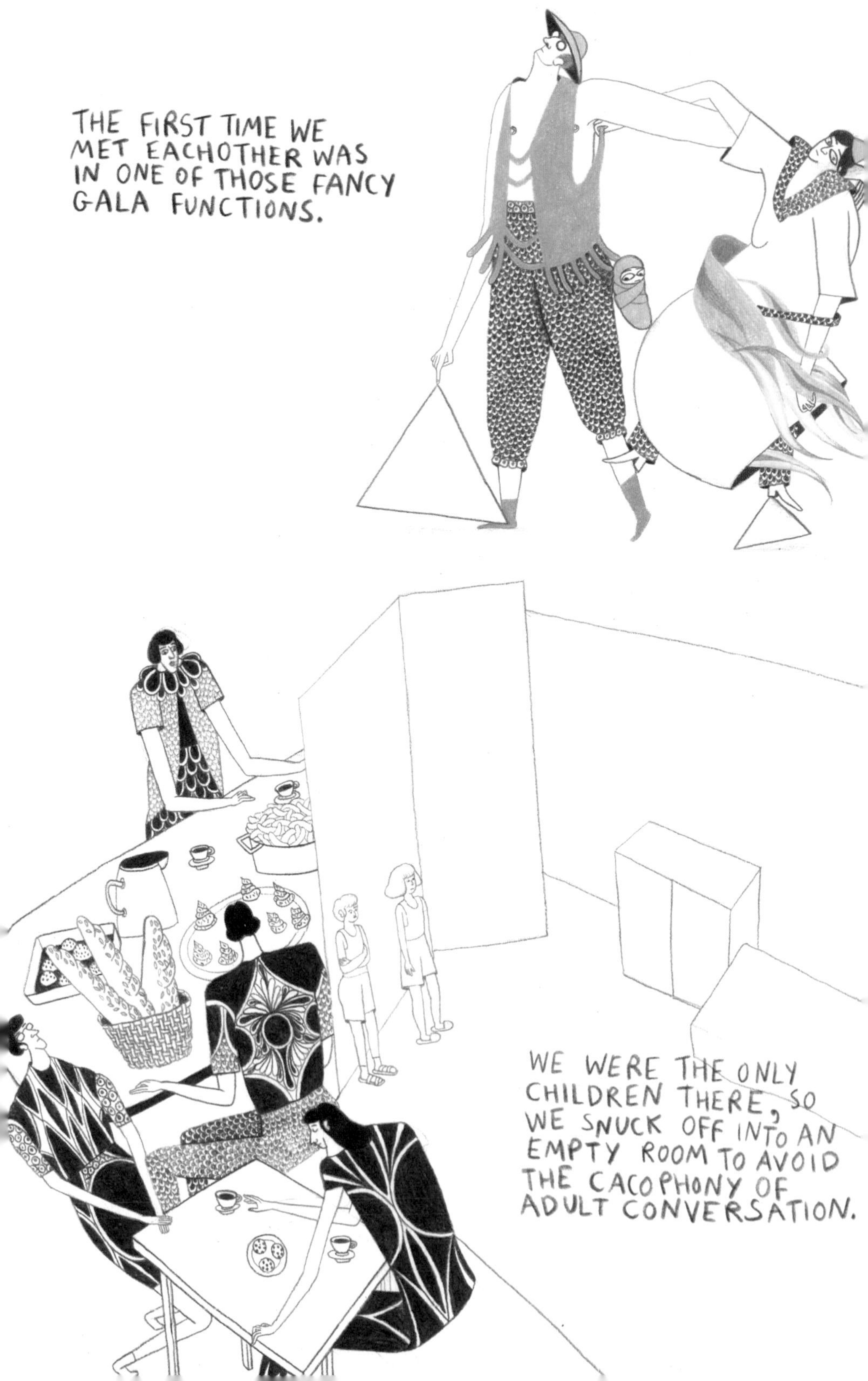
THE FIRST TIME WE MET EACHOTHER WAS IN ONE OF THOSE FANCY GALA FUNCTIONS.
WE WERE THE ONLY CHILDREN THERE, SO WE SNUCK OFF INTO AN EMPTY ROOM TO AVOID THE CACOPHONY OF ADULT CONVERSATION.

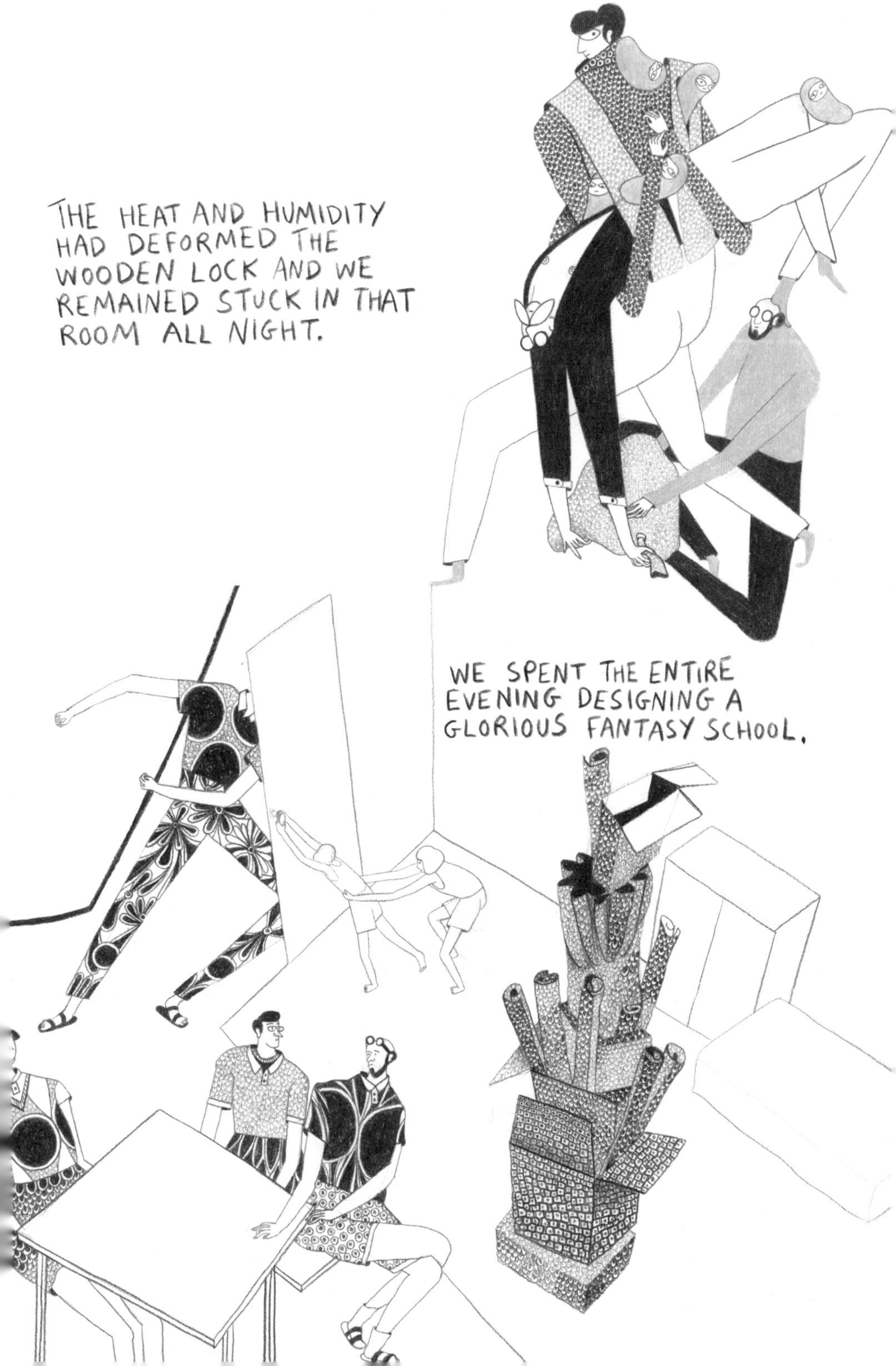
THE HEAT AND HUMIDITY HAD DEFORMED THE WOODEN LOCK AND WE REMAINED STUCK IN THAT ROOM ALL NIGHT.
WE SPENT THE ENTIRE EVENING DESIGNING A GLORIOUS FANTASY SCHOOL.

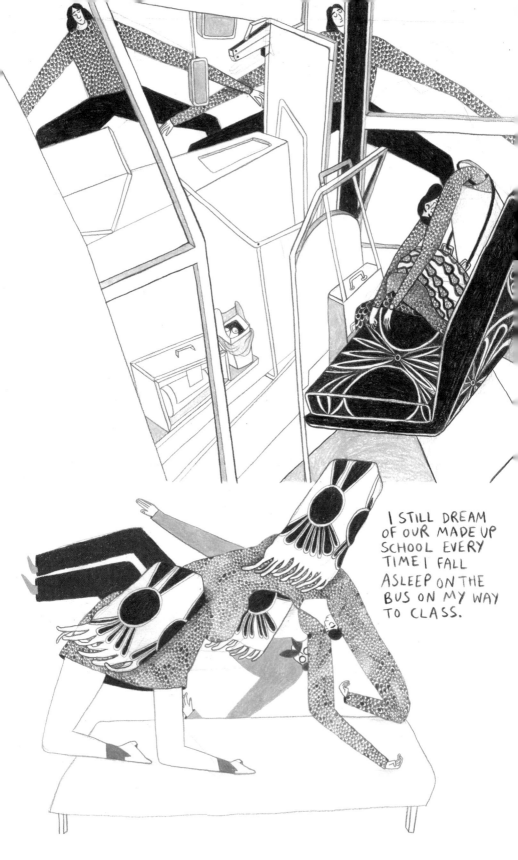

I STILL DREAM OF OUR MADE UP SCHOOL EVERY TIME I FALL ASLEEP ON THE BUS ON MY WAY TO CLASS.

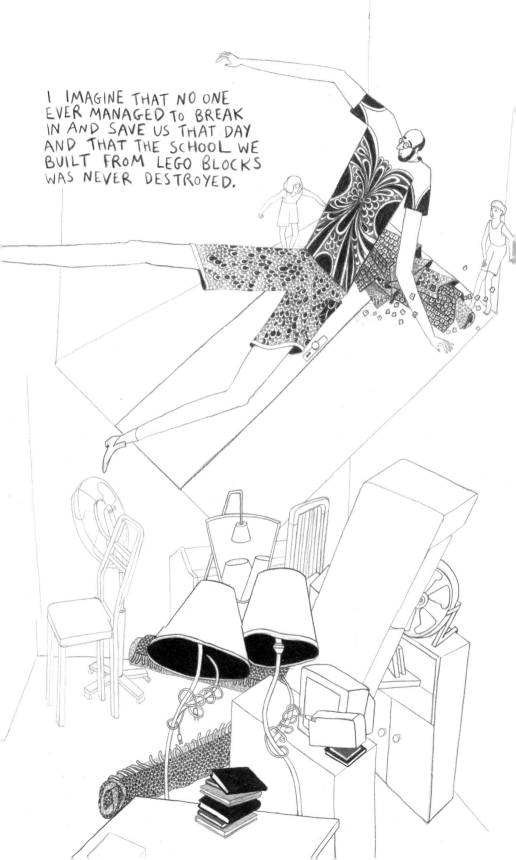

I IMAGINE THAT NO ONE
EVER MANAGED TO BREAK
IN AND SAVE US THAT DAY
AND THAT THE SCHOOL WE
BUILT FROM LEGO BLOCKS
WAS NEVER DESTROYED.

WE SHOULD HAVE KEPT THE RUINS.

WE SHOULD HAVE MADE A MAP
SO WE COULD ONE DAY RETURN.

MY SKELETON WARPS WITH EVERY
TURN THE BUS MAKES.

I DISTRACT MYSELF FROM THE PAIN
BY TRYING TO REMEMBER HOW WE
EVENTUALLY GOT OUT OF THAT ROOM.

WHO WAS THAT MAN THAT GOT US OUT?

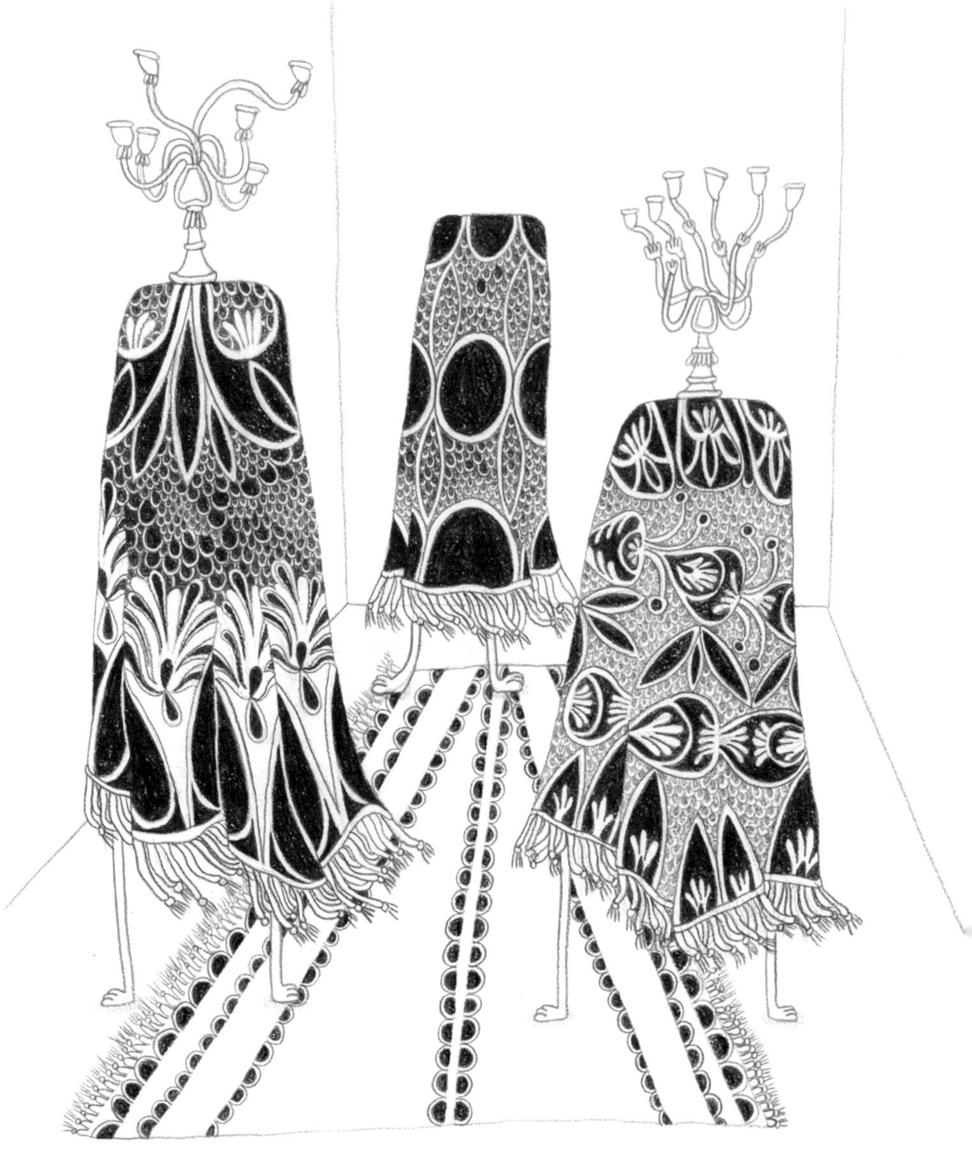

I CAN NO LONGER SIT IN ANY CLASSROOM FOR LONGER THAN AN HOUR, WITHOUT IT TRANSFORMING IN MY IMAGINATION.

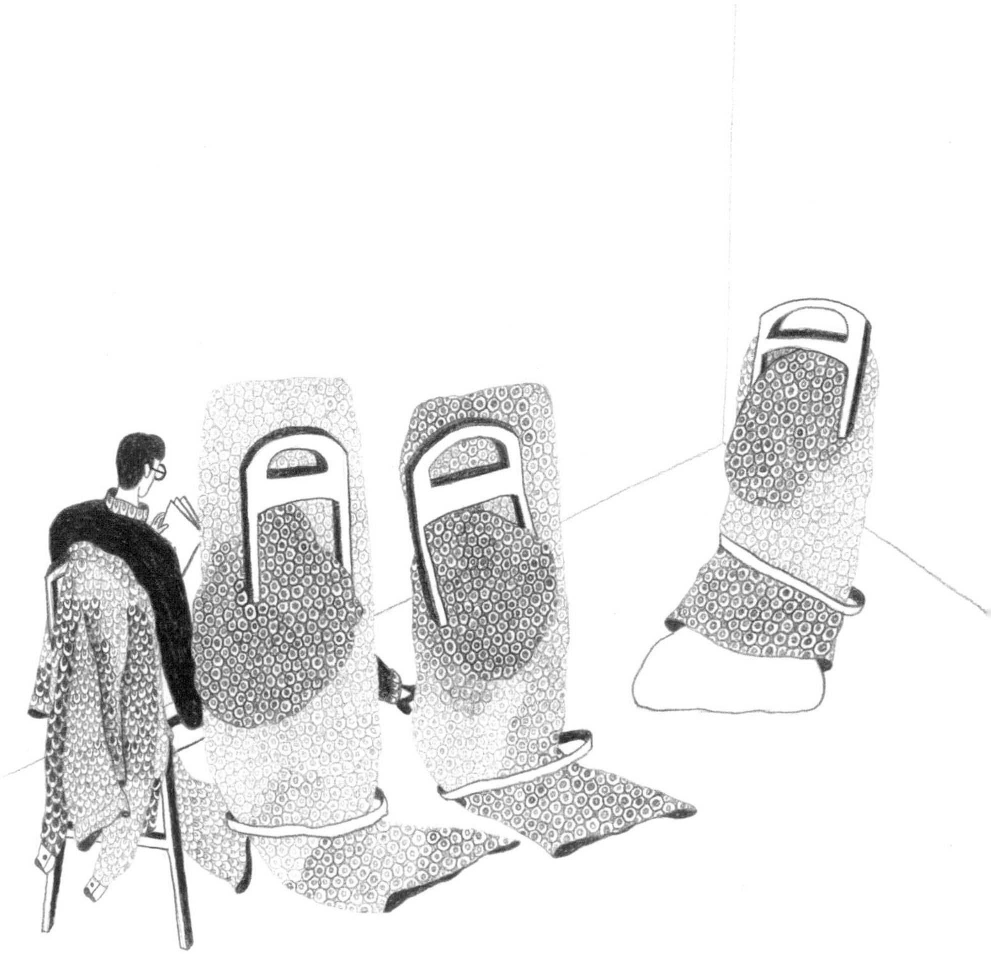

I MAKE PLANS TO LEAVE THEM.
HOW DO YOU LEAVE YOURS?

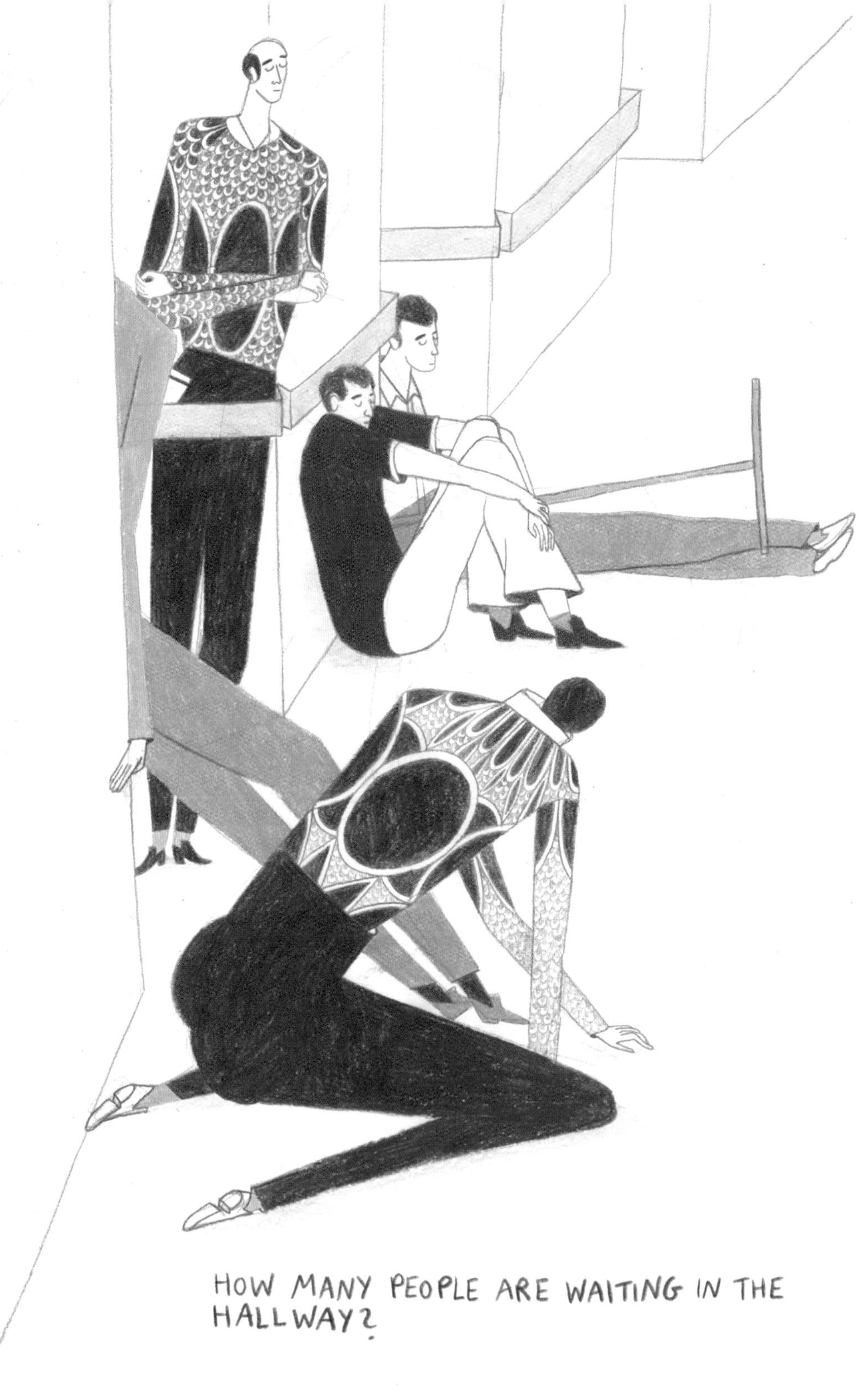

HOW MANY PEOPLE ARE WAITING IN THE HALLWAY?

THE MORE TIME I SPEND MAKING PLANS, THE MORE LIKELY I AM TO BE MAKING PLANS FOR SOMEONE ELSE INSTEAD.

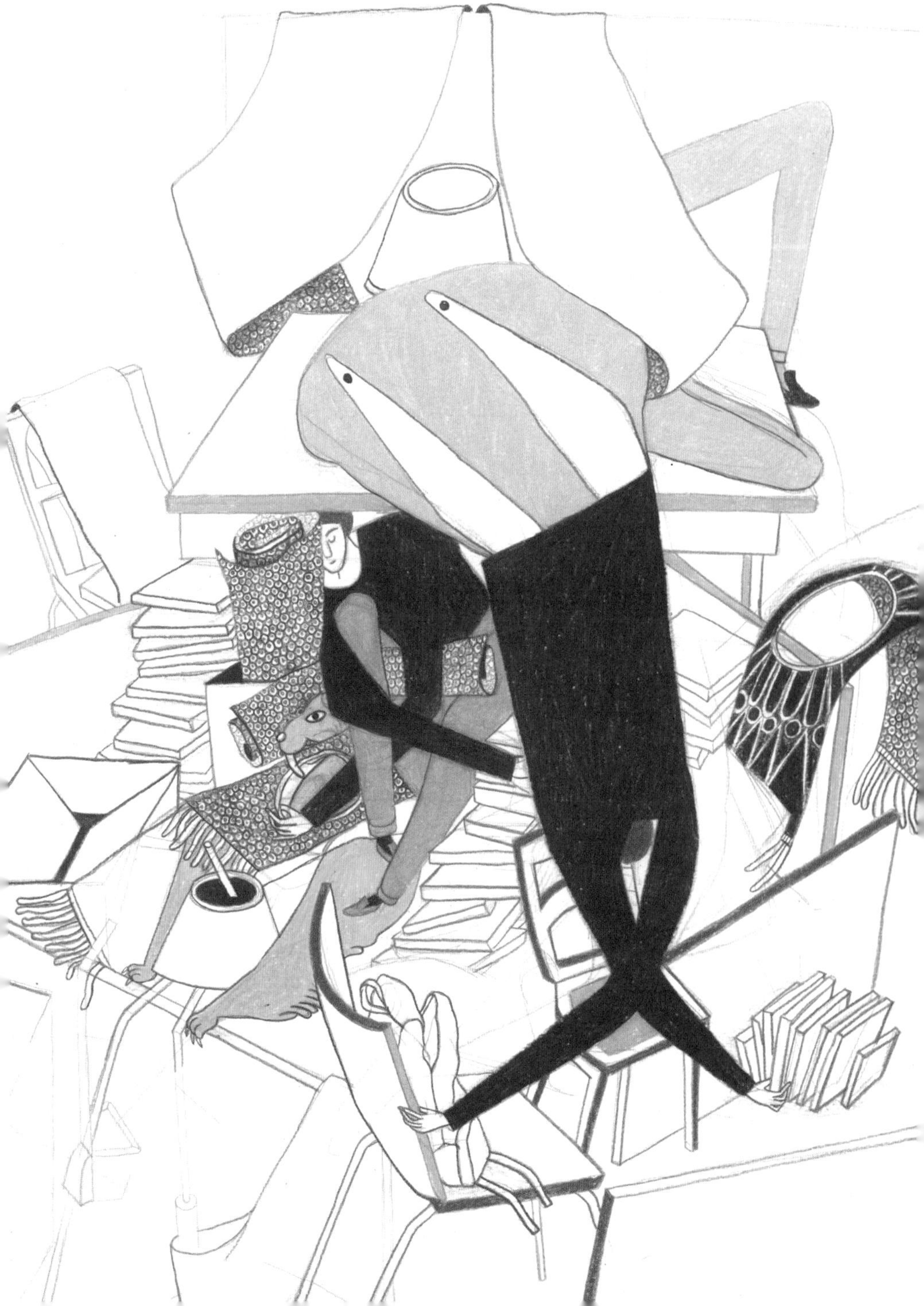

I SEE YOU IN SCHOOL FROM TIME TO TIME, WE CLIMB STAIRS TOGETHER TO REACH VARIOUS FLOORS.

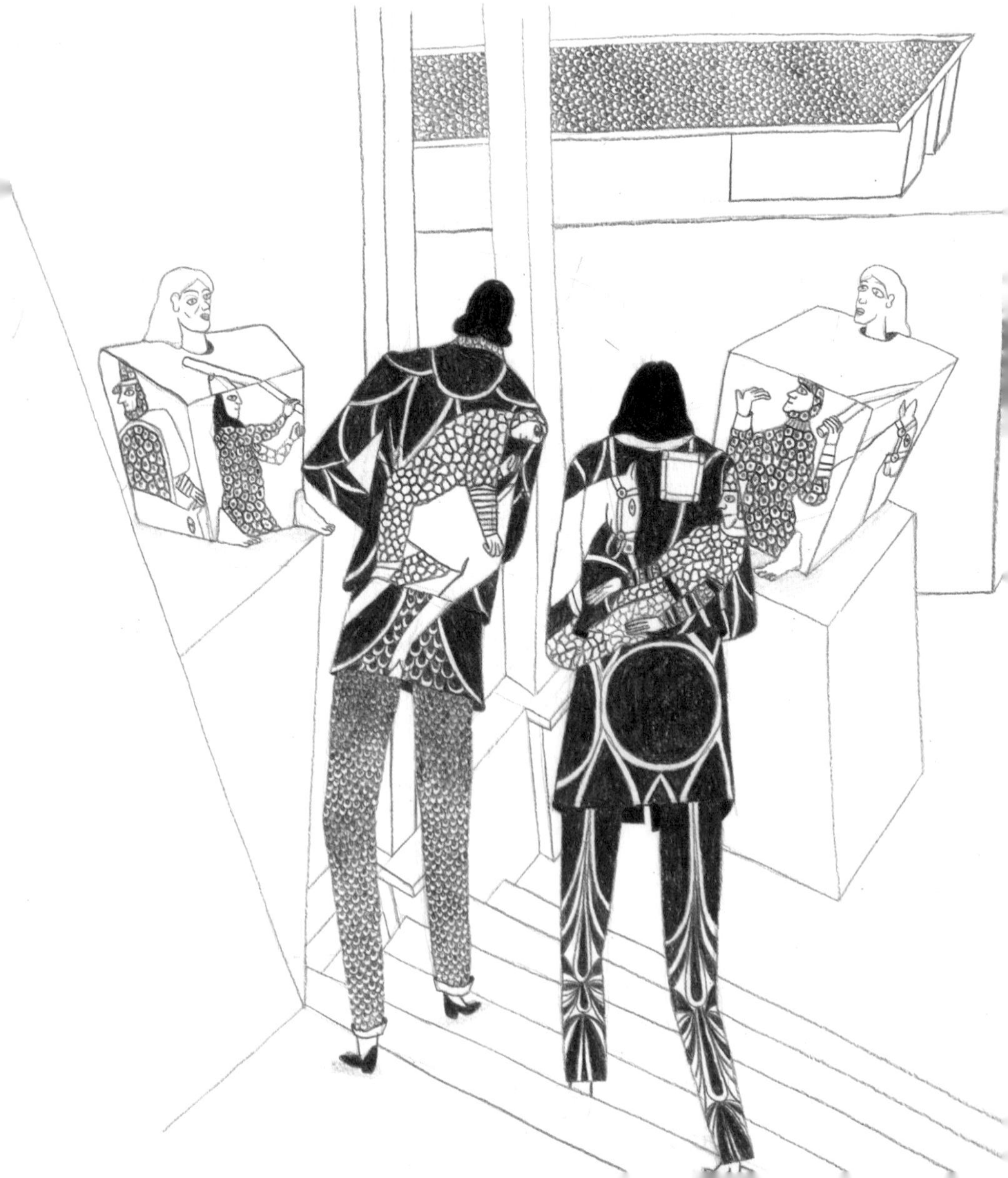

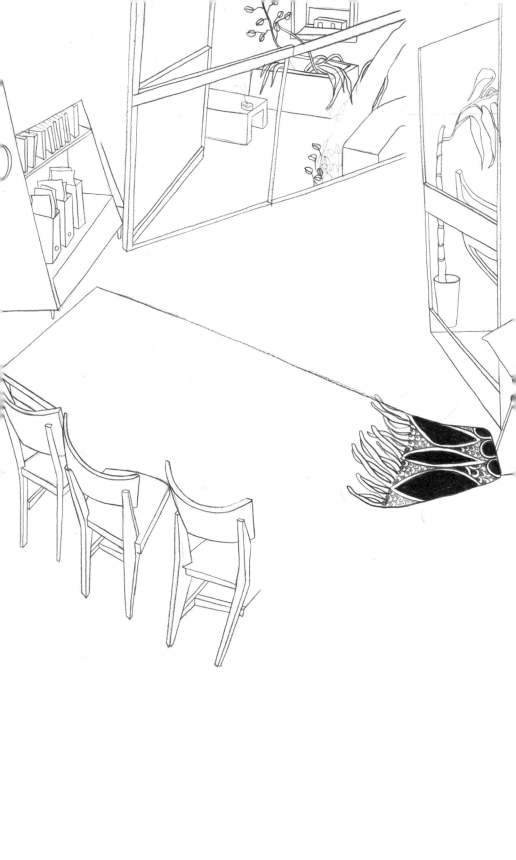

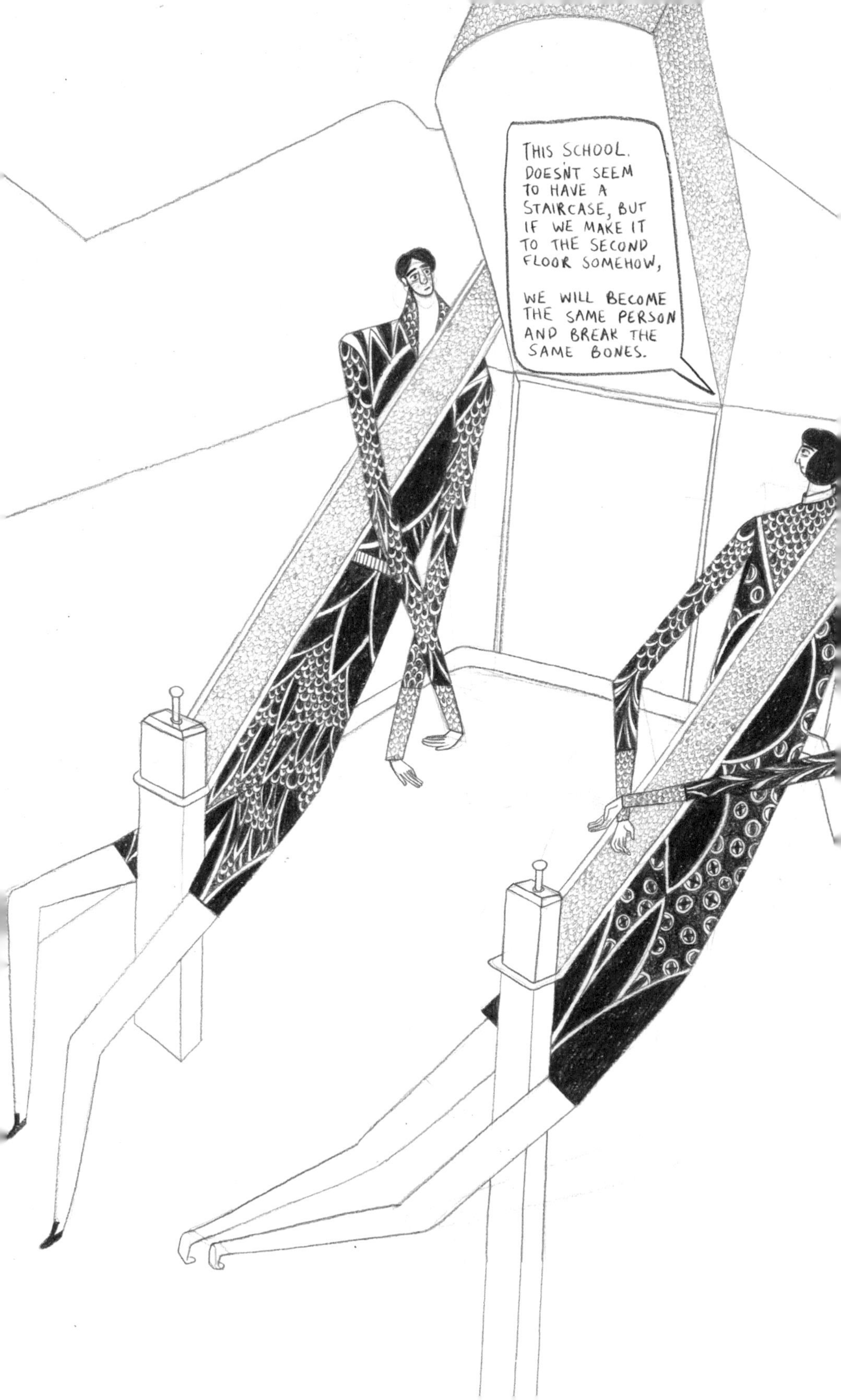
THIS SCHOOL. DOESN'T SEEM TO HAVE A STAIRCASE, BUT IF WE MAKE IT TO THE SECOND FLOOR SOMEHOW,

WE WILL BECOME THE SAME PERSON AND BREAK THE SAME BONES.

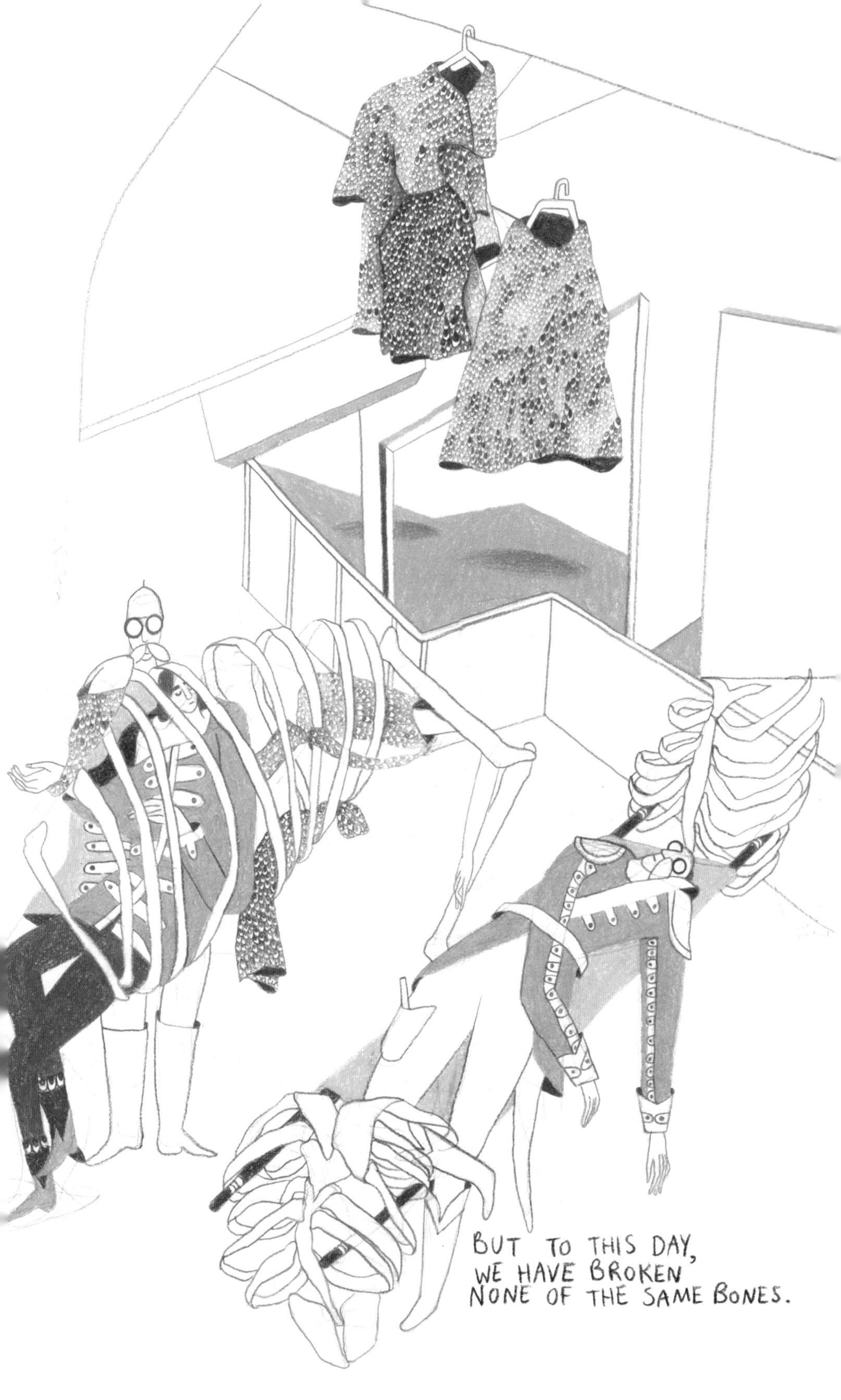
BUT TO THIS DAY,
WE HAVE BROKEN
NONE OF THE SAME BONES.

L.

Might you be available
today circa 3 pm,
South corner?
Not sure of my
availability,
checking on yours,

P.

MARKS ON THE ATTENDANCE SHEET

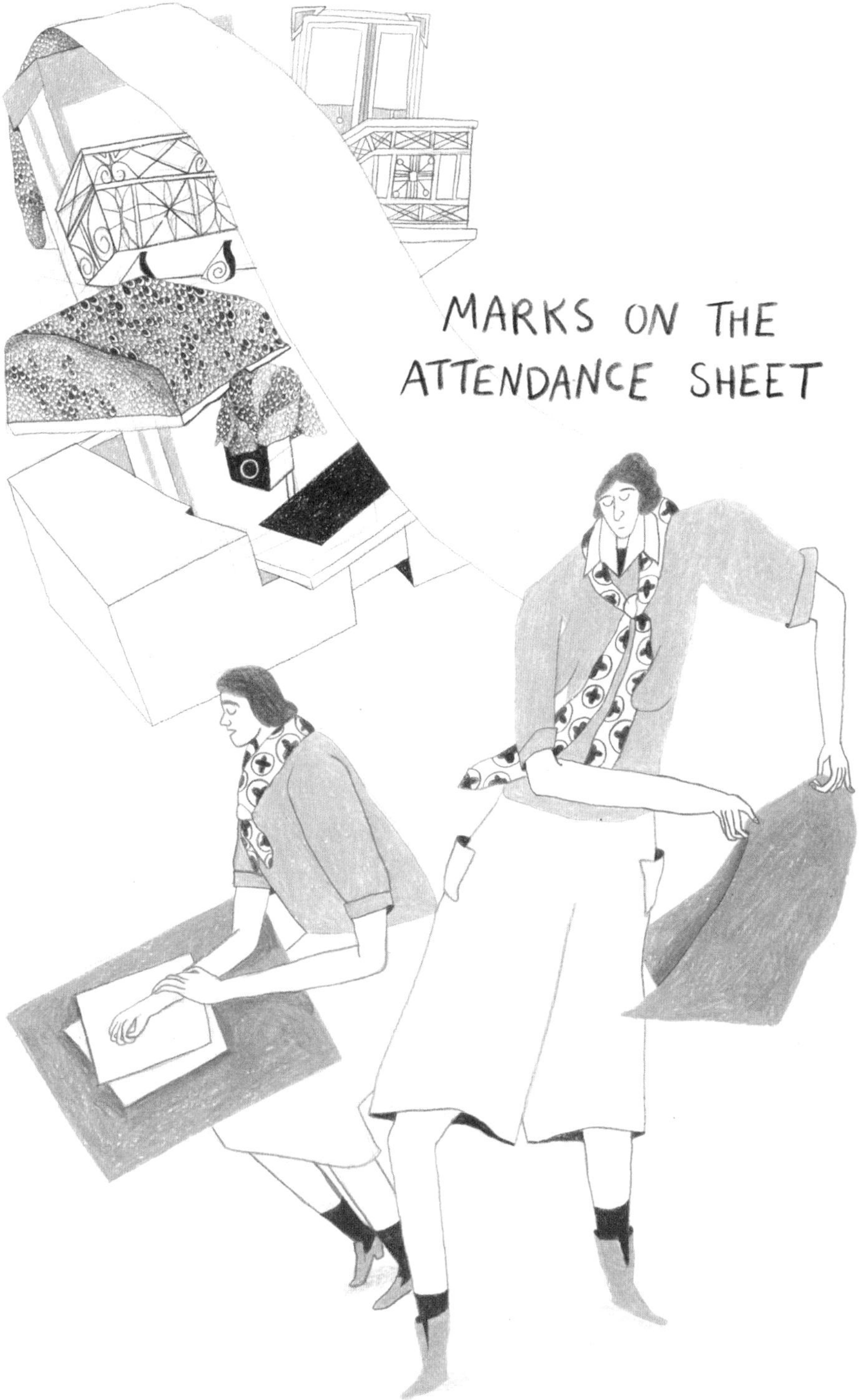

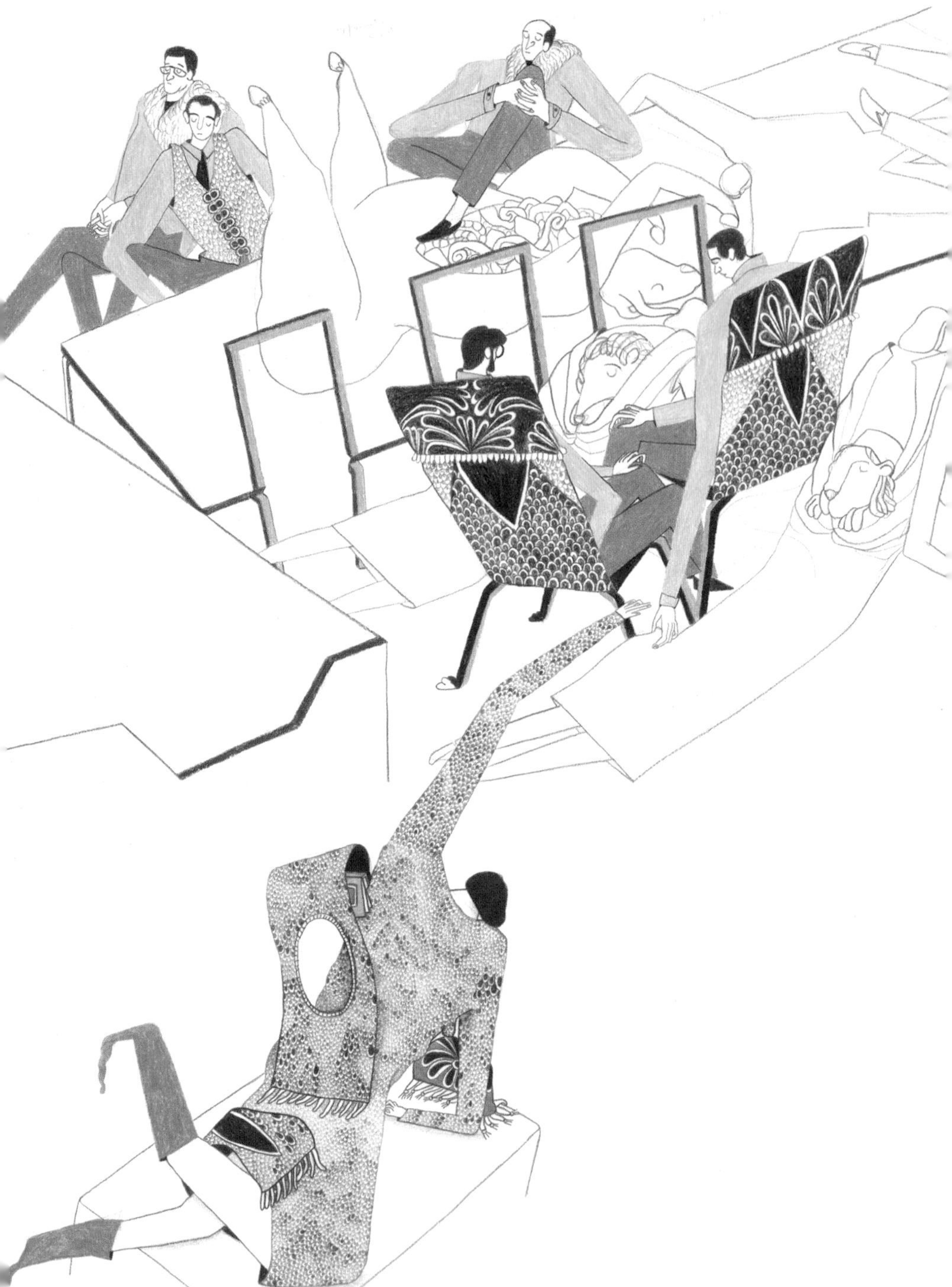

FROM THE MOMENT OF YOUR DISAPPEARANCE, IT BECAME HARDER FOR ME TO TELL WHETHER I AM AWAKE, OR WHEN I AM NO LONGER IN THE UNIVERSITY OR NO LONGER ENTERING CLASSROOMS AND LECTURE HALLS. CLIMBING THE STAIRCASES CAUSES MY EYELIDS TO DROP. I IMAGINE I WAS SWALLOWED BY A HUNDRED YEAR OLD LION, MOVING THROUGH CAMPUS ON THE INSIDE OF HIS ENORMOUS DIGESTIVE TRACT.

NO ONE CAN SEE ME NOW, WANDERING THROUGH THE HALLWAYS, ON ALL FOURS, LOOKING FOR YOU, ALWAYS ARRIVING LATE FOR CLASS SO THAT THE SPELL DOESN'T BREAK IF MY NAME GETS CALLED OUT.

IN EVERY ROOM, I SEE MORE LIONS LURKING, READY TO SWALLOW YOU AS WELL, SO THEY CAN JOIN MY OWN LION'S SIDE.

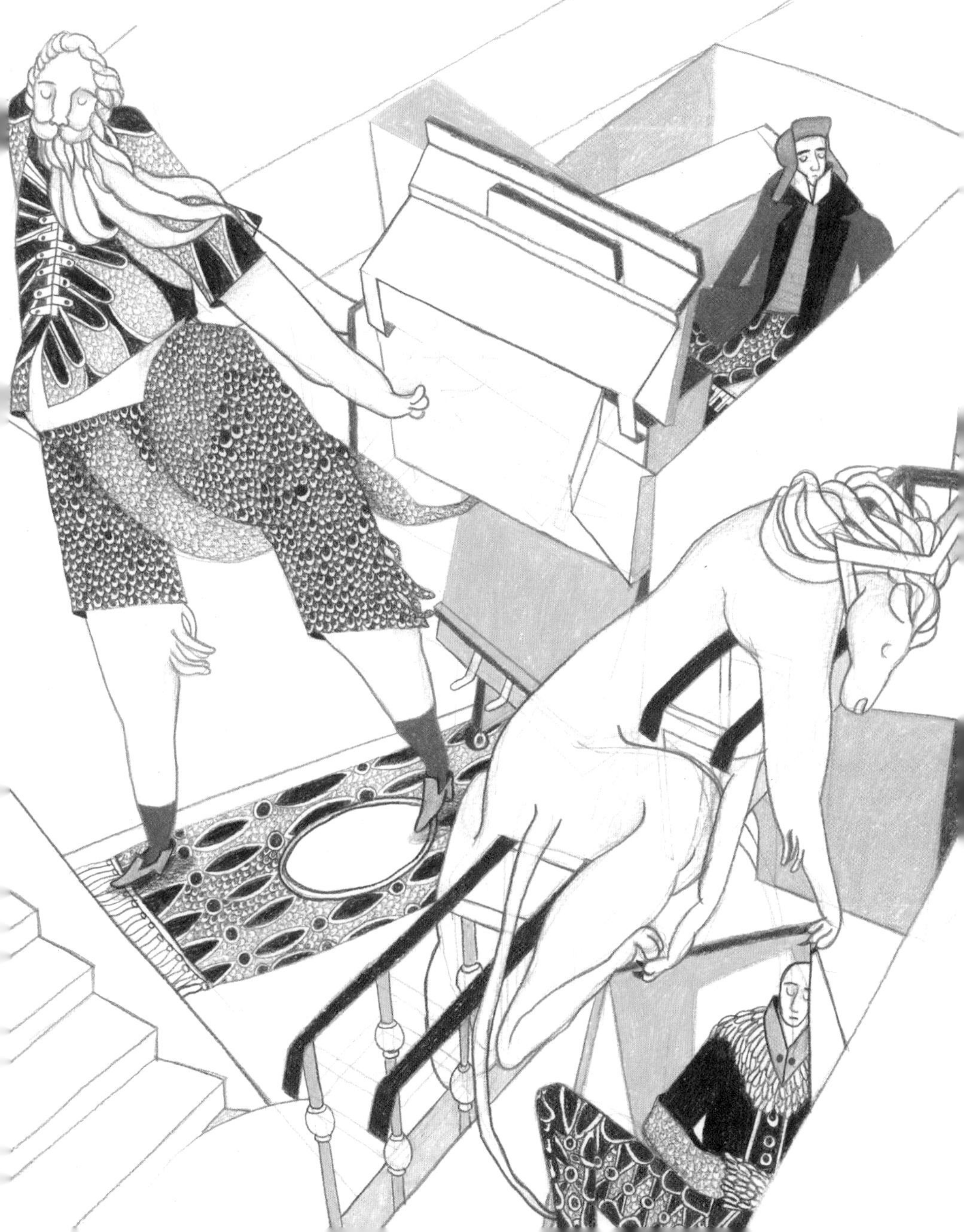

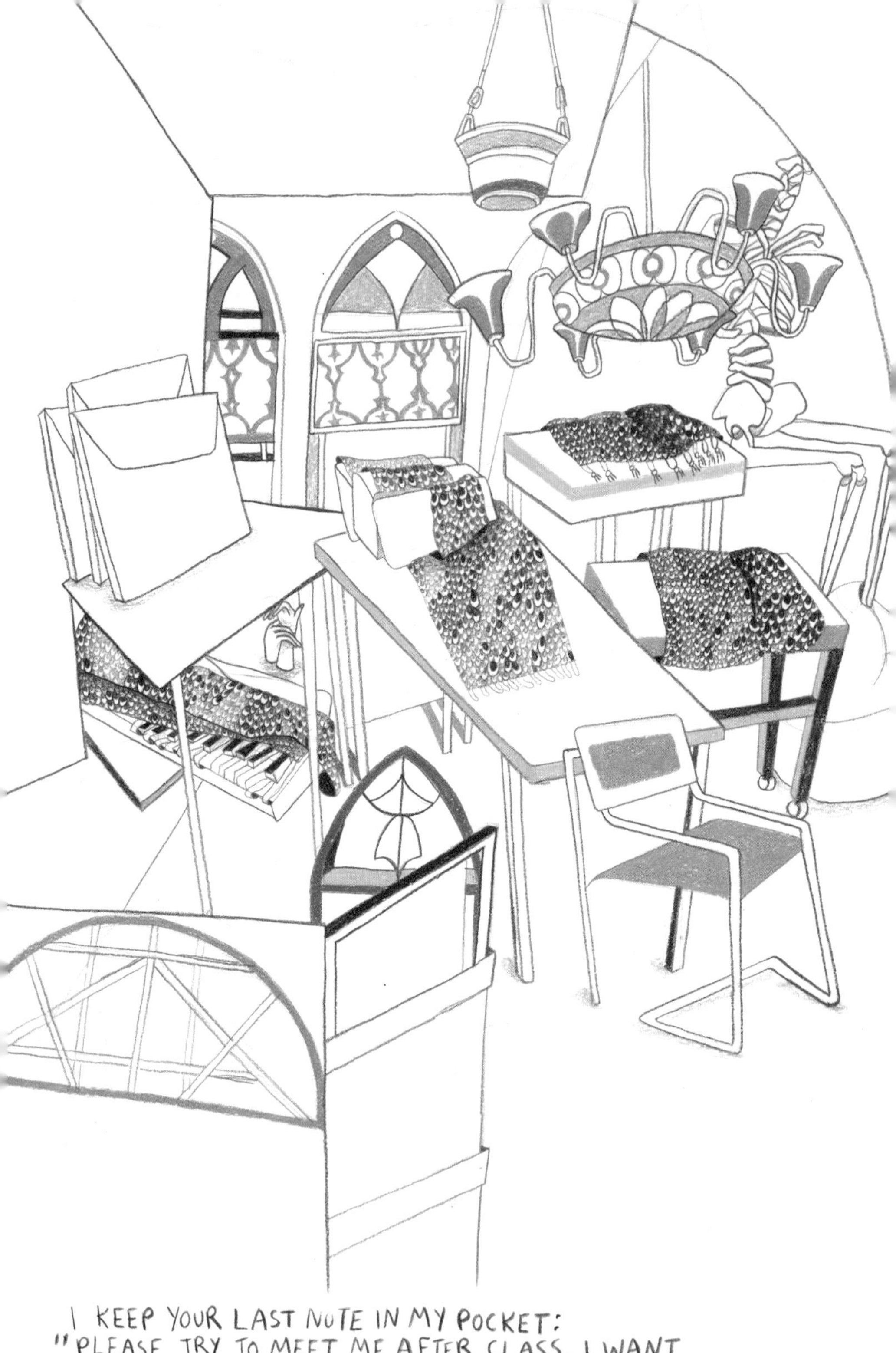

I KEEP YOUR LAST NOTE IN MY POCKET:
"PLEASE TRY TO MEET ME AFTER CLASS. I WANT TO SEE HOW FAR WE CAN BOTH VENTURE OUTSIDE CAMPUS BEFORE WE RUN INTO EACH OTHER!"

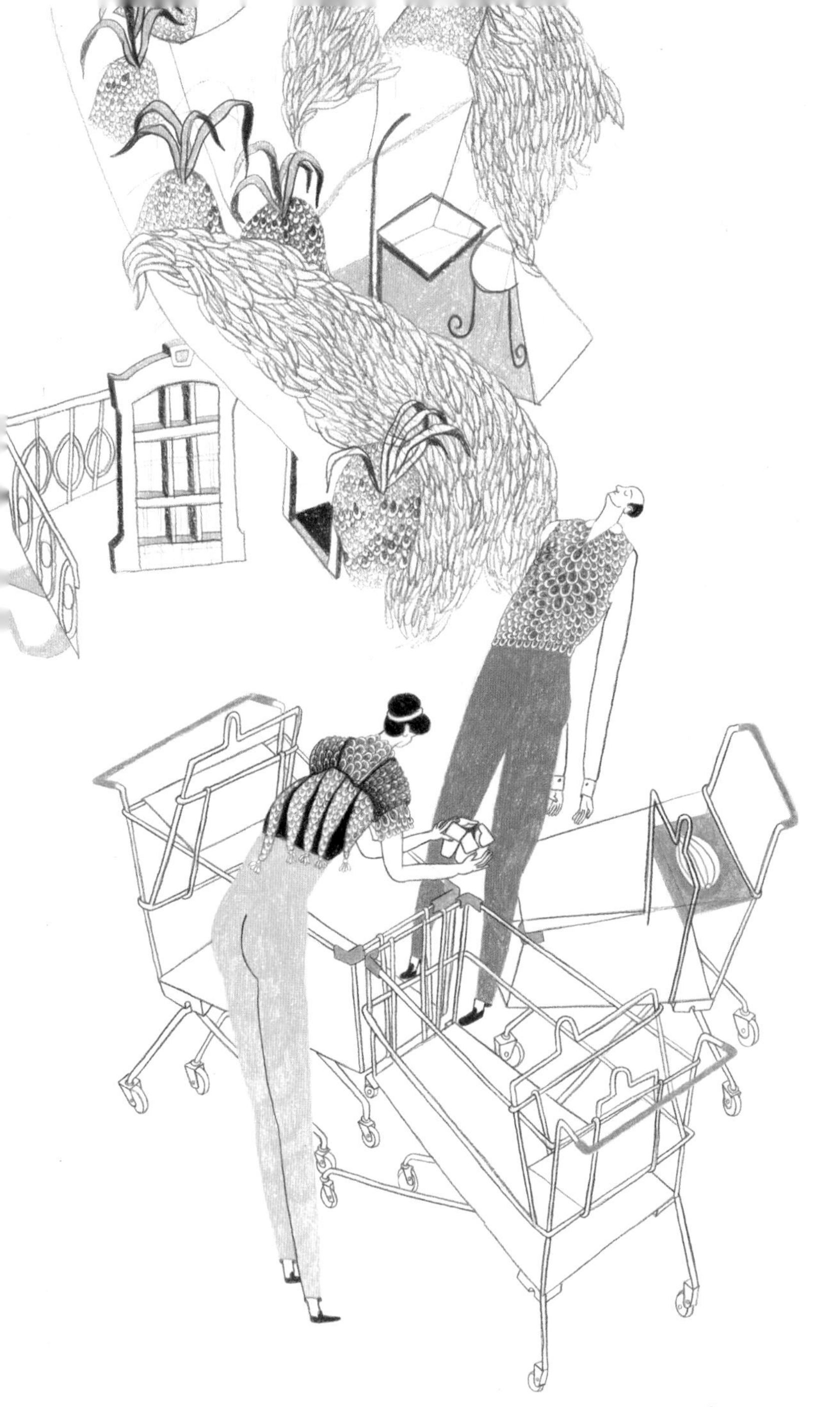

ONCE SOMEONE TRICKED ME INTO A DREAM GUESSING GAME; HE SAID: "START ASKING ME ABOUT MY LATEST DREAM. I WILL ANSWER ONLY YES OR NO." THEN AFTER ASKING HIM THIRTY QUESTIONS, I GOT NOWHERE CLOSE TO KNOWING WHAT HIS DREAM WAS ABOUT. BUT HE KNEW EXACTLY WHAT MINE WAS ABOUT.

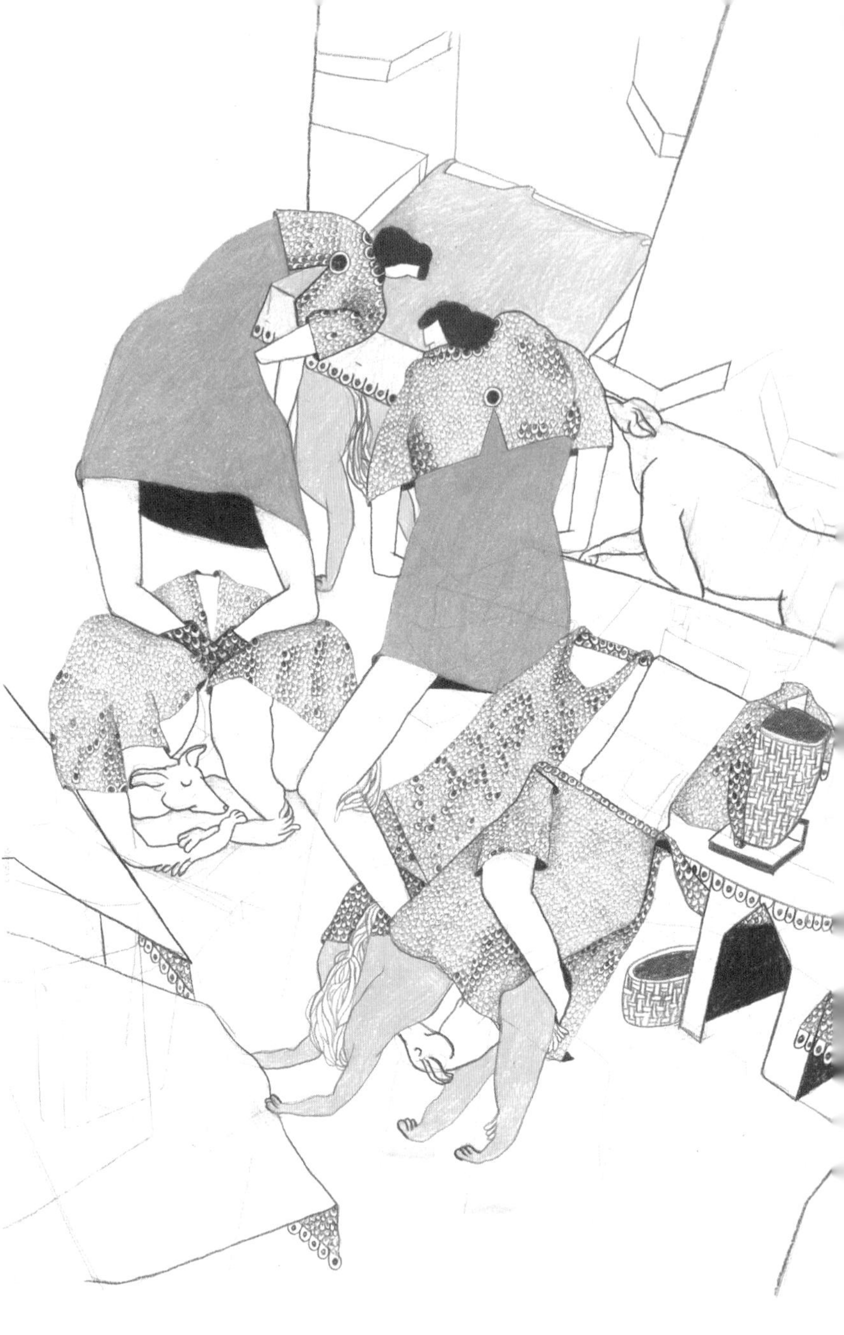

I TOLD YOU THIS STORY A LONG TIME AGO
IN YOUR OFFICE.

AND NOW ANOTHER MAN IS SITTING AT YOUR OLD DESK AND I TRY TO TELL IT ONCE MORE.

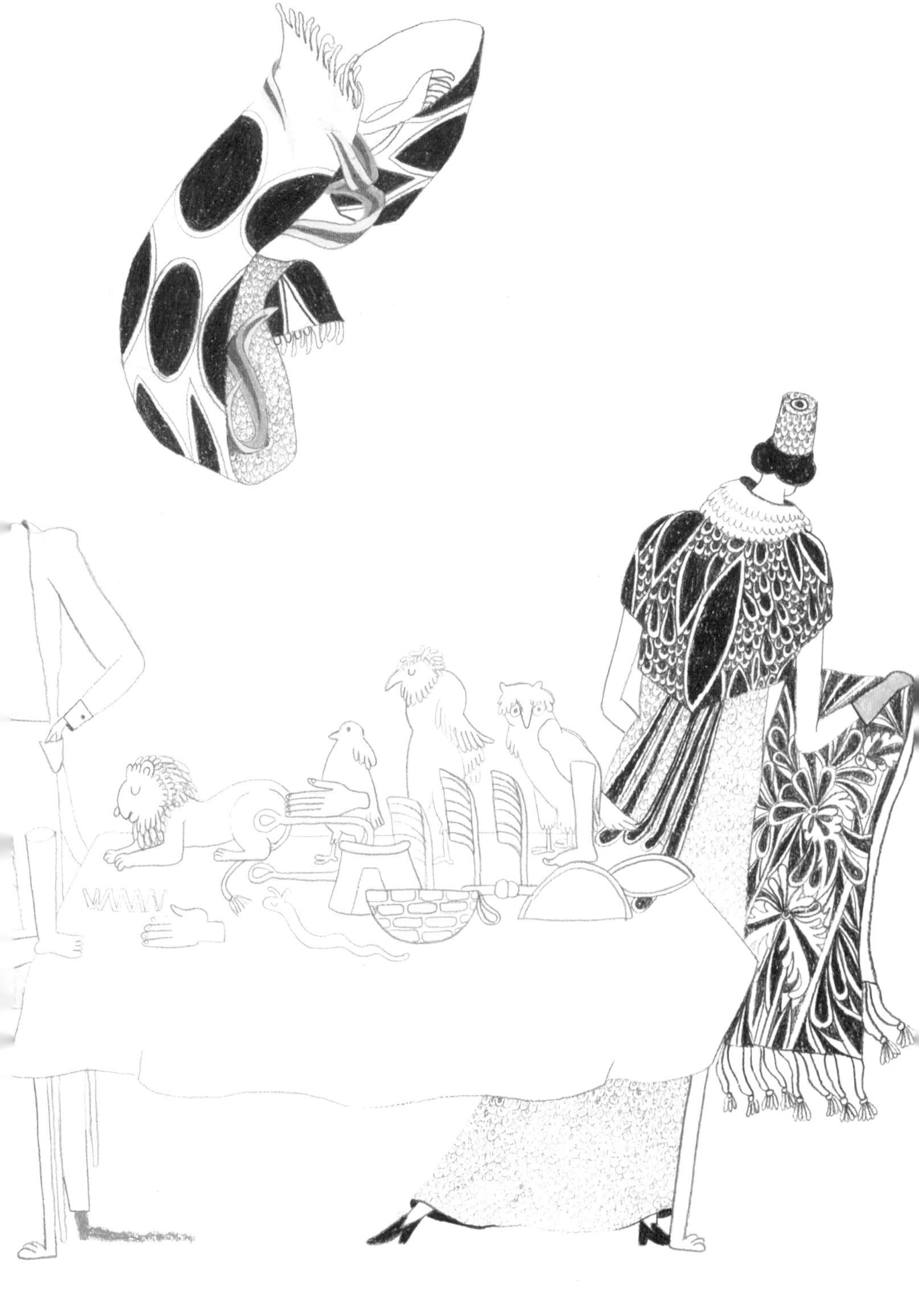

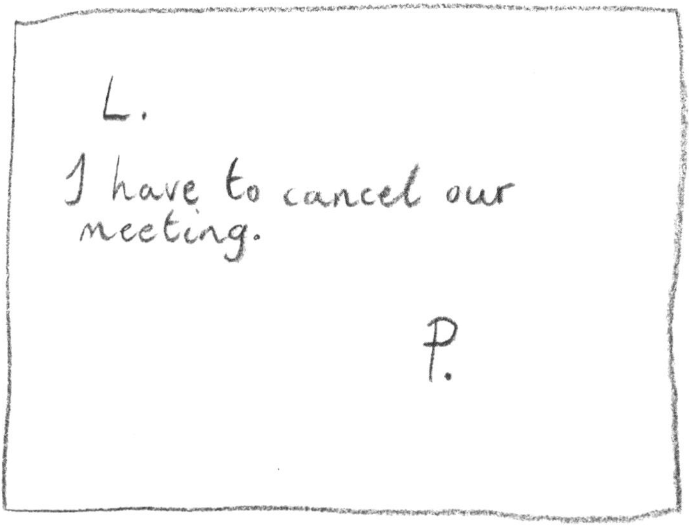
L.
I have to cancel our meeting.
P.

THE CORNERS

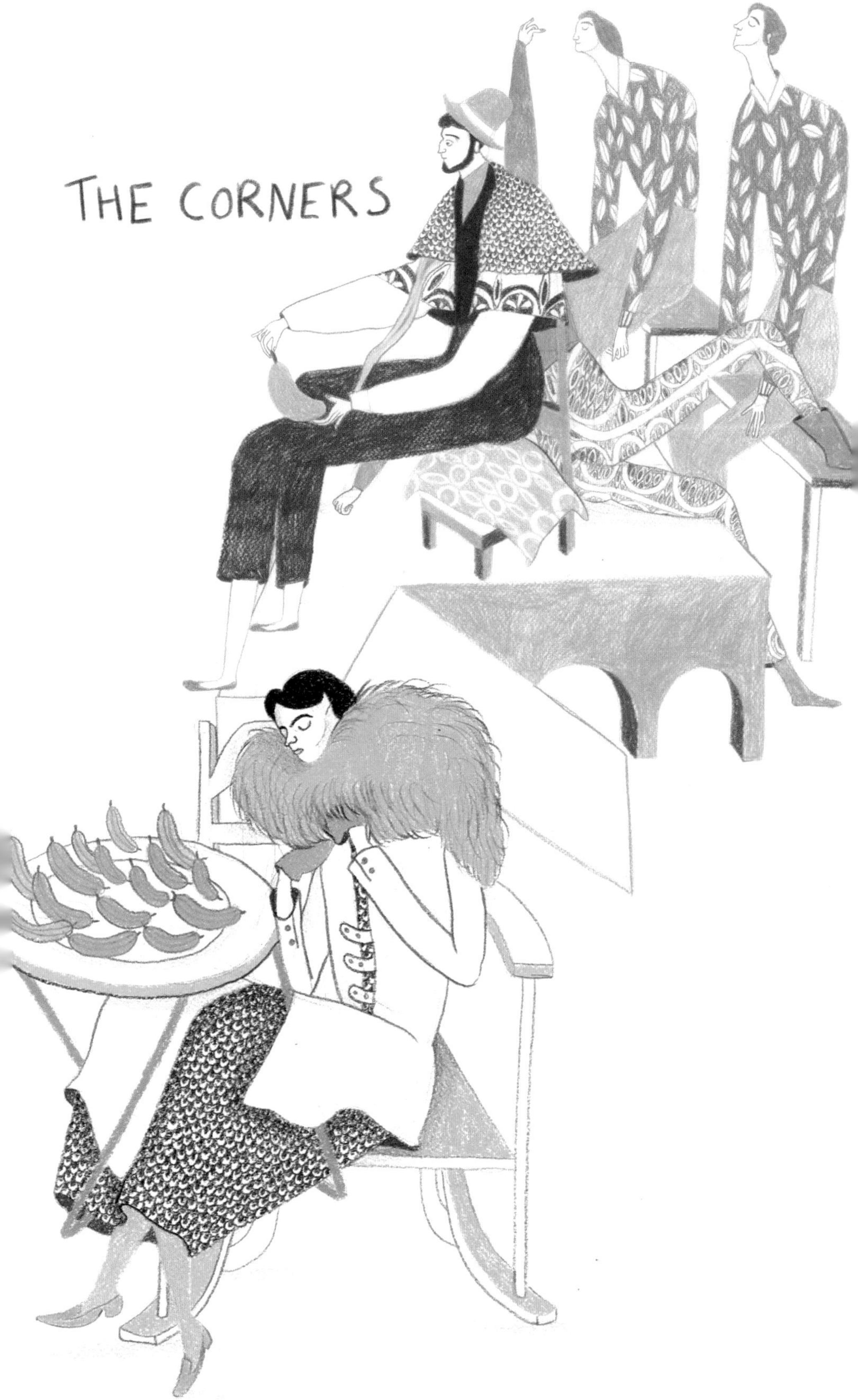

DEAR LIANA,

WHEN I WAS A LITTLE BOY, I ONCE STAYED UP ALL NIGHT READING A BOOK ABOUT THE EXPEDITION TO UNCOVER THE UNDERGROUND IMPERIAL CHINESE ARMY.

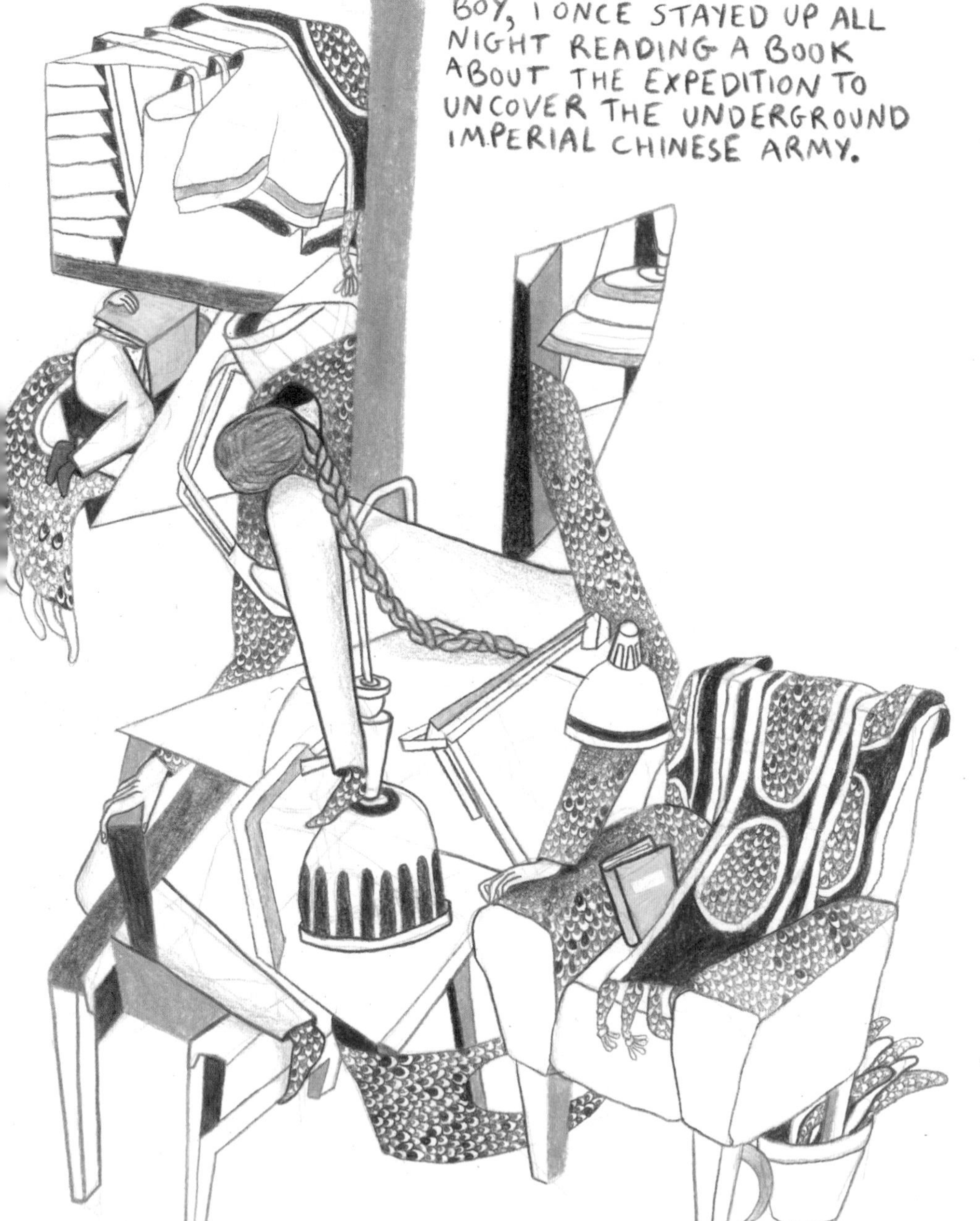

A FEW CHAPTERS IN, I BEGAN TO FEEL TREMORS, AS IF I WAS FOLDING OVER OUR ENTIRE HOUSE BY TURNING THE PAGES. I LOOKED THROUGH THE KEYHOLE AND SAW MY MOTHER BENT OVER HER DESK, AS THOUGH SHE SHARED MY SAME EXACT FEAR.

IN THOSE YEARS, I SPENT A LOT OF TIME STARING OUT OF MY BEDROOM WINDOW, KEEPING A DIARY OF ALL THE COLLISIONS I SPOTTED.

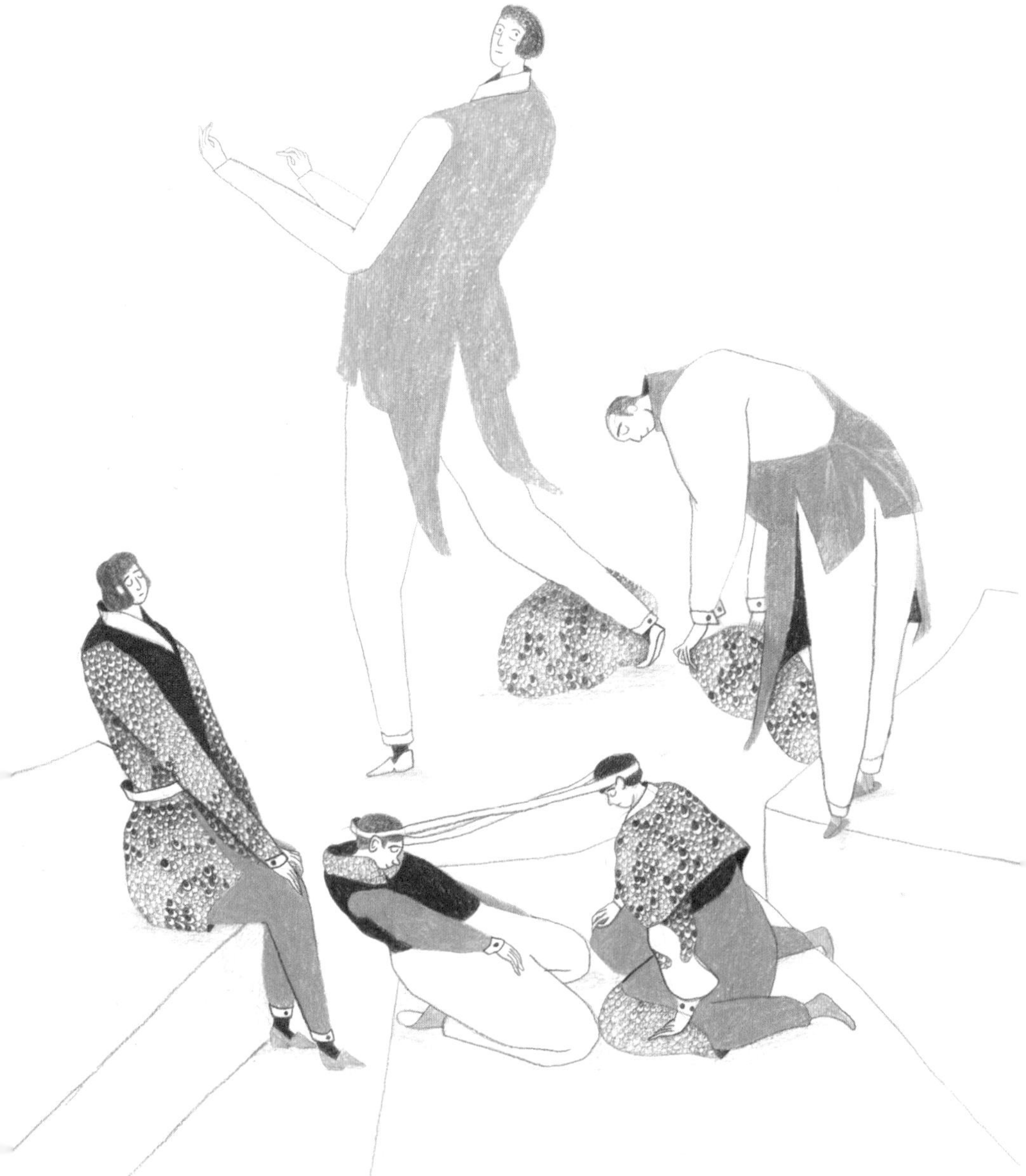

WHEN I GREW UP, I MOVED INTO AN ABANDONED
RAILROAD CAR AND DECIDED TO MAJOR IN
ARCHITECTURE.

I SPENT MY FREE TIME
FROM SCHOOL DESIGNING
BUILDINGS THAT WOULD
BE SUBJECTED TO FLYING
TRAIN CARS, WHICH WOULD
OCCASIONALLY COLLIDE.
MY ROOM WAS VERY
SMALL. I HAD NO DESK,

AND I SAT ON
MY PIANO.

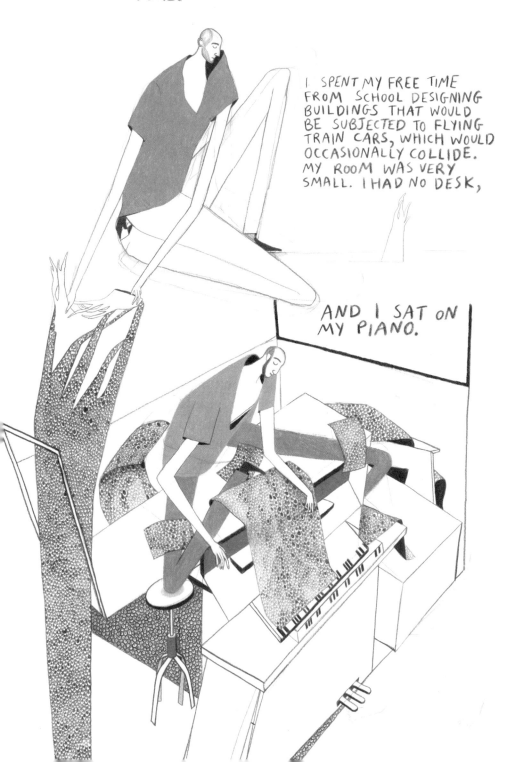

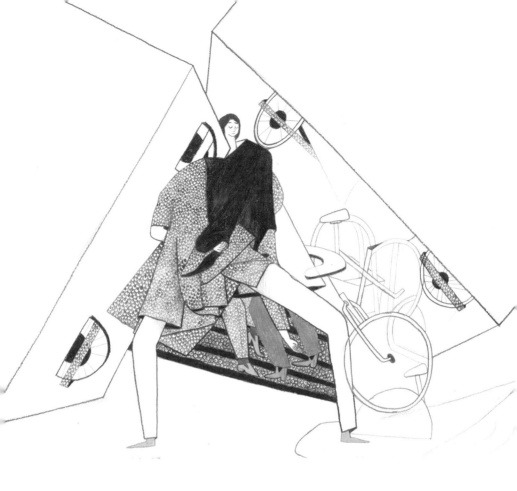

I MET RENATA.
SHE WAS IN ONE OF MY CLASSES.

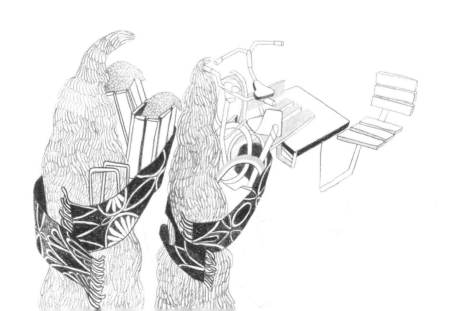

I SHARED MY IDEAS WITH HER AS WE BECAME CLOSE. SHE DISMISSED THEM SAYING NO ONE WOULD EVER AGREE TO SPEND TIME IN A BUILDING WHICH WOULD NOT PROTECT THEM FROM GETTING KNOCKED OVER BY FLYING OBJECTS.

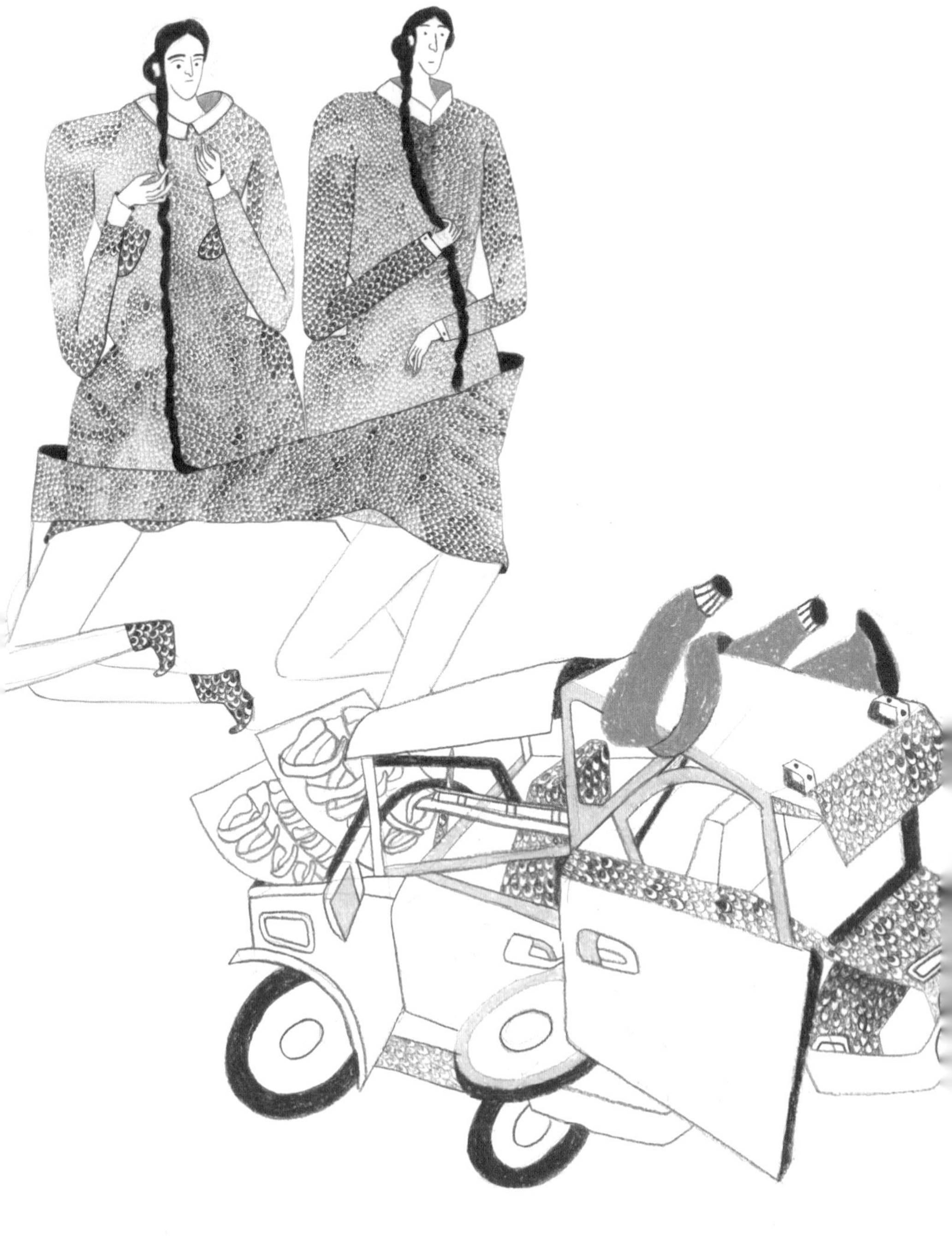

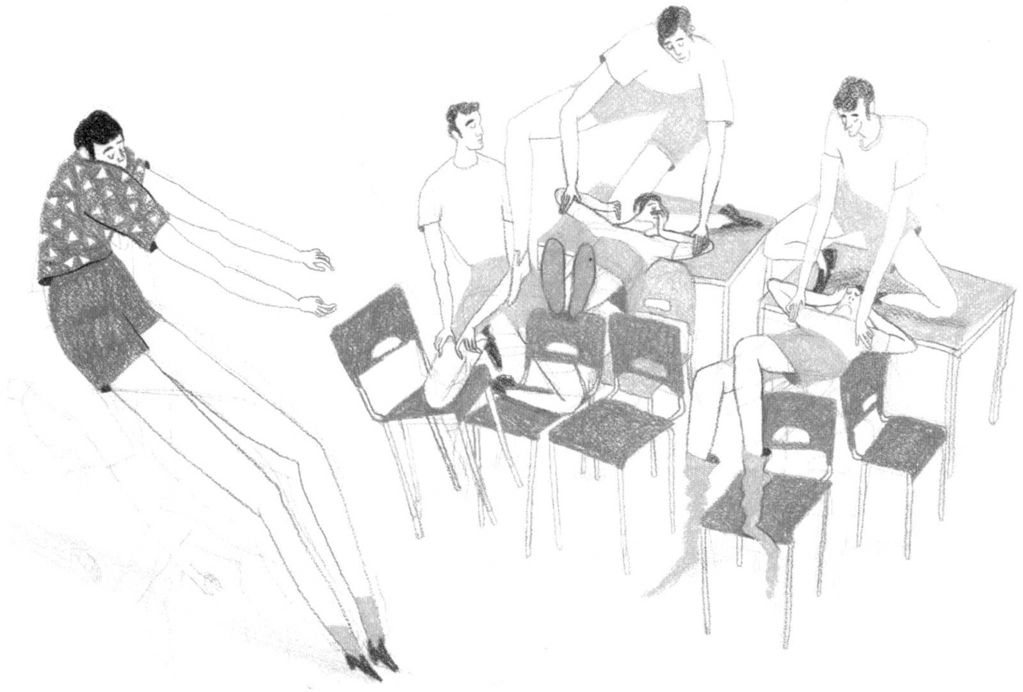

THIS BROKE MY HEART.
BUT SHE WAS PROBABLY RIGHT.

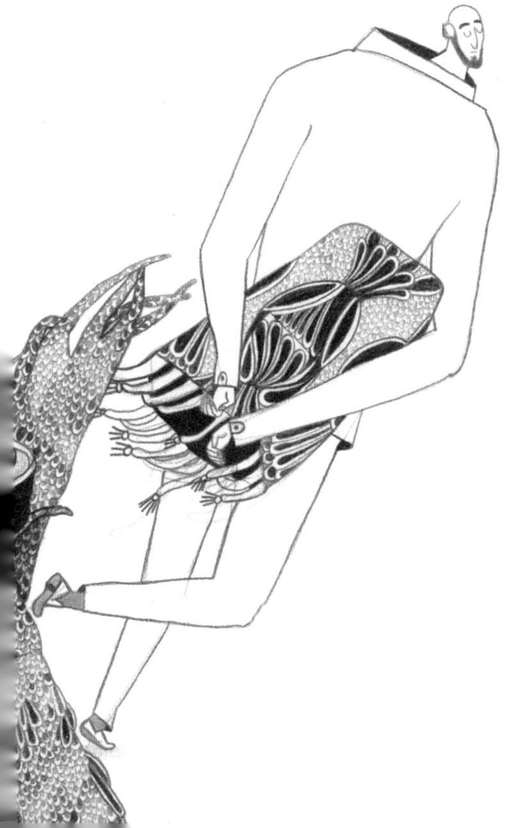

SO I KEPT MY DISTANCE FROM HER,
AND SHREDDED MY PLANS.

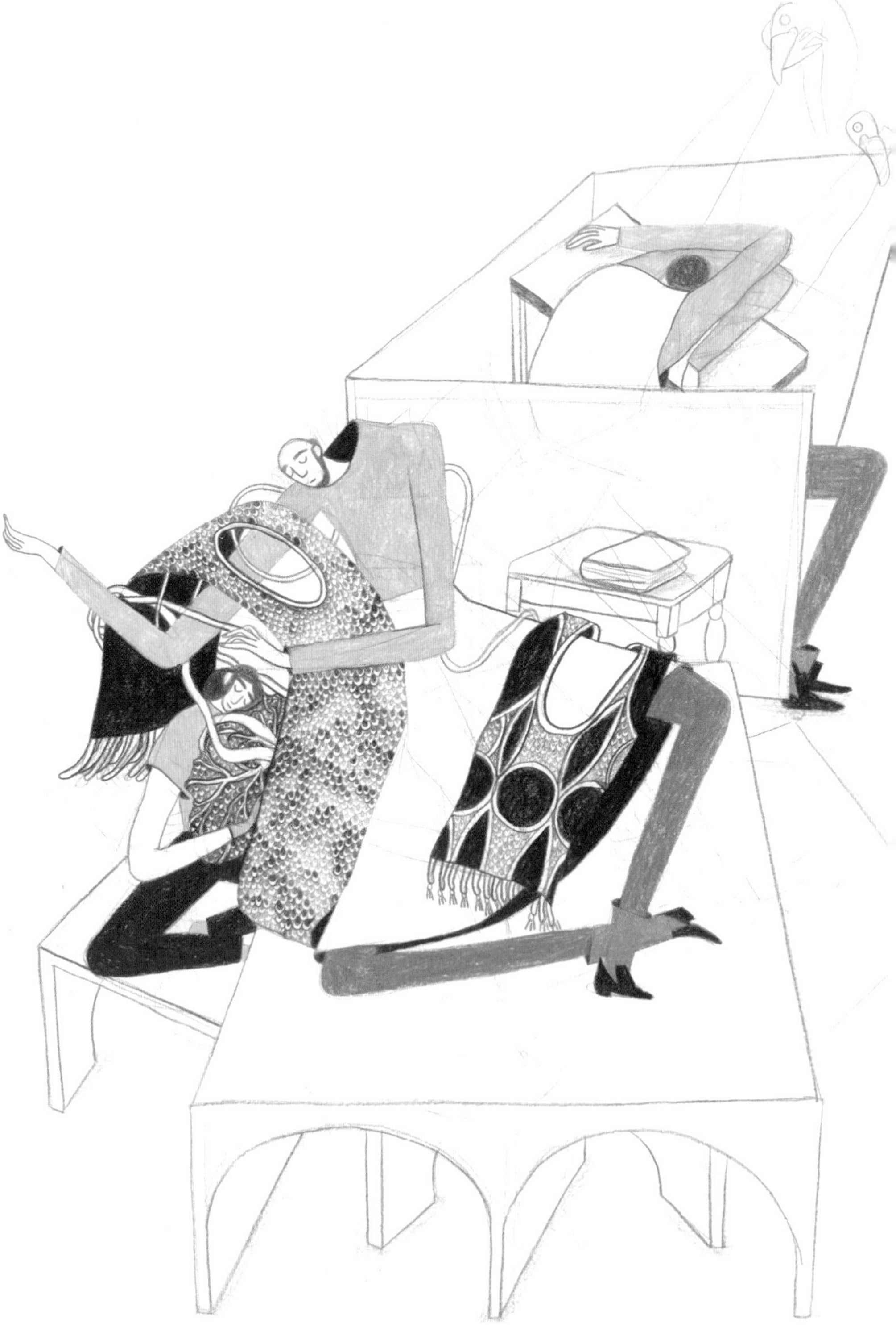

UNTIL ONE NIGHT I DREAMED ABOUT HER
ARRIVING AT SCHOOL IN A BOAT.

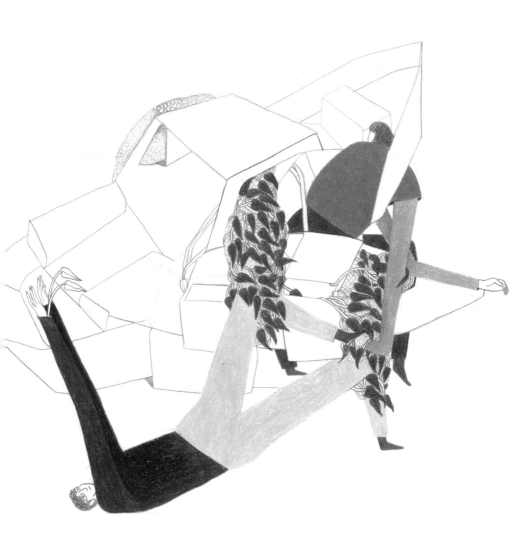

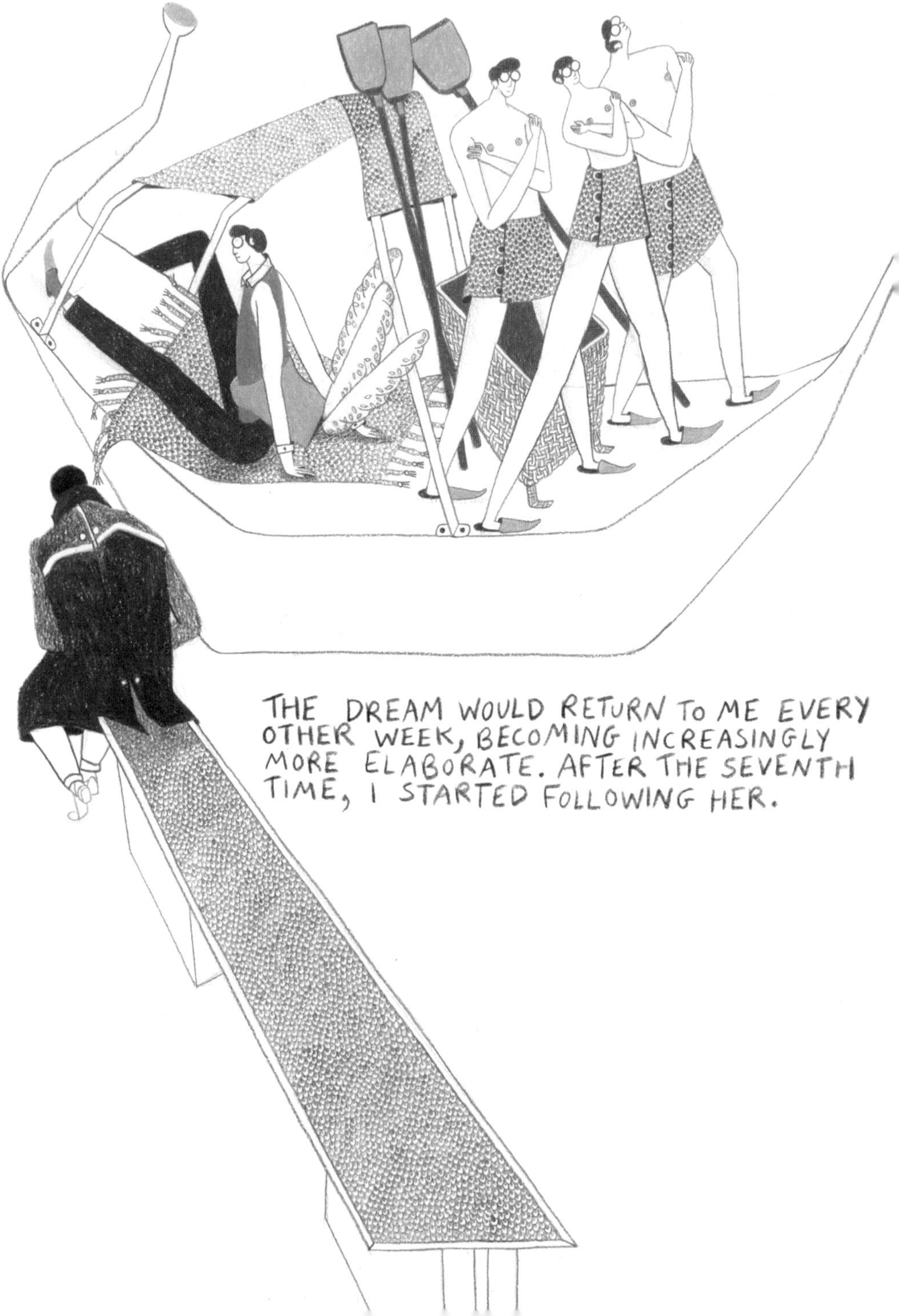
THE DREAM WOULD RETURN TO ME EVERY OTHER WEEK, BECOMING INCREASINGLY MORE ELABORATE. AFTER THE SEVENTH TIME, I STARTED FOLLOWING HER.

ONE TUESDAY AFTERNOON, SHE TOOK UP SMOKING.

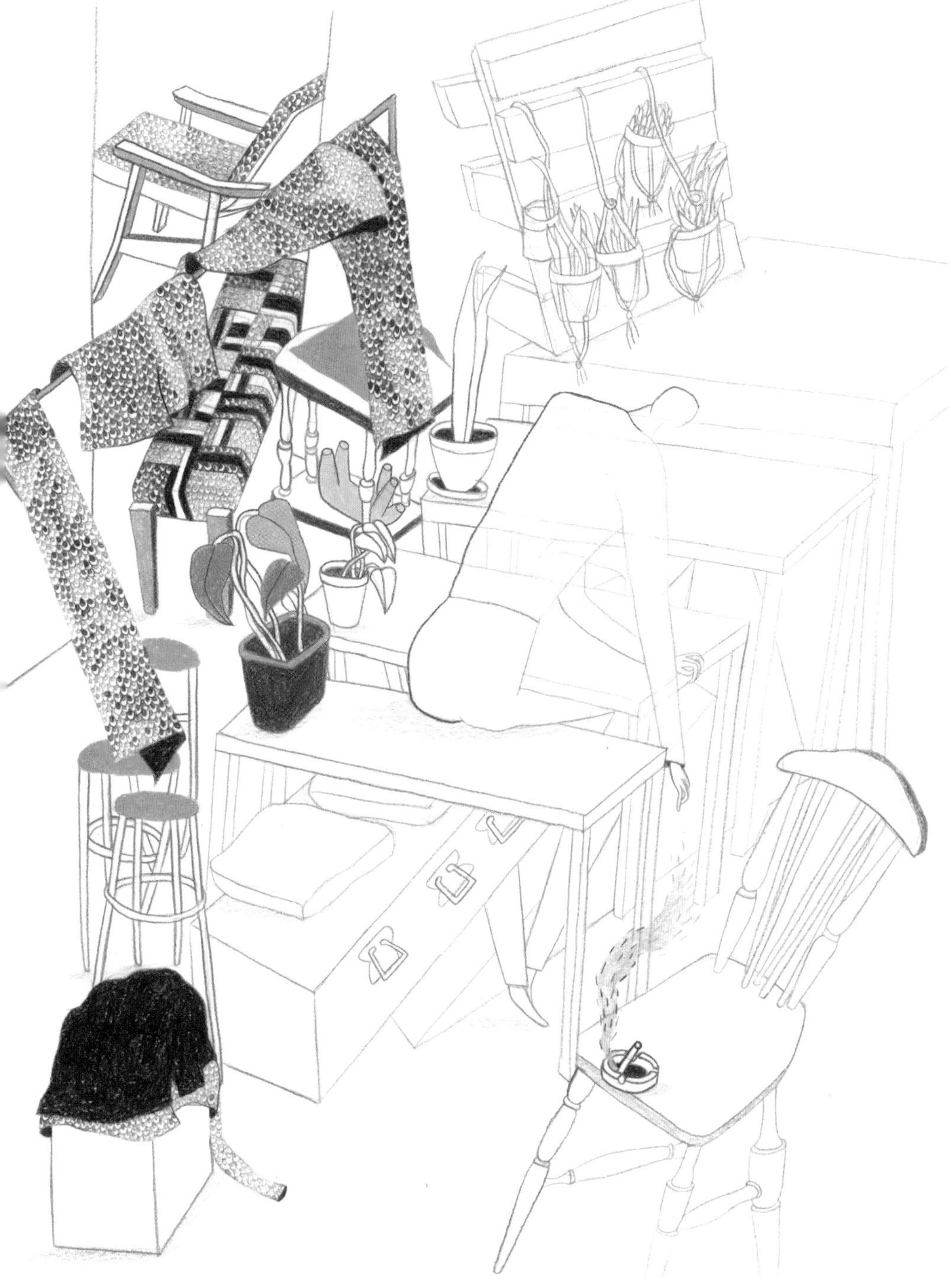

I WAS WATCHING HER FROM A BENCH IN THE NEXT ROOM.

SHE BEGAN DANCING IN HER CHAIR AS THOUGH AVOIDING AN INVISIBLE FLYING TRAIN, LIKE THE ONES I HAD SHOWN HER IN MY SKETCHBOOK.

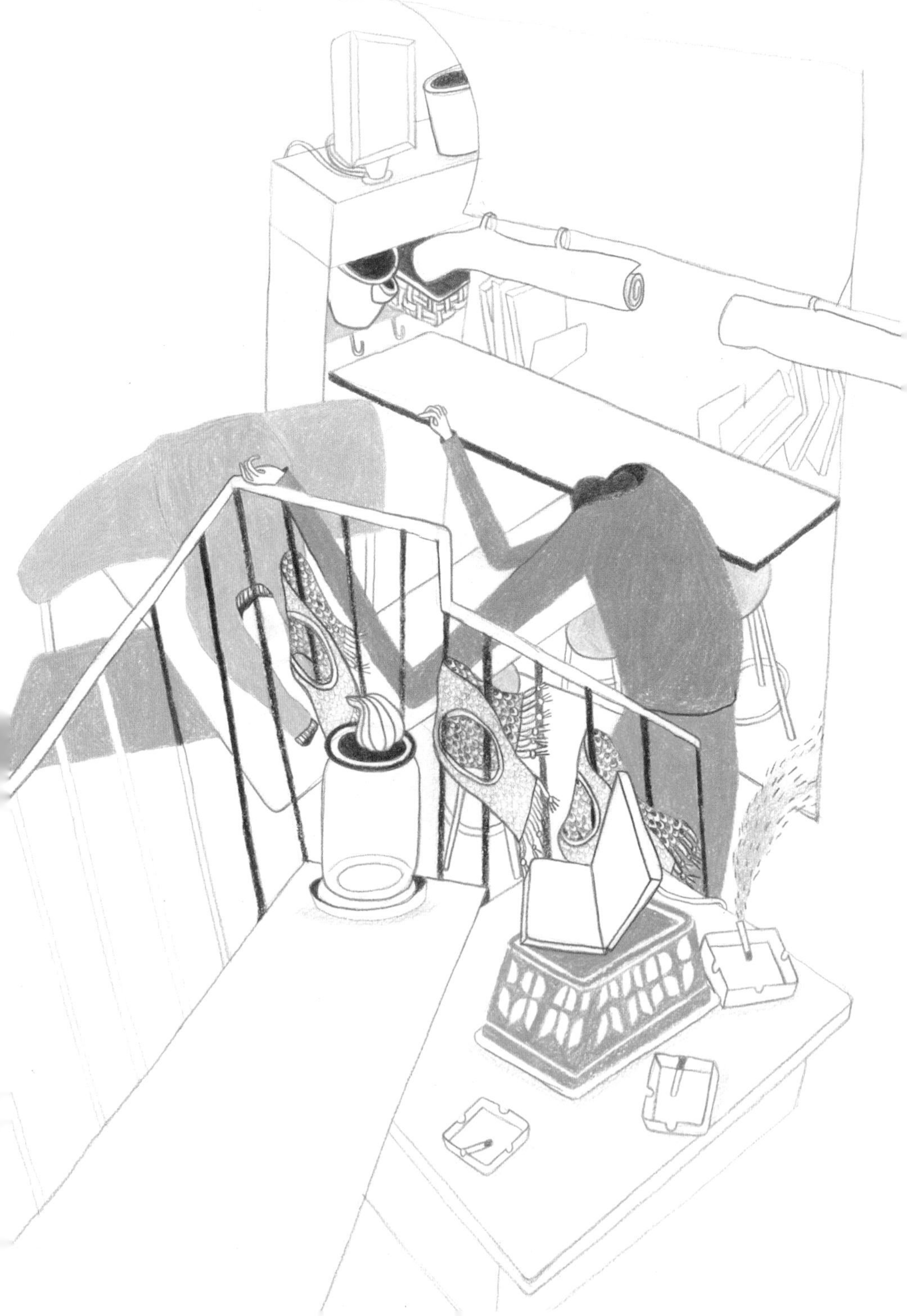

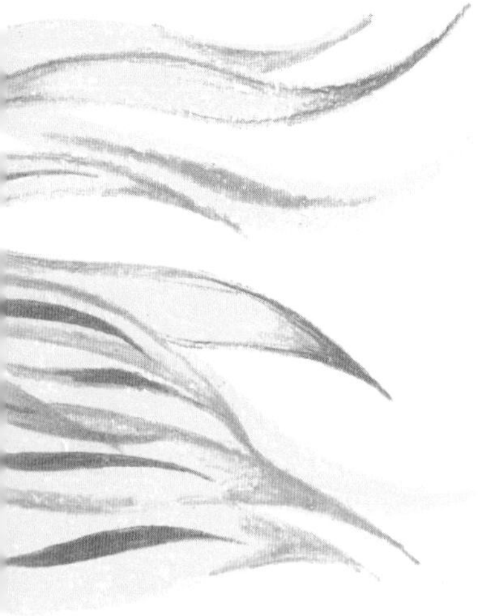

SHE MUST HAVE KNOWN I WAS IN LOVE WITH HER, WATCHING HER BOTH IN MY WAKING HOURS, AND IN MY SLEEP.

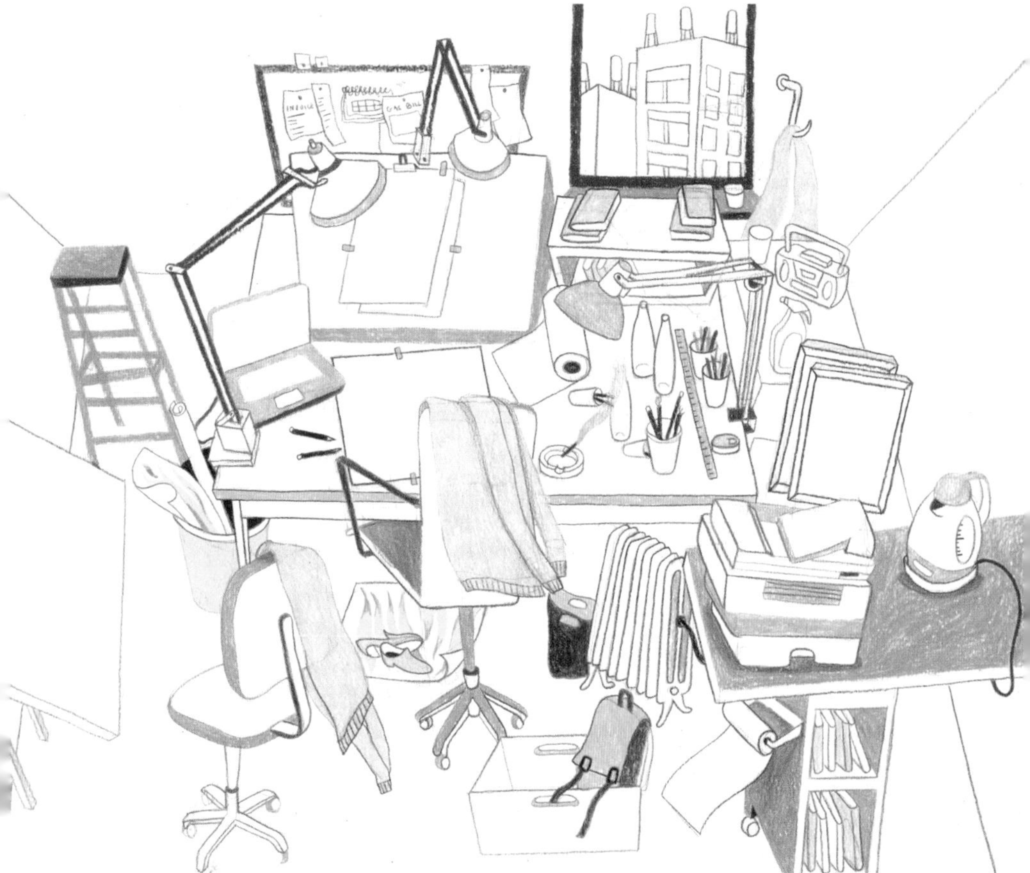

GRADUALLY, SILENTLY, SHE BEGAN TO LEAD ME THROUGH CAMPUS PRETENDING TO SLEEPWALK. SHE WOULD ENTER A ROOM, I WOULD FOLLOW, AND SHE WOULD START DANCING AS THOUGH HER MOVEMENTS WERE INSPIRED BY A FEAR OF INVISIBLE, FLYING OBJECTS.

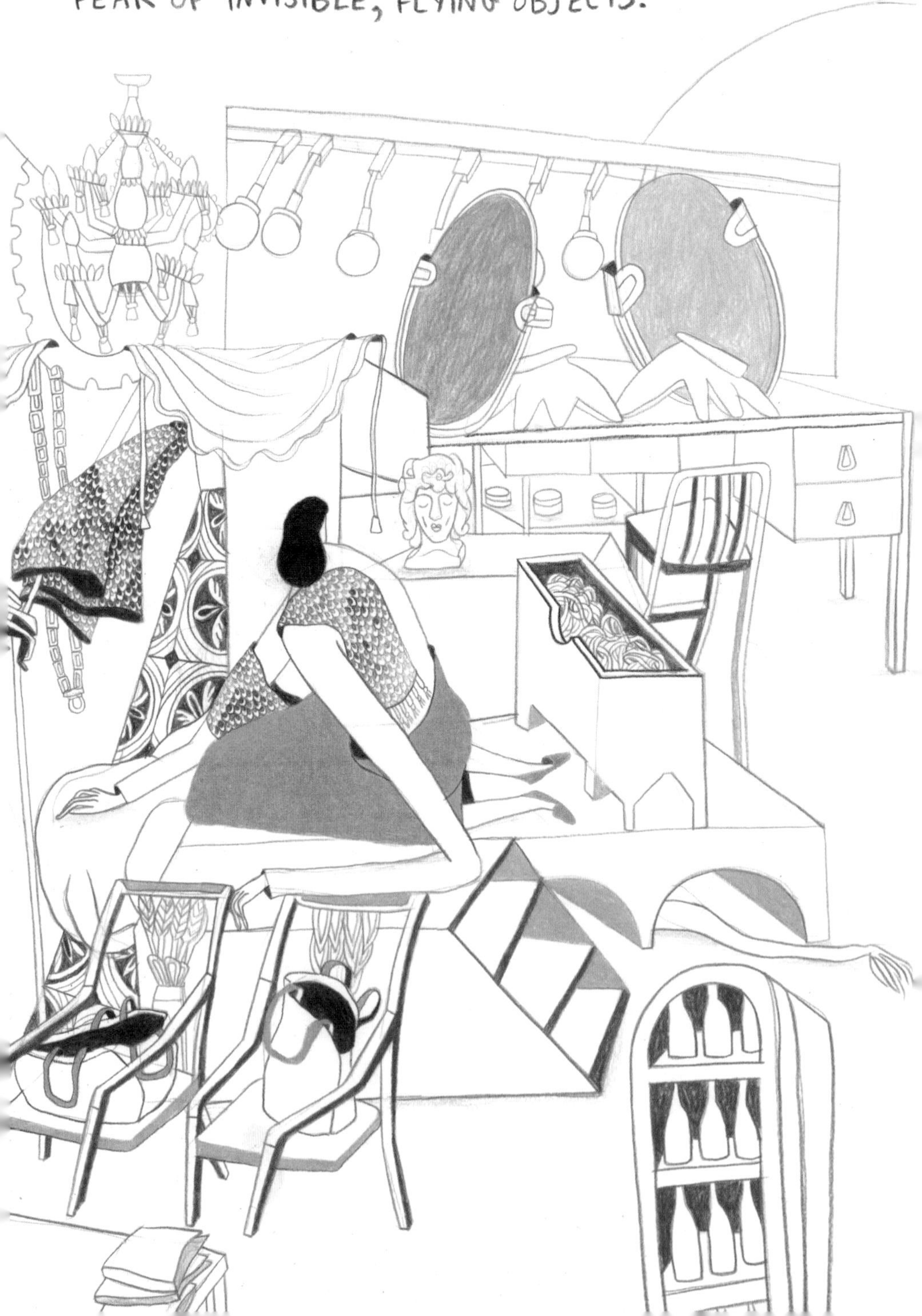

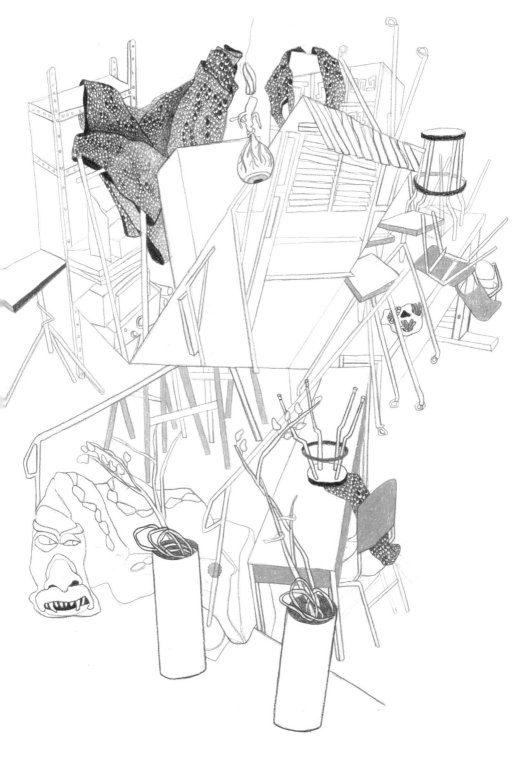

'I WATCHED AS THE ENTIRE SCHOOL CAVED OVER, ROOM BY ROOM, AS SHE BREATHED LIFE INTO MY FANTASIES.'

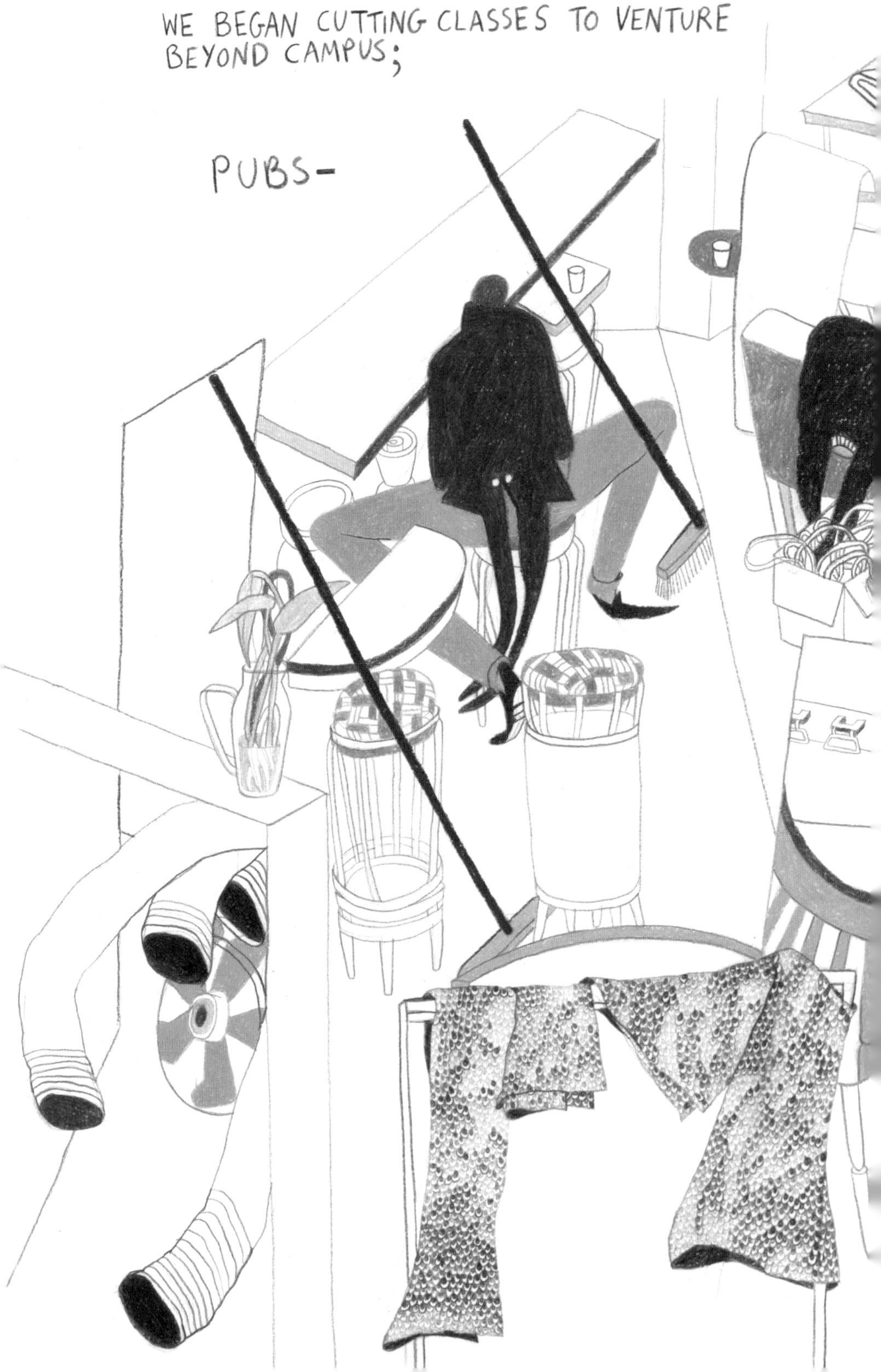
WE BEGAN CUTTING CLASSES TO VENTURE BEYOND CAMPUS;
PUBS-

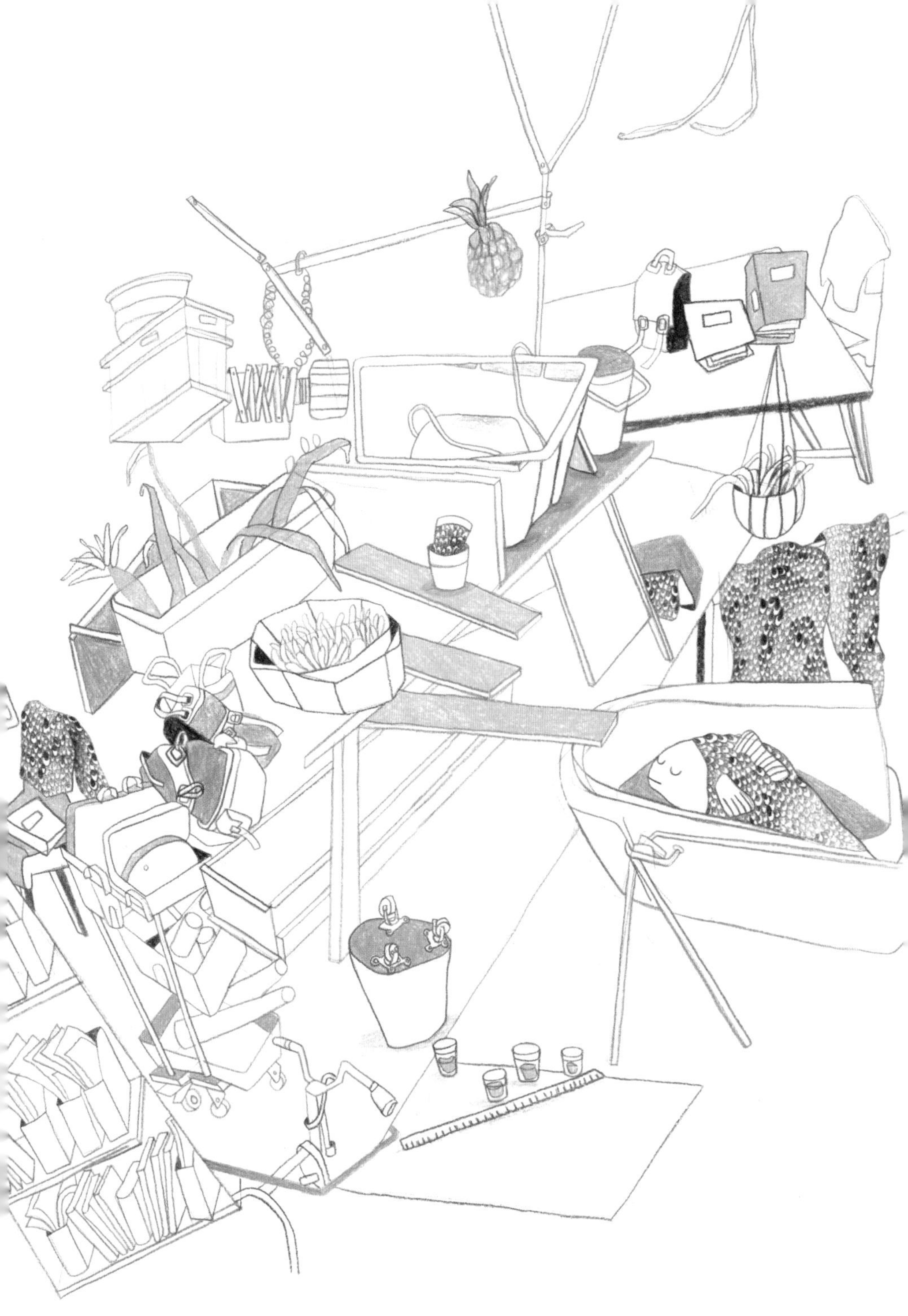

-AND WARE HOUSES

THE MOST VIOLENT OF HER "GHOST-ACCIDENTS" HAPPENED IN A HAIR SALON.

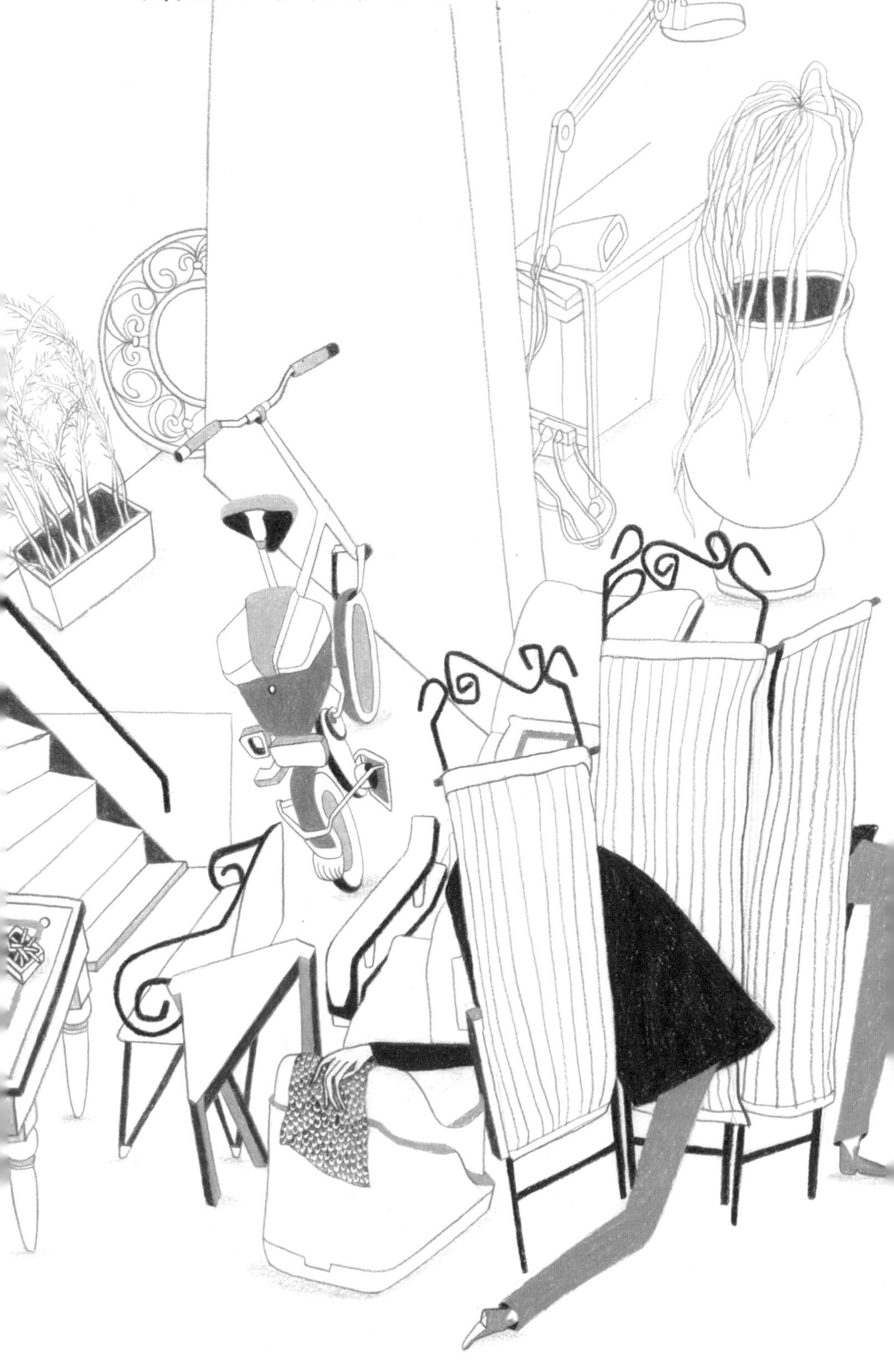

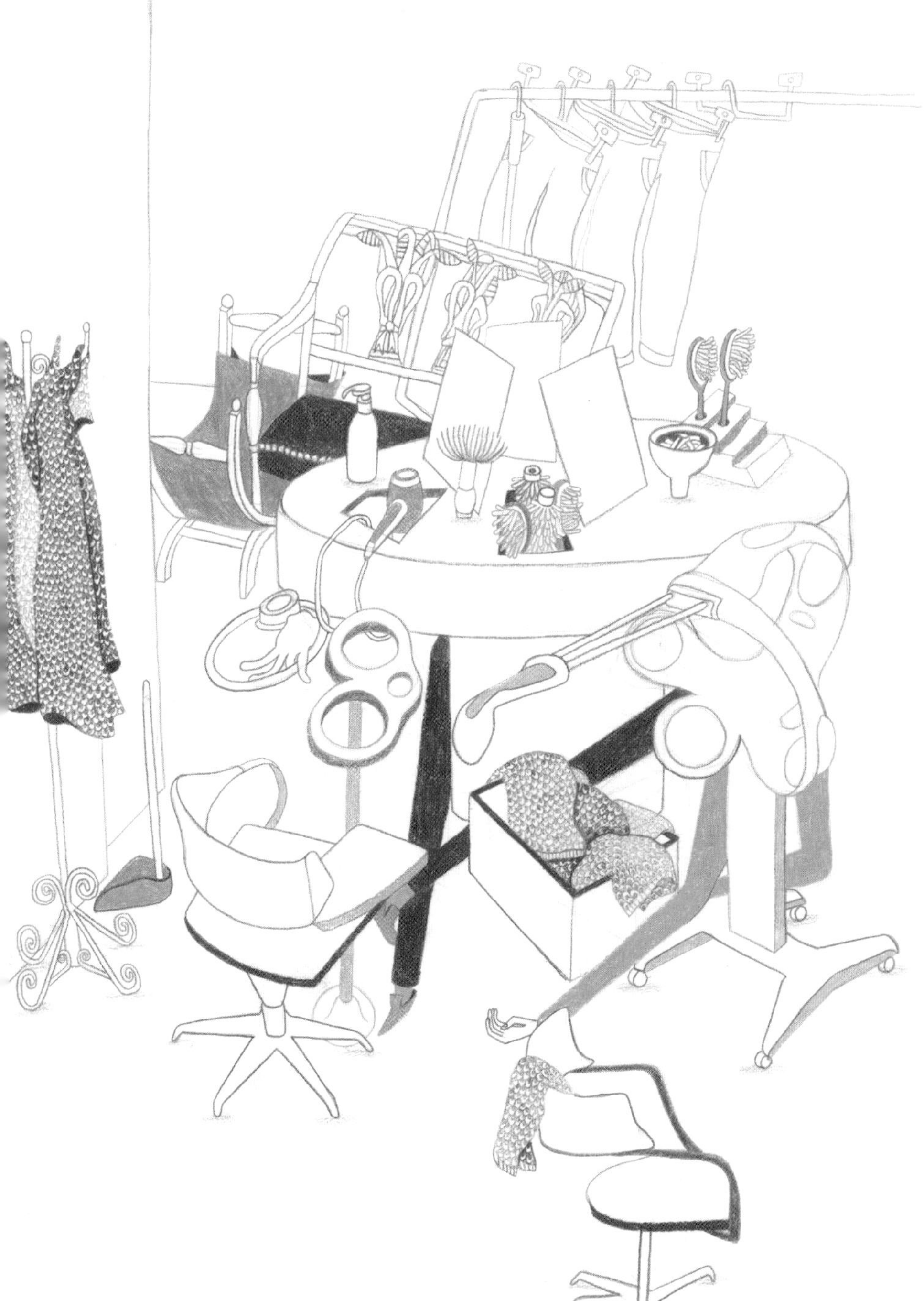

SHE ALMOST DISAPPEARED IN ITS FOLDS.

SHE TUMBLED OVER THE WASHING SINK, CRASHING INTO ANOTHER CUSTOMER AND A GIANT PAIR OF SCISSORS.

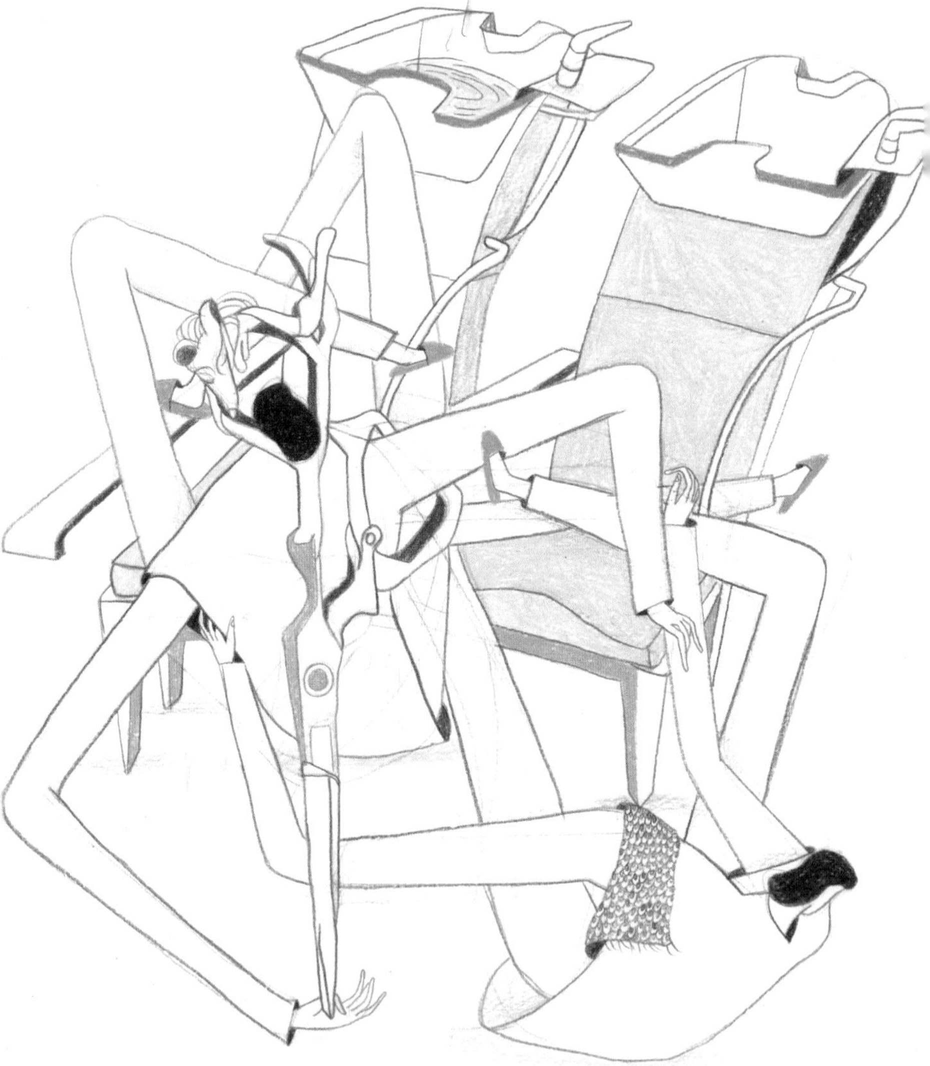

SHE LOST CONSCIOUSNESS. (LATER SHE TOLD ME SHE DREAMT SHE WAS LOST IN A FOREST, HOLDING A PENCIL THAT WAS GROWING RAPIDLY.)

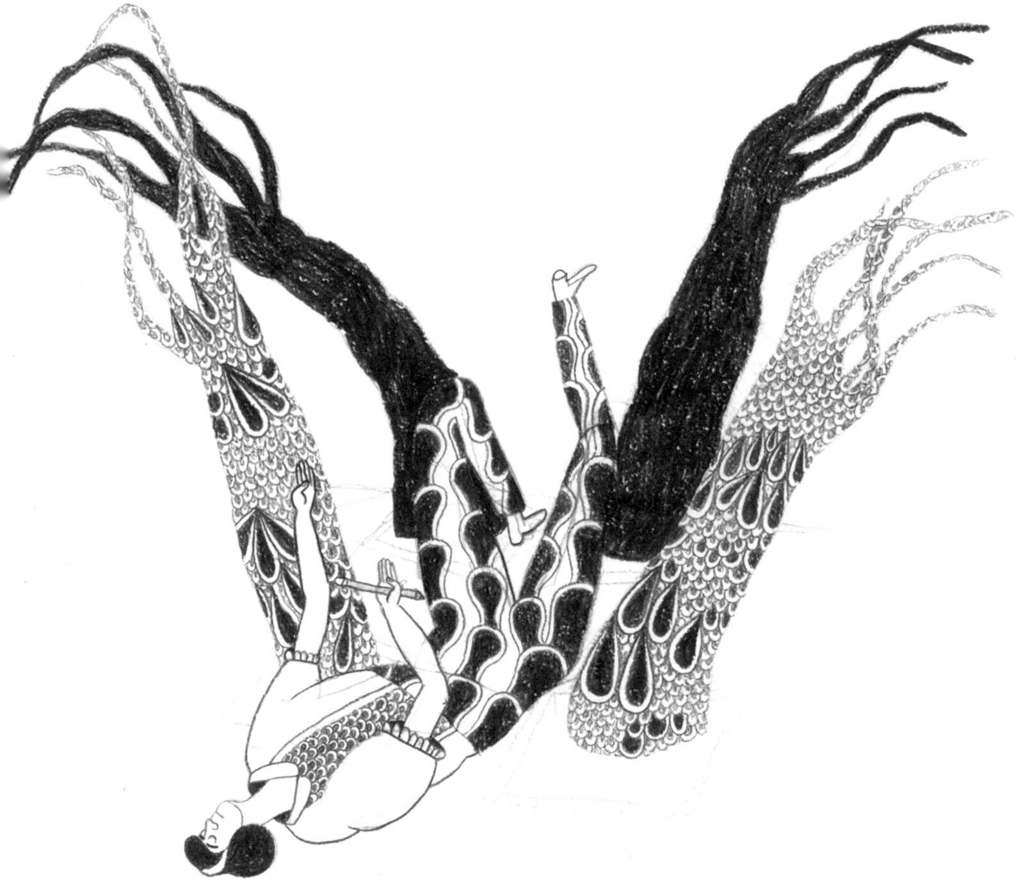

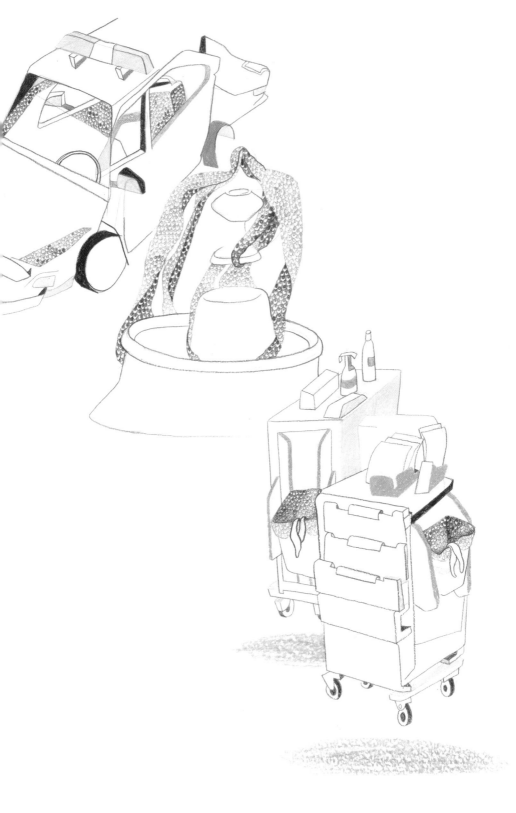

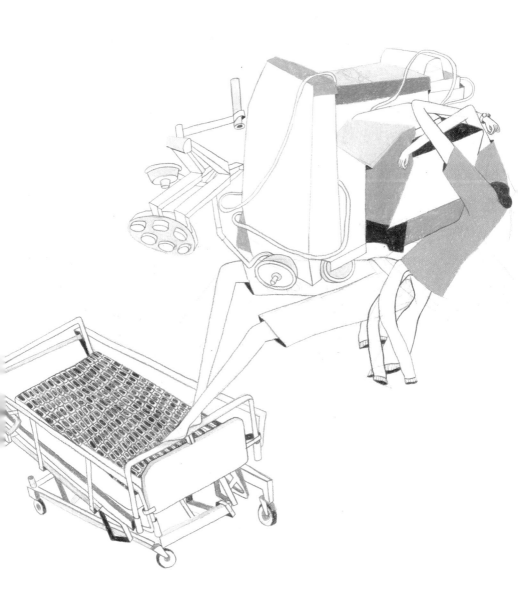

I TOOK HER TO THE HOSPITAL, BUT SHE
KEPT GETTING PUSHED OFF HER BED
AND COULDN'T BE TREATED.

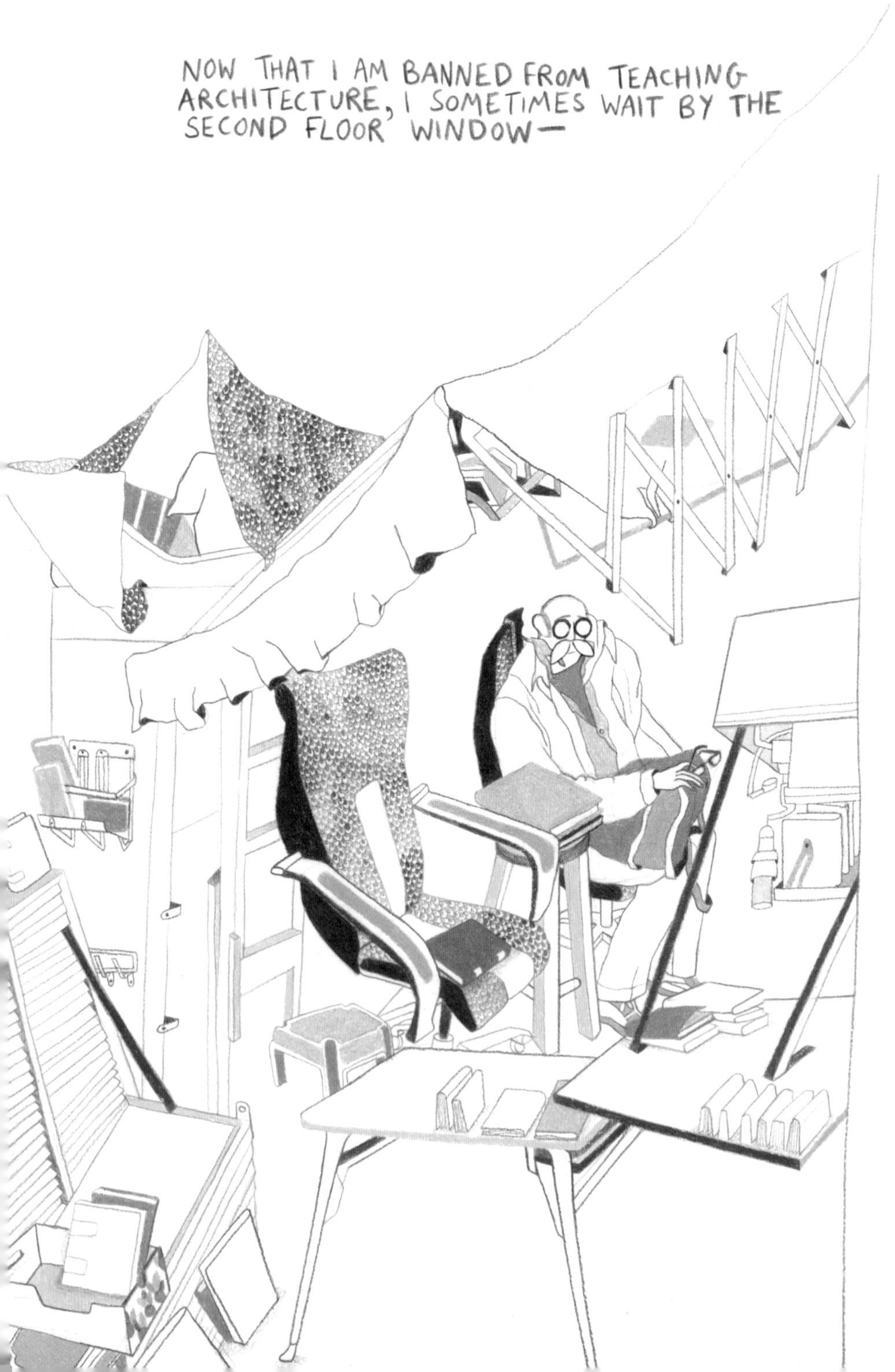
NOW THAT I AM BANNED FROM TEACHING ARCHITECTURE, I SOMETIMES WAIT BY THE SECOND FLOOR WINDOW—

—OR LEAN AGAINST A WALL—

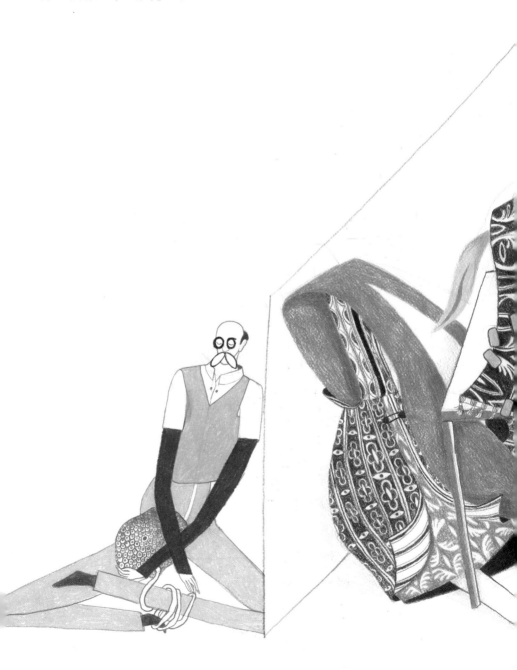

- HOPING TO NOTICE MY LONG FORGOTTEN
IMAGINARY ARMY OF FLYING MACHINES
APPEAR SOME DAY IN THE MOVEMENTS
AND FEARS OF ANOTHER STUDENT.

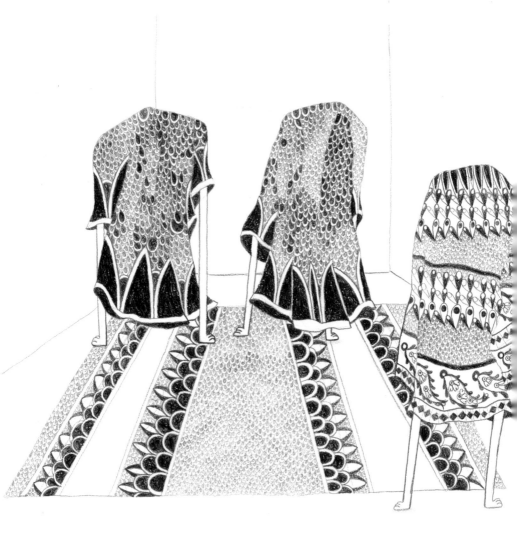

LIANA, PERHAPS I COULD TEACH YOU
TO FEAR THEM AS WELL?

P.

 PLaNS
To MEET

DEAR POTHEL,

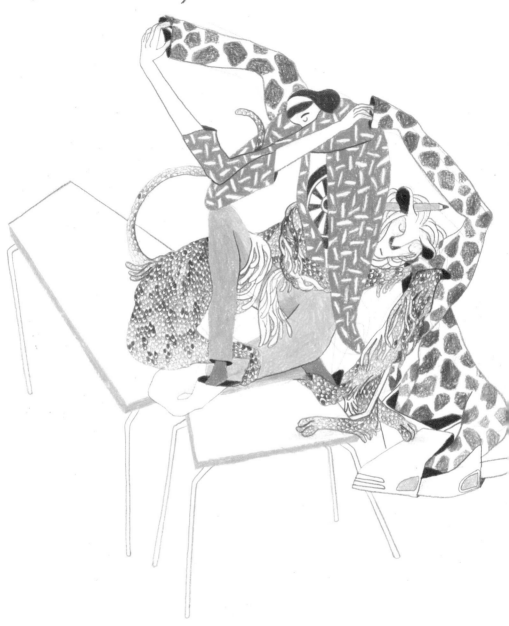

WE WERE TAUGHT ABOUT WOMEN WHO HAVE
TO WALK INTO A LION JUNGLE BEFORE
RETIRING TO BED. THEIR NECKS ARE
PROTECTED WITH TIGHT BRONZE RINGS
WHICH MUSTN'T BE REMOVED, EVEN IN
THEIR SLEEP.

AFTER SEVERAL YEARS, THE WOMEN WHO FIND THEIR WAY OUT OF THE JUNGLE FIND THE MEANS TO CUT AWAY THE RINGS, BUT THEIR NECKS HAVE ALREADY BEEN WEAKENED AND STRETCHED SO FAR THAT THEY CANNOT STAY UPRIGHT WITHOUT THEM.

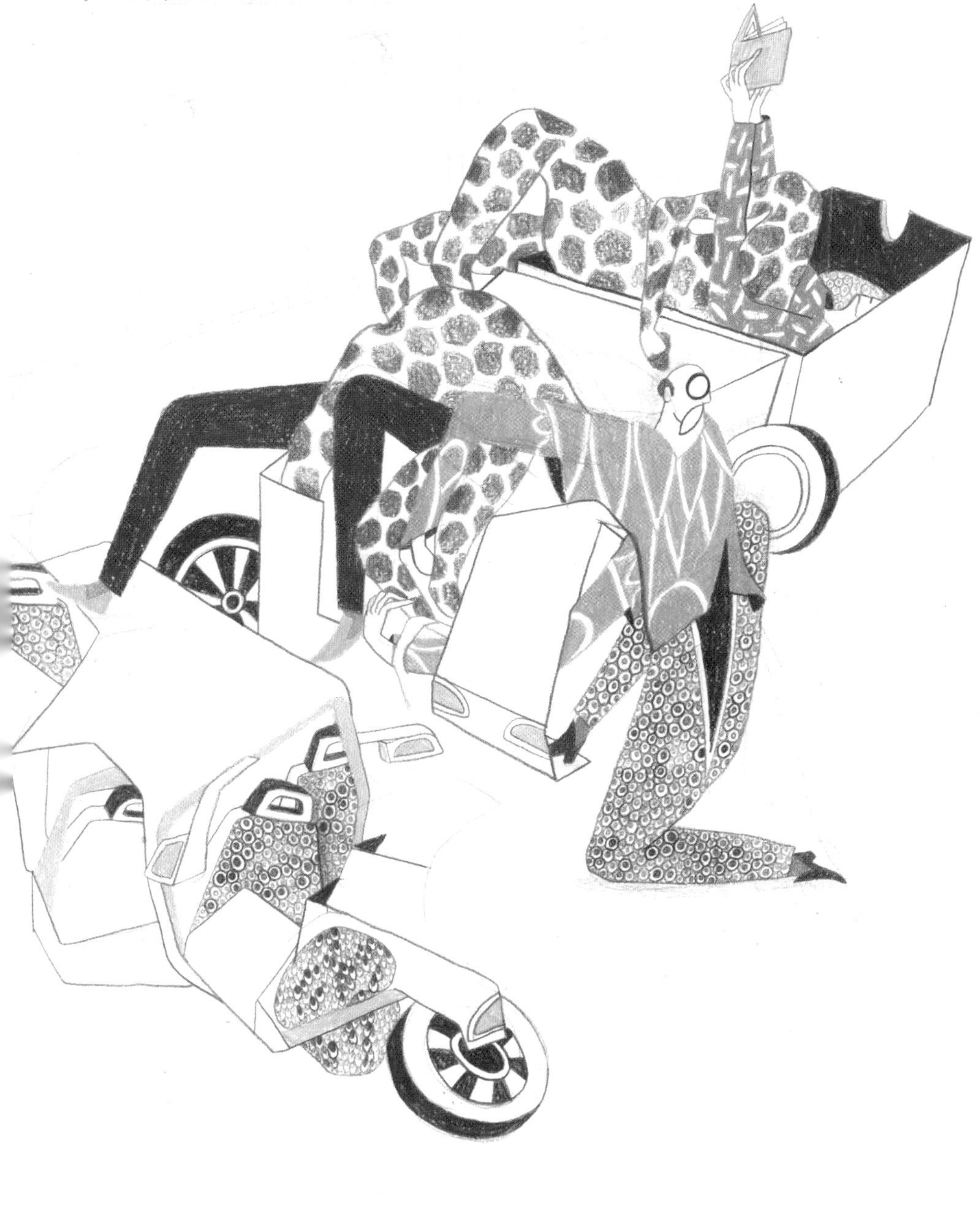

IT IS ONLY A SMALL CONSOLATION TO SLEEP OUTSIDE THE DANGEROUS JUNGLE, BECAUSE THERE ARE NO BROKEN LION TEETH TO COLLECT AS TOKENS FROM THE FOOT OF THEIR BEDS.

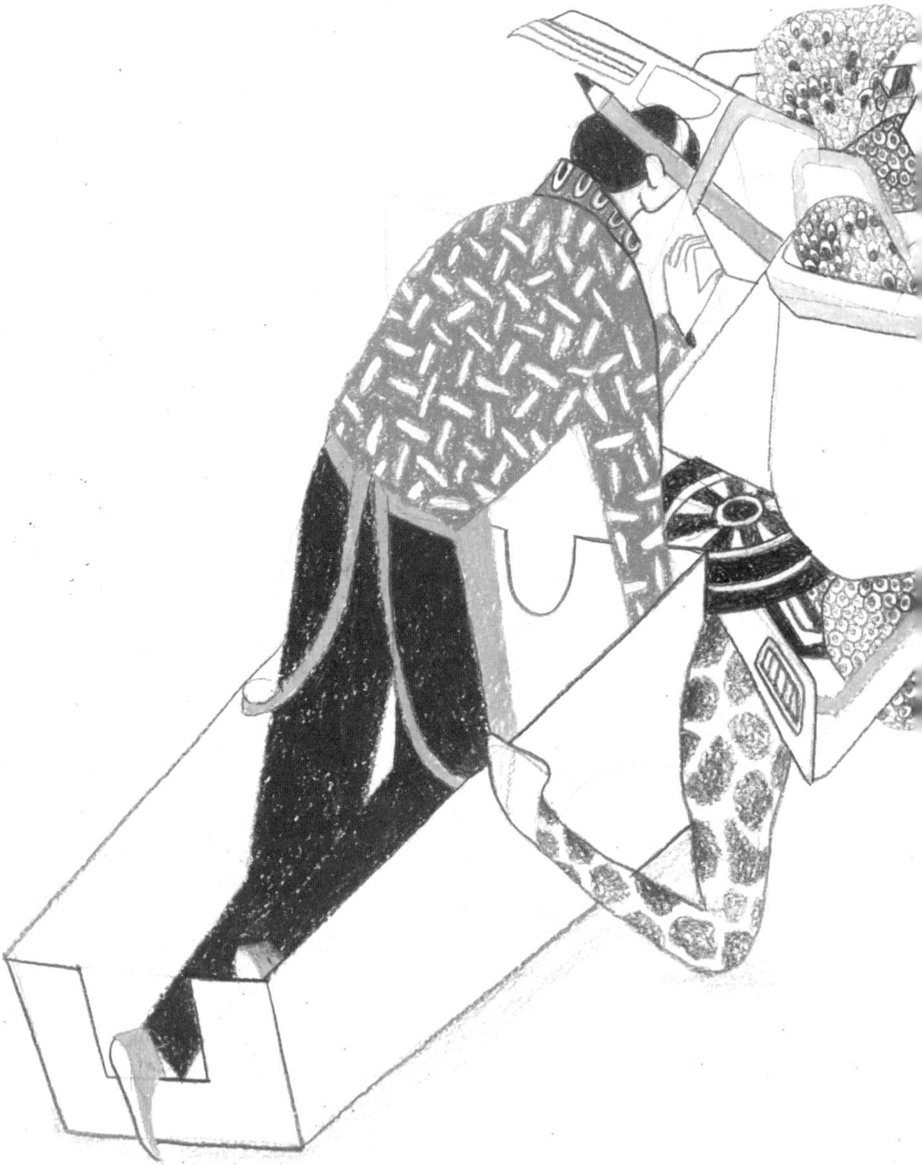

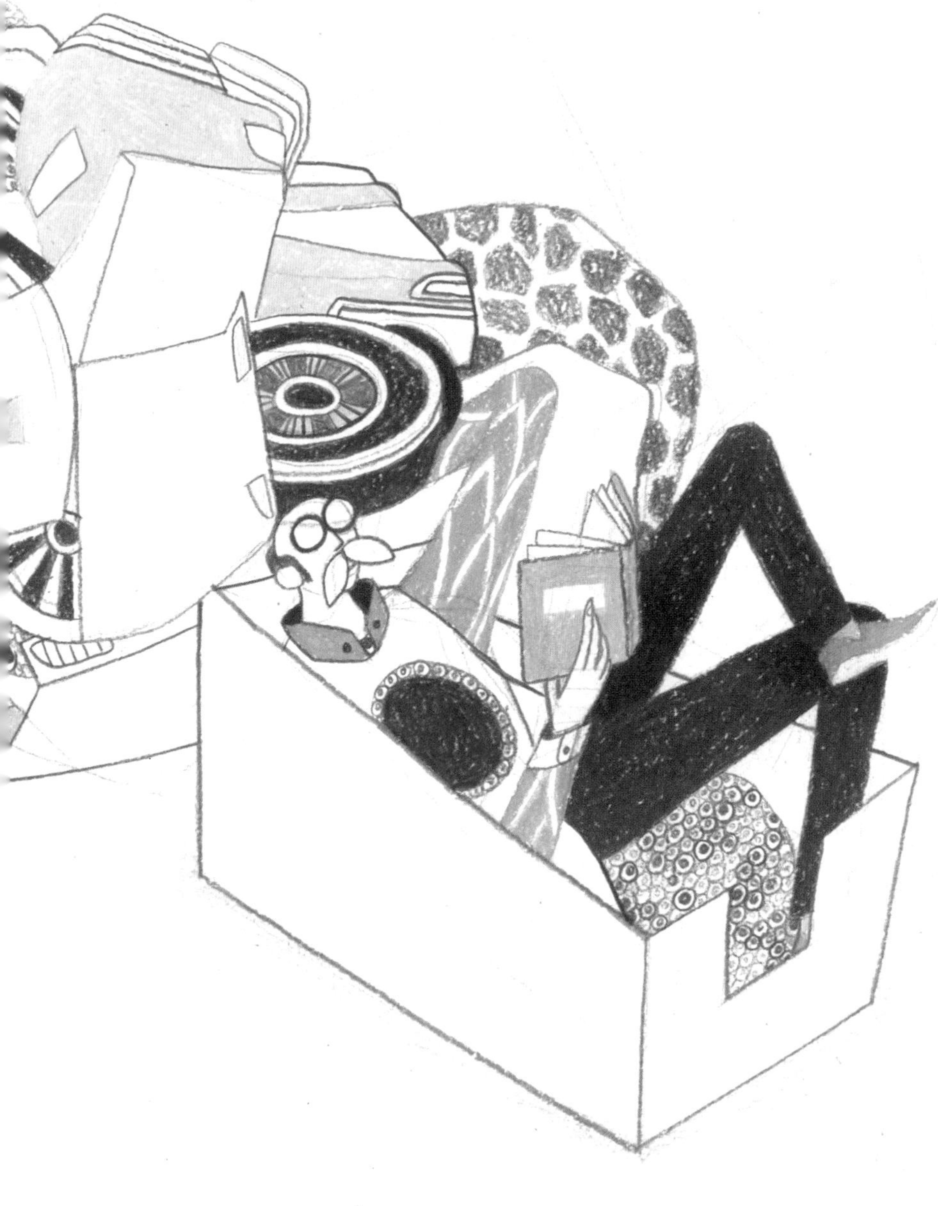

OUTSIDE OF IT, NO NIGHTMARE IS REAL ENOUGH TO KEEP.

IN THIS SCHOOL, TO MAKE THINGS MORE CONVENIENT, FROM THE MOMENT WE ENTER, OUR NECKS SOFTEN AND COLLAPSE SIDEWAYS ONTO OUR LEFT OR RIGHT SHOULDERS AND BEGIN TO STRETCH DOWNWARDS.

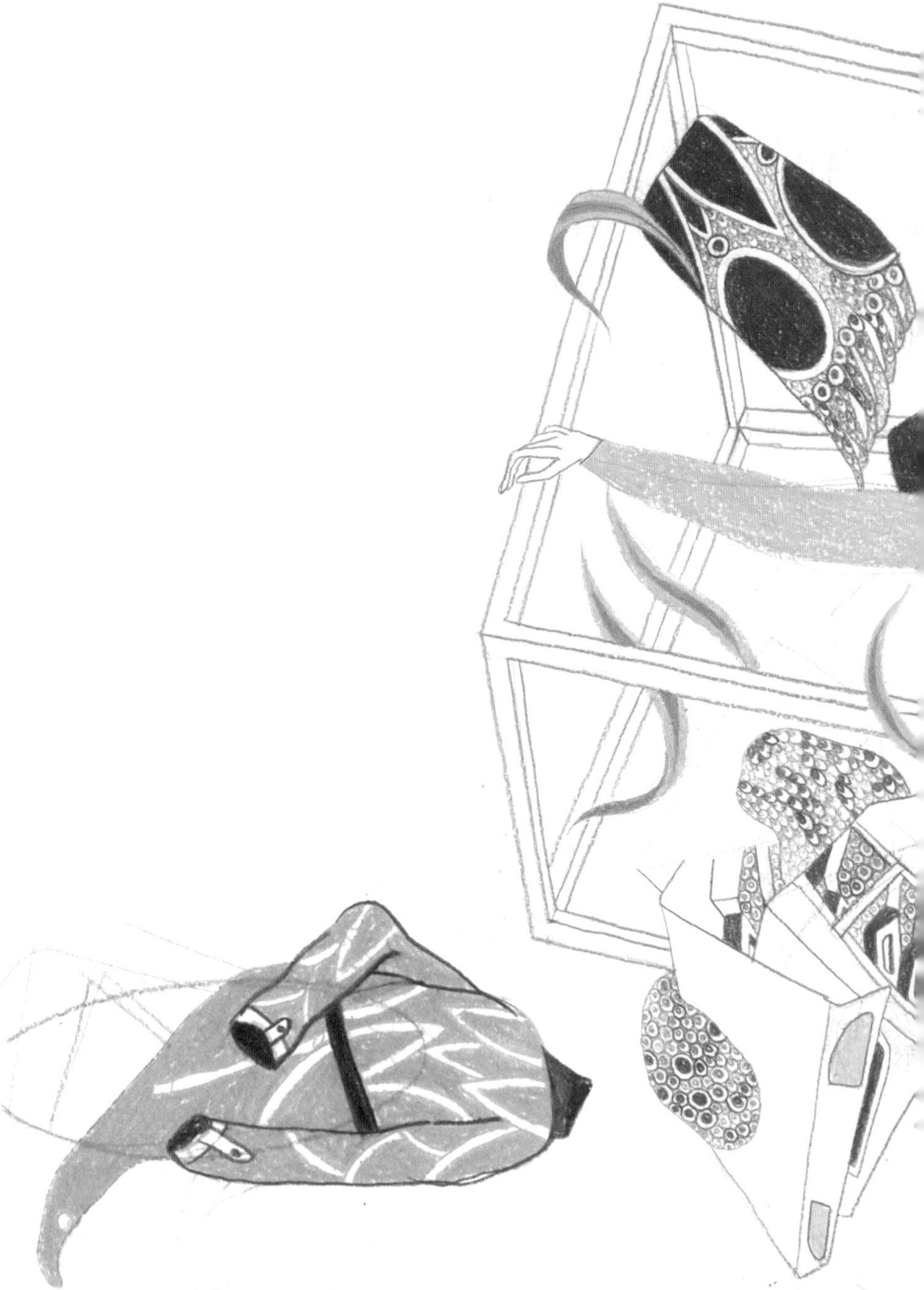

IT'S EASIER FOR EVERYONE, WHEN OUR HEADS ARE ROLLING SLOWLY AROUND THE EDGE OF OUR COLLARS WITHOUT BLOCKING THE VIEW OF THE WHITEBOARD FOR ANY OF THE STUDENTS SITTING BEHIND US.

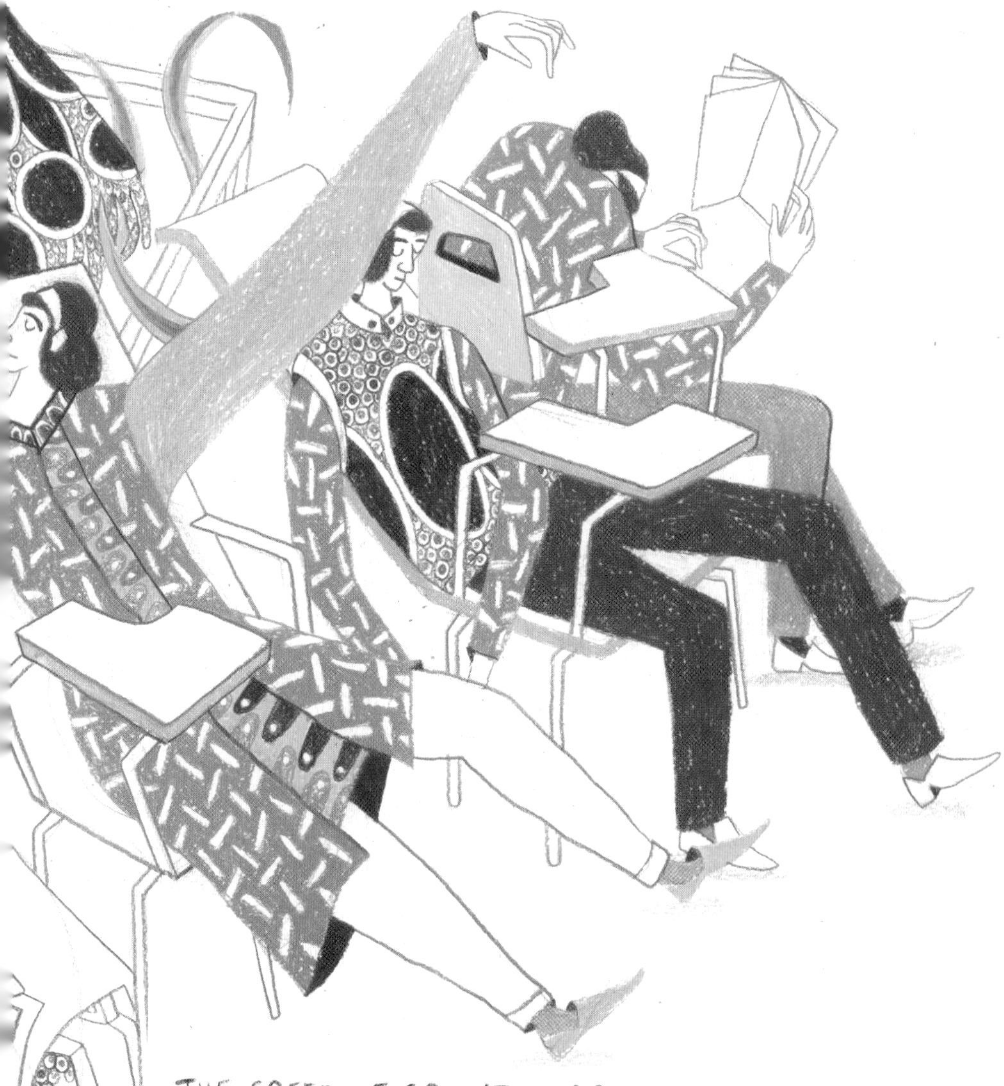

THE SPEED OF GROWTH VARIES FROM STUDENT TO STUDENT. THOUGH I'VE SEEN THE NECKS OF YOUR STUDENTS REACH FULL LENGTH DURING THE FIRST TWO MONTHS OF THEIR FRESHMAN YEAR.

I WAS APPROACHED BY A MAN WHO ASKED
IF I WOULD EVER BE ABLE TO HOLD MY NECK
UPRIGHT. IT WAS JUST BEYOND CAMPUS.
THE GROWTH IS PAUSED WHILE WE ARE
OUTSIDE THE PERIMETERS, BUT IT IS QUITE
APPARENT THAT ALL OF US ARE IN THE
MIDDLE OF A MYSTERIOUS PROCESS.
WE LOOK EXHAUSTED.

I WAS WEAK AND HAD TO LIE DOWN. I COULD
ONLY MAKE A NODDING GESTURE USING MY
FINGERS, FEELING RELIEVED THAT HE DIDNT
ASK ME ABOUT AN ORGAN I WAS ABLE TO
MOVE DIRECTLY.

OR WORSE,
HE COULD HAVE ASKED
ME ABOUT AN ORGAN THAT
COULD MOVE BY ITSELF.

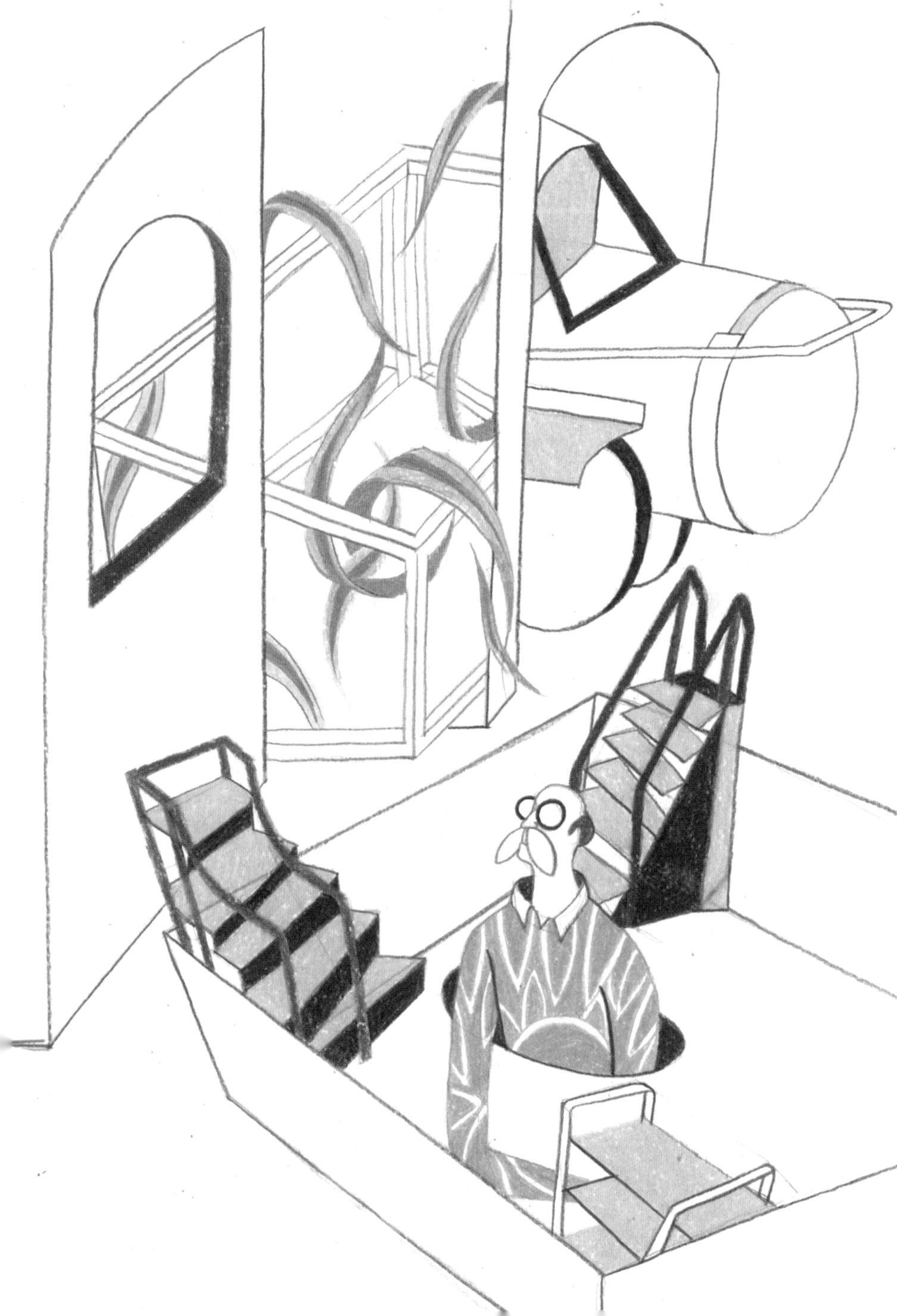

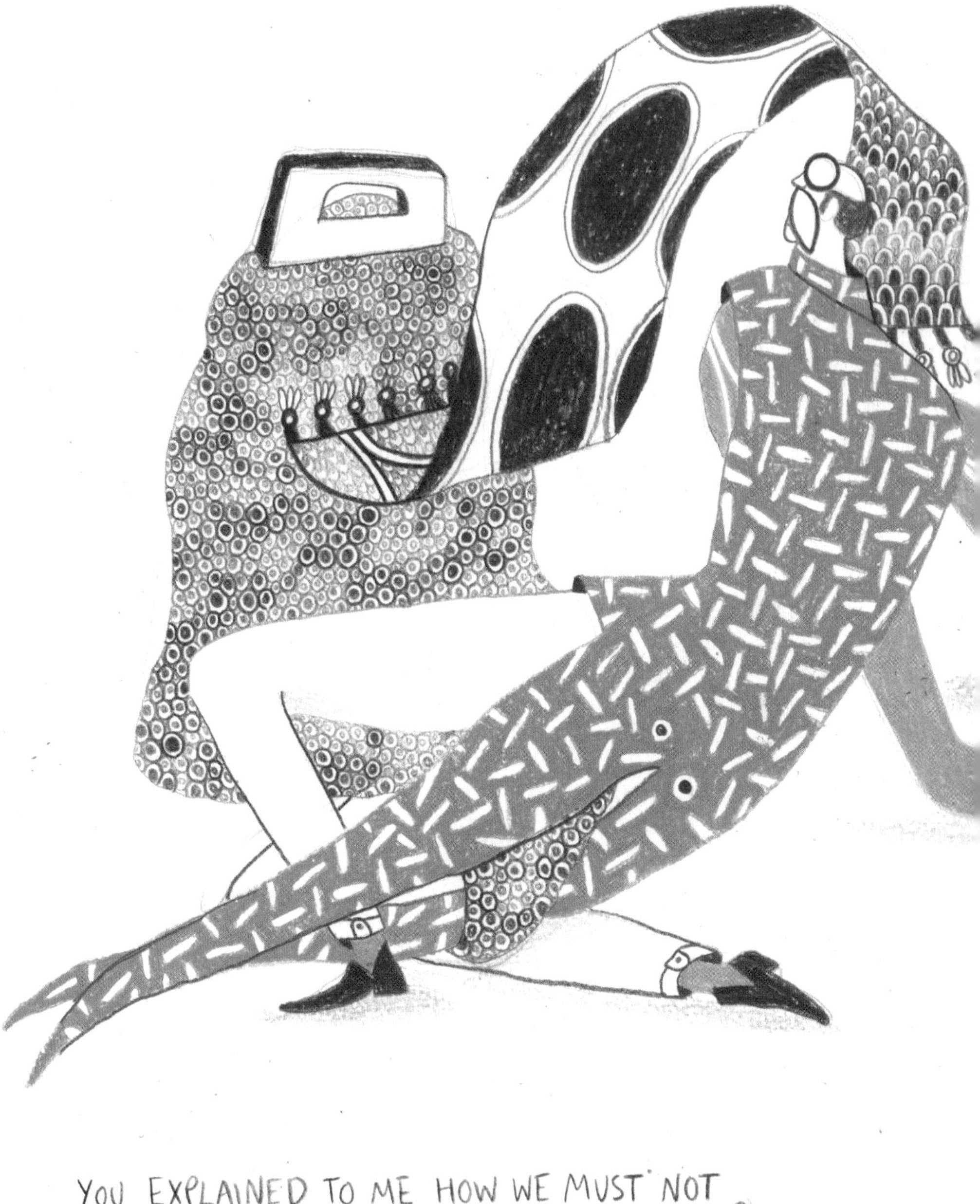

YOU EXPLAINED TO ME HOW WE MUST NOT WALK IN THE MIDDLE OF THE CORRIDOR, LEST WE CAUSE OUR PROFESSORS TO TRIP OVER. LAST WEEK, I HEARD CHATTER FROM THE WELL. TWO STUDENTS WERE DISCUSSING THE NEW GIRL THAT HAD JOINED THEIR CLASS THAT MORNING.

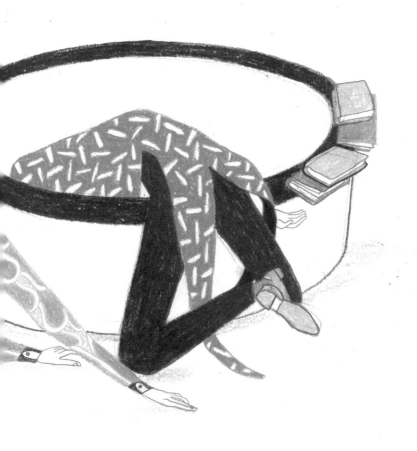

HE COULD RETRACT HER THUMB INTO THE PALM OF
HER HAND, PEELING IT AWAY FROM THE SKIN,
LEAVING BEHIND A LIMP, SACK-LIKE, RUBBER-LIKE
GLOVE, AND THEN POP IT BACK INTO POSITION.
THEY SQUEALED AND SHRIEKED AND I HAD STOPPED
LISTENING TO YOU AND STUCK MY HEAD IN. THOUGH
THEY WEREN'T DISCUSSING THE RULES,
THEIRS WAS A CONVERSATION ABOUT IMPORTANT
ANATOMICAL STRUCTURES.

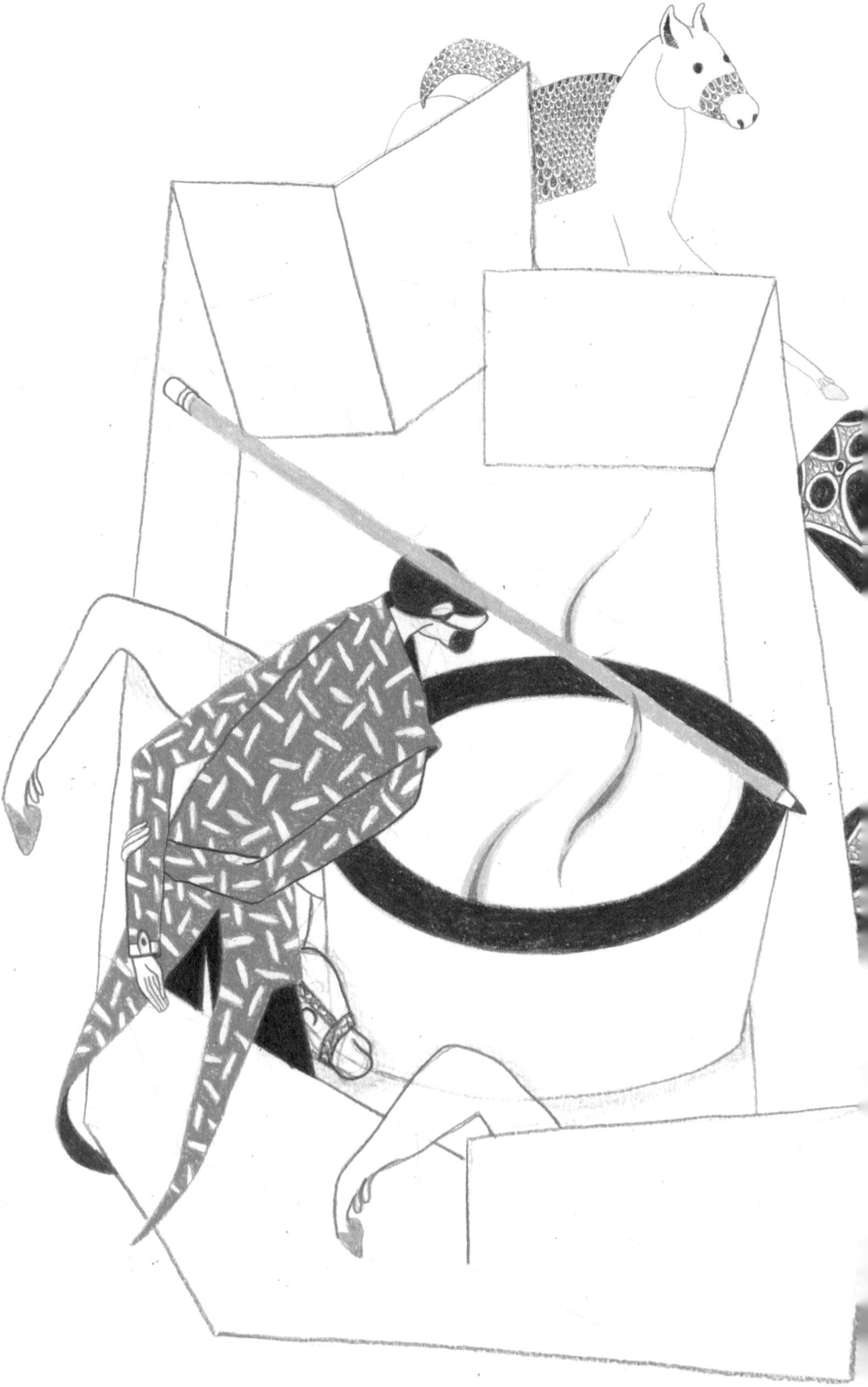

ONE DAY I PLAN TO BE STRUCK OUTSIDE YOUR
OFFICE BY ONE OF THOSE FLYING CARS. I WILL
STRAIGHTEN MY NECK AND IT WILL HIT IT RIGHT
IN THE MIDDLE, WITH PLENTY OF ROOM TO FRAME
A RED RIVER OF BLOOD BEFORE IT SOAKS INTO
SOME DARK ABSORBENT SHIRT FABRIC AND LOSES
ITS THEATRICAL APPEAL.

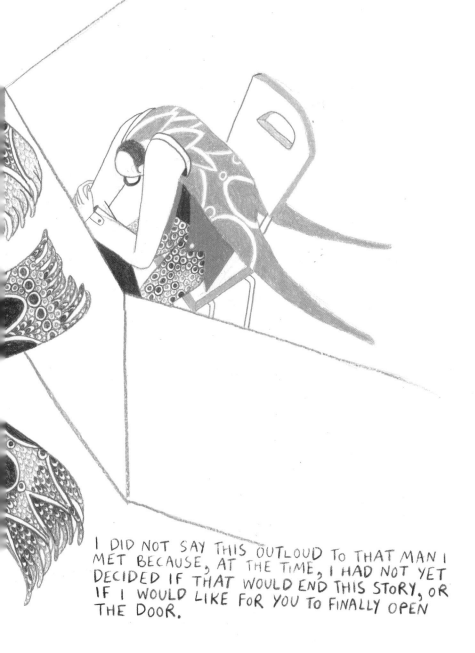

I DID NOT SAY THIS OUTLOUD TO THAT MAN I
MET BECAUSE, AT THE TIME, I HAD NOT YET
DECIDED IF THAT WOULD END THIS STORY, OR
IF I WOULD LIKE FOR YOU TO FINALLY OPEN
THE DOOR.

I MEMORIZED SOME PASSAGES FROM YOUR BOOKS. WHEN THE FLYING CARS HIT, I WILL RECOGNIZE THOSE SCENES UNFOLDING INSIDE ME AS THEIR FORCEFUL, MECHANICAL STRUCTURES REARRANGE MY SKELETON THE WAY YOU TAUGHT US.

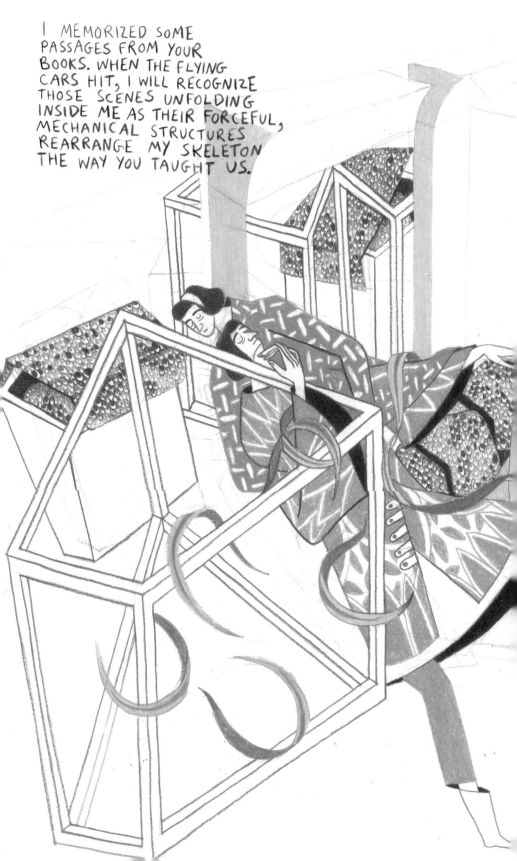

THE CARS WILL BE SURE TO BREAK ME TO THE SIZE OF THE BROKEN PIECES IN YOU. I WILL SEE ALL THE WORDS FALLING OUT OF ME, WHICH I NEVER HAD THE COURAGE TO WRITE. MY LETTERS TO YOU MEANT ALMOST NOTHING, EXCEPT FOR THE EXTREME SPEED WITH WHICH I ANSWERED YOURS.

L.

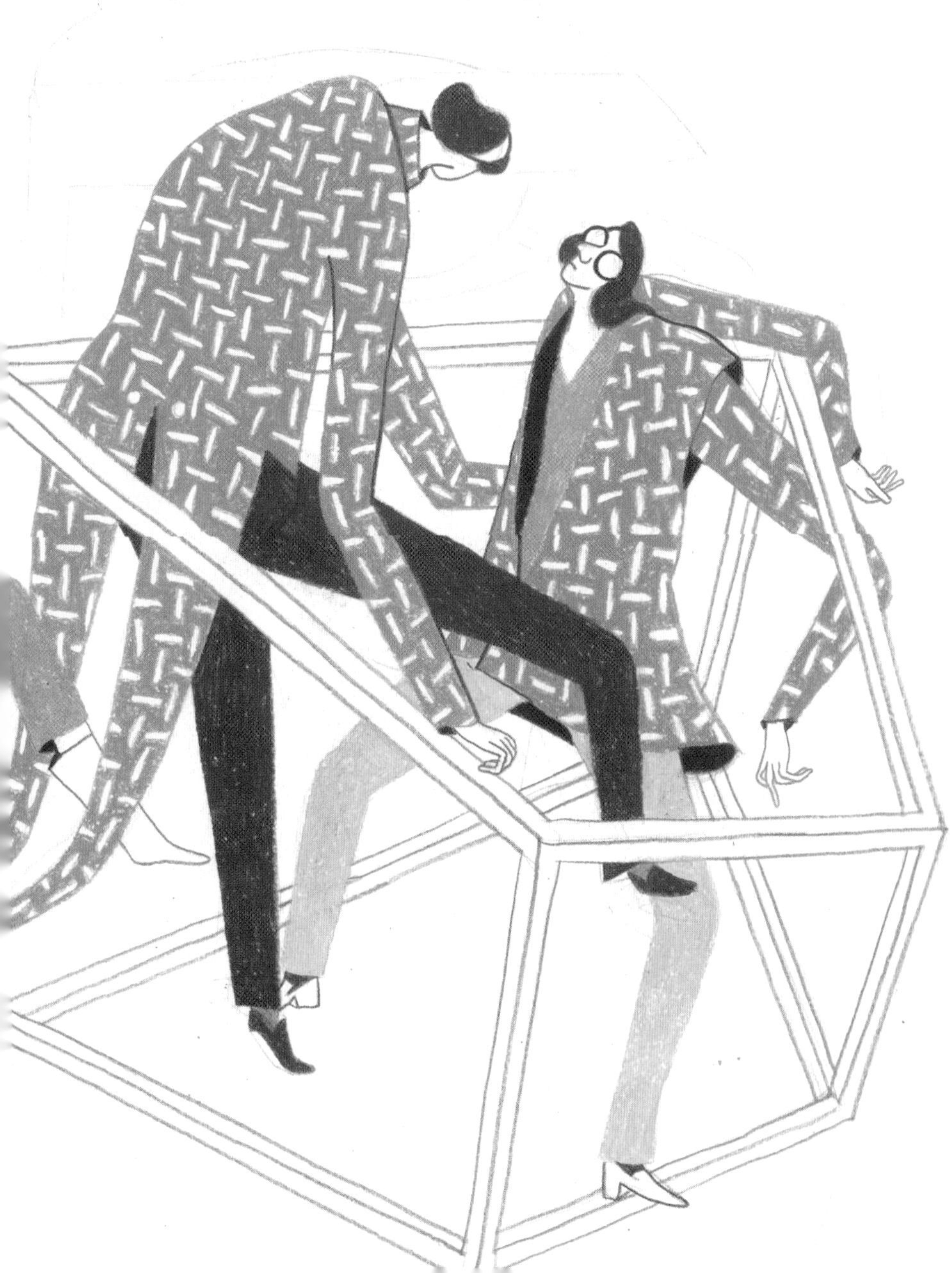

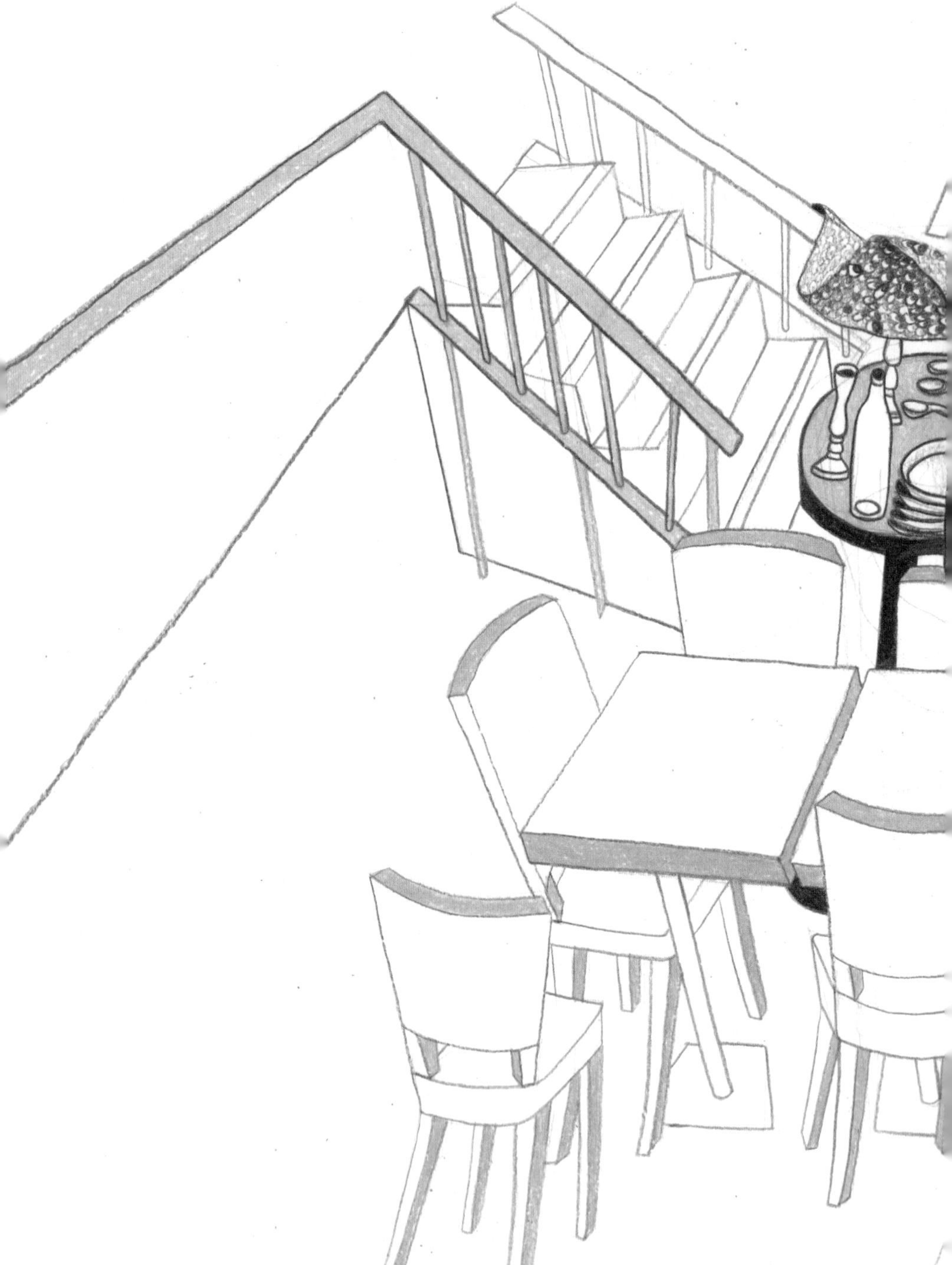

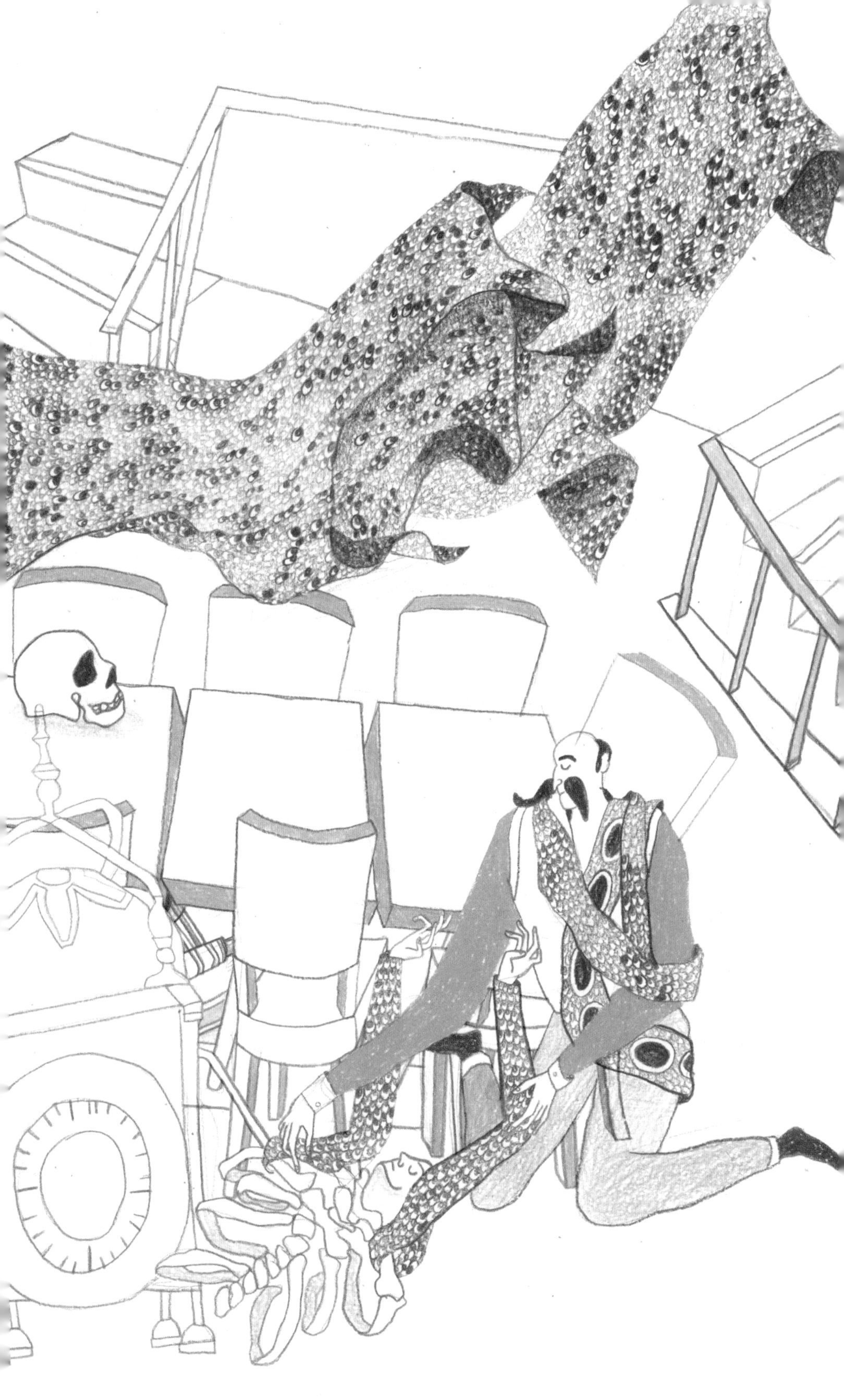

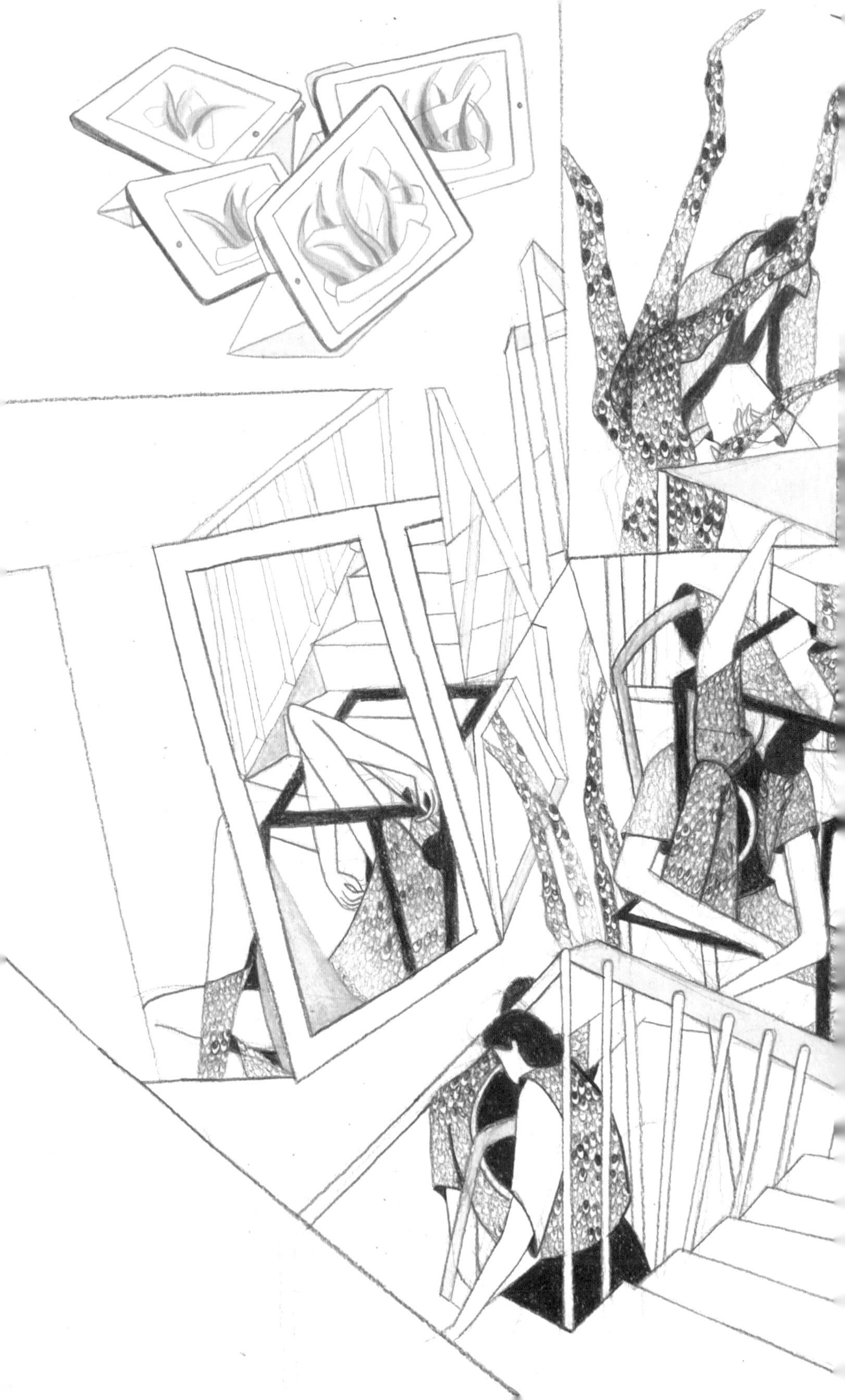

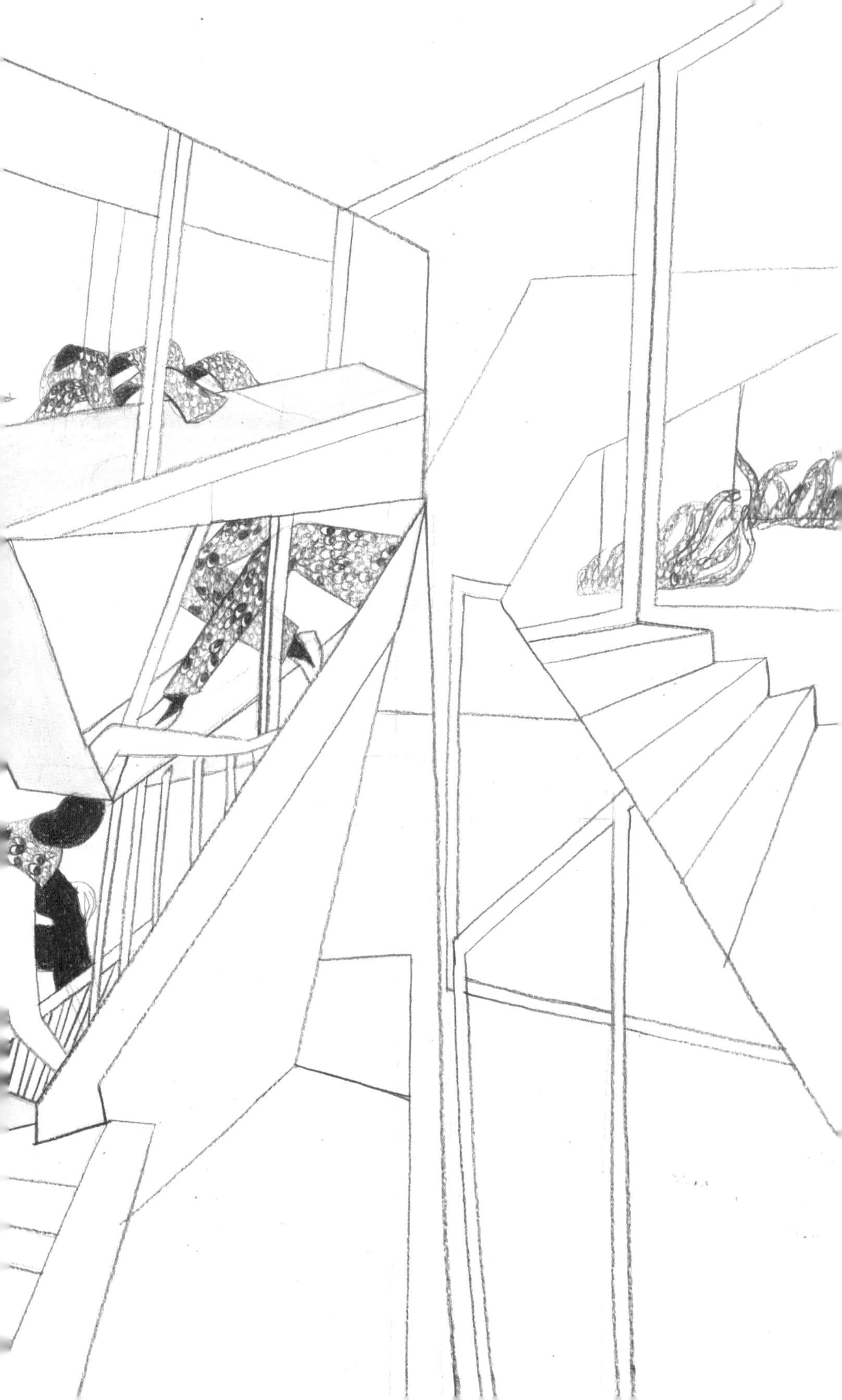

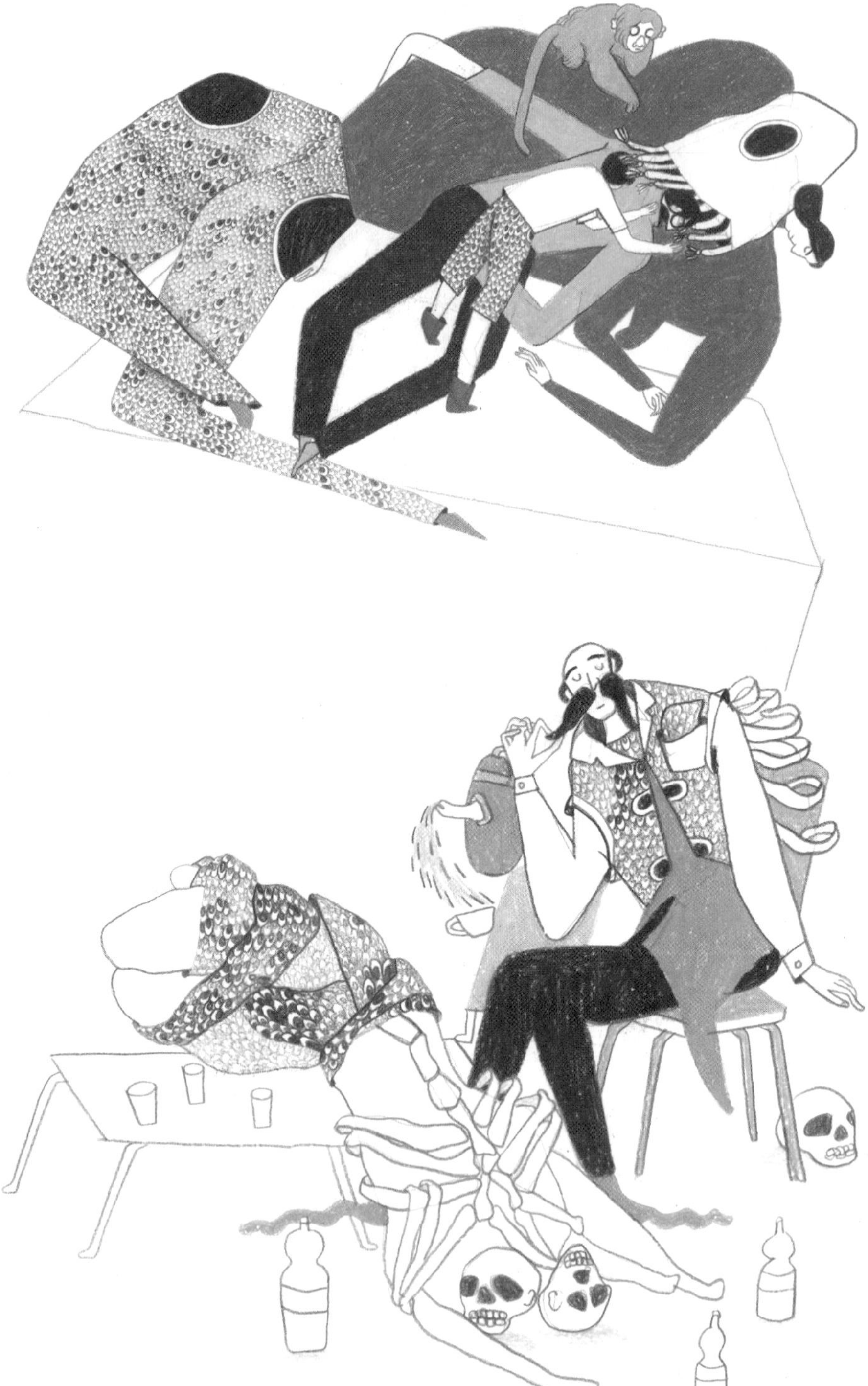